*S*he Stood Fast as Reeve
*U*ntied Her Camisole,
and Then Peeled It Away
from Her Flesh . . .

"Maggie," he said, in a low and ragged voice, and then she felt Reeve's breath on her face and instinctively she tilted her head back to greet his mouth with her own. His forceful but infinitely gentle hands entangled themselves in her hair and he kissed her . . .

As the soul-shattering kiss continued, Maggie felt the straining power of him and trembled for the want of it, even as she recoiled inwardly in fear.

Maggie was powerless to protest, much less flee, and when she felt herself being lowered to a soft bed, she offered no resistance. Reeve's voice was thick, hoarse with needs Maggie couldn't even begin to comprehend. "You're a virgin, then, aren't you, lass?"

Books by Linda Lael Miller

Banner O'Brien
Corbin's Fancy
Desire and Destiny
Fletcher's Woman
Lauralee
Memory's Embrace
Moonfire
Wanton Angel
Willow

Published by POCKET BOOKS

For Nancy —
Great to meet
you

MOONFIRE

Linda Lael Miller

Linda Lael Miller (signature)

POCKET BOOKS

New York   London   Toronto   Sydney   Tokyo

Another *Original* publication of POCKET BOOKS

POCKET BOOKS, a division of Simon & Schuster, Inc.
1230 Avenue of the Americas, New York, N.Y. 10020

ISBN: 0-671-62198-X

First Pocket Books printing May 1988

10 9 8 7 6 5 4 3 2 1

POCKET and colophon are trademarks of Simon & Schuster, Inc.

Printed in the U.S.A.

For Crystal Harworth,
who taught me to hear
the sweet, mystical music that words make

Prologue ❧

Dublin—*September 1867*

A DEFT FLIP OF JAMIE'S WRIST CAUSED THE GOLDEN WATCH to spin at the end of its chain. With a glint of triumph in his ice-blue eyes, he caught the gentleman's timepiece in one grubby palm and grinned.

Reeve, two years older than his brother at fourteen, lacked Jamie's taste for petty larceny. For the sake of the woman and the priest over near the fire—they were about the business of death—he kept his voice low. "Do you want to be transported, you idiot? It's one thing to pinch an onion or a turnip, but a dandy's watch?"

Jamie swallowed hard and glanced toward their mother's cot, which had been set as close as possible to the pitifully inadequate coal fire in the grate. "Herself is wantin' medicine," he said with lame defiance.

"She's past that," Reeve retorted. "There'll be no need of medicine, and we both know it."

The priest was giving last rites by then, and both Jamie and Reeve watched and listened in silence, hating their helplessness and their hunger. Through it all Callie McKenna lay motionless, her eyes closed.

1

At last Father McDougal turned weary-eyed from Callie's cot, his face gaunt and deeply lined. He seemed to carry the troubles of all Ireland on his thin shoulders. As he approached, he reached one slightly tremulous hand into the pocket of his frayed coat.

From his perch on the edge of the table Jamie skittered to his feet. "Is she—"

Father McDougal shook his balding head. "Not yet, lad, but I don't look for Callie to last the night, bless her soul." He paused to cross himself, and then sighed. "She's in God's hands now."

Reeve scowled and folded his arms across his chest; he'd hear no talk of God or his mother's coming happiness in heaven. Where had God been when Callie McKenna was left to scour the scummy floors of taverns and mend the gowns of fancy ladies who didn't think her fit to spit upon?

"Any work to be had on the docks these days, then?" the priest asked pointlessly. He already knew the dismal answer, for there was no work anywhere in Ireland, not in the cities and not on the farms.

Reeve lowered his dark head. He was a sturdy lad, broad in the shoulders and strong despite the hunger that had gnawed at his belly for as long as he could remember. "No work," he muttered. It didn't seem right to mention his plans for the future, not now, with his mother dying.

The elderly priest cleared his throat; Reeve glanced up and saw that Jamie still clutched the watch in one filthy hand. "Stealin' again, are you, boyo?" he demanded more in despair than in anger. "Shameful thing, that. Wrong in the eyes of God."

Jamie's answer was quick and flippant, as Jamie's answers tended to be. "God ain't lookin', now, is He? Not toward me and not toward me poor mum and not toward the whole of Ireland!"

The old man sighed and then, after a moment's hesitation, drew his hand from his pocket and opened his palm to reveal two bits of tarnished brass shaped like coins and punched through at the top. When neither lad responded, he pressed one into Reeve's hand and one into Jamie's and hastily left the cottage.

In the gloom Reeve examined the coin. Thanks to the nuns of St. Patrick's parish, he could read a little, and he made out the words: Blessed is he that considereth the poor.

Shame scalded the back of his throat and throbbed behind his blue-green eyes. "It's a bloody beggar's badge!" he hissed.

Jamie was quiet; both brothers listened to the labored breathing of their mother. She was cold and sick and she was going to die hungry—just as she'd lived.

In a burst of fury and helplessness Reeve hurled the badge across the room. It made a clinking sound as it struck the fireplace.

Jamie set his jaw and started toward the door. "I'll be back," he said softly, speaking not to Reeve but to their mother, "and I swear by all that's holy that I'll bring back bread and tea and whatever else I can find."

"Good lad," Callie replied weakly, a woman wandering in a dream. "He's a good lad, my Jamie. A good lad."

"You're going to beg?" Reeve demanded of his brother in a rasping undertone.

Jamie held up the fancy watch and gave it another arrogant spin. It glinted in the gloom of that tiny hovel. "Aye, Reeve," he answered tightly, "if it comes to that, I'll beg, but first I'll be about makin' a fair swap with the grocer."

A cold premonition quaked in the very core of Reeve McKenna's soul. "Don't do it, Jamie. Sure as the saints, this time they'll collar you."

Jamie's expression was hard, and for the moment he was a man, not a boy. "I'll not see me mother die hungry, Reeve."

Reeve made his way to the hearth, searching for the

3

beggar's badge he'd tossed away only moments before. He'd take it around, to this house and that—for his mother he'd do it, and to save Jamie from the law. He was the elder brother; the task rightly fell to him, intolerable as it was.

"Your luck's sure to run out," he said, searching the floor around the hearth. Just as he caught a glimmer of firelight on the brass, the door of the cottage closed with a smart click and Jamie was gone.

Reeve scrambled across the room, wrenching open the door. The stench of that narrow Dublin street came at him and mingled with the night chill. "Jamie!" he bellowed into the dense fog that covered Dublin like a yellowed muslin shroud. "Jamie, come back!"

It was too late. There was no sign of Jamie; the lad was as quick with his feet as he was with his hands.

Reeve swore and closed the creaky door, running one hand through his hair as he turned back to the dying woman and the dying fire and all his dying hopes.

"Is there word come from your da, then?" Callie asked in a bright voice. She sounded almost like her old self. "It's off to America we'll be, one fine day soon."

Near tears, Reeve knelt beside his mother's cot and took one of her thin, work-roughened hands into his own. "No word yet," he said softly.

Callie's eyes, sea-green like her eldest son's, were fixed on the shadowy ceiling of the hovel where Marcus had left her so many years before. "Never a letter," she said on a long sigh. "Ain't it strange there was never a letter?"

Reeve let his forehead rest against hers for a moment and drew a deep, steadying breath. "Da wasn't much for writin'," he answered gently after a very long time. Privately, he believed his father was either dead or the worst sort of scoundrel, but of course he couldn't say that. Indeed, he wished he'd pretended that there was a letter from America, with passage money for them all. What harm would it have done to lie to Callie now?

It might have been a mercy.

"I'm dying, ain't I?" Callie asked, and her eyes lost their dreamy quality. She was lucid and full of misery.

It was hard for Reeve to speak, impossible for him to lie. He struggled for a few moments before offering a tentative "Father McDougal says you'll go to heaven, sure and straight."

Callie smiled at the prospect. Despite years of suffering, years of waiting and fruitless hope, she believed. Reeve couldn't recall a time when her faith had so much as wavered, though his own was long gone. "Oh, yes," she said. "I'll go to heaven." Her dark hair, without even a strand of gray, fanned out over her coverless pillow, and she arched one finely etched eyebrow. "But what of you and Jamie? Where will you go—to America?"

Reeve shook his head. He could no longer keep back the truth. "I've got a berth on a sailing ship, Ma," he said, and even now he felt a singular excitement at the prospect. "A whaler. Her home port is in New South Wales, at Sydney Town."

Callie's aquamarine eyes widened. "New South Wales! What of Jamie? Will you take him with you?"

Reeve remembered his interview with the captain of the *Sally Dee*—though it had taken place that afternoon, it seemed a thousand years in the past— and felt true despair. The captain had said there was need of only one cabin boy aboard the ship. He'd have a gander at Jamie, and if he looked fit for the sea, there might be a place for him on the next voyage. Beyond that the man could promise nothing.

"I won't leave without him," Reeve vowed solemnly. It was a promise he meant to keep, even if he had to sacrifice his own plans and dreams.

Callie looked relieved, and Reeve wondered if she knew about Jamie's thieving, despite their efforts to

5

hide it from her. "He's a fine boy, my Jamie," she said, "but he ain't so sensible as you, Reeve. He needs lookin' after."

Reeve permitted himself a smile and nodded. "That he does."

"You'll see to him?"

Reeve squeezed his mother's hand. "I'll see to him," he affirmed.

Callie gave a small sigh and closed her eyes to sleep.

Almost an hour passed before Jamie was back, dodging into the cottage, his arms filled with loot. He'd brought tea, a whole loaf of bread still warm from the oven, a cold joint of mutton, and a small bag of coarse white sugar. After casting a look of shame and defiance in his brother's direction, he dropped the food on the table and crossed the room to shovel the last of the coal onto the fire.

Unsettled and anxious, Reeve took the well-used kettle into the street and filled it with water from the neighborhood pump. Back in the cottage, he set it on the hob to boil.

Jamie was slicing the mutton with quick, deft strokes of his pocket knife. "How is Mum?" he asked after a long silence.

Reeve caught his thumbs in the pockets of his tattered trousers. "Lookin' for a letter from Da, she was. Still, after all these years."

Jamie continued to slice the meat for their supper. "You think he's dead?"

"That or just forgetful," Reeve replied with quiet bitterness.

Marcus McKenna's fate in far-off America was a touchy subject between them, and they rarely discussed it. "He had to serve seven years for his passage," Jamie reminded his brother evenly.

"He's had that, Jamie, and four years more. If Da's alive, he's decided not to bother bringin' a wife and two sons over from the Old Sod."

Jamie's jawline tightened, then relaxed. He was a

handsome lad, with his wheat-colored hair and pale blue eyes. "Have you ever thought of goin' to America yourself, Reeve? I mean, if Da could work for his passage, so could we."

Reeve thought of the beggar's badge, still lying on the floor somewhere, a painful reminder of his limited options. "They kept slaves there once," he said. Just the thought made his skin crawl. "Had a war over it too."

Jamie popped a bit of mutton into his mouth and chewed thoughtfully. "You wouldn't be a slave—all that's over now. Workin' off your passage ain't the same at all."

"For a time it is. A man has a master. He's owned, like a carriage or a calf."

"For the likes of us," Jamie pointed out, tearing the fragrant loaf of bread into hunks, "it might be the only way out of Ireland."

"Aye," Reeve replied halfheartedly, thinking of the berth he'd been offered on the *Sally Dee*. Sooner or later he was going to have to speak of it, but the right time hadn't come yet.

When the water came to a whistling boil on the hob, Reeve poured it into the chipped crockery pot. While the savory brew steeped, Jamie gently awakened his mother.

Callie's hands trembled as she reached for the plate her son extended. There was a dazzled expression in her eyes and she cast a quick glance around the cottage, as if thinking that she might have passed on to some other, better life without noticing.

Callie ate little of the meal, but enjoyed two full cups of sugared tea. Later that night, while her sons slept on their pallets on the cottage floor, she died.

She was buried in a pauper's grave, without even a coffin, but Father McDougal was there in the drizzling rain to say the holy words. Reeve listened in a numb rage, hating not only the priest, but the God he served as well. It would have been a comfort to believe that

7

angels had met his mother's soaring spirit and carried her to a place of peace and plenty, but he couldn't quite manage that.

Nor could he weep as Jamie did. There was nothing to do but accept the dismal reality of Callie's death just as it was.

At the edge of the churchyard the grocer waited, flanked by two soldiers of the English crown. "That's him," the fat merchant cried through the downpour. "That's him what give me the watch!"

Reeve started to step between Jamie and the soldiers, but the priest grabbed at his arm. Before he could take the blame on himself, Jamie owned up, his face wet with tears and rain.

"It's me you want," he said.

"Blighter," one soldier muttered to the other as they bound Jamie's wrists behind him. "Sticky-fingered, these micks, every last one of 'em!"

"Wait!" Reeve choked, shaking free of the old priest's grasp. "It's a lie—I'm the one that took the gentleman's watch—"

The second soldier laughed. "Too late for that, lad."

Again Father McDougal caught at Reeve's arm, this time with surprising strength. "There's nothing you can do now. Let them go."

Jamie gave Reeve a nod and a half smile that would linger in his brother's memory for a long time. Then the soldiers dragged him away between them, the fat grocer tottering behind, raving on and on about his own obvious innocence of any crime.

Reeve sank against a tree, and at last he wept—for his mother and for Ireland, for Jamie and for himself.

At home he ate the last of the mutton and the bread and drank the tea. The landlady, a shrill widow, had new tenants for the cottage, so he couldn't stay, and there was nothing to pack, for all Reeve McKenna had in the world were the clothes on his back. Finding the beggar's badge on the floor, he dropped it into his pocket, for even though the talisman was an object of shame, it was a possession, something to own.

For the next few days Reeve tried in vain to see Jamie, but Dublin Gaol was not a place where compassion was practiced, and he was repeatedly refused. Nights, he slept in doorways and alleys.

The day of Jamie's trial—he was called to the docket from among a hundred others like him—Reeve was there in the crowd of spectators. His brother stood proudly, with his chin high and a dancing light in his eyes that seemed not only to ask for trouble but to court it.

The magistrate, who had probably never been hungry a day in his life, made a lofty speech about thievery's inherent evil and sentenced Jamie to be transported for a period of not less than seven years.

Stunned, and half sick with hunger and desperation, Reeve staggered out of the courtroom and into a pouring rain, making his way toward the docks. He could only hope that the *Sally Dee* hadn't sailed without him.

The whaler was still in port, though she was slated to sail within the hour. After one last look around him at the cobbled streets and the crowded taverns and the hovels hunched close together, Reeve turned his back on Dublin forever.

As for Jamie, he'd found his own way to New South Wales, peculiar though it was, and Reeve was sure he'd find his brother again on the streets of Sydney Town.

Chapter 1 ❧

Brisbane—*February 1887*

EMIGRANTS AND FIRST-CLASS PASSENGERS ALIKE STOOD AT the starboard rail of the S.S. *Victoria,* agape at the destruction that greeted them. Gone were the wharves that might have held eager friends and family members waiting to welcome the travelers; cargo, washed away from the docks, bobbed in the sun-spattered blue-green waters. Lavatories floated past, along with what appeared to be an upended cottage, and innumerable rabbits shivered on the few patches of land still visible.

The best part of the city was gone, swept away by the flooded waters of the Brisbane River.

Maggie Chamberlin's heart pounded beneath her dove-gray woolen traveling dress. The thought skittered through her mind that while entirely suitable for the dreary grayness of a London winter, the gown was too warm by half for the heat of February in Australia.

Like the forlorn and frightened rabbits ashore, Maggie trembled. She put her unsuitable frock out of her mind; proper clothing was the least of her problems. Philip Briggs, the man who had persuaded her to make this journey, who had promised to marry her, was nowhere in sight. Suppose he had not survived the disaster?

Maggie realized that she had been clutching the ship's railing for support and relaxed her grip. Her heavy silver-flaxen hair sagged to the nape of her neck, and she raised one hand to secure the pins, a nervous, unconscious gesture that had become a habit.

"A fine bit of business this is," complained Tansy Quinn, the one friend Maggie had made aboard the ship in the five weeks since they'd left London. A small, plump girl with plain brown hair, bright blue eyes, and a beguiling chip in one front tooth, Tansy was emigrating to Australia for the second time in her short but eventful life. She was almost as well-traveled as Maggie, despite her poor beginnings in Liverpool, and, until now, she had exhibited unflagging confidence in her ability to make her way in this strange land where the seasons were turned topsy-turvy and flamboyantly colored birds flew free rather than being confined inside gilded cages in the parlors of the gentry. "Looks as though the lot of it's been washed out to sea."

Maggie's knees were suddenly weak; once again she gripped the railing. Her wide, heavily lashed gray eyes scanned the devastation on shore. Dark despair shimmied up and down her throat and settled over her soul in an ebony fog. There were people waving at the ship from rowboats and dinghies, but not one of them was Philip. She was once again a stranger in a strange land, and there was no one to meet her. She closed her eyes and swallowed, unable to respond to Tansy's comment.

Tansy gave her an oddly reassuring nudge with one elbow. "Don't be lookin' so down-'earted, love. It's a rotten show, but we'll go on to Sydney. Or we could get ourselves jobs at Government 'ouse, down Melbourne way."

Maggie opened her eyes and gave her friend a look

11

that was at once wry and dispirited. Tansy had never believed in Philip Briggs, though she hadn't come right out and said as much; she viewed him with the same kindly disdain older children reserved for St. Nicholas. "Philip specifically told me to meet him here," Maggie said stiffly. "In Brisbane."

"Philip, Philip, Philip," Tansy muttered, shaking her head. The late afternoon sunshine shimmered over the freckles sprinkled across her nose, turning them to gold. "Philip this, Philip that. 'Ere you are, pinin' for that waster after all this time, like some fluttery spinster 'oping for one last chance at a ring and a bed, and you just nineteen!"

"I need Philip," Maggie insisted, thrusting out her chin and fixing her eyes on some point beyond Brisbane and its plight. Then, as an afterthought, she added hastily, "And I love him."

"Some Yank you are," Tansy retorted skeptically. "About as independent as a tit-baby!"

Hot color flooded up over Maggie's well-hidden but shapely bosom and streamed into her face. Her pewter-colored eyes snapped with weary outrage. "I'm as independent as you are, Tansy Quinn, and I'll thank you to remember it!"

"*I,*" huffed Tansy with a quick upturn of her nose, "am not dependin' on some man to make me way easy!"

Maggie bit back a comment about Tansy's shipboard flirtation with a certain young quartermaster and replied coolly, "I can't understand why you hate Philip so when you've never even met him."

There was a softening in Tansy's manner, though she refused to meet Maggie's gaze. "I don't need to meet the bleeder to know 'e's as useless as nipples on a boar. What kind of man drags a girl 'alfway 'round the world and can't even pay 'er passage? You paid a pound for your kit just like the rest of us, Maggie Chamberlin, and you'd best be recallin' what you promised to do in return."

Maggie well remembered her promise: She'd agreed to work at least three years before leaving the country. The contract would be nullified, however, once she became Mrs. Philip Briggs, for if there was one thing Australia wanted more than nannies, servant girls, factory workers, and seamstresses, it was wives for its men. "I haven't forgotten," she said softly, turning away from the rail and the tragedy ashore.

She nearly collided with John Higgins, Tansy's quartermaster. A very tall man with shoulders as narrow as his hips and an eyepatch that gave him a likeness to a pirate, Higgins regarded himself rather too highly for Maggie's taste.

She stepped back, trying to ignore the way the seaman's eyes swept over her person before dodging to Tansy's face. "No point in droppin' anchor here," he imparted with a shrug in his voice that seemed to dismiss Brisbane's suffering as a minor annoyance. "We're off to Sydney Town on the evenin' tide."

"And how far is that?" Maggie asked politely, wishing that she were standing anywhere but downwind of John Higgins, who gave off an odor reminiscent of rancid chicken soup.

"Two days or close to it," Higgins answered. He gave Tansy a surreptitious and entirely improper pinch on her lush posterior and proceeded along the deck, tossing back an offhand "Pity you won't be seein' your Mr. Briggs as soon as you thought" to Maggie.

"Two days," groaned Maggie, overcome by this turn of events, the sad fate that had befallen the city of Brisbane, and the tiff with Tansy. She groped her way back to the compartment that housed nearly one hundred women and sat down on her bunk to think.

There was no point in assuming that Philip had died in the flood. More likely, he had heard of the disaster, guessed that the S.S. *Victoria* would be unable to dock, and very sensibly remained in Sydney, going about his duties in the Royal Theatre.

13

The heat was oppressive, and Maggie unbuttoned her gray woolen dress and stepped out of it, draping the garment carefully over the foot of her berth. Then, wearing only her butter-muslin drawers and matching chemise, she stretched out on the narrow bunk to rest and to dream.

Closing her eyes, she could see Philip's handsome face, his golden brown hair and his amber eyes. She dreamed her way back to the seedy theater in London's West End, back to the tiny dressing room she'd shared with the other players. . . .

Maggie had been powdering her nose when the young Australian she'd heard so much about suddenly appeared in her mirror. His hands—smooth, uncalloused hands they were—poised themselves above her bare, creamy shoulders for a moment, then fell gracefully to his sides. "Miss Chamberlin?" he inquired. "You'll forgive me for intruding, I hope, but I saw your last performance and I just had to speak to you in person."

Maggie stood up hastily and pulled on her shabby silken robe, a garment inherited from her mother. Now faded, the azure blue wrap had once been a glorious thing, as Maggie's mother had been glorious. "Yes?" she answered hesitantly. "What is it?"

An angelic smile curved Philip's soft mouth and lighted his mirthful eyes. "You're an American," he observed in a tone of friendly accusation.

Maggie nodded, her heart hammering against the base of her throat. The robe covered her adequately, and she wore a costume beneath it, but she still felt as though she were wholly naked before this man. She flushed because the sensation was not at all unpleasant, and she stammered out some insensible answer that eluded her ever after.

Philip Briggs laughed, his warm-brandy eyes caressing Maggie, and asked how she liked being an actress.

Maggie shrugged, smitten to an appalling degree. "This is a second-rate theater, after all," she managed to say. And after that, even though she had to be back onstage in less than fifteen minutes, the entire story of her life tumbled out just as though someone had greased her tongue.

She found herself telling Mr. Briggs about her parents, American circus performers, who had died not because of their hazardous acts—Maggie's mother had been an aerialist, her father a lion tamer—but in a train crash high in the mountains of Switzerland. She even told him about her schooling in the States, how she'd been dropped off at a different orphanage every autumn and picked up again in the spring, when the circus came through town.

"You were adopted by your own parents, then?" Philip prompted when the story had ended.

Maggie smiled—oddly, she was both relaxed and excited. She decided at that moment that she loved Mr. Philip Briggs even though she knew next to nothing about him. "At least eight times," she answered. "I hated those winters, but boarding school was out of the question—it cost too much—so I pretended to be an orphan once a year."

Just then another performer peered around the dressing room door, and snapped, "We're on, Chamberlin!"

Now, after spilling virtually every intimate detail of her unconventional life, Maggie became strangely shy. She averted her eyes as she removed her wrap again, revealing the scanty sequin-covered costume, and started for the door.

Gently, Philip caught Maggie's arm. A tingle jolted along her bare limb and, traveling by way of her heart, lodged itself in her throat.

"You'll have dinner with me? After the show?"

Maggie nodded and dashed out of the dressing room into the long, shadowy hallway leading to the wings.

A courtship of the sort only dreamed about by girls of Maggie's station was to follow. Every night Philip took Maggie to supper. He told her about Australia, where he managed several theaters, and, after a few whirlwind weeks, he offered her the two things she wanted most in all the world: marriage and a leading role in Shakespeare's *Taming of the Shrew*. She was entirely too sweet and too pretty for the part of Kate, he assured her, suavely kissing her hand as he made his promises. No, no, she must play Bianca, the gentle sister.

Maggie would have preferred the part of Kate—Bianca seemed to her a dull and dumdazzle character—but she was nobody's fool and she knew how rare it was for a man to offer not only his name but a real job too.

"Say you'll do it, Maggie," Philip pleaded that last evening in a glamorous London supper club she had never expected to enter. "Say you'll come to Australia. I'll meet you in Brisbane—the ship docks there first—and we'll be married the minute you step ashore. We'll honeymoon in Queensland—they have white beaches there, Maggie, and shells as colorful as jewels—and then we'll be off to Sydney—"

Maggie's hesitation was largely pretense; she was certain that she loved Philip Briggs, and there was nothing to hold her in London. She had merely been stranded there after her parents had died in Switzerland; she had no real friends, one good dress, and a tiny room in a back-alley rooming house. She had nothing to lose, it seemed to her.

Opening her eyes, Maggie sighed away the sweet memories and geared herself toward the adventure ahead. Of course Philip was waiting for her in Sydney, ready to marry her and free her from her emigrant's agreement.

Tansy had returned to the compartment and was sitting on her trunk, her tongue caught between her lips, busily writing in her journal. Apparently sensing Maggie's perusal, she pulled in her tongue and sat up very straight.

"Thought you was sleepin'," she said noncommittally.

Maggie had never had a friend quite as loyal as Tansy, and she didn't want to offend her. She yawned and sat upright as well as she could without banging her head on the berth above hers. "I was," Maggie lied. "Will you be seeing Mr. Higgins again after we dock in Sydney?"

"Not likely," Tansy answered. "A seafarin' man ain't for me. Gone too much. I want a bloke what I can cuddle up to of a night."

Maggie smiled and hugged herself, feeling cool and comfortable in her oft-washed and neatly patched chemise. Soon enough she'd have Philip to "cuddle up to of a night." She'd find out what came of a passion such as her own when it was fulfilled in the marriage bed. "Do you suppose it feels good —what men and women do together in the night, I mean?"

Tansy gave a rather bawdy chuckle and whispered, "Lordy, I *know* it feels good. Whether it's in the night or the broad light o' day!"

Maggie colored richly. There was a breeze coming in through the portholes on the far side of the compartment and it rippled pleasantly, sensuously, over her arms and legs. Beneath her chemise her plump breasts seemed to swell in response to it. "You're only boasting, Tansy Quinn! You don't know any such thing!"

"Oh, but I do," insisted Tansy, a sparkle in her blue eyes, her voice low. "There's a groomsman at Government 'ouse, in Melbourne, what can make me 'owl like 'is lordship's best 'ound!"

Maggie was roundly shocked, just as she suspected Tansy had intended her to be, but she was curious too. Vaguely, she remembered lying in her corner of a colorful circus wagon, as a little girl, and hearing odd, muffled moans in the night. She had assumed that her mother or father had eaten one too many sweet apples and gotten a stomachache, but now she wondered. "Go on!" she scoffed, her cheeks stinging.

Tansy was pleased. "So Philip the Wonderful 'asn't 'ad 'is way with you, then. That's something, considerin' 'ow the bleeder's duped you up to now."

"We're back to that again!" Maggie stormed, folding her arms over her chest and jutting out her stubborn chin. "You're just jealous, Tansy Quinn, because there's nobody waiting for you in Sydney!"

"Don't be too sure of that, miss," Tansy retorted loftily. "I 'ad me pick of the lads at Government 'ouse, I did." She paused to sniff. "And I don't talk through me nose, neither, like certain Yanks I could name."

Maggie was stung, just as Tansy had wanted her to be. She turned onto her side, with her face to the wall, and ignored her friend until she went away.

When Tansy and everyone else in the compartment had gone off to have supper, a luxury Maggie's pride forced her to forgo, she got out of her berth and paced. It did bother her, no matter how strenuously she might deny it, that Philip had induced her to travel to Australia as an emigrant instead of as his wife. After all, if something went wrong, if he failed to marry her, she would be obligated to work three years, and since she'd never done anything except perform in secondrate revues in one shoddy London theater, her options would certainly be limited. She would end up scrubbing floors and rinsing chamber pots, sure and certain.

Her fingers trembling just slightly, Maggie pulled her carpetbag from beneath her berth and opened it. Reaching past her spare dress, a woolen even warmer and more somber than the gray one she'd shed a short time before, she brought out her personal papers. There was her birth certificate, proof of her American citizenship—she would need that if she ever decided to return to the United States. That didn't seem likely, given the great distance involved. Along with the certificate was the advertisement Philip had clipped from the London *Times* and presented with a pleased flourish.

Alone, sitting cross-legged on her berth like an Indian, Maggie read the smudged print even though she already knew it by heart.

Free emigration.
Wanted for Australia, young men and women.
Must be over eighteen.

"It only makes sense for you to travel this way, Magpie," Philip had enthused. "You pay a pound for your kit—blankets and sheets and soap, things of that nature. And you'll need to have an emigration form signed by a doctor and a clergyman and the theater manager, proving that you're a good sort and all. Shouldn't be any problem, that. We'll use the money saved on your passage to buy a set of china plates or a fine new rug for the parlor."

Maggie sighed and tucked the tattered newspaper advertisement back among her other papers, turning her attention to a tiny photograph of her parents, taken only months before their deaths. Mama, the daring, fair-haired aerialist, fearless and beautiful. Papa, the handsome lion tamer, in truth as gentle as a lamb. How fiercely they had loved each other and their daughter.

Struck by a loneliness that usually overtook her only by night, Maggie held the treasured photograph close to her heart for a moment, her eyes burning suspiciously. Then, firmly, she took herself in hand. Philip would be waiting for her in Sydney, and he would keep his promises too. She had only to keep her chin up and believe.

With a sniffle Maggie took out her tattered copy of *The Taming of the Shrew* and began to study her lines. It was a largely unnecessary task, considering that she'd long since mastered not only Bianca's speeches but most of Kate's and some of Petruchio's as well, in an effort to fill the long days at sea, but one could not be too thorough when it came to such things.

When Tansy returned from the mess hall, fully an hour later, she brought Maggie's pint ration of tea, along with the heel of a ham and a buttered slice of brown bread, neatly wrapped in a linen napkin that had doubtless been purloined from the first-class dining room.

"It ain't as though I've changed me mind," she said with a toss of her head as Maggie began to eat enthusiastically. "I still think Philip Briggs ain't a patch on a good man like sweet Rory at Government 'ouse, but from 'ere on, I'll keep me opinions to meself."

Maggie's eyes sparkled as she looked up at her friend; she'd believe that when cows sprouted wings, but she also knew an olive branch when she ate one. She finished the bread and ham quickly but took her time with the tea.

"Thank you," she remembered to say when her friend began to look annoyed.

Tansy was instantly mollified. "Some of the passengers is goin' ashore," she confided, "flood or no flood. They're sendin' 'em in dinghies."

Maggie had a sudden picture of Philip standing amid the stranded rabbits and the wreckage of Brisbane, trying to catch sight of her in one of the small boats being lowered from the ship and rowed to shore. As quick as that she was off her berth and scrambling back into her gray woolen dress.

"And where are you off to in such a rush?" Tansy demanded, hands on her hips.

"Why, to Brisbane, of course!" Maggie answered, wrenching her carpetbag from beneath the berth. Her hair was falling about her shoulders in great untidy loops, but there was no time to fuss with it. Carrying all her earthly belongings in that one battered bag, she bounded out of the women's compartment and onto the deck.

Sure enough, there were four dinghies making their way toward shore. The last dazzling light of a tropical sunset blazed on the water, making it very difficult to see.

Suddenly a head wearing a straw bushman's hat appeared over the ship's railing, startling Maggie so badly that she leapt backward a step and gasped, one hand pressed to her bosom.

Aquamarine eyes assessed her boldly from a tanned, ruggedly hewn face, and the man who had climbed the rope ladder dangling down the ship's side swung deftly over the railing to stand facing Maggie.

An insolent smile revealed straight white teeth, and the hat was swept off with a flourish, to show a profusion of tousled black hair. The man was enormous, and even when he bowed a pirate's dashing bow, he still seemed to tower over Maggie.

Having recovered much of her composure by then, Maggie dismissed the bushman with a withering glare and started around him, bent on making her way down that rope ladder, into a dinghy, and across that placid-looking water to Brisbane.

"I'm afraid you're too late, lassie," said John Higgins as he climbed up the ladder and vaulted over the railing. "The last boat's gone."

Maggie's frustration had reached its peak. She stomped one foot and gestured toward the bushman with her free hand. "If this—*gentleman*—came aboard, there must have been a boat to bring him across! And if there was a boat to bring him across—" She paused here to look over the railing. The dinghy that had carried this unconventional passenger over the water was paddling away toward shore. "Come back!" Maggie screamed.

"A Yank," observed the bushman in a tone that bespoke sympathy and tolerance.

21

"Aye," agreed John Higgins with a long-suffering sigh.

Maggie stomped her foot again and then kicked at the ship's side. "Damn, damn, double damn!" she yelled.

"It can't be as bad as all that," said the bushman, presuming to stand beside Maggie at the railing. His grin was beguiling in an obnoxious sort of way, and there was a faint Irish lilt to his voice.

"It ain't," Tansy put in suddenly with a sigh. She had linked her arm through John Higgins's. "That 'orse's—"Tansy paused, clearly remembering her earlier promise to keep her opinion of Maggie's betrothed to herself. "That Mr. Philip Briggs of 'ers will be waitin' in Sydney, I'll wager."

The bushman arched raven-black eyebrows and returned his hat to his head with a deft and innately masculine motion of one sun-bronzed hand. "You've come all this way to meet up with Philip Briggs, have you?"

Maggie's eyes widened as she met the stranger's quietly contemptuous gaze. "Why, yes. Do you know Mr. Briggs?"

A muscle in the Australian's jaw bunched into a knot and then went slack again. "Aye. I know him. He works for me."

Maggie searched her memory and came up with a name Philip had mentioned in passing. "You would be Mr. McKenna, then."

The answer was a nod, so brisk as to be terse and quite ill-mannered. Mr. McKenna's straw hat shadowed his eyes. "I would," he answered. A brassy-gold charm gleamed among the dark swirls of hair visible in the deep V of his shirt.

Maggie realized that she'd been staring, and blinked. She felt oddly alarmed at the coldness the mention of Philip Briggs had engendered in his employer and called upon all her stage experience to smile with confidence. "Then you must know that Philip and I plan to be married."

"Do you now?" asked Mr. McKenna with polite interest. "I'm sure that will be news to most of Sydney."

Maggie had been at sea for five long weeks and now, at last, she'd reached Brisbane, only to be denied the meeting with Philip she'd looked forward to with such bright hopes. And here was her future husband's employer, offering not a word of encouragement or welcome. Was it possible that Philip hadn't mentioned his plans to marry?

A lump formed in Maggie's throat and she gazed toward Brisbane in near despair as the S.S. *Victoria* chugged onward toward Sydney. Tansy and her beau wandered off down the deck, but Mr. McKenna remained, his gaze following Maggie's, his huge frame braced against the railing.

A flock of gray-white birds with lovely pink breasts soared past, a wondrous sight against the twilight sky. Maggie smiled despite all her uncertainties.

"They're called galahs," Mr. McKenna said.

Maggie could not and would not look at her unwanted companion. If she did, she might see pity in his blue-green eyes and that would be unbearable. "They're quite lovely," she said, still watching the beautiful birds as they soared off toward the land. "Are you fleeing the flood, Mr. McKenna?"

"Not really," came the gruff yet gentle reply. "I have business in Sydney."

Maggie drew a deep breath and made herself look into those incredible eyes. "I will find Philip Briggs waiting for me in Sydney, won't I, Mr. McKenna?" she asked.

"You'll find him," the Australian sighed, pulling his hat down farther over his brow.

Hardly more enlightened than before, Maggie squared her shoulders and walked with dignity across the deck and back into the sleeping compartment.

Chapter 2 ❧

DESPITE HIS ROUGH CLOTHING, REEVE MCKENNA TOOK A cabin in the first-class section of the ship. His station in life entitled him to the best and, besides, he felt an odd need to separate himself from that willful Yankee snippet with tangled moonfire hair and eyes the color of a brooding Queensland sky.

Tired and none too clean after a day spent burning off the sugar fields at Seven Sisters, his plantation upriver, Reeve sank down on the edge of the spacious bed bolted to the floor of his cabin and flung his hat away. He kicked off his boots and then stretched out on the fussy satin quilt that covered his berth, smiling to himself.

Loretta. He would think of Loretta. Thoughts of his mistress would surely keep one untidy little Yankee out of his mind.

One by one he assembled Loretta's features in his imagination: dark, glossy hair, wide and impudent brown eyes, ivory complexion, lips as tartly sweet as the fruit of a pomegranate, breasts that could be described only as succulent. . . .

Restlessly, Reeve sighed and cupped strong, callused hands behind his head. Loretta's image faded from his mind like smoke, instantly replaced by the vision of that saucy little chit from America.

What was her name? What was she doing here in Australia, some seventeen thousand miles from her home? Had she given herself to that bastard Briggs, or had some benign fate spared her?

Once again Reeve sighed. What could she have seen in that sniveling waster anyway?

Interested by a rap at the cabin door, Reeve sat bolt upright, as embarrassed as if his thoughts had been shouted in the passageways for all to hear. What the devil did he care whether or not Philip Briggs had had his way with the girl? It was none of his business, and besides, he had Loretta.

The knock sounded again and a tentative masculine voice called, "It's about your bath, Mr. McKenna—"

"The door's open," Reeve responded irritably, swinging his legs over the side of the bed and sitting up.

A steward entered, lugging a glistening copper bathtub and followed by two minions carrying enormous steaming buckets of water. Reeve knew he could find soap and towels in the cabinets affixed to the cabin wall. He gave the men a few coins for their trouble and muttered a dismissal, already peeling off his clothes as the door closed behind them. His smoke-scented shirt and trousers landed in a heap at the foot of his bed.

He fetched a large bar of lard soap from the cabinet as well as a washcloth and several towels, then stepped into the tub. The water was so hot that it made him draw in a sharp breath, but he sank into it without further hesitation, grateful for the ease it gave his aching muscles. If only the dratted thing had been large enough for a man to stretch out in.

Reeve closed his eyes and let his head rest against the high, ornately cast back of the tub. He wished that he'd asked for brandy as well as a bath. Then, except for Loretta, of course, he'd have had all the comforts of home.

There was a second knock at the door, this time a timid one, and Reeve smiled. The steward was back; he would send for a bottle of the ship's best and a good cigar as well.

"Come in," he said, settling deeper into the hot water.

The door opened and instead of the steward's voice he heard a distinctly female "Oh, dear!"

Reeve's eyes flew open and he sat up very straight, his hands instinctively covering his private parts.

It was the Yankee, standing there in the doorway, her mouth agape, her hair freshly brushed and entwined about her head in a complicated coronet involving braids and curls and all manner of feminine fuss. Instead of fleeing, like any normal woman would have done, she simply turned her back, pushed the door closed, and whispered, "I *am* sorry."

Reeve swore under his breath, more stunned than anything. If she was so damned sorry, he wondered to himself, why didn't she leave him to take his bath in peace? "What do you want?" he demanded, after a struggle with his vocal cords.

With her back still turned to Reeve, she shielded her face with one hand. Suddenly, Reeve McKenna would have given all his considerable holdings to know whether or not she was having the good grace to blush. She gave a little shuddering sigh and babbled out, "I didn't mean to interrupt your—your bath, Mr. McKenna. Truly I didn't. It's—it's what you said about my Philip—or perhaps what you didn't say—"

"Good God," Reeve muttered, relaxing a little. Wait till he told Loretta about this episode. He studied the sweet curves of the lady's bottom, her slender waist, the hint of rounded fullness visible beneath the upraised arm.

On second thought, he probably wouldn't mention this to Loretta after all.

The little back straightened in a touching bid for dignity and the head lifted proudly, although the woman didn't turn around to face the man she'd so brazenly intruded upon. "I did apologize," she reminded him tartly.

The gall of the baggage! But then, Yanks were known for their nerve, weren't they?

"What is your name?" Reeve demanded, both because he couldn't think of anything else to say and because he had an intractable need to know what this snippet called herself.

"M-Maggie," she said. "Maggie Chamberlin. About—about my betrothed, Mr. McKenna—"

The humor of the situation was coming home to Reeve by then; he felt his mouth curving into a smile and settled back with a whoosh of water. He even lifted one leg out of the cramped little tub, letting the heel rest against the edge.

"Your betrothed," he said in a leisurely tone. God, his kingdom for a good cigar and a snifter of brandy. "Oh, yes. Philip Briggs."

"Was I wrong in deducing that you dislike my Philip?" sputtered Miss Maggie Chamberlin. "You see, I've come so very far and if I can't marry Mr. Briggs, I shall have to scour floors and empty chamber pots for a period of three years—"

Reeve felt a chuckle rise in his throat and was gentleman enough to swallow it. "I'm not sure that wouldn't be preferable to marrying Briggs," he observed. "Have you been trained as a servant?"

The slim shoulders stiffened. "I should say not! I am an actress, Mr. McKenna, and Philip promised me—"

"Don't tell me, let me guess." Reeve took the bar of soap in hand and began to lather his left armpit. The cooling water reminded him that the bath couldn't last forever. Under the circumstances, he reflected, that was regrettable. "Philip promised you marriage and a role in a play."

Maggie almost forgot herself and turned to stare at Reeve at that moment; fortunately, she stopped just short of complete scandal. "Yes."

Reeve gave a long sigh and soaped his other armpit. He seldom gave a thought to the three theaters he owned; they were nothing more to him than playthings for Loretta, toys to keep her occupied while he traveled between Melbourne, Sydney, and Brisbane, attending to interests ranging from whaling ships and sugar plantations to the breeding and training of Thoroughbred racehorses. "I see," he said after a very long time.

Maggie's voice trembled slightly when she spoke. "If there is something I should know, Mr. McKenna, before I commit myself to marriage, I believe it is your duty to tell me."

Reeve tilted his head forward until it met with the water and industriously lathered his hair. "Have you had any acting experience, Miss Chamberlin?" he was surprised to hear himself ask.

Through dripping water and soapsuds, he saw Maggie Chamberlin stomp one foot in frustration, much as she had done earlier when she learned that there would be no boat to carry her ashore at Brisbane.

"Will you kindly stop skirting my questions, Mr. McKenna?"

Reeve began to rinse his hair with a lusty splashing. "Philip Briggs is a lying, cheating, spineless lowlife with an unnatural attachment to his mother," he said. "And believe me, Miss Chamberlin, he has no more intention of marrying you than I do. Is that direct enough for you?"

Even over the splashing, Reeve heard her suck in a horrified breath.

"You do dislike him!" she cried in wounded resignation.

Reeve reached for a towel to dry his dripping hair and gave Miss Chamberlin's back a wry look. "No," he drawled ironically, annoyed that she cared so much for Philip Briggs that she'd travel more than ten thousand miles and then have the gall to intrude on a man in the middle of a bath, "I was merely trying to convey my esteem for the gentleman."

"There is no need to be rude, Mr. McKenna."

"Don't talk to me about rudeness, Miss Chamberlin. You're the one trespassing here. Or do all American young ladies make a practice of walking in on naked men?"

Unexpectedly, the bundle of determination and gray woolen whirled. High color pulsed in Maggie's cheekbones and her pewter-gray eyes flashed. "I have traveled many thousands of miles, Mr. McKenna, on the strength of a promise from the man I love. I have no money and no references, and if you're telling me the truth about Philip, I shall have no choice but to serve out three years—*three years,* Mr. McKenna—as a household slave! It would have been better to stay in London—at least there I had a role in a revue—"

"So you have had experience as an actress," Reeve replied quietly, settling back in the tub. Due to the soap film on the water, he needed to make no special concession to decency.

Her suspicious gray eyes were fixed on the brass charm Reeve wore around his neck. For some indefinable reason, he covered the talisman with one hand, not wanting Maggie to know what it was.

"I've spent the entire journey learning the part of Bianca, in *The Taming of the Shrew,*" she said, her eyes sliding miserably from Reeve's hand to his face. "Philip promised me that I could play Bianca."

Reeve felt a crushing sympathy for the girl and hid it behind a gruff, "You're more suited, I think, for the part of Kate."

A flicker of hope lit the wondrous gray eyes and then went out like a snuffed flame. "It is most unkind of you to insult me, Mr. McKenna, by calling me a shrew."

Loretta is going to kill me for this, Reeve thought

29

with a remarkable lack of emotion. Slowly, he let his hand fall away from the charm he wore around his neck and ran his fingers through his wet hair. "Quite the contrary, Miss Chamberlin; I was paying you a compliment. Few women have the spirit to play Kate credibly, but you do. The part is yours if you want it."

She backed up to the door, her hands behind her, probably clasping the knob, her lovely eyes wide and suspicious and hopeful. "Please don't tease me, Mr. McKenna—I've come a very long way only to be disappointed, and it would be most cruel of you to make matters worse."

"If you want the role," Reeve answered wearily, settling still deeper into the water and sighing, "Come to Number Fifteen George Street as soon as we dock in Sydney."

The wench didn't leave the room, but lingered, still gazing at Reeve's face, trying, he supposed, to read it. "There is the matter of my agreement to work three years in return for my passage—"

Reeve waved one hand in dismissal, impatient for the chit to be gone. His baser instincts were coming to the fore, probably stirred by the incredible fact that this young woman had inflicted herself upon a naked man and then had the temerity to stay and argue. It seemed to him that a real lady would have fled in a proper state of shame and disgrace. "Good God, Miss Chamberlin," he snarled, "do you never tire of prattling on and on? I'll buy your damnable papers if I have to—just get out of here before I forget my manners and take it upon myself to find out exactly to what extent Philip Briggs has deceived you!"

Once again Maggie's cheeks went from a soft apricot shade to a fierce scarlet. She pulled open the door at last, and fled through it, slamming it closed behind her.

Reeve scowled at the place where she had stood, wondering. Could Maggie Chamberlin possibly have escaped Briggs's more intimate attentions? Given her brass, it didn't seem likely. The idea made him furious, and he flung the bar of soap at the door behind her.

Avoiding Mr. McKenna for the short remainder of the voyage was easy: Maggie had only to keep to her own side of the ship and never let her eyes stray toward the first-class section. She took her meals in the women's compartment, sitting cross-legged on her berth, and her strange mood vexed Tansy into a dither.

She paced back and forth before Maggie's berth, her arms folded across her chest. "You went to Mr. McKenna's cabin, Maggie Chamberlin—I know you did!" she charged in a hissing whisper. "John 'iggins saw you with 'is own eyes! What on earth could you 'ave been thinkin' of to do such a thing? Surely you're not like them women what got off at Thursday Island—"

Tansy's intimation stung Maggie, and she didn't bother to hide the fact. The women who'd left the ship at Thursday Island to be "housekeepers" to lonely men were lightskirts of the crudest sort, after all. Maggie leapt off her berth, her plate clattering forgotten to the floor, and faced Tansy nose-to-nose. "How dare you suggest that I did anything immoral in that cabin, Tansy Quinn!"

Tansy retreated a step, but there was a twinkle in her blue eyes. "I ain't suggestin' anything of the sort, love. It's just that—well—after all your carryin' on about bein' pure for your 'usband come your weddin' night, it looked a bit odd."

All of Maggie's ire escaped her and she sank to her berth like a deflated balloon. "I was desperate," she said. "I had to know why Mr. McKenna behaved so strangely when I introduced myself to him as Philip's intended."

Tansy sat down beside Maggie and shyly took her hand. "What did 'e say, then?"

"Awful things," Maggie replied, sudden tears springing to her eyes and burning there. "Oh, Tansy, he despises Philip!"

Tansy's workworn hand patted Maggie's smooth one and, though tempted, she refrained from saying I told you so. "Coo, but 'e's a 'andsome one, that Mr. Reeve McKenna. Pure man from the soles of 'is feet to the crown of 'is 'ead—I'll wager 'e could make a girl carry on somethin' fearful!"

Though she wouldn't have admitted it on pain of death, Maggie had had the same thought ever since she'd burst into Reeve McKenna's cabin and caught him in his bath. She remembered his broad chest and the dark swirls of wet hair that had covered it, remembered his powerful arms and the mocking light in his blue-green eyes. A strange, melting heat had spread through her on sight of him, and the curious needs left in its wake showed no signs of abating even though a full day and night had passed.

Undaunted by Maggie's failure to answer, Tansy rushed on. "I asked John about 'im, so curious was I, and 'e said McKenna's one of the richest men in Australia—got 'imself over from Ireland when 'e was just a wee lad and made 'is fortune right and proper." Suddenly, the light went out of Tansy's eyes and her smile faded. "'E 'as a mistress, though, and to 'ear John 'iggins tell it, she's as pretty as an angel."

Maggie couldn't think why she wanted to cry, but she did. She wanted to fling herself facedown on her berth and pound her pillow with her fists, too, while kicking her feet and wailing. Of course, she did none of those things; she merely jutted out her chin and said, "He's promised to buy my papers if necessary, and give me a part in *The Taming of the Shrew,* so what do I care if he's got a mistress?"

Tansy's eyes went wide and her mouth dropped

open. "Buy your papers, is it? Give you a part? And what's 'e askin' in return for all this, missy?"

"Nothing," Maggie said stiffly. "Nothing at all."

Tansy clasped a thumb and forefinger to the bridge of her nose and shook her head in frustration. "Lordy, lordy, lordy, I'll get nothin' done for watchin' after you, I can see that!"

Incensed, Maggie got off the berth and ferreted beneath it for her carpetbag. Once she'd found that, she made busy work of arranging and rearranging its meager contents, careful not to speak to Tansy Quinn or even to look at her.

Just after midnight the *Victoria* docked in Sydney Harbor.

Tired and unable to see much in the dense darkness, the one hundred-odd emigrant women left the ship by one ramp while the first-class passengers disembarked via another. Laughter and warm greetings wafted over the dark water, deepening the loneliness of those who had no one to greet them.

For this reason the band of women stayed close together as John Higgins, holding a lamp high above his head, led them into a long, shedlike building, where more lamps shone.

Maggie saw what seemed to be dried seaweed piled up against the walls in heaps and, out of the corner of one eye, a rat skittering across the bare plank floors. There was no furniture, no food, no one to offer a warm welcome.

"Looks like we'll all be piggin' in 'ere together!" Tansy sang out in cheerful tones.

There was a stunned silence at this, Maggie being no more vocal in the face of such a prospect than the other women.

Tansy surveyed her audience with exasperated affection. "Now, don't be lookin' so woebegone, all of you—there'll be wagons come for us in the mornin', bright and early."

Maggie was thinking of what Mr. McKenna had told her in his cabin: that she was to come to Number 15 George Street as soon as the ship docked in Sydney. Given the late hour, the prospect was hardly appealing, but it beat "pigging in" on a bed of scratchy seaweed, with rats for company.

Always one to act on a thought in virtually the same moment it surfaced, Maggie bounded out of the shed on the landward side and along a dimly lighted wooden walkway to the place where the first-class passengers were being helped into sleek buggies and carriages.

In the light of gas-powered streetlights, Maggie searched for Reeve McKenna, having long since given up on the idea that Philip would be waiting here for her, eager to whisk her away to a place where one could have a bath and a clean bed to sleep in. Intuitively, she knew that Tansy had been right about Mr. Briggs, indeed, that Mr. McKenna had spoken the truth concerning him as well. She wondered that her heart had not broken under the knowledge.

There were a good many people milling about in the golden glow of the street lanterns, and it was some time before Maggie spotted Mr. McKenna. When she did, she almost turned away.

A tall woman, clad in a fashionable white silk dress trimmed in the softest wine-colored velvet, with a tiny feathered hat to match, stood scandalously close to him, her gloved hands moving up and down his sides in a most familiar way.

"You still smell of the sugar fields, darling!" the vision trilled, and her laugh rang out in the night like the sound of bells in the far distance. "Oh, but I'm so glad you're here—"

Reeve McKenna muttered, "Loretta," and bent his magnificent head to kiss the woman who clung to him with a thoroughness that made Maggie, watching in horrified fascination, wonder what there was to do while kissing besides touching lips. It was clear enough that something more complicated was going on here, and it was galling not to know what that something was.

"Ah-hem," said Maggie, to let them know that she was there.

Mr. McKenna seemed in no hurry to end the kiss; indeed, his hands encircled the woman's tiny waist and lifted her slightly, the better to mystify untutored onlookers such as Maggie.

Embarrassed and not a little envious, Maggie nevertheless found the courage to clear her throat again, this time more loudly.

It was the woman who broke away from the kiss, putting her small hands to Reeve's chest and twisting her head to one side with a delicate gasp. Deep brown eyes glistened in the lamplight, taking in Maggie's person with dispatch. "Yes?"

By now Maggie wished that she'd stayed in that dreadful shed with Tansy, among the women and the seaweed and the rats. Before she could think of a reply, Mr. McKenna assessed her almost as coolly as his ladyfriend had and said, "In the morning, Miss Chamberlin. In the morning."

Maggie felt like a child; even in the darkness she was painfully conscious of the contrast between her clothes and those of Mr. McKenna's mistress. And there were other differences, too—differences in age, in experience, in sophistication, that were equally hard to bear. "Yes—thank you—" she said stupidly, turning to walk away.

She waited outside the shed until her flaming cheeks had cooled.

"Who on earth was that?" Loretta demanded coyly, keeping the carriage driver waiting, toying with the collar of Reeve's smoke-tinged work shirt.

Reeve was impatient; this was neither the time nor

the place to discuss the Yankee. He wanted to reach the town house, look in on Elisabeth, and then luxuriate in Loretta's uncanny knack for driving him right out of his mind. "Just a girl," he said.

Loretta would not be moved; her feet were rooted to the cobblestones and her dark eyes searched Reeve's face. "'In the morning,' you said. What's going to happen in the morning, Reeve?"

Reeve sighed. At this rate it would be morning before he could indulge the desires that had been plaguing him ever since Miss Maggie Chamberlin had so gracelessly entered his cabin on board the ship. "Philip Briggs promised to marry her, Loretta," he said. "She came all the way from England expecting to be his wife. The least I can do is see that she's properly looked after."

Loretta's hands tightened on Reeve's collar. "I fail to see why it should be your responsibility to clean up after poor Philip."

Reeve had never loved Loretta, but he had liked her, and heartily. Now, strangely, that worthy emotion was fading away. At the look he gave her, Loretta let go her grip on his collar and instead traced the circumference of the brass charm hidden in the thick hair that covered his chest.

"Are you tiring of me, Reeve?" she asked softly, and Reeve realized with a start that perhaps he was. In fact, he had to admit that he wished that it were Maggie Chamberlin coming to his home and his bed.

He was silent, and Loretta wriggled against him, reminding him of her singular skills. Her gaze strayed toward the lighted shed where the emigrants would wait out the long night. There was a wistful expression on her face, visible even in the darkness.

"I see I'll have to be very, very careful to keep you happy, my love," she said. "Very careful indeed."

Reeve, feeling a raw ache where there had once been real affection for Loretta, ushered her somewhat roughly to the carriage and climbed in after her. "How is Elisabeth?" he asked once the vehicle was rolling and rattling over the cobblestones.

Loretta gave a sigh and snuggled a little closer to Reeve on the leather seat, well aware that her breast touched his upper arm as she reached up to take off her hat. "She's been a perfect horror ever since you left," she answered. "Fortunately, your niece is her nanny's problem, not mine."

"That's fortunate indeed," Reeve retorted evenly.

Loretta bristled. "Reeve, you know we agreed that I would have no responsibilities whatsoever where the child is concerned!"

"Elisabeth is alone in the world except for us. Are you completely void of womanly feelings, Loretta?"

"You know very well, Reeve McKenna, that I don't lack for 'womanly feelings.' It's just that I'm an actress of some renown, that's all—I have a reputation—"

"If being my mistress didn't ruin your reputation, why should mothering Elisabeth do it any damage?"

The light of streetlamps along the way caught in the huge tears that had arisen in Loretta's beautiful brown eyes. "What's come over you, Reeve? Why are you being so difficult—is it that girl back there? That emigrant?"

Reeve remained silent.

"So I was right," Loretta whispered in despair. "You want her, don't you, Reeve?"

His answer was a long time in coming; after all, Loretta was his mistress, and had been for several years, and he was not without feeling for her. "Yes," he answered at last, wishing to God that it was in him to lie. "Yes, I want her."

Loretta lifted her hands to her face and began to weep, and Reeve was reminded of her performance in a recent play. She'd cried just that way in the second act, and just as convincingly.

37

When the carriage came to a stop before a splendid white house overlooking Rushcutter's Bay, Reeve got out, helped a distracted Loretta down, and dismissed the driver.

That night, for the first time in years, Loretta and Reeve slept under the same roof without sharing a bed.

Chapter 3 🌿

THE NIGHT HAD BEEN A LONG AND SLEEPLESS ONE FOR Maggie; she'd sat upon a thatch of seaweed next to Tansy throughout, clutching her bag to her bosom lest it be stolen away, and cursing the day Philip Briggs had first drawn breath. If it hadn't been for him, she wouldn't be in this godforsaken place, so far from the rest of the world.

At dawn the wagons Tansy had promised the night before began to arrive in twos and threes, though by this time a good portion of the emigrant women were gone. Maggie had watched them gather their reticules and bags and boxes and creep out, here one, there another, all through the dark hours.

The rattling of wagon wheels on cobblestones awakened Tansy, and she sat up, stretching her arms high above her head and sighing happily. She might have spent the night in a feather bed with linen sheets for all the distress she showed. "Wide awake already, then?" she chimed sunnily, squinting at Maggie and yawning again.

Maggie shook her head at her friend's aplomb and then sighed. Tansy was adaptable, that was all. And if *she* wanted to make a niche for herself in this upside-down, sunshine-in-February place, she'd best learn to be adaptable too. "Most of the women have gone," she said quite unnecessarily, for anyone with eyes could see that the shed was all but empty.

"Streetwalkers," Tansy confided in a blithe whisper. "Never a thought in their 'eads of peelin' potatoes or scrubbin' floors for a livin'."

Maggie's eyes went wide. "You mean, they came here under false pretenses?"

Tansy's regard was steady and completely lacking in venom. "Didn't you?"

Maggie blushed and looked away. "It's hardly the same thing," she protested.

A grand lady swept into the shed at that moment, dressed in a finely made gown of the most disturbing pea-green color Maggie had ever seen. The skirt was smocked between silken stripes of a vile olive shade, and the train was flounced and trimmed in ribbon. A tiny hat with one limp yellow feather dangling to the side capped a head of snow-white hair, carefully coiffed. Kind blue eyes looked out of an eager, generously powered face.

"Good morning, girls," the matron said in an operatic voice touching upon every note in the scale. "My name is Lady Cosgrove and I've come to take you to the Girls' Friendly Society. You shall have baths and hearty breakfasts and then we'll see to your placement."

Maggie started to step forward, to explain that she had an appointment at Number 15 George Street this morning, but she stopped herself. A bath and breakfast sounded very good and besides, if she left too hastily, Lady Cosgrove might decide that she was of an ilk with those women who had sneaked away during the night. That would never do, and anyway, she certainly didn't want to present herself at Mr. McKenna's theater in this state of untidiness.

Without a word she joined Tansy in one of the wagons.

The day was sunny and hot, but Maggie paid little attention to the weather: She was too enthralled with Sydney itself. Far from the outpost of thatched roofs and barefoot natives she had expected, it was a cosmopolitan city with trolley cars, macadamized streets, telephone wires, and towering business buildings. Indeed, it was as modern as New York or London but infinitely cleaner and much more spacious. The waters of the harbor were of a startling aqua color, reminiscent of Mr. Reeve McKenna's eyes.

"Pretty place, ain't it?" Tansy asked, giving Maggie a knowing nudge in the ribs. "The Queen's Jubilee is this year, you know, in June, and there'll be parties and races and illuminations too."

Eventually, the three wagons came to a lumbering stop in front of somber brick house of English-estate proportions. One of the drivers opened the high wrought-iron gates that separated the house and its beautifully kept lawn from the sidewalk, while another proceeded to help the passengers down from their straw-filled wagons just as though they were ladies of the court.

Lady Cosgrove, of course, had arrived first, not in a wagon but in a costly black curricle, and she greeted each emigrant with a warm handshake and a smile as they passed through the gate.

Tansy entered just before Maggie did, giving a little curtsy and muttering, "Your ladyship."

Maggie's knee would not bend; she'd never curtsied in her life, except at the end of a performance, of course. "Pleased to meet you," she said somewhat woodenly, and made to move on up the walk.

But Lady Cosgrove held her hand fast. "An American," she said in a tone that made certain allowances. "Pray, what was your name again?"

Maggie swallowed. "Maggie Chamberlin, ma'am," she answered.

"You're very far from home, my dear."

With anyone else, Maggie might have made a flippant reply of some sort, the fact of distance being such an obvious one, but she liked Lady Cosgrove, sensed that she was a gentle and compassionate person. "Yes, ma'am," she said. If there'd been more time, she might have told her ladyship the whole long story of how she'd come to be in Australia. She felt that warm toward the woman, but there were others, pressing in behind her. "I don't suppose it's any farther than England, though."

Lady Cosgrove smiled at this and released Maggie's hand. "We'll speak again, my dear, after you've had your bath and something to eat."

Maggie nodded, already wondering how she was going to explain to this kindly woman about her appointment in George Street with one Reeve McKenna, and hurried after Tansy.

Over the great double doors, the words GIRLS' FRIENDLY SOCIETY had been carefully scripted, and since Tansy stepped over the threshold without bothering to knock, Maggie followed after her.

Austere-looking maids awaited in the sprawling entryway, their arms stacked with towels and bars of cheap yellow soap.

Still following Tansy's lead, Maggie took two towels and a bar of soap and then mounted the sweeping stairway to the second floor. There, in the first chamber on the right, which looked big enough to serve as a ballroom, hip baths awaited, each tub curtained on three sides for a semblance of privacy.

"Be sure you wash your 'air, now," one of the maids announced to everyone in general, her chapped red hands clasped in front of her in an authoritive fashion. "And if you got bugs, you're to say so. Her ladyship don't want you givin' lice to the fine families of Sydney."

Bugs. Maggie was roundly insulted, but she held her tongue and stepped into one of the cloth cubicles in the second row. There, she set down her carpetbag, towel, and soap, and began to undress. The prospect of a bath was so appealing that she could think of nothing else, not even her appointment in George Street or the fact that Philip Briggs had surely played her false.

By the time she'd thoroughly scrubbed herself, climbed out of the tub, and toweled her hair, Maggie's stomach was rumbling with hunger. Last night's supper, taken aboard the ship, seemed as far in the past as Noah's flood.

To her annoyance as well as her relief, Maggie soon found that her sturdy woolen dress had been taken away, as had her underthings, and replaced by a servant's gown of black bombazine. Drawers, petticoats, and a camisole of unbleached muslin replaced her own unmentionables, and there were prim black stockings as well.

Resigned, Maggie began to dress herself in the clothing provided by the Girls' Friendly Society. Perhaps it wasn't the appropriate garb for an interview at Mr. McKenna's theater, but it was clean and neatly pressed and it felt good against Maggie's freshly bathed skin. Mr. McKenna would simply have to make allowances.

Once she was fully dressed, Maggie took her brush from her carpetbag—at least that and her spare dress and nightgown remained—and did what she could to tame her too-thick, too-curly hair. It was the bane of her existence, that wild and heavy mane; how she'd love to crop it off, short as a boy's, and leave off the fuss of braiding and brushing and pinning forever.

Breakfast was served in the kitchen, a building quite separate from the main house, at long trestle tables with benches for seats. Maggie, like the others, tucked into the steaming hotcakes, salted pork, and fried eggs with an industry born of great hunger.

There was plenty of tea, too, and milk for those who wanted it.

"Now comes the speech," said Tansy with a sigh of resignation, when one of the maids took up a position in front of the fireplace and held high an ornate sheet of paper decorated with flowers and vines and stars and moons.

Hunger appeased, Maggie pushed away her plate and sipped her tea as she listened. The maid announced importantly that a year's faithful and industrious service in a suitable household would bring a girl just such a certificate, inscribed with Lady Cosgrove's own signature. With the certificate, respectable work could be had anywhere in Queensland, Victoria, New South Wales, or Tasmania. Without the certificate, one could expect only disgrace of the worst sort.

Neither Maggie nor any other woman in the room had any doubt whatsoever as to what constituted "disgrace of the worst sort," and the prospect was a sobering one. Suppose Mr. McKenna turned out to be as insincere as Philip Briggs had been, Maggie reflected. She'd be out in the cold, without a certificate to prove herself fit for honest employment. Then what would she do?

Tansy preened beside Maggie. She, of course, had three such certificates already—signed by Lady Cosgrove's various counterparts in Victoria, Queenland, and New South Wales. An idea blossomed in Maggie's mind, but she shoved it aside to listen attentively to The Speech.

Only women of exemplary moral character could expect to earn a certificate, the maid was careful to say. So much for hard and fast rules, Maggie thought, remembering the scandalous stories Tansy had told her about "her Rory at Government House." A wry grin twisted her mouth as she gave Tansy a sidelong glance.

Tansy saw the look and promptly put out her tongue.

The maid's discourse went on endlessly, covering rules of dress, deportment, language, and personal industry. Just when Maggie was beginning to feel sleepy, Lady Cosgrove swept imperiously into the room and took over.

She announced that she would personally interview each girl in turn, beginning with Miss Maggie Chamberlin.

Maggie was at once relieved and alarmed. An expedient conclusion to the required interview might allow her to make her way to Mr. McKenna's offices before he forgot that she existed, but there was a certain distress in being singled out as the first too. Perhaps Lady Cosgrove saw through her pretense. No doubt, the worldly-wise woman had already guessed that Maggie Chamberlin was a fraud, having no intention of serving as a domestic if she could possibly avoid it.

Maggie rose from her seat at the trestle table with an air of confidence that was almost wholly feigned and followed Lady Cosgrove from the crowded, cozy kitchen, across the rear garden, and into the once-grand house.

Her ladyship kept an office in a cubicle adjoining the drawing room, a place cluttered with books and papers and old-fashioned quill pens. The only neatness in evidence came from the lady herself; she was immaculately groomed in every detail.

Lady Cosgrove invited Maggie to take a chair facing the messy French Provincial desk, and she had to shoo an enormous tabby cat off the seat in order to comply.

"Have you ever worked as a domestic servant, my dear girl?" Lady Cosgrove asked forthrightly. So forthrightly, in fact, that Maggie was caught completely off guard.

45

"Well, no," she confessed lamely, without thinking first.

The next question was as gently candid as the first one had been. "How, then, did you support yourself?"

Maggie swallowed hard. "I was an actress, ma'am. In London."

"And how did an American lass find herself in London?"

Quietly, honestly, Maggie explained how she had come to Europe with her parents because they'd been performing with a circus there, and how they'd died so tragically in a train crash.

"Dear me," Lady Cosgrove said with sympathy, "it must have been a frightening situation to find oneself alone in a strange country, without friends."

Not unlike the straits I'm in now, Maggie thought to herself, but she only nodded, conscious of a slight flush in her cheeks.

"You strike me as a most intelligent and well-mannered young woman," observed the elderly lady. "Tell me, can you read and write and figure?"

"Yes," Maggie responded somewhat briskly, surprised by the question.

Lady Cosgrove smiled as the giant tabby cat leapt unceremoniously into her lap and she idly petted the creature. "Don't be so shocked, Miss Chamberlin. Most of those girls out there in our kitchen cannot so much as write their own names. They, of course, will have to resign themselves to domestic service of the most menial nature, but there might be another sort of position entirely for you.

"There is an American gentleman residing in Sydney just now—a widower with two young sons. He's applied to me several times for a governess to look after his children while he attends to his rather extensive interests. I should think he'd be pleased to engage a woman from his own country." Lady Cosgrove left off petting the cat to shuffle through a stack of cards, finally settling upon one with a muttered exclamation. "Yes, here it is. Mr. Duncan Kirk. He keeps offices at Number Twenty George Street; I could telephone him and request an interview if you'd like."

Though Maggie's impulse had been to blurt out her intentions to accept Mr. McKenna's offer of an engagement at one of his theaters, she thought better of it. It was almost providential that Mr. Kirk's offices should be within walking distance of Mr. McKenna's; here was a way she could keep her appointment with that disturbing gentleman without throwing away all chance of obtaining a certificate. No one knew better than she did that fate had a way of slamming doors in a person's face.

"I would like very much to meet with Mr. Kirk, thank you," Maggie said quietly. And if her words weren't entirely true, her gratitude was genuine. Lady Cosgrove obviously took the most thorough care to see that her charges were well placed, and Maggie had seen enough of the world to know how easily a woman in such a position could abuse her authority.

Pleased, Lady Cosgrove unearthed a telephone from the papers that littered her desk and shouted into the receiver, "Give me Mr. Duncan Kirk, if you please."

Maggie suppressed a smile. The telephone was still a new contrivance to people of Lady Cosgrove's generation and they invariably felt the need to compensate for wire-strung distances by speaking loudly. Nonetheless, the interview was arranged and Maggie was dismissed to put up her hair, which had fallen free about her shoulders since her bath.

Back in the upstairs dressing room, Maggie found her bag and got out her brush and pins, making haste to arrange her hair in a fashion that would impress Mr. McKenna and, if need be, Mr. Kirk as well.

There was, a maid came to impart, a carriage waiting to take her to George Street, and would she please hurry. Maggie was already making every effort to hurry, and, minutes later, she bounded out the front gates and through the door the driver was holding open for her.

During the ride to George Street, which lay in the heart of Sydney's business district, Maggie tried to compose her thoughts. As much as Reeve McKenna unnerved her—he was indeed, as Tansy had said, a man from the soles of his feet to the crown of his head—Maggie longed to play the part of Kate in his production of *The Taming of the Shrew.* She wanted it so much, in fact, that the pit of her stomach was jumping and her knees had all the substance of strawberry jelly.

But suppose he was a scoundrel, as men of his obviously lusty nature were wont to be.

Maggie sat up very straight in the cushioned leather carriage seat, taking herself firmly in hand. If Mr. McKenna turned out to be a rascal, the disappointment would be keen, of course, but Maggie had endured worse things, hadn't she? If he had merely been toying with her that day in his cabin, when he'd promised her not only a part she'd coveted all her life but freedom from her work agreement as well, she would, please God, discern the fact immediately and hasten herself to Mr. Duncan Kirk's offices, where she could be fairly certain of obtaining employment.

She settled back in the seat, her hands folded in her lap, her reticule at her feet. It wouldn't be so bad, working as a governess; if there was one thing Maggie Chamberlin loved more than the stage, it was the company of children.

Maggie sighed and smoothed her skirts. Why had she troubled herself? One way or the other, everything would be fine.

Loretta could not concentrate on her lines, even though the role of Lady Macbeth was her favorite, even though she knew the role forward, backward, and inside out. She had to do something about that odd little baggage that had caught Reeve's attention on board ship, and she had to do it fast.

When Philip Briggs came down the theater's main aisle, she marveled at the possibilities she'd overlooked. "Philip!" she trilled, ignoring his surprise at the familiarity of her greeting. In reality, her opinion of the boy was hardly higher than Reeve's, though she tolerated him because he was pretty and because he possessed an endearing talent for flattery.

Small of stature, with lustrous, curly brown-gold hair and ingenuous amber eyes, Philip had a cherubic look about him that the young ladies found irresistible. Loretta smiled to herself. If only it were young ladies that Philip found so attractive.

Today he looked agitated and even despondent, and, as Loretta descended the stage steps to greet him, she caught the scent of good English rum. "What is it, Miss Craig?" he asked, his tone bordering on impatience.

Loretta hid the offense she'd taken at his manner. "Reeve and I were expecting you to present us with a bride today," she said warmly, taking a certain satisfaction in the way the color drained from Philip's angelic face. "Reeve struck lucky, you know, and encountered the lass aboard the *Victoria*. Her name is—" Loretta pretended to search her memory, though in reality Reeve had refused to share that bit of information.

"Maggie," Philip sighed disconsolately. "Maggie Chamberlin. So she did arrive, then?"

"Yes, she did, Philip," Loretta said in stern tones, "and pity that it was, there was no one to greet her. Reeve was quite worried, I don't mind telling you." She paused, drew a deep breath that lifted her fine breasts and flashed in her eyes. *"Too* worried, my dear Philip, as far as you and I are concerned."

49

The pale amber eyes, surrounded by lashes thick enough to be envied even by Loretta, widened. "I didn't think she'd actually travel all this way—it was all a game, a flirtation. I thought she knew that!"

"She believed you, evidently, and she's here. In Sydney. I have reason to believe that she'll be meeting with Reeve at his offices this morning—if she hasn't done so already. What do you intend to do about this situation, Philip?"

Philip retreated a step, his Adam's apple bouncing up and down along his neck. "Do? What on earth can I do, Miss Craig?"

"You can keep your word, insofar as marrying the little twit is concerned. The part about her having a role in a play you can tuck neatly into your—"

"She told Mr. McKenna about that?" Philip choked out, aghast. "The role in *The Taming of the Shrew*, I mean?"

Loretta bridled, smoothing her dark hair with one hand, her skirts with the other. "I merely guessed that," she said haughtily. "So you promised her a part in my play, did you? *My* play? You have some considerable gall, Philip Briggs!"

"It was only—I never dreamed—"

"You will marry Miss Chamberlin, Mr. Briggs, or I'll have your head!"

Philip reached out and grasped a seatback for support. "You know I can't marry her. Mother would be impossible, and besides, I couldn't—I couldn't be a proper husband—"

"That, Mr. Briggs, is your problem. And Miss Chamberlin's. It happens that Reeve is quite taken with this girl and I'll be damned if I'll have her taking over my man as well as my favorite roles! Is that clear, Mr. Briggs? You either marry Maggie Chamberlin or you're out of work, and that, believe me, will just be the start of your woes!"

Philip was walking backward up the aisle, loosening and then tightening his string tie as he moved, and though his throat was working, no sound was coming from his mouth.

"You'll find her at Reeve's office, I would imagine," Loretta said in a cool voice, turning back to the stage and the company of players who stood watching and, at the same time, pretending to be unaware of the scalding ultimatum that had just been given the unfortunate Mr. Briggs. "Make haste," she tossed back over one shoulder, "and my heartiest congratulations on your marriage."

Reeve was just beginning to despair of Maggie Chamberlin when he heard her presenting herself to his secretary, Mr. Coates, in the outer office. Grinning to himself, he made a dash for his chair, behind his august desk, and pretended to be enthralled by the dull list of stock reports lying before him. He even went so far as to frown pensively over numbers he could have recited from memory.

"Mr. McKenna?"

Reeve looked up with feigned distraction and frowned again, as though he didn't quite recall the face or figure that had been burned into his mind like a cattleman's brand. Bombazine. Damnation and spit, they'd dressed her in black bombazine, like a common servant!

"Yes?"

She bit her lower lip and carefully set her disreputable reticule in a chair, approaching the desk as a French aristocrat might have approached the guillotine. "I do hope you remember me—my name is Maggie Chamberlin."

Amused as he was, Reeve was not without sympathy for the lass; it was time to stop teasing her. He rose to his feet in a gentlemanly fashion and gave a slight nod. "Oh, yes—the actress. Won't you sit down?"

Maggie removed her reticule from the chair and dragged the seat forward, practically falling into it. Of course, she rallied instantly; her insolent little chin rose a degree and her cheeks glowed a tropical pink. "I'm here about the role you promised me," she said. "Were you sincere, Mr. McKenna?"

"Sincere" was too idealistic a word for the things this Yankee sprite made him feel, but it wasn't without a certain legitimacy either. "I meant what I said," he replied. And then, after an involuntary inspection of her person, he was compelled to ask, "Where the devil did you get that dress?"

Reeve watched, fascinated, as both relief and fierce pride played in her face. Before she could formulate a reply, the door burst open.

Philip Briggs, the nerveless little rotter, had the unmitigated brass to burst into the room, all bluster and blush, to caterwaul, "Good God, Maggie, what are you doing here?!"

Coolly, if somewhat unsteadily, Maggie Chamberlin rose to her feet. "I'm taking a part, Philip," she said. "An even better one than you offered me."

With uncharacteristic forcefulness Philip grabbed Maggie by the arm and dragged her out of the office, but not out of Reeve's hearing. As he was shoving back his chair to follow, he heard Briggs make his confession.

"I never thought you would actually travel all the way to Australia, Maggie! The plain truth is, I could never be a good husband to you, and I don't have the authority to give you any kind of part!"

There was a sharp sound, like a slap, and Reeve froze behind his desk, grinning. Listening.

"I don't blame you for being angry," Philip went on, more calmly now that he'd gotten his comeuppance. "But you've got to go home, Maggie—back to England, back to the States, anywhere. The theaters are only—only toys for Mr. McKenna's mistress. Unless you're prepared to assume that role, you have no hope of any others."

Reeve's grin faded. Why, that scrawny little pissant!

By God, he'd feed Briggs ten of his own toes, with knees and ankles for good measure.

Cheeks hot, shoulders rigid, Maggie glared at Reeve as he stood in the doorway, pushed her way around him, and snatched up her reticule. He turned to face her. "Maggie—"

She drew back her arm and slammed the reticule into his middle as hard as she could. While Reeve was still doubled over, gasping for breath, Maggie Chamberlin squeezed past him and made what was probably the grandest exit of her career.

Chapter 4 🌿

HALF-BLINDED BY TEARS, TEARS SHE WAS STRUGGLING TO suppress, Maggie walked determinedly in the wrong direction for some distance and then had to retrace her steps. Finally, she stood before Number 20 George Street, which was a block away from Mr. McKenna's offices and on the opposite side of the road. She stood outside for several minutes, drawing deep breaths and dashing at her wet eyes.

Mr. Kirk's offices were on the first floor, and there were desks everywhere, telephones ringing, telegraph keys clicking, typewriters clattering. Maggie was, for a moment, intimidated by all that hectic activity, and she hesitated just inside the revolving door, wringing her hands.

She was not permitted to hesitate long, for a clerk immediately approached her, a fellow with a tight celluloid collar and spectacles. He didn't smile, and there seemed to be a permanent flush in his cheeks. "Miss Chamberlin?"

Maggie, beginning now to regain her equanimity after that unfortunate scene at Mr. McKenna's place of business, managed a slight smile and a nod.

The clerk took her arm with dispatch and half dragged her toward an inner office. "Mr. Kirk will see you now," he said as Maggie hurried to keep up. She hardly had a chance to smooth her skirts and pray that her eyes weren't swollen and red-rimmed before she was thrust into a plush chamber that looked more like a gentleman's study than a place of business.

There were bookshelves filling every wall, except the one that was graced with an ornate ivory fireplace. Beside the impeccably neat desk, a massive piece of polished mahogany, a colorful globe spun on its tall, carved stand, aided by a graceful masculine hand.

The hand was connected, Maggie soon discerned, to a towering, well-built man with chestnut-colored hair and piercing green eyes. He wore a tailored suit of lightweight tweed, and when he smiled, she saw that his teeth were white and even.

"Miss Chamberlin," he observed in a low and smooth voice. "Do come in and sit down."

Hearing an American accent after all her time abroad was balm to Maggie's spirit. She felt herself relaxing slightly, even though there was something about this man, as handsome as he was, that warned her to stay alert.

The clerk drew up a chair for Maggie, much as a waiter in a fine restaurant might have done, and she sat down gratefully. Her knees were wobbling and even though her eyes were dry, there were tears burning in her throat. The incident in Reeve McKenna's office had taken a higher toll than she'd thought.

She started when the office doors closed with a genteel click behind her, and her prospective employer smiled at the reaction.

"My name is Duncan Kirk," he said, slipping out of his costly tweed jacket and sitting down in the enormous leather chair behind his broad and quite intimidating desk. "I presume Lady Cosgrove explained my need to find a governess and companion for my sons?"

Maggie nodded. She had to forget that all her dreams had been dashed in the space of twenty-four hours and pull herself together. If she didn't get this position, she would probably end up as a scullery maid. Or worse. "Yes, sir, she did."

"I am a widower, Miss Chamberlin," Mr. Kirk went on. "My sons are seven and ten years of age and I'm afraid they've suffered some for lack of a mother's guidance. I, of course, am inordinately busy most of the time, and yet I hesitate to send the little scamps away to school, where they might have proper supervision as well as a first-rate education."

Maggie was warming toward Mr. Kirk; his concern for his children touched her, as did the familiar pattern of his speech. "It's very difficult for little people to be away from their homes and families," she agreed, remembering her own years as an intermittent orphan. "Though that's quite the custom in England, I've noticed."

Mr. Kirk settled back in his chair, playing with a small silver ruler he'd taken from his desk. "How do you happen to be here in Australia, Miss Chamberlin?"

Maggie was tiring of that question, but she supposed it was a reasonable one. She explained once again about the circus, her parents' accident, and her subsequent time in England. "How do you happen to be here, Mr. Kirk?" she blurted out once the story had been told.

Caught off guard, Mr. Kirk stared at Maggie for a moment and then laughed aloud. "You are refreshingly forthright, Miss Chamberlin. I came to Australia in the sixties with my father. He'd been, well—disillusioned, you might say—by the War Between the States. He bought mining shares, planning to strike gold. Instead, he found one of the largest opal deposits in the world."

"Your story is certainly more spectacular than my own," Maggie observed guilelessly.

Once again Mr. Kirk gave that disturbing, mellowed-brandy laugh. "I wonder," he said cryptically when he'd recovered. Then, like quicksilver, the conversation changed course. "Have you any references, Miss Chamberlin?"

Maggie's hopes of finding a place for herself began to fade. "No, sir—only those that were required for emigration to this country. I—I've never worked as a governess—"

Mr. Kirk looked alarmingly dour, the ruler propped under his square, clean-shaven chin. "I see. If you weren't a governess, Miss Chamberlin, what were you?"

Maggie gulped, aware of the prejudice some people sustained against performers of any kind. "I was an actress, of sorts."

There was a lengthy silence, during which Maggie could read absolutely nothing from Mr. Kirk's expression, and then he asked, "Do you hope to return to that—profession?"

"No," Maggie lied. She didn't like misleading Mr. Kirk, but the plain fact was that her very survival could depend upon it. "I'm very well educated, sir—I can read and write and cipher as well as anyone—"

"Please stop calling me sir," Mr. Kirk interrupted, somewhat brusquely. "I despise it."

Maggie flushed and looked down at her clenched hands. She couldn't seem to get anything right this morning.

Suddenly Mr. Kirk moved from his chair and strode across the room to one of the bookshelves. From a row of exquisite leatherbound volumes, he took a book and brought it back to Maggie, fairly thrusting it into her hands.

"Read a passage aloud, if you will," he barked, turning his back and clasping his hands behind him to listen, much like a schoolmaster hearing a lesson.

57

Maggie smiled to see that the book was an old friend: Plato's *Republic.* She read a full page without a single hesitation and snapped the volume closed. During the reading she'd felt a rising sense of triumph; the tide of the interview had turned in her favor and she knew it.

"If you'd like the position, it's yours," Mr. Kirk said, now perched on the edge of his desk, his arms folded, and gazing pensively at Maggie as though she were a riddle that he couldn't quite solve.

"Thank you, Mr. Kirk. I'd like the position very much."

"Excellent. Lady Cosgrove will send you around in one of her carriages, no doubt."

Maggie nodded and rose awkwardly from her chair; Mr. Kirk was sitting so close that she feared brushing against him. It was a squeeze, but she managed to stand without the embarrassment of improper intimacy. The smile that quirked her new employer's lips at her effort puzzled and unsettled her, and she hastened to take her leave.

Lady Cosgrove's driver, left waiting far longer than he should have been, due to Maggie's unofficial call on Mr. McKenna, was surly. "Took you long enough, that it did," he snarled.

Maggie gave the driver a saucy look and opened the carriage door herself, since he hadn't bothered to get down from the box and do it for her. Safely inside the luxurious vehicle, she thought of that spineless Philip Briggs and then of the equally impossible Mr. Reeve McKenna, and decided that she detested them both.

Reeve was in a foul mood; Loretta could see that even from a distance. She stepped back from the parlor window, with its splendid view of Rushcutter's Bay, and turned all her attention on little Elisabeth, who sat upon the cool bricks of the hearth, absorbed, as always, in her drawing.

The child was an enigma to Loretta, beautiful with

her dark, dark hair and her uncle's aquamarine eyes. At four, Elisabeth McKenna possessed an uncanny ability to transcribe real life to a series of lines and shadows on paper, but for all that she rarely spoke, except to say "Papa" on occasion.

Reeve had taken the child from doctor to doctor, seeking a cure for his niece as doggedly as he sought his lost brother, Jamie, who had been transported a full twenty years before. There had been no success on either front: The doctors said that there was nothing medically wrong with Elisabeth, that she'd probably suffered some trauma they'd never know about, when her mother abandoned her. As for Jamie McKenna, the best detectives in all of Australia hadn't been able to turn up a trace of him—except for his cast-off child, of course—though they went right on collecting their outrageous fees.

As far as Loretta was concerned, both enterprises were a waste of time as well as money. If Elisabeth delighted in being difficult, so be it. The little scamp needn't think it was any skin off Loretta's nose. And when it came to Jamie, he was probably a ne'er-do-well—if he was alive at all. He hadn't been able to look after his own daughter, in any case. Elisabeth had been found in an orphanage.

The front door opened and Elisabeth's whole countenance was suddenly aglow. She shuffled her everlasting sketchbook and pencils aside and scrambled to her feet, bounding into the entry hall with a cry of glee.

Moments later Reeve came in, carrying Elisabeth in one arm and grinning like the besotted fool he was—when it came to that child. On catching sight of Loretta, his jawline tightened and the smile was gone. Gently, he asked Elisabeth to go and see if Cook was making pie for dinner as promised, and let the child down to the floor.

To Loretta's well-hidden annoyance, Elisabeth raced off to do his bidding.

Loretta decided that the best defense was an offense and asked sweetly, "Am I to assume that your little arrangement with that American girl was nipped in the bud before it could bloom?"

Reeve's face suddenly lost all color and his eyes were hot with anger, searing Loretta's flesh wherever they touched. She turned away to pour brandy for him and for herself, inwardly bracing herself against his fury.

"I wasn't planning to install Maggie in a gilded cage and have my way with her, Loretta. I merely wanted to make sure that she would be looked after."

The chilly calm in Reeve's voice found its way into Loretta's ramrod-straight backbone and caused her to shiver. All the same, she was smiling brightly when she turned around, a crystal snifter of brandy in each hand. "So it's 'Maggie' now, is it?" She extended one of the snifters to Reeve and he slapped it out of her hand, sending it shattering against the face of the fireplace. Loretta retreated a step, taking a healthy sip of her brandy to steady herself and then going boldly on. "Did Philip get there in time to spoil everything? How terrible for you if he did."

"So you did send him." The words Reeve spoke were cold as ice, and yet they scalded.

"It was nothing any other jealous mistress wouldn't have done. Can you honestly blame me for trying to protect my interests?"

For a moment Reeve looked as though he might strike her, something he had never, even in the hottest anger, done before. He raised his hand, then withdrew it, ran it through his hair, and turned away.

"I spoke with Lady Cosgrove a few minutes ago," he said evenly, after a long and ragged silence. "Do you know where Maggie is, Loretta?"

Loretta took another sip of brandy and shrugged. "How could I know, darling?" she countered. She was not the cool and composed woman she seemed; she was playing a part.

"She's taken a post in Duncan Kirk's house," Reeve answered, turning around now, folding his arms and resting his broad back against the mantelpiece. "She's a governess."

Loretta could no longer maintain her facade; she was on dangerous ground now, for Reeve hated Duncan Kirk as he'd never hated another person. The fact that Duncan had inadvertently scored a triumph by taking a woman Reeve wanted into his household would compound Loretta's offense. She allowed a tear to slip down her face.

"Good Lord, Reeve, if you're so bent on having the chit, go over to Duncan's house and collect her! Have your little *affaire d'amour*—you know I'll have no choice but to forgive you!"

Reeve advanced on Loretta suddenly, taking a hard grasp on her chin, forcing her to meet his snapping gaze. "You know what kind of man Duncan Kirk is," he said in a dangerous hiss, "and you know what he'll do to her! Damn it, woman, don't you have a soul?"

"If he seduces her," Loretta spat out, "he certainly won't be the first! Your precious Maggie belonged to Philip Briggs before you knew her, remember!"

Reeve released Loretta so forcefully that she nearly lost her footing. He moved past her, to pour a double shot of rum into a glass and, between swallows, he chuckled. The sound was raw and frightening and Loretta edged away, out of reach.

Finally, he whirled on her, the fiery blue of his eyes warning of his rage even before he spoke. "That will be enough, Loretta. Quite enough."

"Why?" Loretta spouted, wondering at her daring. "Because you can't bear to think of pretty Philip putting his soft hands on her?"

Reeve tossed back the last of his rum before answering with a cutting, "When it comes to women, it's more than Philip's hands that's soft, and you know it as well as I do, Loretta."

The flimsy hope that Reeve might not have considered Philip's personal foible collapsed under his words. She gave a long sigh and searched her mind for something to say that would make Reeve care for her again. Only for her.

"I love you," she said.

"Please," was the caustic reply.

Loretta's voice was shaking and this time her tears were no artifice; they were real. "What do you want of me, Reeve? Just tell me what you want and I'll—"

"I want you to leave."

Loretta's glass fell to the carpet with a *thunk.* "What?"

"I said, I want you to leave. I'll provide for you, of course—you can have the theaters and my solicitor will draw up some kind of agreement for your support, but I want you out of this house, Loretta. Now. Tonight."

"Reeve!" Loretta was standing before him now, clutching at his muscular arms. "In the name of heaven, don't do this! If you want that—that woman, then have her! I'll be waiting when you tire of her, I swear it!"

Something very much like disgust moved onto Reeve's face, sobering Loretta, allowing her to get a hold on her dignity.

"This isn't about Maggie, Loretta. It's me, it's you—" He paused, sighed. "It's over."

"No!"

Reeve gently freed his arms from her grasp and stepped away, turning his back.

Loretta could see by the set of his shoulders that he was waiting for something, braced for something she might say. But what was there to say? She'd tried begging, and it hadn't worked. She'd tried tears and sarcasm with an equal lack of success. What in the name of God did Reeve want of her?

All Loretta had to offer was the venom of a woman scorned. "I'll see you on your knees for this, Reeve

McKenna. And rest assured, sweet Maggie will suffer too. You have my word on that!"

Reeve sighed heavily. "No threats, Loretta. I'm not without a measure of power myself, remember."

Loretta shivered, even though the night was warm. Out of the corner of her eye she saw Elisabeth cowering in a doorway, taking in the scene with an aquamarine stare.

"You'll continue to look after the child, of course," Loretta said stiffly, and Reeve turned to face her with something like contempt moving in his features.

"There was never any question about that," he replied.

With as much dignity as she could muster, Loretta left the room and, after packing most of her clothes and all of her jewelry, she left Reeve's house.

She was far away in the hired carriage Reeve had summoned for her before she realized that it would have been wiser to kiss Elisabeth and weep a few tears over the parting. Only moments too late, Loretta reflected that Reeve's greatest weakness was not Maggie whatever-her-name-was, but Elisabeth.

Mr. Kirk's place was bigger than the mansion housing the Girls' Friendly Society and considerably more imposing. The lawn looked smooth, as if it had been trimmed with embroidery scissors, and there were flower beds and fountains and fragrant rose-bushes pruned to resemble trees.

"Coo!" said Tansy, who had found a place in the next street and was lingering here only to see her friend safely inside the great house. "Think of the parties this gent must 'ave, mind you!"

Maggie swallowed hard and reached out to turn the glistening brass bellknob beside the arched door. Parties were the last thing on her mind this evening; she was thinking of the strange twists and turns fate can take, and just when a person least expects them too. She stood on this doorstep an actress, but the moment she set one foot over the threshold she would become a governess.

Momentarily, the door swung open and a rotund woman dressed in a bombazine dress almost identical to Maggie's appeared in the opening. Her eyes were very small and very bright and they took in every aspect of the new governess's appearance in one quick sweep.

Maggie drew a deep breath. "I'm Maggie— Margaret Chamberlin," she said to break the silence.

"And I'm Mrs. Lavendar, the housekeeper," the woman answered without a whit of friendliness visible anywhere in her vast demeanor. Her gaze shifted to rest suspiciously on Tansy. "What's your business here, lass?" she demanded.

Tansy's chin went up and her eyes were steady on Mrs. Lavendar's doughy face. "I'm only 'ere to tell me friend good-bye, if it's all the same to you, mum."

Mrs. Lavendar receded and quick farewells were said, and then Tansy was moving up the walk as Maggie stepped inside Mr. Duncan Kirk's house for the first time.

Two lads in short pants waited on the stairs, chins propped in grubby palms.

"Here's your new governess, then," said Mrs. Lavendar sharply. Her air was that of one who had better things to do than stand around introducing little boys to their tutor. "Miss Chamberlin's her name."

Two sets of green eyes assessed Maggie, showing neither friendly interest nor devilment, but only tolerance.

"The one on the left is Jeremy," Mrs. Lavendar said, like a student reciting a tiresome lesson, "and the other is Tad. They'll show you to your room—I've work to do in the kitchen."

With that Maggie was left alone with too very handsome redheaded little boys. She put down her reticule and lifted the fingers of both hands to her temples, squinching her eyes shut and pretending to get a message from the spirit world.

When she opened her eyes again, she was pleased to see that both boys were watching her raptly.

"You," she said mystically, pointing to Jeremy, "are seven years old." Her finger moved to Tad. "And you are ten."

"How'd you know that?!" Jeremy demanded, bolting to his feet and clutching the banister with one hand.

Tad stood up, too, only with more decorum, and his face twisted into a mien of skepticism. "Papa told her, stupid."

Maggie stopped in the middle of bending to pick up her reticule and frowned. "Tad Kirk, you must never, ever call your brother stupid. It is rude and, furthermore, it shows a distinct lack of imagination."

"You're stupid too," retorted Tad before bounding off to another part of the vast house and leaving Maggie standing there with her mouth open.

Jeremy, every inch the gentleman, took Maggie's hand in his and tugged, barely giving her a chance to fetch her reticule. "Don't mind him, miss. Tad's a no-gooder some of the time, but mostly he's all right. Come along and I'll show you where your room is."

Maggie suppressed a smile. It was nice to have a champion, however small he might be. "Thank you so much, my good man," she said formally.

Tansy had said that the servants' quarters in most grand houses were on the third floor, so Maggie was much surprised when they didn't proceed beyond the second. She was even more surprised to be led into a spacious chamber with its own small marble fireplace, chintz-covered chairs, a matching mahogany bureau and armoire, and a gigantic four-poster covered with a glistening blue satin spread.

"Surely there's some mistake, Jeremy," Maggie protested, almost afraid to enter the splendid room.

"No mistake," Jeremy said firmly, dragging her over the threshold. "Papa told Mrs. Lavendar to make this room ready and she did, though she fussed over it some. Said you belonged upstairs, like the maids."

"And what did your father reply to that, may I ask?"

Jeremy shrugged. "Don't know, miss. He was speaking over the telephone, so I could hear only Mrs. Lavendar's part. She turned purple as cabbage, but she talked real polite to Papa." The little boy screwed up his freckled face. "Mrs. Lavendar made Tad and me wash our ears then, and they weren't even dirty."

"A strange turn of events, I must say," observed a quite adult male voice from the doorway.

Startled, Maggie pulled free of Jeremy's hand and whirled to face Mr. Kirk. He was standing just inside that magnificent room, endeavoring to clasp a cuff link. He was clad in elegant evening trousers and a ruffled shirt.

Maggie found her voice. "I was just telling Jeremy that there must be some misunderstanding—surely I haven't been assigned a room like this."

"Oh, but you have, Miss Chamberlin," her employer assured her smoothly, his jade-green eyes taking in her somewhat crumpled bombazine dress. "Governesses are not servants."

"Oh," said Maggie, quite at a loss for further comment.

Again the master's gaze swept over her gown, frankly disapproving. "Something will have to be done about your clothing. That dress makes you look like a crow."

Maggie didn't know whether to be insulted or pleased that she wouldn't have to wear the hideous dress. "A crow, sir?" she echoed.

Duncan Kirk arched one chestnut eyebrow. "Didn't I instruct you never to call me sir? Mr. Kirk will do very well, thank you."

"Tad called Miss Chamberlin stupid," Jeremy imparted. Having taken gentlemanly offense, he now sought justice.

"Did he?" returned Mr. Kirk seriously, and Maggie found herself liking him for the twinkle of laughter in his eyes. "By all that's holy, I'll have the lad drawn and quartered at sunrise!"

Jeremy was satisfied with the sentence handed down for his brother and scampered off to pass on the word.

Mr. Kirk had finished with his cuff link and was now adjusting the collar of his immaculate white evening shirt. "I will discipline the boys, Miss Chamberlin," he said. "Tad remembers his mother and he tends to resent women he perceives as any sort of replacement for her."

Maggie wanted to be left alone to think, to rest, to freshen up, and to try to prepare some kind of curriculum for the boys. "Please don't be too harsh with Tad on my account, Mr. Kirk. He'll need time to accept me."

"I suppose so." The man sighed, adding with a slight bow of his head, "Good evening, Miss Chamberlin. Make yourself at home, and please don't plan lessons for the boys for tomorrow. You'll be busy shopping for new clothes. At my expense, of course."

Shopping. As the door closed behind Mr. Kirk, Maggie sat down in one of the chintz-covered chairs. Shopping?

There was something quite improper about all this: the fancy room, the clothes Mr. Kirk was going to buy for her, all of it, but Maggie had had a long and most trying day and she was in no mood to work out what that something was.

Chapter 5 ❧

THE HEAT WAS SWELTERING, AND MAGGIE OPENED ONE OF
her bedroom windows in the hope of catching a
breeze. "February!" she marveled to herself, looking
down on the gaslit cobbled street below. A carriage
was waiting at the gate and, as Maggie watched, she
saw a second vehicle draw up behind it.

Mr. Kirk got out of the first carriage, which had
apparently been about to pull away, and walked back
to the second. Maggie was just turning from the
window, having no wish to eavesdrop, when her
employer's startled "Loretta!" made her whirl around
again. Where had she heard that name and why did it
clutch at her spirit like unseen fingers?

The door of the second coach opened and a woman
stepped down, unaided. Even in the poor light of the
gas-powered streetlamps, Maggie recognized this dra-
matically beautiful dark-haired creature as the lady
who had met Reeve McKenna at the wharf the night
before, when the *Victoria* had docked in Sydney
Harbor.

"Good God," Mr. Kirk exclaimed, and the very
harshness of his tone made Maggie step back behind

the draperies, hopefully out of sight, yet not quite out of hearing. "Loretta, what are you doing here?"

The woman's voice floated on the heavy summer air like notes of music, soft and gossamer. "You look very handsome tonight, Duncan. Dinner at the club?"

"Yes," Mr. Kirk replied stiffly. "Once again, Loretta, what do you want?"

Maggie must have misunderstood Loretta's reply—it did sound as though she answered, "Revenge."

Mr. Kirk laughed at whatever the woman had said, and there was a note of sheer hatred in the sound. Whether that bitter emotion was directed toward the lovely Loretta or not, Maggie couldn't tell, but she was oddly shaken by the depth and ugliness of it and she closed the window just as a tapping sounded at her door.

"Come in," she called distractedly, wondering what or whom Mr. Kirk hated with such virulence and why Reeve McKenna's mistress would call upon him in such a bold fashion.

A very young maid with curly red hair and freckles across her nose came in, struggling through the doorway with a heavy tray. Maggie rushed to relieve the girl of her burden.

"Here's your supper, then," the woman-child said, smiling shyly as Maggie set the tray down on the round wooden table that stood between the two fancy chairs facing the fireplace.

Maggie felt very lonely all of a sudden, and very far from familiar people and places. "Won't you sit down?" she asked, pouring a cup of tea from the small pot on the tray and frowning because there was only one cup. "You look as though you could use a rest."

"Mrs. Lavendar would have my head if I did that, Miss Margaret. Wouldn't be right nor proper."

Maggie smiled over the rim of her teacup. "You know my name," she pointed out, surprised by the formality with which the girl spoke. "What is yours, may I ask?"

The maid cast a nervous glance back toward the open door. "Susan," she answered, in a whisper. "Susan Crockett."

"Well, Susan Crockett, you may address me as Maggie, if you please. No one has ever called me Margaret. I'm not even sure why my mother bothered to give me the name."

Susan paled beneath her freckles and her springy red hair glistened in the light as she shook her head. "I daren't call you anything but what Mrs. Lavendar told me to, and that's Miss Margaret, beggin' your pardon." She took a step closer and kept her voice at whisper level. "'Tis only a month till I get me certificate, you see."

Maggie did see: The importance of earning a certificate had been stressed at the Girls' Friendly Society. What she did not understand was why she should be given a room fit for an honored houseguest instead of a cot upstairs, in the servants' quarters, why she should be served her dinner in her chamber, why Mr. Kirk should feel called upon to provide her with new clothes. Unfortunately, Susan wasn't the person to ask. Maggie would have to keep her questions to herself, at least until Saturday afternoon, when she would have free time. She would then seek out Tansy and find out what she needed to know.

With a brief nod, Susan crept out of the room and closed the door behind her, leaving Maggie to eat her portion of succulent pork pie in solitude. For all her misgivings about her sumptuous quarters and the shopping expedition tomorrow, she was hungry, and she consumed the small pie, vegetables, and biscuits, as well as vanilla pudding.

When her meal was finished, Maggie was ready to fall into bed, but first she needed to wash, and polish her teeth. She put her head out the door and looked up and down the hallway, then made a dash for the bathroom Jeremy had pointed out to her earlier.

It was a startlingly luxurious room, quite half the size of Maggie's bedchamber, with an enormous marble bathtub standing on gracious feet. There was hot and cold running water and a commode with a flushing chain and blue carpet so plush that Maggie's feet fairly disappeared into it. The bathtub's faucet was a sculpture of a Grecian girl holding an urn, and when the spigots were turned on, water poured from the statue's polished vessel.

Delighted, Maggie laughed. She hadn't planned to take a bath, but now the prospect was too charming to ignore. She put the plug in place, carefully bolted the main door and one leading into another room, and purloined a towel and a washcloth from the shelves of a cabinet that reached from floor to ceiling.

The spacious tub and plentitude of hot water were such luxuries to Maggie that she lingered long after she was clean, lying back and dreaming. Perhaps living in this grand house, almost as a member of the family, and working as a governess would be better than acting. Actresses, unless they had achieved considerable renown, were rarely solvent. Here Maggie would have security, with no worrying about how she was going to buy food or pay rent.

Her eyelids were growing heavy and she sighed, completely content and comfortable for the first time in months.

The brisk rattling of the inside door awakened Maggie with a start.

"Margaret!" shouted Mr. Kirk's voice from the other side. "Margaret, are you all right?"

Maggie was so mortified that she didn't even notice that Mr. Kirk had presumed to address her by her given name. In shock, cheeks burning, water splashing everywhere, she lunged for a towel and covered herself before calling back, "Yes—yes, I'm quite all right—I guess I fell asleep—"

A male chuckle sounded from beyond the door. "I

71

see. From now on, please do your sleeping in bed—I was afraid you were drowning. In another minute or so I'd have stormed in there to save you."

Maggie's blush was fierce at the prospect, and she struggled and shimmied into her worn flannel nightgown, making the process more difficult by her haste. Having no earthly idea how to respond to Mr. Kirk's comment, she said nothing at all but merely snatched up her clothes, unlocked both bathroom doors, and ran as fast as she could down the hallway to her own room.

She didn't bother to turn up the lights but simply delved into bed, pulling the smooth linen sheets up over her head. She lay there, half smothering, until she could bear it no longer, and then she bounded up again, pulling open a window, stripping the satin cover from her bed, and finally divesting herself of the nightgown. It was highly improper to sleep naked, but Maggie didn't care. She was not going to lie there roasting.

After several fitful minutes of tossing and turning, Maggie went to sleep and had scandalous dreams about a man with dark hair and blue-green eyes and a charm worn around his neck.

He had been drawn to her room by the force of his imagination; moving as quietly as a ghost, he drew close to the bed, where she lay on her side, the covers disarrayed. One smooth thigh glowed alabaster in the moonlight, though the rest of her was in shadow.

Duncan Kirk swallowed hard. The urge to awaken Maggie, to have her, was almost beyond his power to ignore. He longed to caress those full, rounded breasts, to taste their peaks and feel them harden against his tongue.

Maggie made a whimpering sound and turned restlessly onto her back. The light of the summer moon shimmered over her, fully revealing the breasts Duncan craved, the flat, silken belly, the soft hips that would cradle his. Duncan retreated a step and his right hand trembled, so badly did he want to touch her, to plunder that golden nest of curls and teach her a virgin's pleasure before taking her.

He'd grown painfully hard, but at the memory of what Loretta Craig had confided, Duncan smiled. Reeve McKenna wanted Maggie, just as he himself had wanted her from the moment she'd walked into his office that morning. And knowing that McKenna hungered for her made the prospect of having the little vixen all the sweeter.

But he would not indulge tonight; he didn't dare. The little imp would surely be remorseful in the morning, and she would leave. No, he would wait until it was time to go to the country.

With a lump of raw need lodged tight in his throat, Duncan turned and left the room as quietly as he'd entered it. In the hallway he encountered Mrs. Lavendar, who didn't bother to hide her disapproval.

Duncan met her beady glare steadily and then crossed to his own room, where he was a long time going to sleep.

As she walked to the corner where the trolley car made its regular stop, Maggie was still boggled by the list Mr. Kirk had left for her. The little maid, Susan, hurried along at her side. Susan carried a basket nearly as big as she herself was, for she was going to market, and she pretended that Maggie didn't exist until they'd gotten out of sight of the Kirk house.

When they reached the appointed corner, however, Susan was suddenly all smiles and chatter. "Coo, but Mrs. Lavendar's in a fine dither about all them clothes the master's wantin' you to buy. She says it ain't proper."

Maggie had thoughts along that line herself, especially now that she'd read the list, but she didn't voice them. She only leaned around Susan and her basket to look down the street for the trolley car. There was no sign of it, though Maggie could hear its bell chiming in the distance.

"Tell me true, Miss Margaret," Susan persisted. "Are you really a governess or are you one of them what likes warmin' a gentleman's bed?"

Maggie was preoccupied and it was a moment before Susan's words sank in. When they did, she glared at the girl, her cheeks pulsing, her eyes flashing like the swift silver blade of a knife. "What did you say?" she demanded in a hiss.

Susan stepped back, holding the basket in front of her like a shield, and Maggie subsided.

"I am no man's mistress, Susan Crockett," she said haughtily as the streetcar approached with a clanging of bells and screeching of rails, drawing its power through long metal rods from the wires strung above the street. "And you can tell Mrs. Lavendar and all the maids that I'll not put up with being gossiped about!"

Maggie mounted the streetcar steps first, handing the fare given her by Mrs. Lavendar to the conductor, and took a seat near the back. The car was nearly empty, and sheepishly, Susan sat down beside Maggie.

"I'll be done with the marketin' long before you've bought all the frillies on that list, love. Remember that you're supposed to take the Pitt Street car back home and don't get yourself lost."

Maggie recognized an attempt at friendliness when she heard one and she was not given to grudge-holding, but she sniffed, just to let Susan know that she had overstepped the bounds of acceptable behavior and must take care not to do so again. "I won't get lost," she promised, chin high, voice cool.

The car rattled and clanged along toward the heart of Sydney, and Susan did not find her tongue again until they were passing through a seedy-looking section. There were saloons everywhere, with bawds and no-accounts of every stripe lounging outside, and a din loud enough to compete with the noise of the streetcar filled the air, along with the pungent smell of seeping sewage.

"This is King's Cross," Susan confided behind the shelter of one upraised hand. "See that you don't never come here by yourself, be it night or day."

Maggie was staring wide-eyed at the spectacle of women in dresses that showed not only their legs but their shoulders and most of their bosoms as well. In a doorway a man and woman embraced, the man's hand thrust boldly inside the woman's blouse, cupping her breast.

The sight was disgusting, of course, but it also gave Maggie an odd feeling that made her squirm on the streetcar's hard seat, remembering the shameful dreams of Reeve McKenna she'd had the night before. Dreams? They'd been nightmares, and when Maggie had been jolted awake by sheer shock, she'd have sworn that the scent of shaving lotion tinged the air. . . .

The car made several stops, taking on passengers—housewives and clerks and chattering maids—and then reached the wide street where merchants sold fresh fish, mutton, and vegetables from open stalls. Susan patted Maggie's hand in a reassuring fashion and left the car, swinging her basket at her side.

Maggie smiled as she watched the girl go; she couldn't help liking her.

Downtown Sydney was as daunting as before, with crowds of people streaming in and out of shops and business buildings and the bells of streetcars clanging as if to drown each other out. Skittish horses pulled wagons and carriages and buggies, and women as well as men pedaled past on bicycles.

Taking refuge in the archway of a bank, Maggie got out the careful list Mr. Kirk had provided. Frowning, she read it for the fourth time since it had been given to her at breakfast by a stony-faced Mrs. Lavendar.

Morning dresses, afternoon dresses, evening

dresses. Shoes and slippers. Wrappers and night-gowns, skirts and shirtwaists.

Maggie swallowed hard and folded the list, tucking it carefully into her worn handbag. She was sweltering in a dark green woolen dress that she'd bought sec-ondhand from a stall in the streets of London. Though she longed to be rid of it, she wondered if Mr. Kirk expected more of her than was proper. What man bought nightgowns and wrappers and evening gowns for his children's governess?

Just as she braved the crowded sidewalk again, Maggie felt a strong hand take hold of her arm and before she could voice a protest or even get a look at her assailant's face, she was thrust into the cool, leathery interior of a carriage. Her abductor was none other than Mr. Reeve McKenna, wearing a broad and insolent grin on his deplorably handsome face.

More infuriated than frightened, Maggie lunged for the carriage window, fully intending to put her head out and scream for assistance. When she moved to do this, two iron hands caught her at the hips and wrenched her back, and the carriage seat came up hard against her bottom.

"How dare you?" she hissed, glaring.

The aquamarine eyes glowed with inner laughter, almost as bright as the charm visible in the V of his open-necked shirt. "Suffice it to say that I dare. Period."

"Let me out of this carriage, Mr. McKenna! Imme-diately, please!"

He only chuckled and settled back against the seat, his powerful arms folded across his chest. He wore a white shirt and black trousers and he looked entirely too casual to be about any respectable sort of busi-ness. "You're not being kidnapped, Miss Chamberlin, so kindly compose yourself."

Maggie just gaped at him, too stunned to speak. If this wasn't an abduction, what was it? The nerve of this rascal, grabbing an innocent woman off the streets in the broad light of day. Oh, there were plenty of things she'd say to this rounder once she found her voice again!

The impossibly white teeth flashed in another grin. "That's better, Miss Chamberlin," the knave said indulgently. "Much better."

Maggie swallowed, but when she tried to speak, only a croaking sound came out.

Reeve McKenna ignored her, raising his voice to be heard over the hubbub of Sydney. "What were you reading so intently back there? You were squinting and holding the paper an inch from your nose."

Something—Maggie could not have said what—made her take Mr. Kirk's list from her bag and extend it to her captor. Her voice was back and she'd meant to harangue Reeve McKenna vociferously but, strange as it seemed, she spoke in normal tones. "I've been wondering why a governess would be required to have such clothes," she ventured to say.

McKenna scanned the list several times before he replied, and his frown made creases in his brow. Far more unsettling, however, was the snapping blue-green fury in his eyes. For a moment it seemed that he was about to say something unforgivable—in fact, Maggie braced herself for that very occurrence—but Mr. McKenna only hesitated and then said, "I have no idea. But I thought you said you were an actress, Mag—Miss Chamberlin, not a governess."

Maggie sat up very straight, feeling as though her integrity had been challenged. Susan's remark about women who like warming a gentleman's bed came back to her, stinging her cheeks to a fiery pink. "I have never taught before, Mr. McKenna, but I do like children very much and I am well educated. Since my plans to perform"—she paused to favor the fiend with a scathing look—"fell through, I had to find another way to make a living."

"Have you any understanding at all of what Duncan expects of you?"

Maggie snatched back the list of clothing required for her position. "Quite. Mr. Kirk expects me to train his children in reading, writing, and arithmetic. I intend to teach them history and botany as well."

"Guess what Mr. Kirk plans to teach *you,* Miss Chamberlin: basic anatomy."

Maggie stared blankly for a few moments before catching his meaning. Immediately infuriated, she lunged for the carriage window again, and just as quickly she was pulled back.

"Governesses do not require evening gowns, Miss Chamberlin, nor are their employers generally concerned with their nightclothes. Use your hard little Yankee head! Kirk didn't engage you to teach."

Maggie wanted to deny that hotly, but she remembered her beautifully appointed room and remained silent.

"In any case, you don't need to worry about Kirk, because you are now working for me."

Few things Reeve McKenna could have said would have come as more of a shock. "What?" Maggie rasped.

Smiling again, he drew a folded document from the inside pocket of his vest. "I've bought your papers, my love. You may either play the role of Kate in *The Taming of the Shrew* as you originally planned, or you may serve as a governess to my four-year-old niece. The choice is yours."

"Suppose I choose to go back to Mr. Kirk's house and teach his children, as I promised to do?" Maggie asked, struggling to keep her voice level.

"You will recall that that particular choice wasn't mentioned. That was because it isn't a choice, Maggie. You're as good as indentured to me."

Pale, Maggie reached out for the document and he didn't withhold it. "It isn't possible," she mumbled, her fingers trembling as she unfolded the paper. Some niggling instinct told her that it was not only possible but quite true.

Sure enough, Lady Cosgrove's flourishing signature graced the bottom of a paper that Maggie had signed herself, back in England, promising to work three years in Australia until or unless she married.

"Lady Cosgrove knew I had another position—she arranged it herself."

Mr. McKenna shrugged. "Be that as it may, the papers are legal, Maggie."

Secretly, Maggie found the situation intriguing, in a way she'd rather not have to define, but she was also outraged. "You are reprehensible!" she spat out.

He smiled. "I know," he said proudly.

Maggie was very much at a loss. She read the document very slowly, hoping to find a loophole, and instead came to the disturbing conclusion that she was indeed obliged to work for Mr. McKenna for three full years. "Suppose you abuse me? Will I have no recourse?"

"This is Australia, not the deep jungle, Miss Chamberlin. And I am not in the habit of abusing women!"

She had nettled him and she was glad, though it seemed a pinprick compared to the shenanigan he'd managed to pull. "Your bad manners don't go beyond kidnapping, then?" she asked with scalding sweetness.

"I wouldn't have grabbed you like that if I'd thought you'd listen to reason, you hardheaded—"

"Yankee," Maggie finished for him. Underneath her ire there was a certain relief that she would not have to be beholden to Mr. Duncan Kirk for a fancy bedroom and a new wardrobe of clothes. She would miss the boys, Jeremy and Tad, however; she'd liked them both, even if Tad had called her stupid.

"Why the sad look?" Mr. McKenna demanded, frowning. "Have you already formed an affection for our Mr. Kirk?"

"Actually, no," Maggie replied honestly, "but I do like his boys. I feel terrible about deserting them this way."

79

Mr. McKenna looked distinctly uncomfortable, and it came to Maggie that he had the same weakness she did: children. "They're looking forward to having a teacher, are they?"

Maggie nodded. "I think so."

Reeve let out a long sigh and Maggie was reminded once again of the dreams she'd had the night before. She wondered if men really did those piercingly pleasant things to women. To her utter surprise, Mr. McKenna handed back the document.

"You're free, Maggie. I may hate Duncan Kirk, but I've nothing against those lads of his."

Maggie stared at him, unable to believe that she'd just been handed three full years of her life as easily as that. She might have thanked Reeve McKenna, but he leaned toward her and shook an index finger in her face before she got the chance.

"You've got to promise me one thing, Maggie," he warned, looking dour.

There seemed to be something caught in Maggie's throat, so her voice came out as a squeak. "What?"

"That if you have any trouble with Kirk, any trouble at all, you'll come to me. And don't buy anything on that list but what a governess would wear."

Maggie couldn't resist a smile. "That's two things, but I promise anyway. Thank you, Mr. McKenna."

"My name is Reeve," he replied, at the same time thumping on the carriage wall with his knuckles. The elegant vehicle came to an immediate stop. "And you're welcome."

Maggie was out of the carriage and standing on the sidewalk in a wink. She was free. It was all she could do not to leap for joy. "Thank you again!" she called, jumping so that she could look into the carriage. "Thank you so much!"

"No nightdresses and no evening gowns!" Reeve yelled in response, and then the carriage was moving away.

For a moment, just the fleetest, maddest moment, Maggie considered running after it, brazenly calling out to the driver to stop. But her freedom was too precious and for that reason she simply stood on the sidewalk, staring dumbfoundedly at the disappearing carriage.

After almost a minute Maggie looked around her and realized that she'd been set down in a welter of shops and stores, any one of which would grant unlimited credit on Mr. Duncan Kirk's name.

Mindful of her promise, not to mention her own scruples, Maggie bought six serviceable summer dresses, four badly needed cotton nightgowns, and a new pair of shoes. She would ask Mr. Kirk to deduct the cost from her pay, week by week.

Maggie had boarded the trolley car in Pitt Street, as instructed by Susan, before it occurred to her that her employer might be angry with her for not purchasing all the items on the list. And then she smiled, for it didn't really matter whether Mr. Kirk approved of her decision or not. Thanks to Reeve McKenna, she could once again call her soul her own.

Chapter 6 ❧

Upon returning to Mr. Kirk's town house, tired, elated, and burdened with parcels, Maggie was secretly relieved to learn from Mrs. Lavendar that the master had been called away to a place known as Lightning Ridge, where the largest share of his opals were mined. He would not be back, according to the housekeeper, for some days.

Maggie was beginning to feel a keen dislike for some of the other women employed in that house. In an effort to show that she wasn't uppity, she'd entered the house by way of the rear door, and Mrs. Lavendar, busy at the sink paring vegetables, had been pleased by the gesture, though she tried her best not to show it.

She frowned as she took in the parcels Maggie carried. "The rest being sent, is it?"

Maggie shook her head. "This is all of it, Mrs. Lavendar. I suppose Mr. Kirk will be angry, but I couldn't see buying such fancy things—where would a governess wear evening gowns?"

"Where indeed?" huffed Mrs. Lavendar, but she looked kindly upon Maggie for just the briefest moment. "Well, you'll have some free time, anyway. Mr. Kirk took the boys along with him, so there's no need in your staying around here if you've other things to do."

Maggie started toward the rear stairway, once again feeling rebuffed. As she made her way toward her room, she wondered why Mr. Kirk had not left his sons in her care, so that they might begin their lessons.

The moment she crossed the threshold of that improperly beautiful room, she noticed a letter propped against the base of the bureau's glistening mirror. After unceremoniously dropping her parcels onto the bed with a sigh of relief, she opened the fine cream-colored vellum envelope and read the brief note enclosed. Inside the single sheet of monogrammed paper was a pound note.

> *Margaret, [Mr. Kirk had written] I've taken the boys with me to Lightning Ridge, as Mrs. Lavendar will have told you by now. Since the mines will one day come to them, I feel they should be exposed to the workings of the place at every opportunity. Your first week's pay is included herewith, and I hope that you have had a happy day shopping. I am looking forward to having a hostess under my roof again, as well as a governess. Regards, D. Kirk.*

After pushing back the parcels, Maggie sat down on the edge of her bed, her lower lip caught between her teeth. A hostess? Mr. Kirk hadn't mentioned that duty when she'd accepted this post, but it did explain why he had wanted her to buy such elegant clothes.

Now Maggie felt vaguely ashamed of herself for thinking there had been anything untoward in Mr. Kirk's generous request that she outfit herself with grand gowns and dancing slippers, and she was very glad that she would have an opportunity to carry out his wishes before he returned to Sydney.

The one question that bothered her as she put five of her new dresses away in the armoire and changed into the sixth, a soft blue gown with puffy sleeves and a ruffled hem, was not one that could be easily put aside, however. What did she, Maggie Chamberlin, daughter of circus performers and late of London's second-rate theater circuit, know about serving as a rich man's hostess? What did a hostess do, for that matter, beyond shaking the hands of arriving guests, smiling a lot, and making sure that the servants didn't spill soup in anyone's lap?

Gathering up the empty dress boxes and their wrappings, Maggie pondered these questions as she walked down the hall to the rear stairs and descended into the kitchen.

"Excuse me, but where might I dispose of these things?" she asked of Mrs. Lavendar, who was working at the stove.

"Fireplace," the housekeeper replied succinctly, giving Maggie's dress a quick assessment before pursing her lips and turning back to salting and stirring and lifting pot lids to peer inside at the bubbling contents of each pan. "You've company, Miss Margaret—that woman who was with you the day you came here. I told her to wait in the back garden."

Tansy! Maggie flung the wrappings into the cold cavern of the kitchen fireplace and dashed out through the rear door, eager to see her friend.

Tansy was pacing along a flower-lined walk, her face red at being asked to wait outside like a beggar looking for a handout, but her blue eyes shone when she caught sight of Maggie in her new dress.

"Coo, love—it looks as if ye've fallen into a good thing 'ere!" She reached out one chapped hand to catch the soft cambric of the skirt between her fingers and gave a low whistle through her front teeth.

Conscious of prying eyes and ears, Maggie took her friend firmly by the arm and ushered her farther into the garden. There, beside a fountain with a statue in the center, she demanded urgently, "Tansy, what does a hostess do?"

Tansy's eyes went wide. "A 'ostess? Why, she's a man's wife, love, but for the weddin' license and the tumbles between the sheets. And sometimes—"

Maggie paled slightly and held up both hands to stop her friend in mid-sentence. "Have you ever heard of a governess serving as a hostess as well?"

"Sure." Tansy shrugged. "Leastways, back in England. Is that what you are, then? A 'ostess?"

Quickly, Maggie explained about the list of clothes Mr. Kirk had instructed her to buy and related her doubts regarding the propriety of that. Tansy's eyes grew wider with every word.

"And 'as 'e laid a 'and on you, this bloke?" she wanted to know the moment Maggie had finished speaking.

Maggie was quick to shake her head, her eyes sparkling now as she remembered the good news she had to tell. "I'm a free woman, Tansy. Mr. Reeve McKenna has bought my papers, and he gave them to me!"

Tansy frowned. "Reeve McKenna? That 'andsome one from the ship?"

Maggie nodded. There was no denying that Mr. McKenna was handsome. "And don't ask me what he expects in return, Tansy, because there's nothing."

Tansy found a marble bench and sank down on it, stunned. "Me own news pales by the side of it!" she muttered.

Maggie sat down beside her friend. "What news is that?"

"We're all of us—from the other 'ouse, I mean—takin' the omnibus to Parramatta Saturday noon, when we're done with our work. It's a gay time we'll be 'avin', Maggie, and I wanted you to come along." She took in the new dress thoughtfully. "Though I'm supposin' you're too grand for the likes of us now. You wouldn't care for races and preachin' and picnics and such."

"I would!" protested Maggie, not wanting her status in the Kirk household to alienate Tansy as it had Mrs. Lavendar and Susan Crockett and the rest. "I would too. I'm free at noon Saturday myself, Tansy Quinn, and all day Sunday as well!"

Tansy clasped both Maggie's hands in her own. "Then you'll go? Oh, Maggie-girl, that's grand! We'll 'ave the best time ever! Bring your kit, 'cause we'll be spendin' the night, of course."

"Where will we sleep?" Maggie asked, already mentally packing her "kit," the reticule containing such necessities as soap and tooth polish and a nightdress.

"The gent I work for 'as a property at Parramatta, Maggie, a noble place to 'ear the kitchen girls tell it, and we'll all pig in together in the carriage 'ouse and the barn. There'll be a flock of us, I'll wager, and we'll 'ave such fun!"

"You sound as though you've done this before," Maggie observed with a grin.

"Oh, I 'ave, love—last time I was in Australia we did it every chance. People come from miles around, and there's food and music and dancin'—"

"And preaching?" Maggie asked, surprised. Perhaps she'd been mistaken and Tansy hadn't mentioned that after all.

But she had. "Yes, me friend, but it's tolerable when you know you're going to 'ave a wondrous-good time."

Maggie wasn't so sure that the experience would be "wondrous," but she knew it would be an adventure and she was already looking forward to getting away from this house, where the servants were afraid to talk to her in sight or hearing of the formidable Mrs. Lavendar. "When do we leave?"

"We'll stop for you, me friends and I, at noon

Saturday. Be ready, too, for that old crow that runs the 'ouse is bound to make us wait in the garden!"

Maggie smiled. "I'll be ready."

With a nod Tansy rose to go. "See you are, miss. We've got to catch the streetcar right on time or we'll miss the 'bus to Parramatta."

Good-byes were said and the two young women parted, one returning to a household where all the servants were friends, one about to eat a lonely supper in a room more befitting a princess than a governess or even a hostess.

When she'd finished her meal, Maggie carried the tray back downstairs herself, hoping for a chance to strike up a conversation with Susan or even Mrs. Lavendar. The kitchen was empty, but through an open window Maggie heard the ring of laughter. She looked out as she scraped her dishes and set them neatly in the sink.

Susan and half a dozen other young ladies in bombazine dresses, aprons, and mobcaps were sitting happily on the lawn, chattering and giggling as they ate their suppers. Maggie longed to join them, but she knew that she would not be welcomed, and she turned away sadly, at a loss for something to do. It was far too early to retire and anyway, she didn't think she could bear sitting all alone in that silent room of hers, just twiddling her thumbs and feeling left out.

She decided, since Mr. Kirk was away and Mrs. Lavendar was nowhere in sight, to explore the main floor.

There were the usual parlors, as well as a drawing room and a small study, but it was the library that intrigued Maggie and made her forget that she was an outsider in this household. There were books of every kind, all neatly cataloged and carefully dusted. There was a chess table with a board of inlaid ivory, and two leather-cushioned chairs to attend it.

Maggie sank into one of those chairs, stunned by the beauty of the chess pieces themselves. They were tall and ornately shaped, one side of a shimmering, iridescent white, the other of the rare black opal. The set was surely priceless.

Maggie admired the pieces for a long time, but to her, books were the greater treasure. She caressed their fine bindings with wondering hands, delighting in the scent and weight and texture of them.

She was just opening a remarkable volume of drawings when Mrs. Lavendar startled her with an eloquent, "Ah-hem!"

Maggie blushed guiltily, like a thief caught in Ali Baba's cave, holding the book of drawings close to her bosom. She couldn't think of a single thing to say in her defense.

"I see you're preparing lessons for the lads," Mrs. Lavendar said, surprising Maggie almost as much by her kindness as by her sudden appearance. "Mr. Kirk would like that, I daresay. Take any books you want, and there's paper and pens and such in the desk drawer."

"Thank you," Maggie managed to say.

"Nonsense. Books are a part of your job. Just see they get back to their proper shelf when you're through with them, miss. Mr. Kirk is somewhat choosy about how they're treated!"

Maggie let her eyes wander over the staggering wealth of reading material and sighed. "I should think he would be," she replied, and then, like a child given free rein in a toy shop, she began dashing about, choosing books on botany and history and other subjects she wanted to share with her charges when they returned. She took paper and pens and inks from the desk, too, as well as the book of drawings she had been examining in the first place.

Like a pirate with loot, Maggie dashed up the front stairway, eager to be alone in her room now. On the small table near the fireplace she spread out her booty and sighed with pleasure.

Mrs. Lavendar found her making out a lesson plan

for a study of botany when she entered some minutes later, bringing tea. This gesture of friendliness caught Maggie quite off guard—for the second time that evening she found herself thanking the housekeeper for an unexpected kindness.

Any hopes Maggie might have had of striking up a conversation with the woman were dashed, however, when Mrs. Lavendar simply nodded and hurried out of the room.

Far into the night Maggie labored over her lesson plans, saving the beautiful book of drawings for her own pleasure, when she donned one of her new cotton nightgowns and crawled into bed, propping pillows behind her and wriggling until she was comfortable.

The pleasure Maggie got from that rare book was not exactly the sort she had expected. Closer examination proved that the volume contained a great many renderings of men and women in various stages of lovemaking. Embarrassed but too curious to put the book aside, Maggie settled deeper into the pillows and went right on turning pages, learning more about a subject that had previously mystified her with every flip of the leaves.

The pictures were not ugly or sordid in any way, even though the subjects were nude and engaged in acts of the utmost intimacy. Feeling a warm tingling within the depths of herself, Maggie studied each drawing, sometimes turning the book sideways or even upside down in her effort to understand the rites of pleasure depicted in those pages.

Two of the drawings especially interested Maggie, one showing a woman bending over a man who was sitting in a chair, her breast caught gently in his mouth, her face a study in gentle ecstasy; the other was of a woman leaning back against a wall, eyes closed, lips curved into a tender smile, while a man knelt before her, his face buried in what Maggie sincerely hoped was her belly.

The warm ache between Maggie's legs told her that

the man wasn't kissing the woman's stomach at all, and she slammed the book closed in a spate of short-lived righteous indignation.

Soon enough she was sleeping and dreaming of Reeve McKenna, and this time her erotic dreams had a sweet likeness to the pictures in that frightening, amazing, beautiful book.

Maggie awakened a great deal wiser and feeling pleasantly miserable, craving a relief she could only imagine and certainly wasn't about to seek out. She spent the morning avoiding the volume of drawings and working over her lesson plans. By midday she had a headache and a great need of fresh air. Wearing another of her new dresses, this one a pink cambric with tiny sprigs of green embroidered upon it, she set out for a walk.

Having no particular destination in mind, Maggie walked with a brisk aimlessness that soon carried her into a street she didn't recognize. Was the Kirk town house that way? She turned pensively in the opposite direction. Or that way?

A little girl sat playing on the lawn of a very grand house with pillared porches.

Maggie approached the fence with a smile. "Pardon me," she called brightly, "but do you know the way to Victoria Street? I seem to have lost my way."

The child looked up at Maggie with blue-green eyes so like Reeve McKenna's that she clenched the fence's pickets in both hands and gasped.

The little girl studied Maggie in amicable silence for some time and then went back to her toy, a small, colorfully painted metal horse with wheels.

Maggie knew the child had heard her question and was puzzled by the lack of response. She was about to ask again when the door of the magnificent house opened and Reeve McKenna came out, striding down the walk.

In light of the odd obsession she seemed to be developing for this man, Maggie considered bolting and running. But that was silly; he had given her her freedom, after all, proving that he was not the fiend she had thought, and she did need to learn the way back to the house in Victoria Street.

"Hello," she said, remembering the woman in the book, leaning back against the wall. Hot color flowed into Maggie's face, for in her dream that woman had been herself and the man kneeling to please her had been the one walking toward her at this very moment.

Reeve saw the blush on Maggie's cheeks and smiled a secret smile, as though he knew what she was thinking and was amused by it. Of course, Maggie told herself firmly, he couldn't possibly know.

"I've lost my way," she blurted out when Reeve was suddenly standing just the other side of the fence, his hands close to hers, his chest so near that she could feel the warmth of it. Not daring to look up into his face, she focused on the ever-present brass charm glistening in the dark hair covering his chest.

"I was hoping you'd changed your mind about working for me," Reeve replied, and Maggie could feel his breath on the crown of her head even through her thick hair. She shivered, though she was warm rather than cold. Oh, entirely too warm.

Maggie forced herself to look up into those dangerous aquamarine eyes. "In truth"—she was appalled to hear herself saying this—"I'm at sixes and sevens about that. I did work hard at learning my lines on the way out and—"

At Reeve's slow smile, Maggie's words dried up in her throat. Almost idly, he tangled an index finger in a curl of her hair, just beneath her right ear, where the skin was sensitive.

"And?" he prompted her.

Maggie blushed all over this time, feeling the heat in her face and under her clothes as well. Those damnable pictures towered in her mind, not as drawings, but as flesh and blood. Her flesh and blood, and Reeve's. "Well," she managed to choke out, "none of that matters anyway, now, does it? I've agreed to teach Mr. Kirk's sons and I always keep my word."

"Do you?" The two words, spoken in a low and rumbling tone, somehow affected Maggie like a bold caress.

She stepped back from the fence and from the sweet warmth that seemed to radiate from this man's person. "If you'll just direct me to Victoria Street, please," she said.

"How are you getting on with Duncan?" Reeve asked as though he hadn't heard Maggie's request at all.

She began to feel angry as well as deliciously miserable. "Quite well, since Mr. Kirk's away at the moment," she replied in stiff tones. "He's taken the boys along with him."

"You must be at loose ends," Mr. McKenna ventured to say, and there was no discerning whether he meant the words as a polite comment or an insinuation.

Suddenly, it was very important to Maggie that this man not think of her for a moment as a retiring sort with nothing to do to amuse herself. "On the contrary," she answered evenly, "I'm off to Parramatta, Saturday noon, to have a magnificent time."

Reeve's eyes were steady on her face, or was it expressly her lips that he was looking at? They swelled under his gaze and grew tingly and warm.

"Ummm," he said. And then he seemed to collect himself and turned to point with one hand. "Victoria Street is that way. About six blocks over."

"Thank you," Maggie said, feeling slightly dizzy at the abrupt release from the spell he'd seemed to cast over her. "I am sorry I troubled you."

He grinned. "And I'm sorry for troubling you," he responded.

His meaning was clear as a slap in the face, and Maggie turned away on one heel, fleeing at a brisk walk. She was grateful for the breeze flowing up from the glistening blue waters of Rushcutter's Bay, for it cooled her burning face.

He knew, he knew, he knew. The horrifying thought clattered rhythmically in Maggie's brain like the wheels of a train on their track. Reeve McKenna knew about the peculiar yearning he had aroused in Maggie, and she was mortified.

Maggie walked faster, and Reeve's quiet laughter followed after her like a pesky puppy nipping at her skirts.

Upon reaching the Kirk house, Maggie went upstairs, found the offending book of drawings, and resolutely carried it back to its place in the library. As penance for studying the volume, let alone enjoying it so much, she forced herself to endure ten full pages of the wisdom of Socrates.

Saturday came none too soon, and when Tansy and her chums arrived at midday, Maggie was waiting for them at the garden gate, reticule in hand. In the past three days and nights she'd thought of nothing but Reeve McKenna and the ferocious wanting he'd stirred in her, and she was desperate for distraction.

Tansy quickly introduced all her friends and Maggie remembered none of their names. They set off for the same corner where Maggie and Susan Crockett had boarded a streetcar that eventful day of Maggie's shopping expedition.

They rode to the edge of the city, where they boarded an omnibus drawn by no less than eight horses. There were others bound for the festivities in Parramatta, and soon Tansy had every passenger under seventy singing a lively ditty in perfect rounds. At last, as she sang, Maggie was able to push Reeve McKenna out of her mind.

Darkness had fallen by the time the omnibus reached Parramatta, and Maggie, her throat raw from singing and her bottom sore from the jolting ride over rutted roads, was much relieved.

Now Tansy surrendered the status of leadership to an older girl who had been to the property before. "It's just down this road, not more than a mile," the young woman called to her following.

Torches flared in the darkness up ahead, as well as huge bonfires, and Maggie caught the sounds of laughter and loud and spirited preaching on the night air. A delicious aroma wafted from the camp, quite nullifying the underlying stench of horse dung.

"Supper cooking," Tansy said, reading Maggie's mind. "It's Turk's 'ead, and there's dampers, too, I'm thinkin'."

Maggie stopped so suddenly that she collided with someone behind her. Grudgingly, she began walking again. "What in the name of heaven is Turk's head?" she demanded in a nervous whisper that would brook no evasion.

Tansy laughed. "It's like a pumpkin, only different," she answered after a moment. "They stuff it with fresh rabbit meat and onions and roast it underground. And dampers, since you're bound to ask, is bushman's bread. It's just flour and water, really, but it tastes splendid after bein' cooked in the ashes the way they do."

Maggie's stomach rumbled and she walked a little faster. Soon enough, the group joined hundreds of other people milling about in the companionable torchlit darkness, and they were given plates and eating utensils in return for a few pence.

Abandoned by Tansy, for the moment at least, Maggie filled her plate with dampers and a sizable portion of the rabbit and onion mixture and found a place to sit on the end of a long log facing one of the fires.

The people around her seemed undaunted by the hellfire-and-brimstone preaching coming from one of several tents set up on the grounds; they laughed and told stories as they ate. Vaguely, the happy atmosphere reminded Maggie of other nights, in America, when she'd sat around blazing fires with circus people, listening to their stories.

For a moment she missed her mother and father desperately, but she was soon distracted from this sentimental train of thought, for Reeve McKenna sat down on the log beside her, bold as brass.

"Hello, Maggie," he said as though he had every right to be there, startling her so that she'd nearly choked on her food.

"What are you doing here?" she hissed, keeping her voice to a whisper for a reason she couldn't have explained.

He shrugged. "I never miss the camp meetings," he said.

Maggie gave him a look. Damn the man. It had taken her all this while to get him out of her thoughts and now here he was, intruding. Making her feel that strange, sweet malaise that no other man had ever made her feel. "For the preaching, Mr. McKenna?" she asked, sweetly sarcastic.

Tansy went past just then, holding a plate in one hand and dragging a young man along behind her with the other. Maggie knew intuitively that she'd be left to find a place to sleep on her own and made up her mind to wring Tansy's neck the next time she saw her.

"Actually," Mr. McKenna answered belatedly, "it's the horse racing that I like." He glanced up at the starry sky, the firelight flickering on the rugged planes of his face and catching in the brass medallion at his throat. "Doesn't look like rain."

Given the cloudless state of the sky, that seemed like a silly observation to Maggie, but she kept her opinion to herself.

When she met Reeve's eyes, she saw laughter in their depths. "You don't believe it can rain," he accused her.

"There isn't a cloud in the sky, after all," Maggie replied.

"Storms strike very suddenly in Australia, Miss Chamberlin." The blue-green eyes flecked with firelight held Maggie spellbound. "And when they do, they are torrential."

The ominous words struck a conversely pleasant note deep within Maggie. As sparks from the fire rose toward the black velvet sky, with its spattering of stars, she wondered if this night would be as difficult as the three nights preceding it.

Chapter 7 ❧

As soon as she was able to manage it, Maggie excused herself and escaped Reeve McKenna, anxiously searching the grounds for some sign of Tansy. But there was none; the girl had disappeared into the dense shadows where the flickering fingers of the firelight did not reach.

Now what was she going to do? After a moment's hesitation Maggie ducked into one of the tents where the gospel was being thundered out with vehemence and fury.

"For the Lord your God is a jealous God!" bellowed the short, well-fed preacher pacing the wooden platform at the rear of the tent. Dozens of people sat, watching and listening, on long, splintery benches. Maggie rolled her eyes.

At that moment, as if the Lord meant to reprimand her personally for being a scoffer, thunder split the sky with a deafening crash. Maggie, lurking by the tent's opening, started in fear and then slipped outside to look up. The stars, present only moments before, were now gone, replaced by ugly shifting clouds. Lightning veined across the sky in golden streaks, making a pattern reminiscent of shattered glass.

Less than a second later rain sliced to earth, not in drops or trickles, but in cascades, making a roar the likes of which Maggie had never heard on the canvas roofs of the tents and covered wagons, and turning the enormous bonfires to heaps of sizzling charcoal. People dashed in every direction, taking refuge in and under wagons and inside the tents, laughing as they ran.

Maggie was desperate for shelter—her dress and hair were instantaneously soaked—but not desperate enough to go back inside that tent and hear more about a wrathful God. Cursing Tansy for getting her into this situation in the first place, she stood undecided in the downpour, looking this way and then that.

Suddenly, a strong hand caught hold of her elbow and she was being dragged through the driving rain. Water and her own wet hair streamed down over her face, making it impossible for Maggie to see who was pulling her along, but, as she stumbled behind her guide, through mud reaching nearly to her shins, she had an idea or two.

And she wasn't entirely sure that it wouldn't be better to stand outside in the rain until the storm passed.

After an interminable trek, Maggie made out the gloomy outlines of a covered wagon. Her abductor turned, grasped her firmly by the waist, and hoisted her high in the air. Her bottom landed with a mushy plop on the bed of the wagon, and she scrambled inside because so much water was rushing into her face, she couldn't breathe.

She lay gasping on the floorboards for almost a minute, afraid to look up. Boots moved past her face in the darkness, and then a kerosene lamp flared to life, illuminating the interior of the wagon.

"You'd better get out of those clothes or you'll have

pneumonia before breakfast," warned a placid male voice.

Slowly, Maggie levered herself to a sitting position and, with both hands, swept her sodden hair out of her face. Reeve McKenna sat on the edge of a narrow cot, smiling companionably. At Maggie's glare, he spread his hands wide of his body, as if to ask what he'd said or done that was outside the bounds of social amenity.

She continued to glare, but her teeth were beginning to chatter by then, and she was shivering.

Nonchalantly, Reeve reached to one side and produced Maggie's reticule. He tossed it and it landed at her side with a thump.

"You left this by the fire."

Maggie looked at the reticule, which contained a warm nightdress and a change of clothing, with yearning. She supposed she should thank Mr. McKenna for safeguarding her possessions in such a way, but she couldn't quite bring herself to speak such civil words.

It was then that Maggie was struck by the distinct possibility that her spare clothes were as wet as the ones she wore. Her fingers trembling, she fumbled with the catch until the reticule opened, plunging one anxious hand inside. Sure enough, her new pink and white gingham dress and her best cotton nightgown were soaked.

With a groan of despair, Reeve McKenna's presence having slipped her mind for the moment, Maggie rose as far as her knees, pulling out the spoiled garments for closer inspection.

"I suppose Duncan bought those things for you." The flat words brought the full gravity of her situation home to Maggie. Legs shaky, she got to her feet and stared down at Reeve's expressionless face.

"Yes," she heard herself say. "I'm to be his hostess, you see—"

Reeve stood up, towering over Maggie to such a degree that it hurt her neck to look up at him. One of his hands snatched the sopping wet nightgown from her, a thumb and forefinger assessing the weight of the delicate fabric. "You'll be greeting his guests in your nightdress, will you?"

Maggie was a moment grasping the implications of what he'd said. The rain pounded at the taut canvas top of the wagon, dripping through here and there, and still Maggie thought she could hear the beat of her own heart.

She faced Reeve with what proud dignity she could conjure up under the circumstances. "Of course not," she replied weakly, and then she reached out and grabbed the garment back.

Without so much as a word of warning, Reeve turned away, lifted the glass chimney of the lamp he'd lit earlier, and extinguished the flame. The wagon went dark as the cellars of hell, and Maggie drew in a swift, stunned breath.

"What do you think you're doing?" she demanded of the gloom. She couldn't see an inch in any direction; it was safe neither to stand fast nor to flee.

"Do you want the whole of the camp to watch you undress?" Reeve retorted from somewhere in the black desolation that surrounded Maggie.

"I have no intention of undressing!"

"Brave words," Reeve responded, unconcerned. "The trouble is, Yank, that you're wet to the skin and cold as a banker's heart in the bargain." Some unidentifiable but dry garment flew through the blackness and Maggie clutched at it. Flannel. Warm, blessedly dry flannel.

Shivering, Maggie felt the article of clothing and determined that it was a man's shirt. "I'm leaving," she said, making no move to do so. The only thing more dangerous than the inside of that wagon, of course, was the storm that raged outside.

"Get out of your wet things, Miss Chamberlin," Reeve ordered wearily, "or I'll take you out of them myself."

Maggie had absolutely no doubt that Reeve Mc-Kenna would make good on his threat should he be driven to it, and she was shivering hard now, cold to the very marrow of her bones. "What assurance d-do I have that you're not pl-planning to light that lamp or—"

"If I lit the lamp, you'd be putting on a show for anyone stupid enough to be outside," Reeve answered, "and if I wanted to seduce you, I'd never have thrown away a perfect opportunity to keep you under my roof by giving you your emigration papers, now, would I?"

Maggie saw reason in his words and began unbuttoning her dress. Given the cold numbness that had beset her fingers, she had the devil's own time trying to work the bits of mother-of-pearl through the tiny openings provided.

Finally, in utter frustration, she spat out, "Damn, damn, and triple damn!"

Reeve chuckled in the darkness, and she sensed rather than heard his drawing nearer to her. Unerringly, he found her buttons and began undoing them without the slightest problem, even though he had to be every bit as wet and cold as Maggie was.

"You are fond of that phrase, aren't you, Yank?" he said.

Against Maggie's sodden camisole his knuckles felt warm and hard as they worked. She was stricken speechless by the magnitude of the situation she'd gotten herself into and the strange stirrings that Reeve's touch engendered deep within her. "Wh-what do you mean?" she asked lamely, unable to turn and flee into the rain as she should have.

His hands were at her waist now, unfastening the last of those cursed buttons. "You said something similar on the ship when you found out you couldn't go ashore in one of the dinghies."

Maggie had heard Reeve's words, but she couldn't make sense of them. Her attention was focused on the

101

hands she could not see, now slipping under the shoulders of her dress and moving it away. She shivered again, and not with cold, but with wonder at the hot, biting sweetness that possessed the most secret part of her.

She stood fast as Reeve untied her camisole and then peeled it away from her flesh, which was chilled on the surface and scalding hot underneath. His thumbs grazed her hardened nipples, whether by accident or design Maggie could not tell, and she gave an involuntary groan at the pleasure the motion spawned.

"Maggie," he said in a low and ragged voice, and then she felt his breath on her face and instinctively she tilted her head back to greet his mouth with her own. His forceful but infinitely gentle hands entangled themselves in her dripping hair and he kissed her.

Maggie was stunned by the tender warmth of his lips moving against hers, moist and undemanding. She shivered when the tip of his tongue encircled her mouth in one swift, featherlight foray, bidding it to open for him. Maggie responded by parting her lips in response to his mild command and nestling close to him. Her nipples tightened even more on contact with the cold, rain-drenched barrier of his shirtfront.

His fingers moved along the slender, moisture-beaded curve of her back, warming her, exciting her more with each pass over her flesh. Then, with the soul-shattering kiss continuing, Reeve caught his hands under her bottom and lifted her flush with the full force of his need. Even through her petticoat and drawers, all the clothing left to her except for shoes and stockings, Maggie felt the straining power of him and trembled for the want of it even as she recoiled inwardly in fear.

Reeve's hand suddenly came up beneath Maggie's chin and clamped around her jaw, and it was as though he were battling his own will to break away from the kiss.

He half groaned and half growled an expletive and stepped away from her. But soon enough his hands were back, briefly cupping Maggie's full and throbbing breasts, then sliding down the sides of her waist to dispense with her petticoats and drawers.

Maggie was powerless to protest, much less flee, and when she felt herself being lowered to a soft bed covered in woolly blankets, she offered no resistance. She closed her eyes as she felt Reeve removing her shoes, rolling down her practical ribbed stockings with a sensual lassitude that heightened Maggie's need to a pitch that made her toss restlessly on the bedclothes.

Reeve's voice was thick with the brogue Maggie had heard only hints of before, and hoarse with needs she couldn't even begin to comprehend. "You're a virgin, then, aren't you, lass?"

Maggie could not speak; he knew her answer because one of his hands had come to rest alongside her cheek and he felt her feverish nod.

"Then I'll not be takin' you this night," he vowed in the dense gloom. Maggie couldn't tell whether the roaring in her ears was the sound of the rain outside or just the rushing of her own blood.

She did know that her disappointment would have been fathomless but for the fact that Reeve's thumbs were once again brushing her nipples. She'd lost all sense of propriety by then; her need of whatever Reeve was promising with his nearness and his touch was primal.

Reeve chuckled at her eagerness; when she regained her senses, Maggie promised herself, she'd call him to account for that. "You'll 'ave the pleasure, lass," he vowed in that same thick brogue, "without the ruinin'."

His mouth closed over one of Maggie's distended

nipples then, sucking for a moment and then withdrawing. Maggie gave a little cry and clutched both her hands together at the back of his head, pressing Reeve back to her breasts.

He laughed before enjoying her again, this time with a lusty avarice that made Maggie writhe in pleasure, her head thrust back, her lips parted, her breath coming in short, rasping gasps.

Reeve had his fill at the first breast and then took leisurely nourishment at the second. Maggie was almost delirious with wanting as it was; when Reeve's fingers brushed over the downy place at the junction of her thighs, promising much in their passing, she groaned aloud and, of their own accord, her hips bolted from the bed in response to his touch.

A low sound in Reeve's throat indicated his amusement, and his mouth left her breast to tease her with a kiss so light as to cause Maggie to wonder if she'd imagined it. And then Reeve's lips were moving against hers. "The rain 'as stopped," he said. "If you aren't quiet, lass, everyone in camp will know just what it is that I'm doin'—"

Maggie's hands were still locked in his hair, and her body throbbed in restless yearning on the blankets. His fingers brought her yet another new torment, sweet and achy and fierce. "I'll b-be quiet—I promise —I promise!"

Reeve chuckled again and then he was moving away, his lips brushing along her chin, the quivering satin expanse of her neck, her breasts, and her stomach. And then, to her utter surprise, his fingers gave way to his mouth.

Maggie's hips were flung high by some savage instinct as he nuzzled her, tasted her with brief fiery strokes of his tongue, and then claimed her fully. His hands held the shivering plumpness of her bottom high while he consumed her, and Maggie clapped both her own hands over her mouth in a desperate effort to muffle the low, lusty cry of welcome that spiraled up from the very core of her soul to rattle in her throat.

She had thought, in the first jarring realization of what Reeve was doing, that this was the summit of pleasure, the fulfillment. Instead, it turned out to be only a hint of the explosive tumult that was to come.

Maggie's heart hammered and her breath tore back and forth through the latticework of her fingers, and the sensation at the joining of her thighs became unendurably pleasurable. At the same time she craved the mysterious satisfaction her body strained toward, she fought to escape it. But Reeve held her fast in his hands, raising her hips higher and higher as he tongued and sucked her toward madness, and Maggie's own legs betrayed her, knees widening to give him greater access, heels digging into the mattress in a frantic, entrenching motion.

And then it happened, that fiery explosion ignited at the very essence of her womanhood and fanning out to pound at her hips, tingle in her breasts, and make the hair at the nape of her neck, sodden as it was, stand on end. Her hands were not enough to quiet the long, low cry of release that escaped her; Maggie wrenched the pillow from beneath her head and clasped it over her face.

Slowly, Reeve lowered her shivering hips back to the bed; reluctantly, he rolled his tongue around that sensitive nubbin of flesh once more before withdrawing.

Maggie lay trembling, too shaken and too embarrassed to come out from under the pillow. "Oh, Lord," she moaned, "what have I done?"

She felt Reeve rise off the bed, heard his rueful chuckle and then his answer. "Nothing that'll do you any lasting harm," he said. "I, on the other hand, may never be the same."

The brogue was gone. Even as Maggie noted that fact, she wondered why she cared and pressed the pillow down harder.

Before she knew it, the pillow was snatched away, and landed with a soft thump on the other side of the wagon somewhere. "You won't undo what's happened by smothering yourself," Reeve pointed out.

Maggie sat bolt upright, forgetting her mortification and the delicious, sated feeling possessing her body in a disturbing realization that while she might as well have been blind for all she could make out in that pitlike darkness, Reeve had been able to see. "You must have the eyes of a cat!"

Reeve laughed, but the sound was harsh somehow, as though he might be suffering pain of some sort. "The pillow slip is white, Maggie. Besides, you struck me with it when you pulled it out from under your head to—"

Maggie wailed with embarrassment and wriggled underneath the covers. If the pillow slip showed white in the darkness, her skin probably did too.

"You saw me!" she accused him through the blankets.

"I did more than see you, my love," Reeve responded. She was once again conscious of the rain; it grew louder.

Maggie tore the blankets from over her face, forgetting that her body might glow in the gloom like a pale light. "You're leaving me alone?" she hissed.

"If I don't, Yank, we'll both be sorry," Reeve answered, and then there was a splashing sound as he leapt down from the wagon. The driving thrum of the rain was muffled a little when he closed the canvas curtain.

Maggie lay down again, pulling the covers up to her nose. The sensible thing to do, of course, would be to get out of Reeve McKenna's narrow bed, put her clothes back on, wet or not, and leave. The trouble was that the sensible approach had a distinct lack of appeal. Wet clothes would be cold clothes, and the rain was still beating down outside. If Maggie left the warm, though admittedly scandalous sanctuary of the wagon, exactly where could she go?

Finding Tansy would be impossible, since there were a thousand and one places the little devil could be, and the thought of throwing herself on the mercy of one of those fire-and-brimstone preachers was the worst prospect of all. Far worse than anything Reeve could do even if he were to return to the wagon in a rage of lust.

Snuggling under the covers, her hair an unruly mess around her head, Maggie smiled as she imagined Reeve in a rage of lust. The prospect was intriguing.

The covers warming her, her body feeling all soft and boneless and profoundly cherished in the bargain, Maggie yawned and closed her eyes. Within moments she was sleeping, untroubled by dreams of any kind, erotic or otherwise.

There were other places Reeve could have slept, other places where the needs that tore at him might have been appeased, but in the end, after wandering for nearly an hour in the rain, he went back to his own wagon and crept inside.

Maggie was sleeping; he knew that from the soft meter of her breathing. Reeve smiled to himself as he stripped away his wet clothes and flung them into a corner of the wagon. There was only one bed and it was too damned cold to sleep on the floor, so he crawled into the narrow berth beside Maggie and huddled close to her. He'd just have to control himself, that was all.

She stirred as his icy flesh pressed against her, but didn't awaken. Reeve was filled with tenderness—Maggie was exhausted—and he was gentle as he laid one possessive, protective arm over her and ordered himself to sleep.

Maggie's plump little posterior wriggled against him as she stirred in her sleep, and Reeve swallowed a groan as he felt himself growing hard again. The effects of an hour's walk in the frigid rain had just been undone.

A shudder went through him and then he sneezed, shaking the whole bed. As luck would have it, Maggie awakened and he felt her turning toward him, the peaks of her breasts brushing his chest and making matters generally worse.

"You've caught a cold," she scolded softly, sleepily, her small, smooth hand moving up and down his arm in an effort to warm him.

She was doing a lot more than warming him, but Reeve couldn't think of a way to withdraw without getting out from underneath the blankets, and he wasn't about to do that. Even chivalry, he reflected, has its limits.

"Maggie, stop it," he pleaded hoarsely. And then, unable to help himself, he exploded with another thunderous sneeze.

Maggie snuggled closer, trying to share her warmth, and Reeve was so moved by the ingenuous charity of the motion that his throat thickened into an impassible knot, making it impossible for him to warn her.

Her hand moved along his hip in a circling motion, hesitated, and then progressed to his left buttock. His manhood ached, taut and hard, and he groaned.

Maggie's hand came back to his hip, and then she was massaging his thigh, at times coming perilously close to the part of him that most needed, most craved touching.

Reeve could bear no more, and he grasped Maggie's wrist in his hand to stop the sweet torment.

"Don't you want me to touch you?" she whispered, sounding puzzled and hurt.

"Believe me, Maggie," Reeve breathed, "I do."

"Then why did you grab my hand like that?"

"It was your interest I was looking after, Yank, and not my own. If you'd kept that up much longer, I'd have finished what we started earlier."

He could sense her surprise, her wonder, and again he was filled with a tenderness so all-encompassing as to be painful.

"You mean there's more? We didn't—we didn't do everything?"

A low, startled laugh erupted from Reeve's throat. "You thought that was everything?" he asked in a hoarse whisper when he was able to speak coherently.

He heard the tears gathering in her throat before he reached up with a gentle hand and felt them on her face. "You *did* think that was everything," he said gently, answering his own question.

Maggie's forehead was tucked against his chest; then he felt her nod and his fingers delved into the damp, tangled hair at the back of her head. Unable to resist her for another moment, Reeve made her lift her face for his kiss.

It betrayed all his hunger, that kiss, a hunger he'd never felt for any other woman, Loretta included. God, even weeks of lonely nights on board a whaler had never driven him to a need like this.

His tongue sought admittance; Maggie opened for it, greeted it with her own shy sparring. His groan echoed in her mouth and he shifted, so that he lay above her, his elbows keeping his full weight from resting upon her.

Reeve's mind spun like a child's boat on a stormy sea. Some instinct made Maggie part her legs for him and he rested between them, allowing his shaft to press its throbbing length into the flesh of her belly.

Dear God in heaven, he needed her, but even in his fever to have her he remembered that this was Maggie, not Loretta. Maggie was a virgin, and if he thrust into her too suddenly, too forcefully, he would hurt her.

"Maggie," he breathed raggedly, his face buried in the sweet softness of her neck, "Maggie."

Her hands were caressing the taut muscles of his back, soothing his soul and, at the same time, inflaming his flesh. He felt, through the wall of his chest, a soft whimper escape her, and then heard it pass his ear.

Instantly, Reeve lifted himself again, so that no part of him except his lower legs was touching her. "Did I hurt you?" he whispered.

Her soft hair tickled his face as she shook her head back and forth. "No, Reeve—you didn't hurt me." Her hands were slipping, light as gossamer, up and down his back again. "Let me hold you. You're so cold."

"Strange," Reeve managed to reply, "I'd swear I have a fever."

Maggie's cool hand rose to his forehead, smoothing back the damp hair he'd dried briefly with a cloth before getting into bed. He saw her alabaster brow furrow in the dense darkness. "People die of fever," she fretted softly.

Reeve felt his heart swell to the point of breaking. "It isn't that kind of fever, love," he said.

She was kissing the underside of his jaw; if she didn't stop soon, Reeve wasn't going to be able to keep from taking her much longer.

"What else is there to do," she asked, her lips tracing the length of his neck now, "besides what we did before?"

Unable to answer audibly, Reeve shifted so that his manhood again pressed its length into her soft stomach.

"You want to put that inside me!" Maggie almost crowed in the tone of one who has just had an Olympian revelation.

Reeve covered her mouth with his, even though it was a belated effort. "Be quiet," he said, and the whisper echoed.

She sent the words back to him on a soft giggle and Reeve was lost. He slid down her body, as far as her breasts, and began the pleasuring that would prepare her for his taking.

Chapter 8 ❧

ON SOME LEVEL OF HER MIND, MAGGIE KNEW THAT WHAT took place in the next few minutes might prove to be the worst mistake of her life, but she was unable to act on that knowledge. She had no desire to stop Reeve from feasting at her breasts, no desire to stop him from kissing her shivering middle. And then his mouth was on hers and she could feel his powerful shaft nudging at the portal of her womanhood.

"Are you sure, Maggie?" he asked, just barely inside her.

Maggie was sure. She felt herself expanding to welcome him, and the expansion was a burning ache that only his taking could relieve. Wildly, her fingers clutching at Reeve's back, she nodded her head.

He entered her slowly, by careful degrees, and each advance increased Maggie's pleasure a thousandfold. She tried to raise her hips so that he would take her fully, but Reeve would permit no deviation from the pace he was setting. Finally, he reached a barrier of some sort and there was a brief, searing pain as he passed it. Maggie gasped and he did not move deeper inside her until several moments had gone by.

Reeve reached beneath Maggie and cupped her bottom in his hands, lifting her slightly, and then he was wholly, gloriously hers. Maggie trembled, her hands tangling in his hair, forcing him to bend his head for her kiss.

While they kissed, their tongues fighting a fierce and friendly war, Reeve began a rhythm of pleasure that drove all semblance of rational thought from Maggie's mind. He withdrew slowly, then delved deep, then withdrew again. And each time he pulled away, Maggie wanted to weep for the need of him.

His slow pace was excruciatingly sweet, commanding, and, at the same time, gentle. Maggie had only to give herself up to the wondrous sensations that possessed her, for Reeve guided the motion of her hips with his hands.

Each time their joining deepened, Maggie moaned. There were kisses, some brief and frantic, some long and hungry, and all the while Reeve's body set the pace for hers. The passion grew until it filled Maggie, swirling through her mind, swelling her lush breasts and hardening their peaks. She grasped at Reeve's shoulders, pleading, "Reeve—Reeve—"

And then the riot of sensations tearing through her culminated in one shuddering, desperate eruption of feeling, of needing, of loving. At the same time Maggie cried out in her pleasure, the skies replied with a deafening salvo of thunder.

Reeve was still approaching his own pinnacle of release; he groaned and began to move faster and faster along the velvety channel that teased and taunted even as it caressed. There was no thunder to mask the cry of despairing rapture that tore itself from his throat.

Maggie reveled in the shuddering exhaustion that caused his body to fall to hers, warm and heavy and perspiring from exertion. She wrapped her arms around Reeve's heaving middle and held him close.

Only when Reeve rolled to his side, his breathing

still ragged, did Maggie release him, and then she idly caressed his arm with one hand.

Moments later she slept, cuddled close to Reeve, and she had no way of knowing that he lay awake for hours, staring up at the shadowy canvas roof that protected them from the rain.

The first thing Maggie was conscious of was a soreness in her most private place, an innocuous, gentle kind of pain. She squirmed deeper into the covers, aware now of the blinding sunlight that turned her closed lids pink. It was much too warm beneath the blankets, so Maggie threw them off, delighting in the cool caress of a morning breeze along her naked skin.

It was then that she remembered, and her eyes flew open and she sat upright in the narrow bed. Reeve was gone, and her clothes had been carefully draped over a trunk in the corner to dry.

Cheeks crimson, Maggie scrambled out of the bed, snatched up her still-damp drawers and camisole, and shimmied into them. Then she put on her stockings and her shoes and the pink and white gingham dress that had been packed so carefully in her reticule. It was shamefully wrinkled now, and slightly wet, but Maggie got into it anyway.

She was just attempting to button the gown, when Reeve suddenly vaulted into the wagon from the back. Maggie flushed and averted her eyes from his face, afraid to see mockery there, or revulsion, or remorse.

He approached her from behind, his fingers warm as they did up the buttons she'd been unable to reach. When he'd done that, he pushed aside her flowing, snarled hair and bent to kiss the nape of her neck.

Maggie stiffened against him, against the terrible needs he stirred within her so easily. Without looking at Reeve, she found her reticule and brought out her hairbrush, trying to tame her hopelessly tangled hair.

Still silent, Reeve took the brush from her hands,

sat down on the bed where they'd done such scandalous things the night before, and pulled a startled Maggie onto his lap. When she struggled to rise, he restrained her, his arm hard around her middle.

And then he began to brush her hair.

Maggie had never thought that having a man hold her on his lap and brush her hair could be a sensual thing; indeed, she'd never thought of a man doing those things at all. But it was an intimacy so tender as to almost take her breath away.

Maggie trembled slightly. His thighs were hard as granite beneath her own soft ones and a sweet, mysterious excitement shot through her.

Reeve paused, no longer working at the tangles and snarls in her hair. "Cold?"

"Yes," Maggie lied, sitting up a little straighter.

Reeve chuckled and went back to his gentle work. "Your hair is just the color of moonlight on white opal," he said thoughtfully after a few moments, all evidence of amusement gone from his tone.

Maggie didn't know what to say to that, and she wasn't sure she could trust herself to speak anyway, so she kept her peace. Reeve continued to brush her hair, and when he'd finished, a long time later, he laid aside the brush and, with a tender boldness, cupped his hands over Maggie's breasts for a moment.

She shivered at the delectable sensations this inspired and then bolted from Reeve's lap because she knew where such caresses could lead.

"How am I going to leave this wagon without everyone for miles around knowing that I spent the night here?" she demanded in a tone of practical petulance.

Reeve grinned and rose slowly to his feet, standing within inches of Maggie and clearly enjoying the obvious discomfort this caused her. "Not many people will notice, Maggie. Provided you put up your hair, that is, and stop blushing."

Maggie swallowed hard and then made an involved business of finding her hairpins, which were scattered from one end of Reeve McKenna's bed to the other. "I wasn't blushing," she said, still bent over as she collected the last few pins.

Brazenly, Reeve reached out and caressed her rounded bottom, and heat surged through her. She was ashamed of the knowledge that, should this man kiss her again, should he touch her breasts, she would surely allow him to take her. Right there in broad daylight, on that narrow, rumpled bed.

It was knowing that that made Maggie whirl and slap Reeve McKenna soundly across the face, the blow making a satisfying noise.

Instantly, Reeve caught both her wrists behind her in one of his hands. With the other he stroked her right breast, grinning as he felt the nipple harden beneath its covering of muslin and thin cotton. Still keeping Maggie prisoner by clasping her hands together, he bent and nipped gently at the hidden point with his teeth.

Maggie moaned and closed her eyes. There was no need for Reeve to restrain her; she was powerless to move away. But still he held her, tormenting the other breast with his tongue and his teeth while with his free hand he lifted her skirts. She trembled as she felt the ties of her drawers give way, groaned when Reeve's hand slid inside to caress her. He left her breast to kiss the length of her neck then, while his fingers remained where they were, fondling, flicking, rolling the nubbin of flesh between them.

"Oh, God," Maggie gasped as her body suddenly convulsed in a swift, searing spasm of pleasure.

He laughed softly, continuing to stroke Maggie even as she shuddered in the aching aftermath of his small conquering. "If you ever slap me again, Maggie," he said, gently rolling her earlobe between his teeth, "this will be your punishment."

Maggie could feel the awesome need building within her again and she whimpered, "Oh, no, Reeve, please—not a second time—"

His fondling was relentless and brutally pleasurable for Maggie. She found herself bent far backward over Reeve's arm, surrendering to the magic his hand ignited while his teeth again tormented breasts that craved to be bared to him and were not.

"Oooooh," she moaned as the second pinnacle was reached, and her hips spasmed in response to Reeve's skillful touch.

When the tumult had ended, Reeve withdrew his hand from Maggie's drawers, let her skirts fall back into place, lifted her so that she again stood upright. She stared at him, dazed by the glory of the moments just past.

And Reeve gave her a hard swat on the bottom, turned, and left the wagon, whistling. Damn and double damn, the man was *whistling!*

Maggie pressed her hands to her cheeks in an effort to cool them and stood stock-still until her breathing was normal again. Then, not wanting to hide inside Reeve's wagon all day, she climbed bravely out the back.

The sky was a deep, rain-washed blue, the sun bright as polished brass. People milled about everywhere, talking and eating as they moved between puddles of muddy water. Almost immediately, Maggie spotted Tansy, standing by one of the new bonfires, casually warming her hands.

Maggie stormed toward her friend, furious beyond all good sense. If Tansy hadn't disappeared the way she had, Maggie might not have ended up in Reeve's wagon. She might not have given up the most precious thing a woman could offer a man. "Tansy Quinn," she demanded in a scathing whisper, "where have you been?"

Tansy looked at Maggie and then at the wagon she'd

crawled out of, a knowing, saucy gleam in her blue eyes. "I was doin' the same thing you were doin', only in the barn," she answered, bold and brazen as you please.

Maggie stiffened, her face burning. Unable to think of an answer to Tansy's remark, she remained silent.

Tansy drew nearer, catching Maggie's rigid arm in her hand and ushering her away from the fire and the people waiting there for their breakfast. "You're the luckiest of us all, Maggie Chamberlin," she confided in a delighted whisper. "Imagine beddin' a man like that!"

Unfortunately, Maggie didn't have to imagine bedding a man like Reeve. But neither did she have to admit to anything. "It so happens that nothing of the sort took place last night. Nothing at all. Mr. McKenna simply allowed me to sleep in his wagon because I'd been caught in the rain and had nowhere else to go!"

Tansy nodded sagely, her eyes revealing utter skepticism. "Aye, love. That must be why I heard you moanin' the man's name when I came by the wagon earlier this mornin' to find you." She bent a little closer to Maggie as she propelled her between enormous pools of rainwater. "What in the name of 'eaven was the bloke doin' to you to make you carry on like that?"

Completely mortified, Maggie pulled her arm free and stood, still and stubborn, glaring down into Tansy's upturned face. "Anything you thought you heard must have come from your own lewd imagination!" she accused her friend hotly. "Either that, or you were lurking behind the wrong wagon!"

Tansy held up both hands in a gesture of peace, but her eyes twinkled and her lips twitched just a little as she struggled to keep from giggling. "All right, love, if you want to pretend it didn't 'appen, I guess that's fine by me, but you shouldn't be so free with the feelings of a friend like meself, 'cause in nine months or so, you might be needin' one."

All the color drained from Maggie's livid face. Not once had she thought that she might be carrying Reeve McKenna's child; now the prospect was horrifying.

Tansy took both Maggie's hands in her own. "Don't be frettin' now, love. The time for that is when your curse should come and doesn't."

Maggie's knees felt weak as she tried to calculate when her next flow was due. She had two weeks to wait! Two long, hellish weeks before she would know the fate that might be bearing down on her even now. "I feel sick," she said.

Tansy again took hold of Maggie's elbow, this time squiring her back toward the crackling bonfire. "Fiddlesticks, you're only scared," she argued, "and a mite 'ungry, too, probably. Come and 'ave some breakfast with me and we'll watch the 'orse races."

Maggie didn't want to watch the horse races; it seemed to her that Reeve had mentioned coming to the camp meeting for the express purpose of doing just that, and she wasn't ready to face him again, under any circumstances. "I couldn't eat."

Tansy didn't listen; it occurred to Maggie that her friend never listened. She left Maggie to join a queue at the food table and came back minutes later with two plates.

Maggie followed helplessly after her as she led the way to an improvised racetrack, carved right out of the farmer's pasture, and found a place to sit on one of the long, wet logs that had been provided for spectators. In the center of the track were any number of horses, some Maggie recognized as Thoroughbreds, some, Tansy explained, were brombies, wild Australian horses that had been captured and tamed.

Hardly aware of what she was doing, Maggie ate her breakfast as she watched the preparations for the first race. Reeve was there, holding the bridle of an enormous coal-black stallion while a slight figure scrambled up into the English saddle.

Tansy had apparently followed Maggie's gaze. "Bloke I was cuddlin' with last night says 'e 'as a place 'ereabouts, your Reeve McKenna."

Maggie whirled, nearly upsetting her plate and what remained of its contents. "A place?"

"Sure." Tansy shrugged. "A man with 'is money probably 'as more 'ouses than you and I got 'airpins. A body does wonder why Mr. McKenna'd bed you in a wagon, though, when 'e could 'ave taken you to a nice, warm 'ouse!"

It was all Maggie could do not to clout her friend over the head with her breakfast plate. She wouldn't have admitted for anything in the world that she was wondering the same thing Tansy was. "Will you keep your voice down?" she hissed, all too aware that some of the people around them were watching her with amusement, curiosity, or reproof.

Maggie's head was aching and her food was beginning to roil in her stomach. "What time does the 'bus go back to Sydney?" she asked miserably.

"There'll be one at two and another at four," Tansy answered distractedly, her attention on the riders and the horses that were getting ready to race.

Maggie's mind was made up in that moment. Taking Tansy's plate and stacking it on top of her own, she stepped awkwardly over the log. "I'll take these back," she said coolly.

Tansy had turned, shielding her eyes from the bright sun with one hand. "But you'll miss the start of the race!" she cried.

Maggie only shrugged and walked purposefully away. She intended to miss far more than the race.

After disposing of the plates, Maggie went back to the wagon where Reeve McKenna had so pleasured her, and she snatched up her reticule. It was an easy matter to repack yesterday's dress and the nightgown and her hairbrush, and soon she was walking along the muddy, rutted road to Parramatta, leaving the camp meeting and all its questionable splendors behind her.

Along the way Maggie saw a grand house that she hadn't noticed on arriving the day before and wondered if it was Reeve's. She decided it was and felt her cheeks burn a bright pink. She walked faster now, paying no heed to the puddles that glistened on the road. A cot in a covered wagon was the place he'd considered fitting for the deflowering of Miss Maggie Chamberlin; no sense mussing a real bed with the likes of one gullible little "Yank."

By the time she reached the country inn where the omnibus would stop, Maggie had worked herself into a miff of puddle-stomping proportions. Her shoes and the hem of her new dress were muddy and wet and her mood was intractable. Even though the innkeeper warranted that it would be a good two hours before the 'bus came and went, Maggie insisted on purchasing her ticket. That done, she sat down in the inn's cozy lobby to wait. And to silently berate herself for being such a wanton fool.

Muddy to his knees and exultant over Samaritan's easy win at the races, Reeve strode toward the wagon where he'd spent the most pleasurable night of his life, certain that Maggie would be there.

She wasn't, nor was that pathetic little case she carried around, virtually all her worldly goods stored inside. Some of Reeve's exultation faded away.

"Mr. McKenna?" inquired a female voice from the back of the wagon.

Reeve turned to see the young woman who had been Maggie's companion on board the *Victoria*. He couldn't remember her name, if he'd ever known it. "Yes?" he snapped, worried and annoyed.

"Excuse me, sir, but I was 'opin' you'd seen Maggie in your travels—Maggie Chamberlin?"

Reeve was interested now; he left the wagon to stand facing the girl in the bright sunshine and the mud. "I'm afraid I haven't," he said.

The moppet stomped one foot, splashing muddy water everywhere. "Drat that chit—sometimes I wonder why I 'ave 'er for me friend! She's gone off to the inn at Parramatta, she 'as, lookin' to catch the early 'bus! And me 'ere, not knowin' whether she's been nabbed by bushrangers or what!"

Reeve bit back a smile and glanced toward the sun, gauging its position. It would be a long time before the first omnibus left for Sydney. "Don't worry, miss— I'll see that Maggie gets safely home," he said, and then he took off at a sprint for the pasture where the races had been held.

Maggie spotted the rider at quite a distance. Of course she knew it was Reeve McKenna on the back of that splendid stallion, but the land stretched away from the inn unfettered, which made trying to flee imprudent.

Reaching the inn, Reeve dismounted and tethered the magnificent animal to the hitching rail just to the right of the porch steps. His blue-green eyes were mischievous as they assessed Maggie's disgruntled person, and his teeth flashed white in a grin. "Going home, Miss Chamberlin? And without so much as a good-bye for your first lover ever?"

Maggie's temper flared, as did the color in her cheeks. Determined not to let this man guess what an effect he had on her, she hugged herself and turned away, stomping to the far end of the porch.

He simply followed her, and when she tried to escape, he leaned close and pinned her to the porch railing in a most scandalous fashion. "Give me your ticket, Maggie," he said in a voice as intimate as a caress, "and I'll get your money back."

Maggie moved to squeeze past him, but instead felt

greater pressure both from Reeve McKenna in front and the porch railing in back. Her pulse leapt and her breath quickened, as the whole situation was most embarrassing. "I need my ticket," she said in barely more than a whisper. "I'm going back to Sydney on the omnibus."

"You're going back to Sydney with me," Reeve said flatly.

Maggie couldn't free herself, so she squeezed her eyes shut in an effort to blot Reeve McKenna from existence. He simply remained where he was, pressing close to her in that indecent way, and when Maggie was finally forced to open her eyes, he was watching her with amusement.

"You gave back my papers, remember?" she pointed out when she could trust herself to speak. "I'm a free woman and if I want to go back to Sydney by myself, I most certainly will!"

"Papers?" Reeve echoed stupidly. And then he reached into his shirt pocket and drew out a packet of documents, documents he had to have taken from Maggie's reticule while she slept. "These papers?"

"Damn you." Maggie gasped, pushing at Reeve's chest with her hands. "You're not only a seducer, you're a thief!"

Reeve threw back his head and laughed at that. "A seducer? Maggie, Maggie—what quaint words you use." He arched one dark eyebrow and then went on. "May I remind you that I made every effort to keep my distance after I got into bed with you last night? You were the one who insisted on touching me."

Maggie was at a loss for words and, further, she was worried that someone would see her in this compromising position. She tried to look around Reeve's shoulder, certain that she'd die on the spot if anyone had overheard their conversation.

Unexpectedly, Reeve relented a little and stepped back so that Maggie could breathe a bit more freely.

"Come home with me, Maggie," he said, his voice gruff and yet oddly persuasive. "We can go to Sydney in the morning."

"That," Maggie blustered, trembling all over because she was so angry and because a part of her wanted to go home with Reeve McKenna and let him do what he would to her, "is an indecent proposal!"

"You weren't worried about indecent proposals this morning," he pointed out.

The reminder of their shameless behavior in the wagon stung its way through Maggie's veins like poison. She drew back her reticule to strike him, but he only took it from her and set it down on the rough board floor of the porch.

Her eyes were riveted on Reeve's shirt pocket, where he'd put the precious papers that meant the difference between freedom and slavery. "I would like my documents back, please," she said evenly.

"Certainly," Reeve replied with a slight bow of his head, but he made no move to hand over the papers.

Acting on sheer bravado, Maggie held out her hand. Reeve took it, snatching up her reticule with his free hand in the same motion, and dragged her toward the impatient stallion tethered to the hitching post. He untied the animal with one deft pull on the reins.

"What do you think you're doing?" Maggie croaked as she was swung unceremoniously onto the beast's back, with Reeve behind her only a moment later.

"Miss Chamberlin," he said, his voice grating past her ear in a low rush, "I'm going to do the right thing in spite of you."

The stallion danced and tossed its enormous head as Reeve reined it in the direction of the road, and Maggie, clutching the horse's raven-black mane in both hands, was suddenly glad for the strong arm that at once encircled her waist and held her reticule.

"C-carrying me off against my will is not the right thing!" she pointed out, her voice unnaturally high because she'd never ridden any animal more spirited than an elderly circus horse, and she was afraid.

"Seeing you safely home is the least I can do," Reeve argued, pausing to give her a brief nip on the earlobe that sent waves of delicious shivers flowing through her, "after having my way with you last night."

Maggie held on tighter and squeezed her eyes shut again as the great horse bounded into a gallop.

"And then, of course," Reeve went on as though they were sitting together in a rocking chair instead of on the back of that terrifyingly powerful stallion, "there was this morning."

Both to Maggie's relief and her alarm, Reeve's house proved to be close by, though it wasn't the one she had seen earlier. It was a sprawling building of red brick, with a glassed-in sunporch at one end and a fanlight over the door. There were flowers and well-tended shrubs growing in the yard and, if it hadn't been for her circumstances, Maggie would have been charmed.

Reeve dismounted and lifted Maggie down after him, and just as she was shaking out her skirts in a disgruntled effort at gaining some dignity, two little black-skinned girls appeared, gazing adoringly at Reeve and smiling broad, toothy smiles.

"Goodness and Mercy," Reeve confided in a whisper.

"Who?" Maggie asked.

Reeve did not bother to repeat the girls' unforgettable names. "Their parents were afflicted by the teachings of certain English missionaries," he added. "Every time I come to Parramatta, they glue themselves to my heels. Wherever I go, they go."

Maggie was enchanted, as she always was by children. Forgetting her own perilous situation, she smiled at the beautiful little girls.

Reeve took her arm and ushered her up the stairs

leading to his front door. He glanced backward, as did Maggie, and saw that his tiny admirers were in hot pursuit.

He sighed heavily as he opened the door. "Surely," he teased, "Goodness and Mercy shall follow me all the days of my life."

Chapter 9 🌿

REEVE HAD NO MORE THAN OPENED THE FRONT DOOR TO his house when another little girl, the same child Maggie had seen playing on his lawn in Sydney, literally hurled herself into his arms with a joyous shriek. "Papa!"

The affection between Reeve and the child was obvious. He held her close. Over his broad shoulder she gave Maggie a thorough, implacable inspection with her blue-green eyes.

Reeve turned slightly, there in that spacious, well-lighted entryway, and said, "Maggie, this is Elisabeth."

Automatically, Maggie offered her hand. Elisabeth merely looked at Maggie's face for a moment, not deigning to loosen her arms from around Reeve's neck. Although this would have been a snub in the adult world, there was no unfriendliness in the child's manner.

"Hello, Elisabeth," Maggie said politely, and her smile was genuine.

"She rarely talks," Reeve pointed out when they had reached an enormous parlor and the silence had stretched out too far for his liking. He set Elisabeth on her feet and she scampered away. "The only thing she says with any regularity is 'Papa.'"

Maggie was so concerned that she hardly took in the understated elegance of her surroundings. "But she must be four, at least—"

Reeve gestured offhandedly for Maggie to take a seat, and then strode off across the long, uncluttered room as she sank into a barrel-back chair facing the massive fieldstone fireplace.

When he returned, he held a glass of some amber-colored liquid in his hand. Maggie resisted a telling glance at the clock on the mantelpiece, but she did arch one eyebrow. It was surely too early in the day for liquor.

Reeve chuckled at her reaction as he sat down in a chair facing hers. "I'm assuming that you would prefer tea to this particular sort of refreshment," he said, and before Maggie could stiffly confirm that she would indeed prefer tea, a black woman appeared in the parlor, carrying a tray.

The woman set the tray on a table beside Maggie's chair and left the room again without a word or a look at either Reeve or his houseguest.

"The mother of Goodness and Mercy, I presume?" Maggie asked just to make conversation and wondering to herself just how one should behave in such an unorthodox situation.

Reeve smiled. "I believe Kala is related to them in some way, though she isn't their mother. The Aborigines define relationships in their own fashion."

Maggie's eyes went wide. "Aborigines? But I thought they were wild people, roaming the Outback—"

"Many of them are," Reeve broke in quietly. "They're a wandering people and they do have a tendency to just drop everything and leave, should the spirit move them."

Before Maggie could make a response to that, a

127

short, balding man with an air of authority came striding into the room. He carried a round-brimmed hat in one hand and his small, colorless eyes took in Maggie's countenance with an expression that bordered on disapproval.

Reeve set his drink aside, seeming just the least bit self-conscious, and Maggie understood when she took a second look at the stranger. He was wearing a clerical collar. Standing, Reeve said with a cordial nod, "Reverend Collins."

The reverend nodded back. "Time I was moving on," he said in a thick Australian accent. "Of course, I couldn't go without telling you that I passed the stormy night in great comfort, thanks to your kindly offer of a roof over my head."

Maggie slanted a look at Reeve, knowing now why he hadn't brought her to this house the night before, and took a sip of her tea.

Reeve shook hands with Reverend Collins. "I'm glad you were at ease," he said. He was just about to present Maggie properly, when the minister turned and left the room.

It was a rebuff; Maggie might as well have been invisible. Nettled, she looked Reeve McKenna squarely in the eye when he sat back down in his chair. "You don't strike me as a religious man," she said.

He smiled. "I'm not. I was planning on staying at the campsite anyway, since Samaritan was going to race today. Reverend Collins came from some distance, and he didn't have a wagon."

Maggie stole a glance at the clock on the mantelpiece. It was making a whirring sound as it geared up to strike the hour. One ponderous bong followed another. "I've missed the omnibus," she muttered, annoyed.

"You'll be back in Sydney before Duncan is, so don't worry," Reeve responded, his tones clipped.

"You don't like Mr. Kirk, do you?" Maggie wanted to know, watching Reeve very closely.

She saw his features tighten, noticed the involuntary leap of a muscle along his jawline. "That is an understatement," he replied. "Duncan may seem charming and genteel, but he's no fit companion for an innocent young woman."

Maggie's throat constricted and she looked down at her hands, the teacup she held rattling ever so slightly in its saucer. When she lifted her eyes, they were fiery with the knowledge of all she'd lost. "And you are?" she asked pointedly.

Reeve McKenna let out a long, ragged sigh. "I'm sorry, Maggie—about everything."

It hurt Maggie a little that he regretted what had happened, but she wouldn't have revealed that for anything. "Which is surely why you abducted me from the inn and brought me here," she said with saucy contempt.

Dark eyebrows arched in a tanned, ruggedly hewn face. "You think I want to—as you put it—seduce you again?"

Maggie went red and set the teacup and saucer aside, lest she drop them. "What else should I think?" she hissed, not wanting anyone to overhear.

Reeve settled back in his chair and regarded Maggie's flushed face and stiff countenance for a long time, his lips twitching slightly, his eyes laughing outright. Just when she was about to leap out of her chair and slap him silly, he assumed a serious expression and said, "You're quite wrong. I regret what happened and I brought you here simply to prove to you that you're safe with me."

"Safe?!" Maggie blurted out. "How can you say that after last night?"

Once again Reeve sighed. "I lost my head—I wanted you so damned much, and you didn't exactly try to discourage me—"

Maggie's blush returned. "Why did you steal my papers?" she demanded.

To her utter surprise, Reeve reached out and took both her hands into his own. He spoke with quiet sincerity. "It occurred to me that Duncan might find them and put them to a use that doesn't bear mentioning. You're still free, though—I'll make no demands on you."

Maggie had neither the strength nor the wit to free her hands. "But you're not planning to return the papers, either, are you?"

Regretfully, Reeve shook his head. "I think they're safer in my keeping. If Duncan were to get his hands on them—"

"Mr. Kirk," Maggie began pointedly, her shoulders aching because they were so stiff, "has been a perfect gentleman. And that, Mr. McKenna, is certainly more than I can say for you!"

Reeve chuckled, though there was no sign of amusement in his eyes. "There are worse things than not being a gentleman, Yank."

Maggie finally managed to pull her hands from his. "Lady Cosgrove would never have sent me to Mr. Kirk's house if she thought there was any danger!"

Reeve took up his drink again, and he finished it off before answering. "Lady Cosgrove is not familiar with Duncan's true nature. I am."

Maggie remembered Reeve's beautiful mistress and all that had happened during the night, and she glared. "I don't see how his 'true nature' could be any worse than yours. Does he keep a mistress and then seduce other women behind her back?"

Reeve's jawline grew taut and then he thrust himself out of his chair with a suddenness that made Maggie start. But he only moved away, standing with his back to her, his gaze fixed on the empty fireplace. "Loretta is no longer my mistress," he said in a voice so low that Maggie had to strain to hear him. "When I realized how much I wanted you, I asked her to leave my house."

Maggie could imagine what it must feel like to know this magnificent man on an intimate basis and then be shunted out of his life without warning when he found someone new to dally with. If she gave in to Reeve McKenna and the feelings he stirred inside her, she would one day find herself in Loretta's position, and the possibility didn't bear considering. "I won't be your courtesan, Mr. McKenna, so it appears that you have acted hastily."

He turned slightly to regard Maggie with a sober expression that was somehow tainted with mockery at one and the same time. "I'm not the only one who has acted rashly, Miss Chamberlin. You gave me something last night that the man you marry will sorely miss."

Even though the words had not been spoken in anger or contempt, they wounded Maggie because they were all too true. She was probably ruined for a decent man. She forced back tears, not willing to show Reeve any more weakness than she already had.

Reeve came and crouched before her chair, his voice gentle. "Have you considered the possibility, Maggie, that you may be carrying my child?"

Maggie's eyes were shimmering when she lifted them to his face. Still unable to speak, she nodded.

"If you find out that you are pregnant, I want you to come to me immediately."

"W-why?" Maggie managed to ask. She was thousands of miles from home, she was poor, she was facing a prospect that had driven other women to desperate lengths. The misery of it was quite nearly too much to bear.

Again, he took her hands. "Because I'll marry you, Yank," he said with quiet patience, as though he'd expected Maggie to know that a wealthy, powerful man such as himself would be interested in making a servant girl his true and legal wife.

131

"You can't be serious."

"I am serious. Nothing in the world could matter to me as much as a child of my own."

Maggie felt a certain sadness at his words, odd as it was. She wanted, on some level, to be the person who mattered most to Reeve McKenna. "But you have Elisabeth—"

"I love Elisabeth," he answered softly, "but she isn't my daughter; she's my niece."

Maggie swallowed. "But she calls you Papa."

"That's only because she doesn't remember my brother." Reeve's eyes had a faraway look in them now; unconsciously, he fingered the brass medallion he was never without.

Suddenly, despite all her other problems, Maggie's concern was focused on that strange bit of brass hanging from its golden chain. "What is that?" she asked in a whisper.

Reeve let the medallion fall against his chest again. "I guess it's a good luck charm," he said, and that curious distance, tantamount to pain, was still visible in his eyes.

"Tell me about your brother," Maggie ventured, guessing that Reeve's brother and that odd talisman were somehow linked.

"Jamie and I were separated, years ago, on the trip out here from Dublin. I've been looking for him ever since." Reeve rose, went back to his chair, and sank into it with a sigh that was almost forlorn. "I've hired detectives, gone everywhere I could think of myself—"

"But you never found him," Maggie finished for him, saddened.

Reeve shook his head. His eyes were averted and his throat worked as he struggled to control some indefinable emotion.

"Elisabeth is his child?" Maggie pressed, though gently.

Reeve's eyes swung to hers and he nodded. "The detectives found her, in Brisbane, in an orphanage. The people there told me that Elisabeth's mother hadn't been married to Jamie, though she'd left papers saying that he was the father of her child."

Maggie had no doubt that Elisabeth was truly a McKenna; her aquamarine eyes were proof of that. "Why did this woman abandon Elisabeth?"

"She was sick," Reeve replied on a distracted sigh. "According to the nuns at the orphanage, she died soon after she'd left Elisabeth with them."

"Perhaps Elisabeth herself remembers something?"

Reeve looked at Maggie as though she were mad, but she knew that his annoyance was based in his deep disappointment at not finding his brother and not in anything she'd said or done. "Elisabeth was two at the time, and if she remembers anything, she can't or won't talk about it."

Maggie didn't ask if the little girl had been examined by a doctor; she knew this was something that a man as thorough as Reeve would not have overlooked. "Perhaps there was some trauma—"

Reeve nodded. "But what?" he demanded hoarsely. "What could steal away a child's will to speak? And where was Jamie when all this was happening?"

Maggie looked down at her hands, not wanting to suggest the obvious: that death rather than choice might have separated Jamie McKenna from his child and the woman who had borne her.

"He isn't dead," Reeve said in a low voice that challenged Maggie's secret suspicions. "If he were, I'd know it!"

Maggie was silent. She hoped that Reeve was right, that somewhere, somehow, Jamie McKenna was alive and well, waiting to be found.

"Are you hungry?" The question was so trivial, so ordinary, that it jolted Maggie out of her uncomfortable reflections.

133

"Yes, a little," she answered honestly.

It was uncanny, but the black woman, clearly Reeve's housekeeper, appeared again at just that moment. He asked for fruit and bread, and the simple fare was brought immediately.

Maggie ate in silence, wondering how she was going to get herself back to Sydney before Reeve could compromise her again, and when the meal was over, he suddenly took her hand and pulled her outside. They rounded the grand brick house to the rear garden and there, to Maggie's delight, sat an enormous kangaroo.

"This is Mathilda," Reeve said by way of introduction. Mathilda regarded Maggie with interest.

Maggie was awed. "Is she tame?"

At Reeve's nod Maggie approached the fascinating creature and reached out tentatively to touch it. Mathilda's fur felt coarse instead of soft, and if there was a baby hidden in her pouch, Maggie couldn't see it, though she did cast several polite glances in that direction.

Suddenly bored with the American, Mathilda turned and hopped off across the open field, moving at a speed that left Maggie openmouthed with wonder and delight. If only she'd had someone to write to, someone to tell.

There was sadness in her eyes when she turned back to face Reeve again. He understood loneliness; Maggie sensed that and she was comforted. Suddenly, it was as important to her that Reeve find his lost brother as it was to him.

"Elisabeth likes animals," he said, taking Maggie's hand in a way that seemed perfectly natural. "She has a few stray wallabies by the barn. Would you like to see them?"

Maggie nodded eagerly, and Reeve led her around the back of the barn, where a wire pen had been built. Reddish-brown wallabies, much smaller versions of kangaroos, hopped about inside the pen, and there was a folded blanket suspended from the back of an old chair.

Before Maggie could ask what it was for, a tiny bright-eyed head appeared above the edge of the blanket, peering cautiously this way and that.

"He's an orphan," Reeve explained quietly. "He needed a warm pouch, so Elisabeth and I made one for him."

In a way, Reeve's admission of this gentle act touched Maggie's spirit even more deeply than his lovemaking had. She couldn't speak for a moment, and her eyes were swimming with silly, sentimental tears.

If Reeve noticed, he pretended that he hadn't, though his hand tightened on Maggie's and, behind them, Goodness and Mercy giggled.

Reeve let go of Maggie's hand and whirled, making a good-natured growling sound and stalking toward the delighted little girls. Their beautiful dark eyes shining, they shrieked with laughter and scampered away.

Maggie was sure they hadn't gone far. She wondered if Elisabeth ever spoke to them when there were no adults around to hear.

The sky was beginning to grow dark and cloudy, and a swift wind came up from the south. In unspoken agreement Maggie and Reeve returned to the house, this time through a rear door.

The kitchen, roomy and immaculate, was empty. Maggie didn't protest when Reeve led her up the rear stairway without a word of explanation, and she was, to her shame, actually disappointed when he deposited her in front of a door on the second floor and ordered her to make up for some of the rest she'd lost the night before.

All the same, Maggie was tired and, yawning, she opened the door and went in. The room was not large, but it was pleasant and airy, with a colorful patchwork quilt on a carefully polished brass bed. There was a rocking chair and, wealth upon wealth, a small shelf stuffed with books.

Maggie helped herself to one after dutifully removing her muddy shoes, and stretched out on the bed. She was asleep before she'd reached the end of the first page.

Reeve paced the parlor as he would have paced the study had he been in Sydney, fighting whatever it was inside him that made him crave the silken feel of Maggie's flesh trembling against his own. Never in all his life had he been as obsessed with a woman as he was with this saucy, gray-eyed Yankee snippet, and he didn't like the feeling, as treacherously pleasant as it was.

Kala entered the room silently, as she entered every room, and squatted in front of the fireplace to light the fire she'd laid earlier. The wind howled outside, sending huge droplets of rain lashing against the windows. When a blaze was crackling on the hearth, Kala left again.

She was a mystery to Reeve, ageless, as though she might have existed since the Dreamtime, the time of Aboriginal legend, before the start of recorded history. Kala might have been twenty, and she might have been a hundred and twenty, and because he didn't want to think about Maggie Chamberlin, Reeve pondered his silent housekeeper.

An insistent pounding at the front door brought him out of his wanderings; to save Kala the trouble, he made his way into the entry hall and answered the knock himself.

Few things would have surprised him more than finding Loretta standing on his porch, wet to the skin. A wagon, probably hired at the inn, was just pulling away, the driver's back hunched against the thundering rain.

"Aren't you going to let me in?" Loretta asked

sweetly, her lips curved in a smile that belied her sodden clothes, her drenched hair, and the forlorn feather drooping from the side of her once fashionable hat.

Reeve stepped back to admit her, having no other choice. "What are you doing here?" he managed to demand as Loretta made a beeline to the parlor fireplace.

She shook out her skirts and then tossed a smile back over one shoulder, countering Reeve's question with one of her own. "Are my clothes still upstairs in our room, or have you tossed them out?"

Reeve scowled, wishing he could find it within himself to toss Loretta, as well as her damned clothes, out into the storm. "I don't come here very often, Loretta," he said evenly. "So your clothes are just where you left them."

Loretta was shaking out her voluminous skirts again, leaving puddles of rainwater on the hearth. "Good," she sighed softly, and then she countered that gentleness by flinging back her head and yelling, "Kala!"

Reeve winced, but before he could protest Loretta's officious manner, Kala had appeared, silent as always, her expression questioning.

"I want a hot bath drawn," Loretta dictated snappishly, "and I'll have a glass of sherry the moment I'm settled in the tub. Once you've brought that, you may lay out—let's see—my blue lawn gown. The one with the feathers stitched to the neckline."

"Loretta—" Reeve began in a dangerous rumbling voice as Kala hurried off to start the bathwater running.

Loretta turned, her face puckered into a childish pout. "Oh, Reeve—surely you wouldn't deny me the comforts of your home on such a nasty night! I don't have anywhere else to go, after all—"

"You have the inn. And I'm taking you there as

137

soon as you've changed clothes, so you might want to put on something more practical than lawn and feathers!"

Loretta's dark eyes snapped. "So it's true! You have brought that little Yankee scrap into this house!"

Loretta's network of efficient informants never ceased to amaze Reeve. "Surely you didn't come all the way from Sydney just to see if Maggie would be here?"

"Of course I didn't. I knew you were here to race Samaritan and I came to try to talk some sense into you."

Reeve kept his distance, his arms folded across his chest, one eyebrow rising in silent question.

"I can't accept that it's over," Loretta said briskly. "You loved me once and I'll make you love me again."

"I never loved you and you never loved me, Loretta," Reeve pointed out. "We agreed on that from the beginning, didn't we?"

Theatrical tears swelled in Loretta's eyes, shimmering in the firelight. "My feelings have changed."

"Actually, it's your fortunes that have changed, isn't it? Have you found your allowance inadequate for your needs, my dear?"

"You're a beast," Loretta muttered miserably, going so far as to let her shoulders sag and lower her head a little. "How can you say such things, after all I've been to you?"

Reeve sighed. There were times when it was impossible to reach this woman. "Take your bath, Loretta," he said in exasperation. "Drink your sherry. Then prepare yourself for a trip to the inn, because you're not spending the night in this house."

A tear slipped down Loretta's cheek—or was it a raindrop? Either way, she turned in a swirl of outraged femininity and swept up the stairs to lounge in Reeve's spacious marble bathtub.

Reeve nursed a foolish hope that she would be gone

before Maggie awakened from her nap, knowing all the while that the wish would not be granted.

Maggie woke to the sound of a woman singing. The voice was full and rich, obviously that of a trained professional. She knew without question that Loretta Craig had come home.

Despair thickened in her throat, making it ache, but she would not cry. She tossed back the quilt that had covered her, sat up, and began the laborious task of putting her shoes back on. When she'd done that, she smoothed her hair, now slipping from its pins, and stood.

In the hallway outside her room the singing was louder, and Maggie could make out the words. Something quite fitting, about being a bird in a gilded cage.

Squaring her shoulders and lifting her chin, Maggie made her way down the front staircase. *Please, God,* she prayed silently, *don't let me cry in front of Reeve or that woman. I'll be virtuous to the end of my life if You'll just not let me cry.*

When Maggie reached the bottom of the stairs, she was dry-eyed. Catching sight of Reeve pacing back and forth in the parlor just to her left, she hoped she truly would be able to be virtuous for the next twenty or thirty years.

"Maggie," he said almost forlornly as she crossed the threshold and stood facing him, her hands caught together in front of her in a dignified manner.

Maggie drew a deep breath. "If you'll just drive me to the inn, and give back my ticket to travel on the omnibus—"

Reeve shook his head. "Loretta will be leaving, not you."

Maggie lifted her chin another jot. "You misunderstand, Mr. McKenna. The decision has already been made, and if you won't take me to the Parramatta Inn in your carriage, I shall walk."

"In this rain? You must be out of your mind!"

139

Maggie was not out of her mind. She knew when she'd made a mistake, and she knew how to correct it. She left the parlor, and found her cloak and her reticule in the entryway. Draping the cloak around her shoulders and clasping the reticule in one hand, she opened the front door, crossed the porch, and walked out into the rain.

Chapter 10 🌿

THE WIND LASHED MAGGIE'S SKIRTS TO HER ANKLES, making her cloak flow out behind her, and the rain nearly blinded her, though it felt warm as bathwater against her skin. She paused at the foot of Reeve McKenna's front walk, trying to remember whether the Parramatta Inn lay to the east or to the west.

She was still pondering this dilemma, her lower lip caught between her teeth, when Reeve suddenly appeared in front of her, grasping both her shoulders in his hands. She was not surprised, nor was she angry. Maggie was merely numb.

Reeve's dark hair was dripping, his shirt so wet that Maggie could see through it. He shouted to be heard over the pounding rain, giving her small, periodic shakes. "Do you want to catch your death, you little idiot?!"

Maggie raised her chin. Her hair clung to her head like a sodden cap, and the rain was deafening, making craters in the deep puddles that lay all around. A loamy, fertile scent filled her nostrils. "Let me go," she said.

Reeve couldn't possibly have heard her, but he

reacted all the same. Without warning or ceremony he shifted his hands from Maggie's shoulders to her waist and hoisted her off the ground and over his shoulder. A second later he was striding back toward the house.

Maggie was too stunned to do anything at first, but soon enough she was kicking and struggling and shrieking words she'd learned years before from the circus people. None of her efforts brought anything more than a smart slap to her bottom as Reeve carried her back into the entryway and then the parlor. There, before the fire, he set her on her feet and summarily began removing her clothes.

Maggie tried to fight, but it was hopeless. Every attempt to scratch, slap, or kick was dodged or fended off, and her screams of fury were trapped in her throat.

Finally, when only her camisole, drawers, and shoes remained to her, Reeve clasped Maggie's chin in one hand and caught her wrists together behind her back with the other. "Enough," he said in a warning rasp, and Maggie went still.

"What a perfectly charming scene!" chimed a woman's voice from somewhere beyond the mountainlike barrier of Reeve's massive shoulders.

Loretta. Maggie wanted to die, knowing that that woman was witnessing her humiliation. She closed her eyes and swallowed, trying to brace herself for the moments to come. A woolen throw of some sort was draped around her, and Maggie looked up into Reeve's face and saw understanding there.

He turned to face his mistress, his towering frame blocking Maggie's view of the woman, and asked cordially, "Are you ready to leave for the inn, Loretta?"

Loretta's laughter had a sharp edge. "And leave this poor child here, unchaperoned? Why, Reeve, darling, that would be unthinkable!"

Reeve's voice was taut; Maggie peered around one

142

of his arms, glad that she couldn't see his face. "No need," he said succinctly. "Kala is here, after all."

Loretta was wearing a floaty blue dress trimmed at bodice and hem with the softest of feathers. Her hair, gleaming like ebony in the firelight, hung freely to her waist, giving her the look of a beautiful witch. Involuntarily, Maggie shivered.

"Kala!" hooted the woman scorned, her hands on her hips now, her gaze searing Maggie as she argued with Reeve. "That Aboriginal woman? Good Lord, Reeve, you can't be serious! She could never be a proper chaperon and you know it!"

"Are you going to go willingly," Reeve asked in a dangerously charitable tone, "or do I have to carry you?"

A flush climbed from Loretta's magnificent bosom to her hairline. "You really are unreasonable."

Maggie couldn't be sure, of course, but some sixth sense told her that while Reeve was smiling at Loretta, the smile was cold and even cruel. "Yes," he answered.

Loretta subsided, her lower lip thrust out in a subtle pout, her arms folded across her chest. She'd lost, temporarily, and she knew it.

Maggie was gloating a little, inwardly at least, and so she was startled when Reeve suddenly rounded on her, his index finger waggling an inch from the tip of her nose. "You try leaving here while I'm gone, Yank," he warned ominously, "and I'll take you across my knee. Is that clear?"

Maggie swallowed. It was clear, if totally unreasonable and unfair, and she had no choice but to nod.

"Good," Reeve said brusquely, and he strode over to Loretta, caught her by one arm, and propelled her up the stairs.

Huddled in the woolen throw, Maggie made an exasperated sound in her throat and sank to her knees on the stone hearth, staring into the leaping flames of the fire. She heard the rattle of dishes on a tray and looked up to see that Kala had brought her another pot of tea, along with several sugar cakes.

Resigned, Maggie toddled over to the low table in front of the settee, the blanket still wrapped around her, and poured herself a cup of tea. She was just sinking her teeth into one of the sugar cakes when Reeve and Loretta came down the stairs again.

Apparently Reeve did not plan to leave Loretta alone with Maggie while he hitched up his carriage, for he went toward the rear of the house, dragging the warmly cloaked and rigid woman along with him.

Disconsolately, Maggie consumed the rest of her sugar cake and then choked down some tea. Thus fortified, she went up the stairs, meaning to crawl back into that bed where she'd napped earlier to try to forget what a mare's nest she'd gotten herself into.

Kala was standing in the hallway when Maggie reached the second floor, and she beckoned. Maggie went toward her questioningly, clutching the blanket around her, beginning to shiver now that she was far from the fire.

Kala indicated the doorway behind her and Maggie stepped through to find a steaming, scented bath waiting. There were fluffy towels stacked on a low shelf within reach of the marble tub, and fresh soap had been set out.

Maggie glanced gratefully at Kala, who smiled and slipped out, closing the door behind her.

Cold, tired, and overwrought, Maggie found that bath irresistible, even though she knew that she should not avail herself of any of the treacherous comforts of Reeve McKenna's house. What she should do, in fact, was put on whatever dry clothes she could find and make her way to the inn, rain or no rain. But the pull of that hot, aromatic water was almost mystical; Maggie could not resist it.

She let the blanket fall to the floor, awkwardly removed her shoes and the sodden stockings beneath, and peeled away her clammy camisole and drawers.

She was just sinking into the glorious luxury of her bath when the door opened again.

Gasping, braced for a confrontation with her host, Maggie sat rigidly upright in the luscious water, her arms covering her breasts.

But her visitor was only Kala, bringing a single delicate crystal glass on a small tray. Some deep purple liquid sparkled in the tiny goblet, promising sweetness and warmth.

Maggie settled back in the spacious tub, thanked Kala as she set the tray down within reach, and lunged forward to clasp the glass the moment the woman was gone.

The drink was a cordial of some sort, tasting of grapes and sugar. Each delicate sip deepened Maggie's state of languor until she was yawning, her body so fluid as to seem a part of the lulling, sweet-smelling water.

Exhausted by the rigors of taking Loretta somewhere she hadn't wanted to go, specifically the Parramatta Inn, wet and cold and annoyed, Reeve made his way up the stairs, unbuttoning his shirt as he went. By the time he reached the door of the bathroom, he was down to his trousers. His boots and shirt and socks were strung out in a trail on the hallway floor.

Maggie was sleeping in the bathtub, her insouciant little nose barely an inch above the water. Reeve drew in a ragged breath and sank back against the door, the sane, reasonable part of him battling another, less civilized one. "Maggie?"

She stirred, stretching her arms high above her head and giving Reeve an enticing view of her full pink-tipped breasts. He groaned inwardly and closed his eyes, but the sweet image followed him, made the wanting of Maggie Chamberlin a grinding ache.

Just then Maggie opened sleepy gray eyes and, of all things, she smiled and purred his name.

Reeve gaped, this being the last reaction he'd expected from this kicking, clawing little hellcat, but he understood when he caught sight of the empty glass perched on the side of the tub.

The tenderness that filled him displaced his passion, at least temporarily. One cordial wouldn't have affected a more sophisticated woman, but it had rendered Maggie helpless. He laughed low in his throat, and approached the tub.

Catching Maggie under both arms, he lifted her to her feet and held her against his bare chest with one arm while he reached for a towel with his free hand. She giggled, her head lolling against his shoulder, as he wrapped the towel around her and gently lifted her into his arms.

In her bedroom he set her down on the edge of the bed, intending to unpin her hair and ruffle it partially dry with the towel, but she fell over the moment he let go of her, giggling again, one breast escaping its covering to taunt Reeve with its sweet, inviting peak.

He suppressed an urge to bend and touch that straining morsel with his tongue, laughed despite the fact that he was in more pain than he ever remembered suffering, and hauled Maggie back to a sitting position. Her head sagged against his middle while he pulled the pins from her hair, and a searing jolt of need went through him, stiffening both his manhood and his resolve to do the decent thing.

Awkwardly, Reeve dried Maggie's flowing hair as best he could, then he tucked her under the covers and reached out to extinguish the lamp Kala had left burning on the bedside table.

Maggie made a crooning sound and thrust both hands up onto the pillow, causing her breasts to bob free of the blankets and torment Reeve anew. He couldn't resist taking them full in his hands and caressing them for a moment before gently replacing the blankets.

Her lashes thick on her cheeks, Maggie wriggled and gave a regretful whimper, her arms outstretched to Reeve even though she wasn't fully awake. In anguish Reeve put out the kerosene lamp and left the room.

There was a burning, pulsing ache deep within Maggie's middle, finally driving her to a half-wakefulness. She sat up in bed.

Had she only dreamed that there was a storm? Silvery moonlight flowed in through a nearby window, pooling around her. She stretched her arms and yawned, and then her hands came tentatively to her breasts. She cupped the warm, tingling mounds in her palms for a moment, craving Reeve, offering them up to him even though he was not there.

Scrambling out of bed, wrapping the quilt around her, Maggie paced. The friction of her pacing made the throbbing in her middle worse, so she stopped near the door and opened it.

The hallway was quiet and, of course, empty. Still half besotted from the cordial, Maggie found herself creeping out of her room.

She was sure she hadn't made a sound but, all the same, a door near the bathroom opened with a soft suddenness, and she heard Reeve whisper hoarsely, "Maggie?"

Boldly, Maggie followed the whisper, and when she reached Reeve's doorway, she simply stood there, looking up at him.

"Go back to your room," he said softly, desperately.

Maggie shook her head and somehow the quilt slipped away from her shoulders, landing in a moon-washed heap at her feet.

Reeve's eyes swept over her naked curves with a reluctant hunger, as though they were rebelling against the orders of his mind. "Oh, God," he breathed, and then he caught hold of Maggie's hand and pulled her into his room, dragging the disgarded quilt in as an afterthought.

147

"Hello," she said.

"You're drunk," Reeve responded, trying to keep his distance. He was wearing nothing but the smattering of moonlight slipping in through the windows, and Maggie watched in sleepy wonder as he grew to a splendid stiffness under her gaze.

Feeling a half-witted sort of marvel at her own audacity, even as she was driven forward by some imp within her, Maggie took a step closer to Reeve. He was standing beside his bed and, for just a moment, he looked as though he might be poised to run.

"Maggie, in the name of heaven," he pleaded in a harsh voice, "go back to your room."

Maggie stayed where she was, frozen in place by the splendor of him.

Reeve's hand trembled slightly as he reached out and took something from the bedside table. There was the distinctive sound and scent of a match being struck, and light flared on the planes of his face as he lit a cheroot and drew deeply of the smoke. The heat of his gaze warmed Maggie, thawed her stricken muscles. Without thinking, she lifted her hands to her breasts again because they felt sore and heavy.

At that moment Reeve snuffed out the cheroot he'd just lit and, with a primitive groan, strode across the room to Maggie. He seemed enraged as he took her waist in his hands, lifted her off the floor, and hurled her backward onto his bed.

She lay sprawled on the covers, her eyes wide, her heart hammering at her rib cage. She couldn't have spoken if all the world had hung in the balance.

"Did that sober you up?" Reeve demanded, glaring down at her.

Maggie was excited. She smiled, knowing that she had won a battle it would have been more advisable to lose. Deliberately, she raised her arms above her head and indulged in a languorous, kittenlike stretch.

Reeve swore, propelled to her by some force he could no longer resist. His hands brushed the length of her thighs, parting them, setting them a-quiver. His jawline was hard with a helpless anger, and his fingers gently caressed the down at the joining of her legs.

Maggie moaned and tossed her head from side to side, already senseless with the pleasure he wrought.

Kneeling beside her on the bed now, Reeve continued his rhythmic plundering even as he bent his head to touch the peak of her breast with his tongue. She arched convulsively, making a soft whimpering sound in her throat.

"Oh, this is just the beginning, Yank," Reeve promised with gruff devoutness, his breath warm on the skin of her breast. "Just the beginning. I'll teach you to tempt me."

With that he took Maggie's swollen nipple into his mouth, teasing it with his tongue and the gentle scraping of his teeth. And still he caressed the rosebud that bloomed beneath his fingers, first softly, then with a roughness that made Maggie thrust her legs farther and farther apart.

"You're a hardheaded little wench," Reeve said between tonguings of her breast, "but you'll have learned your lesson by the time I'm through with you."

Maggie's hands tangled in Reeve's hair, and she shivered as his mouth coursed downward over her stomach slowly, so slowly. But his greed was sudden and startling and Maggie cried out with pleasure as his fingers left her totally vulnerable to the attentions of his mouth.

"Lesson—number—one," he breathed between furtive nibbles that set Maggie's hips twisting and dragged a crooning whine from her throat. No matter how she moved, she could not escape the sweet torment he induced.

Something erupted within Maggie like a volcano, and her response was so lusty that Reeve clamped one hand over her mouth to stifle her cries of release. Shivering and sated, she expected him to leave her, but he didn't. Soon another tumult was building inside her, terrifying heat and motion.

Three times he drove her to shattering explosion, and she was exhausted when he finally left her, but the respite was brief. He kissed her deeply, hungrily, and then he turned onto his back and pulled Maggie after him, sliding her upward until he had ready access to her breasts.

As he sucked, Maggie writhed against him in involuntary pleasure, never knowing how she was sealing her fate.

She was wild with need and with a desire to repay him, and that gave her the strength to break free, to slide down until she was kneeling on the floor. Instinctively, Maggie guessed what the most effective vengeance would be, and the cry Reeve gave, the tangling of his fingers in her hair, proved that she'd been right.

Maggie pleasured him until, with a rumbling growl, he suddenly pulled her back onto the bed. She landed astraddle of him, his manhood prodding at her swelling dampness, seeking entrance. Maggie took him in with one fierce motion of her hips, flinging back her head in glorious submission as his hands closed over her breasts.

Reeve's hips began to rise and fall beneath Maggie, and with each withdrawal she suffered the profoundest despair, with each deep, returning thrust, she knew undiluted joy. This fierce parrying went on for a long time, until both Reeve and Maggie were groaning in the singular delirium that is love.

Their crises were simultaneous, sundering their souls from their bodies, bonding them together into one entity. Inevitably, though, they became two people again, and even that separation was sweet.

Maggie was so weak that even after her breathing had returned to normal, even after her body had ceased its shuddering, she couldn't trust her legs to carry her back to her own bed. She snuggled close to

Reeve and he held her, his hand moving tenderly up and down her back until she slept.

Bright sunlight glared through Maggie's lids, forcing her to wake up. She opened her eyes to find Reeve lying beside her, watching her with a sober expression that instantly turned to a teasing amusement.

It was then that Maggie remembered what a wanton she'd been, and she blushed, the color rolling up her body from the tips of her toes to finally lap at her forehead like a tide. "It was the cordial," she protested lamely.

Reeve threw back his head and laughed. "The hell it was," he replied.

Maggie moved to push him away, but before she could, he was suspended above her, his weight pinning her arms to her sides. She squirmed, furious. "Let me go!" she hissed.

"Not yet," he said, his lips playing with hers. "Oh, no, Yank—not yet."

Maggie was beginning to want him again and that, after the night just past, was more than she could bear. She started to protest, but her words were trapped in his mouth as he kissed her, and her resolve was greatly weakened by the way he gently moved his hips against hers.

Presently, he drew back from her mouth, but his hips remained solidly in place and his beautiful blue-green eyes laughed into Maggie's snapping gray ones. "Let me love you, Maggie, or I swear I'll make you beg."

Maggie knew that he could make her do just that; he'd done it over and over again the night before, and she found the prospect unappealing. Besides, she could feel the heated length of him pressing against her skin. "Oooooh," she moaned, for that was all the protest she could manage, and when Reeve entered her, slowly and tenderly, she welcomed him.

* * *

Sydney seemed somehow changed since Maggie had seen it last; it was less intimidating, less strange, and far more beautiful, with its sparkling harbor and bustling streets.

As Reeve's carriage rattled over the macadam, bringing her back to Victoria Street, Mrs. Lavendar, and her duties, however, Maggie's high spirits began to sag a little. During the long ride from Parramatta, Reeve had been with her, but he'd thought it better that she arrive at the Kirk house alone and had gotten out of the carriage in front of his office downtown.

Now, as the carriage came to a stop in front of Duncan Kirk's house, Maggie was feeling a very real need to go back to Reeve and plead with him to take her in as his mistress.

She was instantly ashamed of that, and as she alighted from the carriage, her reticule in hand, Maggie kept her chin high. No one had to know, if she didn't let on, that she was forever changed, and she wasn't likely to confide what had happened even to Tansy, who probably knew anyway.

After a brief thank-you to the driver, Maggie went through the Kirk gate, up the walk, and around the side of the house. As one of Mrs. Lavendar's serfs, she didn't dare enter by any way except the rear.

Only it wasn't Mrs. Lavendar that Maggie found in the kitchen, but Mr. Duncan Kirk himself. He was standing by the table, his hands gripping the back of a chair so tightly that his knuckles were white, his green eyes snapping.

"You came home in Reeve McKenna's carriage," he said in an expressionless voice that made Maggie pause and clutch her reticule in front of her like a shield.

Maggie bit her lower lip, wondering how anyone could tell one carriage from another. They all looked the same to her, except for the ones belonging to the gentry back in England, of course—they had crests on their doors. "Yes," she finally admitted.

For a moment the green eyes assessed her, and Maggie prayed there was no way that Mr. Kirk could discern what she and Reeve had done. Then, in a clipped voice, he told her, "Get your things together. We're leaving for Melbourne on the evening train."

"Mel-Melbourne?" Maggie echoed, puzzled.

"I have business there, with the governor, and I may have to remain for some time. I would like you and the boys to be with me."

Maggie didn't want to leave Sydney, and Reeve, but neither did she truly want to live as Loretta Craig had. And she still had to earn her own living. "All right," she said meekly, then, unable to bear Mr. Kirk's perusal any longer, she dashed past him and up the stairs to her room.

Mrs. Lavendar was there, packing the clothes Maggie had bought at Mr. Kirk's request into an enormous leather trunk with the smell of newness still about it.

"Hello," she said somewhat breathlessly to the broad bombazine-covered back.

Mrs. Lavendar stiffened. "So that Irishman is done with you, is he?" she asked.

Maggie was as stunned as if the woman had slapped her. "I beg your pardon," she said, staring.

The housekeeper turned, her eyes keen, seeing through Maggie's flesh to her spirit. "You've made a terrible mistake, lass," she warned, and Maggie couldn't tell whether the words were meant to be friendly or sinister. "A terrible mistake."

Maggie let go of her reticule and it made a thumping sound as it struck the floor. "What on earth do you mean?" she asked, meaning to brazen it out and pretend that Mrs. Lavendar's insinuation was unfounded.

Mrs. Lavendar turned back to her packing. "I'll not be explaining to you, miss. You'll have to find out for yourself."

Maggie remembered some of the things Reeve had

said about her employer and it struck her that the malice he'd expressed might be returned, in spades, by Mr. Kirk. "They're enemies," she muttered more to herself than to Mrs. Lavendar.

"From the first day they met," Mrs. Lavendar replied, apparently forgetting her vow not to explain. "If I were you, lass, I wouldn't go to Melbourne. In fact, I'd leave this house and never come back."

Maggie rounded the housekeeper's bulk then, to face her, annoyed. "I've got to earn my living, Mrs. Lavendar," she said coldly. "Just like you do."

"Mr. McKenna will take care of your living," Mrs. Lavendar retorted, undaunted, "as long as you please him."

"This is nonsense!" Maggie cried, too proud to admit to the truth even in the face of this woman's obvious knowledge. "I was stranded at Parramatta and Mr. McKenna was kind enough to send me home in his carriage!"

Mrs. Lavendar nodded sagely. "If that's your story, miss, then so be it. I've warned you and that's all I can do." With that the housekeeper left the room.

Trying to ignore the dread she felt, Maggie went about packing the last of her new clothes.

Chapter 11 🙖

THE TRIP TO MELBOURNE WAS A LONG ONE, AND BY THE time the train had reached its destination, Maggie and her two young charges were rummy with fatigue and dawn was breaking, pink and gray. Mr. Kirk, who had spent the night in the club car, was in fine spirits nonetheless. Except for the clinging scent of cigar smoke, he was as impeccably groomed as ever. To Maggie's relief, his glowering mood had apparently passed.

A carriage was waiting at Melbourne Station and, after Maggie and the two boys were settled inside, Mr. Kirk took the seat across from them. His shrewd emerald eyes swept over Maggie's dress once and flashed with some singular annoyance, but he seemed determined to be pleasant.

As the carriage rolled over paved streets, Mr. Kirk pointed out this building and that, the most impressive, by far, being Government House. It was truly a palace, with many windows and more archways than Maggie could count, along with a high, square tower that seemed to touch the sky.

Jeremy and Tad were unimpressed, having been to Melbourne before, but Maggie could barely contain her eagerness to explore the city, particularly the manicured grounds and gardens of Government House.

"As my hostess," Mr. Kirk said pointedly as the grand structure disappeared behind the carriage, "you'll be presented to the governor on a number of occasions. It's proper to address him as 'Your Lordship.'"

Maggie was painfully conscious of the simple cotton dress she wore; now she understood why Mr. Kirk had instructed her to buy evening dresses. She flushed and lowered her eyes, unable, for the moment, to speak.

Mr. Kirk laughed softly. "I've made another list," he said, extending a folded paper to Maggie. "This time, will you please do as I ask and buy the proper clothing?"

Maggie took the paper and shyly raised her eyes to Mr. Kirk's handsome, freshly shaven face. She nodded.

"Excellent. As soon as we've reached the house and the boys are settled, I would like to speak with you privately, Miss Chamberlin. In my study."

Maggie felt a tremor of alarm, though she managed to keep her sleepy smile firmly in place and her chin up. Now she was going to get a lecture about the Parramatta episode; she only hoped that, unlike Mrs. Lavendar, Mr. Kirk hadn't divined the truth of it all.

Soon enough the carriage came to a lurching stop in front of a house as every bit as splendid as the Kirk residence in Sydney. Maggie drew in her breath at the sight of its glistening white walls, showy gardens, and shimmering windows.

Mr. Kirk left the carriage first, followed immediately by his two boisterous sons, who ran whooping and hollering through the open gate and up the wide flagstone walk. Maggie could see that she was going to have to work with the children's manners as well as their sums and spelling.

Her employer took her hand in a grip so tight that it was almost painful as she moved to alight, and his gaze, companionable only moments before, seared her. "My study," he said in a quiet voice. "Fifteen minutes."

Maggie swallowed a "yes, sir" and nodded her head. "I'll be there," she answered, and her legs seemed a bit unsteady as she stepped down to the ground.

"See that you are," Duncan Kirk replied, and then he released Maggie's hand and she felt him watching her as she fled toward the open front door of the house. Not daring to look back, she bolted through the doorway and found Jeremy and Tad sliding down an elegant oaken banister, carrying on like banshees.

"Enough!" Maggie snapped in a not-to-be-ignored tone, and both boys stopped where they were, watching her with wide green eyes.

She drew a deep breath, regretting that she'd spoken so sharply, and began again. "Please show me where your rooms are."

With a sulky glower rather reminiscent of his father's, Tad raced off to parts unknown, in blatant rebellion. It was Jeremy who took Maggie's hand and said, "This way, please, Miss Chamberlin. Shall I tell on Tad? Papa will give him a trouncing if I do."

Maggie bit back a smile. "Mustn't be a tattletale, Jeremy. I'll deal with Tad myself, if you don't mind."

Jeremy nodded solemnly, and Maggie knew that he was wondering how she intended to manage such a feat. Indeed, Maggie was pondering that question herself. Tad was a difficult boy, and, for all her love of little ones, she'd had no real experience with problem children.

In this house, unlike the one in Sydney, the boys did not have separate rooms. Instead, there was, on the third floor, a nursery area, complete with a schoolroom, sitting room, cramped quarters for a governess, and a rather austere-looking bedchamber for Jeremy and Tad.

"Will we start our lessons today, miss?" Jeremy asked, yawning as he hoisted himself onto one of the two matching beds and sat with his feet dangling.

Maggie felt sleepy herself since she hadn't been able to rest on the train, and forced back a yawn of her own. "Perhaps this afternoon," she said. "For now, I want you to rest."

For just a moment Jeremy looked as though he might lodge a protest, but he quickly remembered his status as a young gentleman. "All right," he said on a long-suffering sigh, thrusting himself backward onto the bed.

Smiling, Maggie removed his shoes and covered him gently, her hand stroking his bright auburn hair back from his face. A warm feeling of love welled inside her for the little boy, and she was wondering whether or not it would be proper to kiss him, when he said in a piping little voice, "Could you please give me a good-night kiss, miss, the way Mum used to do?"

Maggie felt tears gathering in her throat and wondered what Mrs. Kirk had been like. She bent and placed a gentle kiss on Jeremy's freckled forehead. "Like that?" she asked softly.

He nodded, his eyelids obviously growing heavy. "Yes, miss, just like that," he said, and then, as quickly as that, he was asleep.

"You don't need to think you're ever going to kiss *me,*" Tad remarked from the doorway. "Besides, it isn't time for good-nights, it's morning."

Maggie took a moment to compose herself before turning to face her other pupil. He was standing in the doorway, leaning indolently against the jamb, but his face and the expression in his eyes showed Maggie a vulnerability she'd only suspected was there before. "Hello, Tad," she said, ignoring his challenge.

"Are you going to tell Papa that I ran off?" Tad

158

demanded, watching Maggie with both suspicion and hope.

The mention of Mr. Kirk reminded Maggie of the setdown she was about to receive in the study. "Absolutely not," she said. "But I would appreciate it if you would tell me where your father's study is."

Tad looked pleased and, conversely, worried. "You're in trouble, ain't you?"

"That was a terrible abuse of the King's English, Tad Kirk, and I will thank you to rephrase it."

Tad gave a sigh. "You're in trouble, aren't you, miss?" he asked. Then, stubbornly, he added, "We don't have a king. We have a queen now—this year is her Golden Jubilee."

Maggie was developing a headache. She was hungry and tired and unnerved at the prospect of the coming interview with Duncan Kirk, but she was determined to reach Tad somehow, to win his respect if not his affection. For this reason she did not take the trouble to explain that the King's English is always the King's English, no matter who might be on the throne at the time. "We'll be discussing Her Majesty's reign in our lessons."

Tad frowned. "I don't call her that, you know," he confided. "I'm half American, and Americans don't have kings and queens."

"I realize that," Maggie responded circumspectly.

"Papa's going to take us there to visit one day. To America, I mean."

Maggie was smoothing her skirts and her hair, wondering if the stated fifteen minutes had passed. "I envy you," she said truthfully. "I'm not sure I'll ever find my way back."

Without speaking, Tad crossed the room and took Maggie's arm. In a gentlemanly fashion he led her out of the bedchamber, along the hallway, and down the first set of stairs. Maggie knew that he was escorting her to his father's study and she was touched at his attempt to be as mannerly as his brother was.

They were standing outside a massive set of double doors on the second floor before Tad released his hold on Maggie's elbow and whispered somberly, "I hate it when I get called to Papa's study. I always get my hide tanned."

Maggie was careful not to smile, and she bent slightly to whisper back, "I'm a bit nervous myself."

"You'll be all right," Tad assured her manfully. And then he was on his way back up the stairs, covering a yawn with one hand.

Maggie took a moment to straighten her shoulders and draw a deep breath, then she lifted her hand and knocked softly at one of the study doors. There was always the chance that Mr. Kirk had forgotten about the intended lecture and left the house on business.

There was no such luck. "Come in, Miss Chamberlin," called a somewhat weary male voice from the other side of those towering doors.

Maggie dragged in another restorative breath and turned one of the brass knobs, stepping into a spacious room graced with Oriental rugs, brass fixtures, bookshelves, and a desk. Mr. Kirk leaned against that massive, ornately carved desk, his arms folded across his chest.

"Sit down, Miss Chamberlin," he said peremptorily, and before Maggie could rebel, she found herself obediently sinking into a leather chair.

His face expressionless, Mr. Kirk drew a folded paper from the inside pocket of his suit coat and held it out. "Do you know what this is?" he asked.

Maggie took the paper and unfolded it, recognizing it as a certificate of the sort so highly touted at Lady Cosgrove's establishment. If properly signed and witnessed, the document assured a young woman of future employment. The flowery certificate was, of course, completely blank.

Her throat suddenly too tight to permit speech, Maggie merely nodded her head.

"Good," Mr. Kirk answered in a clipped tone,

taking back the paper, refolding it, and slipping it back into his pocket. "From this day forward, Miss Chamberlin, your behavior will be exemplary, I trust. There will be no more dalliances with Reeve McKenna or any other man, and when I give you instructions, you will follow them."

Maggie's face went bright pink. How on earth could Mr. Kirk know that she'd been with Reeve at Parramatta? He must have had spies there. At that instant Maggie remembered seeing Loretta Craig get out of a carriage one night, remembered eavesdropping on a part of the conversation Miss Craig and Mr. Kirk had shared. Maggie went rigid in her chair.

"Tomorrow night," Mr. Kirk went on, his arms still folded, his gaze locked with Maggie's, "you and I will dine at Government House. I shall expect you to be dressed properly, Miss Chamberlin."

Maggie swallowed hard. She had no idea what a lady would wear for such an occasion, and she opened her mouth to say so.

Mr. Kirk stopped her with a brusque, "I have arranged for one of my friends to accompany you to the shops this afternoon. You will buy as she instructs you to buy, Miss Chamberlin. Is that clear?"

Maggie's cheeks were burning and she knew there was insurrection snapping in her eyes. She stood up slowly, planning to tell Mr. Kirk that she liked neither his arbitrary tone nor his manner, but once again he spoke before she could get a word out.

"You will find me to be a most generous and understanding employer, Miss Chamberlin," Duncan Kirk said, "but if you disobey me, you will also discover that I can be ruthless. I will not tolerate any more trysts or rebellions, minor or otherwise."

Maggie knew only too well the choices that would be left to her if Mr. Kirk should terminate her employment, leaving her without a signed certificate to serve as a reference. She would end up either on the streets or in some love nest provided by Reeve

McKenna, and both prospects were patently unacceptable. As much as she'd flowered in that man's bed, she had no intention of becoming his plaything, to be coddled and pampered for a time and then tossed away as Loretta had been tossed away. She wouldn't be able to bear that.

"Your friend wouldn't be Loretta Craig, by any chance?" Maggie asked coldly, her chin high as she rose out of her chair and stood facing Mr. Kirk.

He smiled a slow, obnoxious smile. "Loretta is only one of my friends. It's Lady Rosalind Simmons who'll be taking you shopping. I think you'll like her."

Maggie doubted that, but there didn't seem to be any other choice than to let this Lady Simmons oversee the shopping expedition. She'd taken this position and now, since Mr. McKenna had reclaimed her emigration papers, she was going to have to make the best of things. "I'll be ready when Lady Simmons arrives," she said evenly.

"Excellent," said Mr. Kirk with a slight nod of his head.

Maggie turned away without being excused and swept as far as the doorway before pausing to look back at her employer. She expected to see anger in his face; instead, she found amusement. And that made her furious. "I trust," she said in bitingly polite tones, "that there will, at some point, be time for teaching your sons, Mr. Kirk?"

He laughed. "I promise you, Miss Chamberlin—you'll have more time with the boys than you could possibly want."

Having no way to respond to that outlandish statement, Maggie turned in a whirl and stormed out of the study and up the staircase to the third floor. In the nursery both Jeremy and Tad were sleeping soundly on their beds.

Mechanically, Maggie covered Tad as she had covered Jeremy earlier, then went into her tiny room.

There, she flung herself down onto the narrow bed and pounded at the pillow with her fists.

The telephone on Duncan's desk gave a jangling ring; not an uncommon occurrence, of course, though he had hoped for a few minutes to relish the spark in Maggie Chamberlin's gray eyes when he'd told her what was what.

Annoyed, Duncan grabbed up the cumbersome receiver and demanded, "Yes?"

There was a low male laugh at the other end of the line, a laugh Duncan recognized all too well. "Hello, Kirk," said Reeve McKenna.

Duncan considered slamming down the receiver, and then thought better of the motion. Here was a chance, after all, to get under McKenna's skin. "How are things in Sydney?" he asked as companionably as if he had been speaking to a friend and not a man he'd just as soon see dead.

Again, that familiar laugh sounded. "Sydney? You only wish I were in Sydney, old friend. I'm in Melbourne, as it happens."

Duncan yearned to sit down, and then remembered that he was already sitting. He rubbed his eyes with a thumb and forefinger while he tried to assemble himself. "Melbourne," he echoed stupidly, hating himself the moment the word was out of his mouth.

"Loretta couldn't wait to tell me that you were planning a trip," Reeve said smoothly. "That's the trouble with Loretta, her loyalties are flexible."

Duncan let out a long breath but said nothing. When he got his hands on Miss Craig's pretty neck, he vowed to himself, he was going to wring it.

"Of course," Reeve went on in that dangerously affable way of his, "we're going to have to discuss this situation. In person."

Duncan sighed. "Yes."

"Where?"

"Anywhere but here," Duncan responded.

"The club?"

Duncan nodded distractedly, then realized that Reeve couldn't see him. "Yes. Five o'clock?" He made the words sound cordial.

"Now," Reeve argued, and with a click the call was disconnected.

Seething, Duncan left his study to order a carriage brought around.

Lady Simmons was neither a dour old matron nor a doxy. By turns, Maggie had expected her to be both. Instead, she was a pretty young woman with fashionably styled black hair and a quick, ingenuous smile.

"I know where all the best shops are," she told Maggie warmly as they rode away from the Kirk house in an elegant carriage. "And Harry says that there's nobody better at spending money than I am."

In spite of the situation, Maggie found herself liking Lady Simmons, who insisted on being addressed as Rosalind. She was, Maggie quickly learned, a duchess; she and her titled husband had decided to spend several years in Australia as an adventure. They had two children, several English estates, and four dogs, of whom Rosalind spoke almost as fondly as she did of the future Duke of Devonshire and his younger sister, Polly.

"Have you and Duncan been friends for a long time?" Maggie asked when there was an opening to speak.

"I do love your American accent!" Rosalind trilled, beaming. "And yes, Harry and I have known Duncan for some years. We have shares in several of his opal mines."

Maggie nodded numbly. Even though she'd spent some time in England, she had never been within touching distance of a bona fide member of the gentry, and she was a little overwhelmed.

"You'll enjoy dining at Government House,"

Rosalind went on after taking a breath. "And of course there are the boat races in the harbor and there will be quite a celebration in June, when Her Majesty's Jubilee—"

Maggie found her voice. "I'm really only a governess," she pointed out, meaning to imply that she would probably not be included in events the gentry would be enjoying.

Rosalind peered at Maggie with narrowed blue eyes, looking honestly puzzled. "A governess? Why, Harry and I both had the impression that—oh, never mind."

Maggie stiffened in her seat, her hands clasped together in her lap. "What impression did you have, please?" she asked with quiet insistence.

"Well, since you're so pretty, and you're an American and everything—well, we did think that Duncan might be planning to—to marry you."

Maggie drew in such a quick breath that she nearly choked on it. "I'm a governess," she repeated when she could trust herself to speak. "And I'm also to serve as a hostess of some sort."

Rosalind assessed Maggie with wry friendliness. "Well, well, well. A hostess, is it? I thought Duncan was buying you a trousseau."

Maggie leaned forward slightly in her seat, keeping her voice to a whisper even though she knew that no one could possibly overhear. "It is—well—proper, isn't it? My serving as Mr. Kirk's hostess?"

Rosalind giggled. "Of course it's proper. That clever Duncan—if you were anything besides a hostess or a governess, he'd have to have a chaperon in the house!"

Maggie was hardly comforted by this remark. "You don't mean that Mr. Kirk might have—have designs on me, do you?"

Rosalind's pretty blue eyes danced. "My dear, Duncan has designs on all of us," she said.

Maggie groaned and sank back in her seat, her eyes

closed, and Rosalind reached over to give her hand a pat that was undoubtedly meant to be reassuring.

"Duncan is a gentleman," she said.

Maggie remembered the green fire in Duncan Kirk's eyes when he'd laid down the law in his study only a few hours before, and she wondered whether Rosalind Simmons knew what she was talking about.

For the rest of the afternoon she followed the energetic young duchess from one shop to another. Several gowns were bought ready-made, while dozens more were ordered. Shoes were selected, as well as handbags for both daytime and evening; parasols and perfumes were bought. Maggie estimated the cost of this expedition and developed yet another headache.

By the time she and Rosalind returned to the Kirk residence, which was within a stone's throw of Government House, Maggie was exhausted. Burdened with as many packages as she could carry, she hurried to her small room off the nursery, only to find a maid there, stripping the blankets and sheets from the bed.

Her mind spinning with the implications of that, Maggie let her parcels fall to the floor with a series of loud clumps. The only thing worse than having to stay under Duncan Kirk's roof for a full year would be having to leave it, that very day, in disgrace.

"What are you doing?" Maggie croaked.

The maid was already kneeling on the floor, reaching for the boxes Maggie had dropped. "Why, I'm pickin' up your things, miss. Anyone could see that!"

If it hadn't been for the rigors of the day, Maggie would have laughed. "I meant, why were you stripping the bed?"

The young maid looked up, her eyes bright. One work-roughened hand caressed a silver dress box in a gesture of wonder. "The master wants you to sleep on the second floor, miss," she said, cocking her head to one side. She had a mop of tightly curled brown hair that seemed determined to swallow up her mobcap, and her nose turned up at the end. "You just go on

down there now—Cook's sending up your supper—
and I'll bring your things along later.''

Maggie opened her mouth to protest, then closed it
again. She'd no strength left for doing battle with "the
master" and his arbitrary decisions. For now, for
tonight, he'd won.

"Which room is mine?" Maggie asked in a defeated
tone.

"The one at the far end of the hallway, miss. Away
from the stairs."

Maggie left the small room that had been good
enough for other governesses and distractedly
smoothed the beds Jeremy and Tad had left rumpled
from their naps. She wondered where they were and if
she'd ever get a chance to teach them. Or were they
simply an excuse, as the title "hostess" might be, for
Duncan to keep Maggie under his roof, ordering her
about and dressing her up like an expensive doll.

Maggie cursed Philip Briggs for bringing her to this
place so far from the rest of the world, and there were
tears of anger, weariness, and frustration in her eyes
when she made her way down the stairs and along the
second floor hallway.

This room, like its counterpart in Sydney, was
entirely too sumptuous for a governess; at the windows it had soft blue velvet draperies trimmed with
gold tassels. The spread on the massive mahogany bed
was of some gauzy white fabric, and plush pillows of
all shapes and sizes and colors gave it the dissolutely
luxurious look of a harem couch.

Maggie stopped cold in the doorway. She could not
turn to the streets, of course, but she did wonder if it
would really be so terrible to be Reeve McKenna's
mistress. Sure, one day he might tire of her and cast
her aside, but in the meantime she would have food to
eat and clothes to wear, not to mention long nights of
ecstasy almost too keen to be borne. . . .

"Do you like the room?" inquired a low voice,
directly behind her.

Maggie whirled to find herself standing within inches of Mr. Kirk. He smelled of bay rum and good whiskey, and his green eyes were not threatening or angry, but full of laughter.

"It does seem—well—a little fancy—" Maggie managed to say.

Duncan laughed softly and his hands rested on Maggie's upper arms for a moment before falling away as he remembered his manners. "You're worried about what I might expect in return—is that it? I should have guessed that Rosalind would fill your head with all kinds of silly ideas about my predatory nature."

Maggie swallowed and took a step in retreat, thus putting herself inside the too-luxurious room. "She did say that you have designs on all women," she confessed, her eyes wide.

Duncan laughed again, this time throwing his head back, and his eyes shone as they assessed Maggie's flushed face and poised-to-flee stance. "She exaggerates."

Maggie didn't know what to say to that, so she took another step backward and just watched Mr. Kirk's face. She saw the amusement drain away, leaving sadness in its wake.

"I loved my wife very much, Miss Chamberlin," he said quietly, and then, with that statement hanging in the air behind him, he turned and left Maggie's room.

Chapter 12 🦢

FIRST THING THE NEXT MORNING, MAGGIE SUMMONED Jeremy and Tad to the schoolroom on the third floor and began their lessons. She was not surprised to find that both boys were very bright, though Tad, the older of the two, was less than enthusiastic about staying in and doing sums when there was a whole world outside just waiting to be explored.

When Maggie had gauged the mathematical abilities of both boys, she ferreted out a few materials from a cupboard at one end of the long room and set them to drawing maps of Australia.

"Papa has houses here, here, and here," Jeremy said, stabbing at widely separated places on the map with the point of his pencil.

"And here," Tad added, making an unwanted mark on Jeremy's map and getting a glowering look for his trouble. "Mum liked this one best. She said Queensland was like paradise."

Maggie was very curious about the late Mrs. Kirk, but of course she didn't want to pry, so she simply said, "I imagine your mother was very beautiful."

Both boys nodded solemnly.

"Her name was Elena and she died giving birth to our third child," put in an icy male voice from the doorway behind Maggie. "Is there anything else you'd like to know, Miss Chamberlin?"

Maggie whirled to face Mr. Kirk, and she was shocked at the rigid fury she saw in every line of his body. "I'm sorry," she said softly, though she wasn't exactly sure what she'd done wrong.

In the space of a second or so Duncan relaxed. "No, Miss Chamberlin," he said sheepishly. "I'm the one who should apologize. I guess I'm still a little sensitive where Elena is concerned."

Maggie nodded, not knowing what to say. She was no stranger to grief herself, having lost both her parents in one tragic accident, and she knew that it made people do and say very odd things at times.

"Come and see our maps, Papa," Jeremy entreated his father. "We've made Australia."

Maggie was pleased with the attention Mr. Kirk paid to each map, carefully studying every line and place name and mountain range. When he had quietly lauded both boys' efforts, he sent them downstairs to have their lunch.

After the children had raced out of the schoolroom, Duncan lingered over one of the maps, his hands braced against the low tabletop. In the sunlight streaming in through the windows, his hair gleamed a golden red. "Elena was very beautiful," he said without looking at Maggie. "Would you like to see her portrait?"

"Very much," Maggie said quietly. In many ways Duncan Kirk frightened her, but now she found herself feeling real compassion for him. She had expected to be led to some other room; instead, Mr. Kirk took a small golden item, much like a watchcase, from his vest pocket and opened it.

Maggie looked inside and saw a miniature of a woman with very dark eyes and pale hair almost the color of her own. Elena was smiling in the portrait, something that was unusual given the seriousness of having one's likeness done, and she was, indeed, beautiful.

"She passed away two years ago," Duncan said quietly, as though he were still baffled by the unfairness of her passing. "Our infant daughter perished with her."

Maggie didn't know what to say in the face of such a tragic loss, so she remained silent, trying to convey her sympathy by the expression in her eyes.

Mr. Kirk's pensive look was gone in an instant; almost briskly, he snapped the small portrait case closed and dropped it back into his pocket. His green eyes were clear as he took in Maggie's prim shirtwaist and skirt, and he smiled. "I'd like to see what you plan to wear to Government House tonight," he said.

The reminder of the evening ahead both excited and unnerved Maggie. How was she to show Mr. Kirk the gown Rosalind had recommended without asking him to her room? That, of course, would be unthinkable. "It's blue silk," she said, "trimmed with millions of tiny crystal beads—"

Duncan smiled at Maggie's emphasis on the word *millions* and folded his arms. "I want to see the dress," he repeated.

Maggie opened her mouth to argue that she still planned to give the boys a lesson in botany and have them practice their penmanship, but Mr. Kirk cut her off a second time.

"Put on the gown, please, Miss Chamberlin. I'll be in my study." With that Mr. Kirk was striding out of the schoolroom, leaving Maggie behind to simmer. The man was utterly imperious, demanding that she model a dress for him in the middle of the school day!

Nonetheless, Maggie went down to the second floor bedroom where she had slept so fitfully the night before, took the glitteringly beautiful gown from its place in the armoire, and put it on.

The garment was, beyond a doubt, the loveliest

thing Maggie had ever seen, let alone owned. Its midnight-blue skirts whispered as she walked, and the crystal beads, spread liberally over the low-cut bodice as well as the skirt, sparkled like diamonds in the light.

Maggie tugged at the bodice, wanting it to show less of her natural endowments, but it resisted, reaching no higher than two scant inches above her nipples. With a sigh she left her room and hurried toward the study. Best to get this over with and return to botany and penmanship.

The doors to the study stood slightly ajar, and Maggie stepped through them after one short knock. Mr. Kirk, working at his desk, looked up at her in amazement, his mouth open, his eyes burning.

"You wanted to see the dress," Maggie said, her patience wearing thin.

Mr. Kirk dropped his pen, heedless of the ink that splattered from its point over his papers, and stood up. "My God," he breathed.

Maggie couldn't help being flattered, though she did her best to hide it. She harbored a secret wish that Reeve McKenna could see her in that magnificent, twinkling gown. "May I go now?" she asked coolly, her chin at an obstinate angle.

"You may not," Duncan breathed, and then he gave his head a slight shake, as if to clear it, and sank back into his leather chair.

Maggie sighed. Perhaps she was to be a "hostess" at night, but it was daytime and, as far as she was concerned, she was still a governess. "The boys' lessons are waiting—"

"The boys are eating," Mr. Kirk broke in, and there was just the hint of a smile at his lips and in his eyes. "They've had enough schoolwork for one day, anyway. I want them to get some fresh air."

Maggie didn't see how she could be expected to educate Jeremy and Tad if they were allowed only half days for their schoolwork, but something in Mr.

Kirk's manner made her hesitant to argue. He was behaving rather oddly, though not, she had to admit, any more so than usual. "I'll take the boys to the park then, or perhaps to the menagerie."

"You will rest," Mr. Kirk corrected her, as he was forever doing. "Tonight's festivities will go on until the early hours of the morning."

"But—"

"Miss Chamberlin." The words were spoken as a weary warning, and Duncan Kirk was already absorbed in his paperwork again.

Maggie went back to her room to change and found a maid waiting there, setting out a plate and silverware from a luncheon tray. She assessed Maggie's dress with round eyes and muttered, "Coo, ain't you the elegant one, miss!"

Suddenly lonely for Tansy, Maggie swept around behind the changing screen in the far corner of the room and began taking off the gown. The maid, the same young girl Maggie had encountered the day before in the nursery, came right behind her and insisted on helping.

Resigned to eating and then following Duncan Kirk's order to rest, Maggie put on a wrapper instead of donning her shirtwaist and slim black skirt again, and she took down her hair as well. The young maid brushed the silvery-blond tresses while Maggie ate, then tucked her into bed as though she were a child.

Maggie had not expected to sleep, but she did, and soundly. When she awakened, her cheeks were pink from the erotic dreams she'd had, all of them featuring Reeve McKenna. She splashed cool water over her face until her flesh was once again its normal temperature, but there was nothing she could do about the tingling ache in her middle. She got out paper and a pen and started a letter to Tansy.

The task proved impossible, given that Maggie could think of nothing but that obnoxious Irishman and the way his hands had felt on her body those wondrous nights in Parramatta, so she put her governess clothes back on and went for a walk. By the time she'd circled the block three times at an industrious pace, she was calmer.

Returning to Duncan Kirk's house by the rear entrance, of course, Maggie encountered his housekeeper for the first time. Unlike Mrs. Lavendar, this woman was voluptuous but not obese, and her heavy hair was a coppery color, her skin a flawless white. There was a lush, sensual quality about her, and one look from under her dense lashes convinced Maggie that she had no intention of becoming friendly with the new governess.

Nonetheless, Maggie tried, being a gregarious soul. "My name is Margaret Chamberlin," she said.

"Bridget," replied the housekeeper in a terse tone. "Bridget O'Malley."

Maggie wanted to wring her hands, but she forced herself to keep them at her sides. "Have you worked here long?"

Bridget O'Malley's look was enough to quell even the boldest. "Long enough," she answered, her eyes moving over Maggie with undisguised contempt. "Don't be using the back door in the future, miss," she said. "You're a little better than the rest of us, so Dunc—Mr. Kirk will expect you to come in and out in front, like the gentry."

Maggie felt as though she'd just been soundly slapped, but she was hurt rather than angry. Why was it that none of these people were willing to accept her as what she was, another domestic servant? "Mrs. O'Malley—"

"Miss O'Malley," snapped the housekeeper, putting a curious emphasis on the "miss."

Completely thwarted now, Maggie subsided, her cheeks flaring with color. She wished that Tansy were there, that she had a friend with whom she could talk and laugh. Her feeling of isolation was all but intolerable.

"The master was asking about you earlier," Bridget said, concentrating on the dishes she was washing. "You'll go and see what he wants, if you know what's good for you."

Maggie lifted her chin, recovering from the rebuff now. She'd gotten through nineteen years without Bridget O'Malley's friendship, and she could get through a hundred and nineteen more. "Thank you," she said coldly, and then she swept out of the kitchen in the same imperious way she'd seen Rosalind leave shops that had not carried suitable merchandise.

When she reached the second floor, she was nothing less than amazed to find Duncan Kirk there, with Tad clinging to his back and Jeremy to his middle. All three were laughing, and it was a moment before Maggie realized that she'd interrupted a sort of hallway wrestling match. Some of the sting of her encounter with Bridget ebbed away, and she found herself smiling.

Duncan's face sobered when he caught sight of Maggie and, at an unspoken signal, both Jeremy and Tad stepped away from him, suddenly silent. "Well, Miss Chamberlin," Mr. Kirk said in a low and curiously stricken voice, "you've returned."

Maggie felt as though she'd been caught doing something underhanded. "I was only out walking," she said.

Duncan laughed softly and then laid a hand to each of his sons' shoulders. "Go and wash up for supper," he told them, and they vanished immediately, leaving Maggie alone in the hallway with their father.

For a long and singularly uncomfortable moment, Duncan simply watched Maggie. It was as though he could see deep inside her and discern her most private thoughts. Maggie blushed because too many of those thoughts were of Reeve McKenna, and too many of them were scandalous.

"You know, don't you," Duncan finally said, "that you are very, very beautiful?"

Maggie knew nothing of the sort; she was pretty, she thought, but too young and unsophisticated to be really beautiful. "I've got absolutely no idea how to behave at dinner tonight!" she blurted out, partly to change the subject and partly because she really was afraid of making a fool of herself at Government House.

Duncan arched one eyebrow and folded his arms, letting one shoulder rest against the hallway wall. He was blocking Maggie's way to her room and she suspected that he was doing it on purpose. "Nothing more is required of you, Miss Chamberlin, than that you conduct yourself as a lady."

"But I'm not a lady!" Maggie cried desperately.

Duncan shrugged. "You were an actress in London; play the role of a lady, then."

Maggie had not thought of that, but it seemed a good idea. She would watch Rosalind and the other female guests and do as they did. Brightening a little, she started around Duncan, only to be stopped by his hand gripping her arm. For a moment his fingers caressed the skin beneath the short puffy sleeve of her blouse, but then he let Maggie go so swiftly that she was left wondering if she hadn't imagined the entire episode.

As many of these patently dull affairs as he'd attended, Reeve was jarred out of his cynical languor by the sight of Maggie, strolling into Government House on Duncan Kirk's arm. She was wearing an indigo dress that sparkled in the soft lighting and her silver-honey hair was swept up, revealing her long, graceful neck. Reeve remembered running his lips along that neck, and something deep inside him tightened painfully. He set aside his wineglass and strode toward Maggie, completely forgetting the buxom young thing he'd been charming moments before.

The front of Maggie's dress, Reeve decided, revealed far too much. Why, one good tug at that glittering bodice and . . .

"Hello, Maggie," he said, coming to a stop directly in front of her.

The expression on her face as she looked up at him was one of utter surprise. "Reeve!" she gasped, then color flooded her cheeks and she tossed one glance at Duncan, who was glowering. "H-how have you been?"

Reeve was in no mood for small talk. He wanted to cover Maggie's full bosom before any other man could look. More than that, he wanted to take her somewhere private and bare those delectable breasts, preferably in the moonlight, to taste their pink-confection tips, hear Maggie whimper in response, feel her fingers entangling themselves in his hair. He darted one look at Duncan—it conveyed a silent reiteration of their conversation at the club the day before—then demanded in a polite undertone, "What the hell do you think you're doing, wearing a dress like that in public?"

Maggie's color heightened again, moving up over the lush rounding of her breasts, flooding along her neck, seeping into her face. Her lips moved, but no sound came out.

"Good God, Reeve," Duncan hissed, "even for you, that was a plebeian thing to say!"

"I presume you bought it?" Reeve asked of Maggie's escort. The last thing in the world he cared about was Duncan's opinion of his manners.

Maggie finally found her voice. "This gown is the very height of fashion," she whispered angrily, and there was a storm brewing in her thundercloud eyes. "It came all the way from Paris!"

"Just the thing for a governess to wear," Reeve retorted dryly. "What are you teaching your students, Miss Chamberlin? Wild abandon?"

Duncan looked both pained and annoyed, while Maggie seemed ready to explode with fury. Reeve loved baiting her, and despite his feelings about her dress, he had to fight to keep himself from grinning.

"Passion becomes you," he added.

Maggie's reaction was anything but disappointing. Her beautiful breasts heaved up and down, threatening to burst free of the scant band of silk that restrained them, and her eyes flashed with pewter lightning. At her side, one hand flexed as though she'd like nothing better than to slap Reeve with all the power she possessed. Of course, she was pretending to be a lady, so she didn't dare do anything rash, and Reeve enjoyed her helplessness, temporary and uncharacteristic though it was.

Duncan had apparently decided to pretend that Reeve wasn't there. He pulled Maggie toward the reception line forming just inside the main parlor and said out of one side of his mouth, "Remember to address the governor as 'Your Lordship' and curtsy."

"I will *not* curtsy!" Maggie vowed in a scathing whisper, and Reeve smiled to himself as he stepped into the reception line behind the two of them. Usually he avoided such tedious exercises in formality, but this was going to be too good to miss.

True to her word, Maggie did not curtsy to either the governor or his wife, though she did incline her head slightly. Reeve held his breath for a moment, sure that she'd fall out of her dress in front of God and everybody, but the sparkly blue silk retained its tenuous grasp on her bosom.

At dinner, served in the largest of several dining rooms, Reeve contrived to be seated directly across from Maggie and her much annoyed partner, Duncan. If anything interesting happened, he wanted to be on hand.

Duncan scowled across the table as Reeve seated his own dinner partner, a saucy, dark-haired vixen who had once been his mistress, while Maggie ignored him studiously. He had to admire the way she fitted herself to her surroundings; even though Reeve was sure Maggie had never attended a social event of this magnitude, she took her cues from the other women at the table with a sublime subtlety, always using the right fork, the right gesture, the right word.

The sumptuous meal was nearly over before Maggie allowed Reeve to catch her eye, and she flushed deeply when he winked. If it wouldn't have been the pinnacle of bad manners, Reeve would have laughed out loud.

There was dancing after dinner in the enormous mirrored ballroom upstairs, and Reeve watched Maggie whirl about with Duncan as long as he could bear it. Then, when Kirk slipped away to the terrace to converse with a few of his investors, Reeve made his way to Maggie's side before any of several other men with the same idea could manage.

Without waiting for a yes or a no, Reeve swept her into the swirling stream of a waltz, delighting in the ire that flared in her eyes and the color glowing on her cheekbones.

"Your decision to follow Duncan to Melbourne must have been an impulsive one," he said, his social smile fixed in place, his voice even, "since you didn't bother to tell me about it."

Snapping pewter eyes met his gaze squarely. "I don't have to report my every move to you, Reeve McKenna," she said with dignity. Behind her the room was a tangle of jewellike colors as other women danced in their splendid dresses.

Expressively, Reeve glanced down at the swell of alabaster bosom revealed by Maggie's dress. He still wanted to tie a dinner napkin around her neck, but he wasn't above enjoying the view. "That's quite a gown," he said. "Did Duncan choose it for you?"

"I'm quite capable of selecting my own clothing, thank you very much," was the chilly reply.

Reeve maneuvered her toward the open doorway of one of the many terraces, and before she could grasp what was happening, he was pulling Maggie across the stone balcony and down the set of steps that led to the gardens.

They were moon-washed, those gardens, almost spooky in an ethereal sort of way. The shadows and strange forms made Maggie draw a little closer to Reeve instead of running away, as she would have at any other time.

"Mr. Kirk will be furious," she said lamely, gazing up at Reeve, her skin glowing like white opal in the moonlight.

Reeve gave a gruff chuckle, barely able to keep his hands to himself. God in heaven, this woman was beautiful, and the fact that she didn't seem to know it made her all the more attractive. "Duncan will be busy with his investors for at least an hour. He probably doesn't even know you're gone."

Maggie sighed and sat down carefully on a stone bench drenched with the eerie light. She might have been a sprite or a spirit, sitting there, such an unearthly beauty she was, but Reeve knew only too well that she was made of flesh and blood.

"I don't suppose you'd like to give back my emigration papers," she said hopefully.

Reeve sat down on the bench beside her, straddling it. "Did I neglect to return them?" he asked innocently. The papers were locked in his office safe in Sydney.

Maggie's temper flared again. "You know perfectly well that you took them from me at Parramatta!" she whispered furiously.

"You don't need to whisper," Reeve pointed out affably. "There's no one to hear you."

She swallowed, looking at once worried and intrigued. "No one?"

Reeve nodded. The night air was cool and fragrant with flowers, and the sounds of the governor's party drifted over the grounds. "Are you going to marry me, Maggie?"

Maggie's mouth dropped open and her eyes went wide. "Marry you?" she echoed.

"You do remember my proposal at Parramatta, don't you?"

She recovered instantly from her surprise and again looked as though she would like to slap Reeve. Or worse. "I'm not pregnant," she said stiffly.

Reeve was disappointed, though, of course, he hid that fact. Maggie was not the sort to be kept as a mistress; she would have to be taken as a wife. To his own surprise, Reeve was more than willing to do that. "That can be remedied easily enough," he heard himself say.

Maggie was staring at him. "Why would you want to marry me if you didn't have to?"

He almost laughed. Why, indeed. "Frankly, Maggie, I like the idea of being able to bed you where and when I want to."

He'd shocked her again, but before Maggie could speak, he did what he'd been longing to do ever since she'd walked into Government House earlier that evening. He reached out and caught the fingers of one hand in her bodice, giving it a slight tug.

She gasped when her breasts bounced free of the dress, swelling proudly in the moonlight, their tips tightening under Reeve's gaze. Maggie made no move to cover herself; her eyes were closed and her breathing was quick.

Enchanted beyond good sense and certainly beyond good manners, Reeve reached out and cupped her breasts in his hands, gently kneading her fullness and her warmth. She shivered against his palms, and her eyes rolled open slowly, as if from a deep and delicious sleep. "Reeve—"

He bent his head to one breast, lifting it with his hand, and drank deeply of her. She moaned and wound her fingers in his hair, pressing him close, reveling in her nurturing.

When the first spate of greed had been sated, Reeve relaxed a little, tonguing the peak of Maggie's quivering breast instead of sucking hungrily as he'd done

181

before. She made a sound that was part croon and part groan as he enjoyed her.

A sudden gust of laughter from the direction of the governor's mansion restored Reeve's good sense. He drew back from the sweet bounty that was Maggie and carefully put her bodice back in place.

"Marry me, Maggie," he said hoarsely, "before I lose my mind completely."

She was holding her chin high, though there was a touching vulnerability in her eyes. "Do you love me?" she asked.

"I don't think so," Reeve answered, wondering even as he spoke.

Maggie was trying to smooth her bodice, which looked as though it had been lowered and then raised again, and Reeve knew she was hoping to hide the expression on her face. "Well, I don't love you either," she said.

Reeve bit back a smile. "Fair enough. Lots of people marry without love, you know, and they're perfectly happy."

The gray eyes were hollow when they slid to Reeve's face. "I could never be happy with a man who didn't love me," Maggie said candidly. "Never."

Reeve wanted to draw Maggie close and hold her, but he didn't dare. Damn it, why had he never learned to lie? "Maybe, after a time, we would come to love each other."

"I'm not about to take the chance!" Maggie said spiritedly, and then she bolted off the bench and started walking back toward Government House.

Reeve considered stopping her, then decided against it. Since he couldn't honestly offer Maggie what she wanted most, he had to learn to leave her alone. He left Government House without a word to anyone, including his host and hostess. In the morning, at first light, he intended to leave for Sydney.

Chapter 13 🍃

DUNCAN KIRK'S RAGE WAS WELL HIDDEN, BUT MAGGIE could sense it beneath his suave smile and elegant manner as they danced. She tried not to look for Reeve among the dozens of other guests, but she couldn't help it.

By the end of the night Maggie's feet were aching and so was her heart. Here she'd let Reeve take all those liberties in the garden, and he didn't even love her. That was unfortunate indeed, for if there was one thing in the world Maggie was sure of, it was that she cared for him in a deep and lasting way. Perhaps, she reflected somberly, as Duncan spun her around and around Government House's spectacular ballroom, she should have accepted Reeve's proposal and worried about love later.

She shook her head as if answering a question only she could hear. No, she'd done the right thing by refusing. Marrying for any reason other than love would be a terrible mistake.

Suddenly, Duncan's fingers tightened at the side of Maggie's waist and, startled, she looked up into his eyes. They were serious and angry, even though his mouth was smiling.

"Would you mind letting me in on this little debate," he asked coldly, "or is it one-sided?"

Maggie flushed, thinking back on her disappearance earlier in the evening and all that had happened in the garden. She did hope that no one had seen and reported the sordid details to Duncan Kirk. "I was just thinking," she said somewhat defensively.

"You've been doing a lot of that since you vanished from the ballroom a little while ago," Kirk replied without missing so much as a step in the sweeping waltz they were engaged in. He looked around, and when his eyes came back to Maggie's face, they were angry. "Were you with McKenna? It's the oddest thing, but I haven't seen him since he danced with you."

Maggie resented not only Kirk's implication, true as it was, but his tone as well. Besides, she was still nettled at the pinch he'd given her in the receiving line when she'd refused to curtsy to the governor. "Mr. McKenna," she said, "has asked for my hand in marriage."

Duncan Kirk suddenly went rigid, stopping there in the middle of the ballroom, his face going crimson and then ghostly pale all in the space of a moment. "What?" he rasped.

Maggie regretted speaking so rashly, for there was something dangerous in this man's bearing and in his eyes, but she had no choice now but to carry on. She lifted her chin. "I believe you heard me," she said, and her voice was remarkably even, considering that she was quaking inside.

Without another word Duncan half propelled and half thrust her through the crowd, his grip painful on her arm. He nodded tersely at the governor and his wife, then fairly hurled Maggie into the great entryway. There were two maids there, fussing with cloaks and coats, but Maggie doubted that Duncan had even noticed them. To people like himself, such lowly creatures were all but invisible.

"What did you tell McKenna?" he demanded in a raspy whisper, and now both his hands were clasping Maggie's upper arms, hurting her.

She tried to squirm free and Duncan's grip tightened so harshly that she winced. Dear heaven, what she wouldn't have given to have Reeve appear then, but he was nowhere in sight. "Please," she said breathlessly.

Duncan loosened his grasp slightly, but instead of releasing Maggie, he gave her a fierce little shake. "Margaret," he warned her.

"I—I told him I couldn't m-marry him," Maggie faltered, tears brimming in her eyes. "Y-you see, he doesn't love me."

As if he'd somehow sensed that Maggie's tears had their root in Reeve's honest admission that he cherished no deep feelings for her instead of in the pain he was causing her with his hands, Duncan spun her about and virtually hurled her toward the door.

The two maids were watching with wide, sympathetic eyes, their color high. But Maggie knew that they couldn't help her; to Duncan, they were no more important than the pattern on the wallpaper. The door was open to the warm summer night and Maggie stumbled through it.

She would have lifted her skirts and run if Duncan hadn't retained his hold on her, dragging her toward the long line of carriages waiting at the base of the broad lawn. Within minutes Maggie was flung into one of the rigs.

"Home, sir?" she heard the driver ask of Kirk, who lingered at the doorway of the carriage, his eyes strange and colorless in the moonlight that shone directly onto his face.

"No," Duncan said crisply after what seemed to Maggie a small eternity of indecision. "The lady and I will take a ride. A long, leisurely ride."

The driver chortled in the darkness. "Yes, sir!" he said jubilantly. Fat lot of help he'd be, Maggie thought, folding her arms and trying to melt into one shadowy corner.

Duncan climbed into the vehicle and slammed the flimsy door behind him, taking the seat facing Maggie's and glaring at her. "You have sorely taxed my patience, Maggie," he said finally, when the vehicle had been under way for some time.

"Miss Chamberlin to you," Maggie said. She might have sounded saucy and flippant, but inside she was terrified. Making her own way in the world for so long had taught her that bravado was more advisable than whimpering.

Duncan reached out suddenly, clasping her wrist in one hand and wrenching her out of her seat. She bumped her head on the low roof of the carriage and landed unceremoniously on his lap.

Instantly, she began to struggle, but she could not escape those iron hands which had caught her wrists together behind her back. "I'll scream!" Maggie threatened in a breathless whisper.

"That," said Duncan flatly, "would amuse my driver very much. Why don't you do it?"

Maggie had never been so suddenly, searingly angry in all her life. Her fear was displaced by a pounding sense of outrage and, without thinking first, she spit into Kirk's face.

He went rigid and, in that awful moment, Maggie realized what a dreadful mistake she'd made. She squirmed to be free, but Duncan restrained her with only one hand, taking a handkerchief from the inside pocket of his coat with the other and slowly drying his face.

"I'm sorry," Maggie said lamely.

Duncan tucked his handkerchief back into his pocket. "I seriously doubt that, Maggie, but you will be sorry shortly. No question about it."

A shiver went through Maggie. How on earth did she manage to get herself into these situations? First she'd traveled halfway around the world to marry a man who'd only been toying with her affections. Then she'd spent not one night but two in Reeve McKenna's bed. And now she was trapped inside a darkened carriage with a brute whose sole aim in life seemed to be to make her sorry she'd ever been born.

"I'm willing to forget that this ever happened," she said reasonably, "if you'll just let me go."

She felt the hoarse laughter ripple through Duncan Kirk's powerful body before she heard it escape his throat in a grating burst that was quickly stilled. "That is very generous of you," he said.

Maggie bit her lower lip. She'd exhausted all her bravado; now she was just plain scared. Not only that, but his grip on her wrists was making them hurt. "Why are you doing this?" she asked softly.

The question seemed to reach Kirk as none of her struggling or her impudence had. He let go of Maggie, even allowed her to leap back to her own seat, where she sat shivering despite the warmth of the night.

"McKenna was right," he muttered, "passion becomes you."

The man was insane. Maggie reached subtly for the handle of the carriage door, mentally calculating her chances of escaping a moving vehicle without breaking every bone in her body. They didn't add up to a comforting figure. "P-passion?" she echoed, still groping for the little lever couched somewhere in the padded leather interior of the door.

Duncan gave a ragged sigh and Maggie saw him lift one hand to his face. The motion was almost despondent. "Never mind. Miss Chamberlin, will you forgive me?"

Not until the day I die, Maggie thought, but she wasn't fool enough to say that out loud. It seemed wiser to go along with whatever Kirk might say, then leap to freedom and make a run for it if the carriage slowed at all. She couldn't think of a single thing that would be safe to say, so she kept her peace, still fidgeting for the door handle.

Finally, she found it. Realizing that she'd been holding her breath, she let it out.

"I won't try to make excuses for my behavior," Kirk went on, "for there are none."

Maggie was only half listening; her attention was focused on the sounds of tinny piano music and raucous laughter coming from outside. Underneath, she thought she detected the gentle whoosh of an incoming tide. She was near the harbor then, and in an area where men came to drink and revel. She remembered that part of Sydney that she and the maid, Sally Crockett, had ridden through on the trolley car. If this place was like that one, she was probably safer inside the carriage.

On the other hand . . .

Suddenly, the rig came to a lurching stop and the driver began shouting at someone who had gotten in his way. Without taking another moment to consider, Maggie wrenched open the door and leapt out.

As luck would have it, the toe of her slipper caught in the hem of her gown, and she went rolling across a hard-packed dirt road instead of landing at a dead run as she'd hoped to do. Finally, when she'd stopped trundling end over end, she came, bruised and scraped and rumpled, to a stop against a pair of scuffed and muddy boots. Untangling herself from her skirts, Maggie looked not at the wearer of the boots, but back over her shoulder.

Duncan was striding toward her, and while he might have felt sorry minutes before, there was no sign of remorse in his moon-washed features now. He resembled a devil, and his plans for Maggie would be worked in hell.

Hardly daring to hope, she looked up at the man against whose boots she'd landed with such dash and flare. He was tall and he wore a slouchy leather hat and a vest, but that was about all Maggie could tell about him from her position. She did catch a glint of brass or gold at his throat, and for a moment her heart did a wild leap, but instinctively she knew that, whoever this man was, he couldn't be Reeve.

He bent and, with one work-hardened hand, hauled Maggie to her feet. She huddled against him, staring at Duncan, who reached out for her with a grasping motion that made Maggie remember how he'd hurt her inside the carriage.

"No," she whispered, and the stranger held her close to his chest.

"Let her go," Duncan ordered peremptorily. "This is a private matter!"

The stranger's arm was hard as steel, though he held Maggie gently. "Did you throw her out of that carriage, mate," he asked, "or did she jump?"

Maggie turned her head and felt a cold metal circle press against her cheek. The man's chest was hairy and warm and hard, and she clung to him mostly because of the medallion he wore. "I jumped," she whispered miserably.

Duncan's rage pounded against Maggie's being like a hot tide threatening to drown her. "Margaret," he said, "come here."

Maggie shook her head, and the hair on her rescuer's chest tickled the end of her nose.

"It doesn't look as if she wants to do that, now, does it?" the stranger asked, the words rumbling from deep inside his chest. "I'd advise you to go on about your business, mate, before I'm forced to knuckle your head."

Behind Maggie, Duncan gave a raspy, exasperated sigh and then swore. He hadn't minded manhandling her, but it was clear enough that he had his reservations about fighting the man with the medallion and the floppy hat.

"Maggie, think of the children," he said, trying to sound reasonable.

The man holding Maggie stiffened. "Children?" he asked.

Maggie knew what he was thinking, that Duncan was her husband and that they had little ones at home and that he was interfering in something very private. She grabbed hold of the leather vest with both hands and shivered, refusing to let go.

"The boys love you, Maggie," Duncan went on, pressing his advantage. "You can't desert them now."

Slowly, the stranger's hands came up to cover Maggie's and gently pry them from his vest. He was about to abandon her, she knew it, and she wailed desperately, "You don't understand! I'm not his children's mother, I'm their nanny!"

The reluctant guardian angel stepped back and Maggie could see that his face was hard and handsome, his hair slightly too long, his eyes a clear azure blue. He assessed her dress, with its abundant view of her cleavage and its glittering beads of crystal. "I've never seen a nanny who owned a dress like that," he said.

"Exactly," agreed Duncan.

The tall man's blue eyes narrowed in a leathery face. His teeth were even and white as a Massachusetts snow. "What are you meaning to do to her, mate?"

Duncan sighed a husbandly sigh. "For starters," he said, "I believe I'll blister her bustle for nearly getting herself killed like that. She tends to be dramatic, our Maggie."

"I'm not your Maggie!" the object of this idiotic conversation shrieked.

Unbelievably, the stranger chuckled. "I can see she's a spirited sort," he agreed, and he stepped away, leaving Maggie vulnerable to Duncan.

"Please!" she cried.

Duncan was too smart to be rough with her, though his fingers bit into the flesh on her elbow where he grasped her. He was smiling and speaking in soothing tones as he ushered her back toward the carriage.

In a last-ditch effort to save herself from God knew what, Maggie looked back at the stranger, her eyes fixed on the medallion he wore around his neck. She hadn't been able to get a good look at it in the darkness, but if there was the remotest chance . . .

"I know a man named Reeve McKenna who wears a brass talisman around his neck!" she called back over one shoulder as Duncan propelled her along.

Even in the darkness Maggie saw the man's body go rigid. "Wait a minute," he said in a low voice.

Duncan pretended not to hear. The carriage door was hanging open and he virtually flung Maggie through it. Before he could follow, however, the stranger came forward and spun Duncan around with one easy motion of his hand.

"I said wait," he repeated.

"I'm in love with Reeve McKenna," Maggie spouted from inside the carriage. "This man hates him for some reason, and he's bound and determined to keep us apart."

Duncan cursed roundly.

"Are you married to this man or not?" the man demanded of Maggie, his stubbly jawline tight in the dim light flowing from noisy saloons and the moon itself.

"I swear I'm not. It's—it's Reeve I want to marry." That was true enough. Maggie did want to marry Reeve McKenna, even if it was impossible.

"If you're lying to me, miss," the rescuer warned, "there'll be no need of this bloke turning you over his knee, for I'll do it myself."

Just then Duncan reached the end of his patience. He took a wild swing at the man, and then the driver, who had been content to look on until now, leapt down from the box to enter the fray. It was two against one, but the fellow wearing the medallion like Reeve's held his own easily. He sent Duncan slamming backward against the carriage and brought the driver low with one fierce thrust of his knee.

Maggie hurled herself out of the carriage and into those sturdy arms. He immediately dragged her off toward one of the saloons, pulling her up the outside stairs after him and flinging her into a room there. The damage to Duncan and his driver must have been serious, for neither of them gave chase.

But Maggie was past thought of Duncan now, wondering what new scrape she'd gotten into by throwing herself to the mercy of an utter stranger. She might have imagined the gentleness with which he'd held her, after all, as well as the chivalry he'd shown in defending her. Her heart was beating double time when he lit a lamp, and a small, seedy room dominated by a messy brass bed leapt into view.

She turned to face her unlikely champion with a nervous smile, her heart wedged into her throat, making it quite impossible for her to speak.

Her host pulled off his hat and Maggie saw that his hair was a very light brown. He made no move to come toward her.

"Tell me how you know Reeve," he demanded.

Maggie's bravado was returning, even though her hair was falling down around her shoulders and her dress was torn. Remembering how low cut it was, she raised her hands to cover her breasts, just in case. "First," she said imperiously, "you must tell me who you are."

The stranger hesitated for a very long time, so long that Maggie began to fear that he'd rescued her from Duncan just so he could ravish her himself. This little room would be the perfect place for it, and even if Maggie screamed, no one would come to her aid. "James," he said finally. "My name is James."

Remembering what Reeve had told her at Parramatta, Maggie gasped, "Jamie?"

Jamie let out a long sigh and leaned back against a grimy wall, his arms folded across his broad chest. "Aye," he said very reluctantly. "Jamie McKenna."

Maggie forgot all the danger and sank down to sit on the rumpled bed, her knees weak. "Do you know," she began in a whisper, "that your brother's been searching for you for twenty years?"

"I know." Jamie sighed. "Believe me, it hasn't always been easy to keep from being found."

Maggie thought of Elisabeth, but some instinct warned her not to mention Jamie's little girl just yet. She stared at him, baffled. "But why would you hide from your own brother? Do you hate him?"

"God, no," Jamie breathed. "I could never hate Reeve."

"Then, why—"

"I 'ave me own reasons," Jamie broke in, lapsing into that lilting brogue the way Maggie had once heard his brother do. "Now, you'll be answerin' a few questions for me, lass."

Maggie's lower lip was protruding; she folded her arms stubbornly and fidgeted a little. "I asked first," she complained.

Jamie threw back his head and shouted with laughter, and even when he'd recovered himself, his eyes were still glistening with amusement. The brogue, with Reeve a sign of stress or passion, was gone as quickly as it had come. "Where are you from, anyway?" he demanded. Before Maggie could answer, he waggled an index finger and said, "No, wait—I know. You're from the rebel colonies. By God, you're a Yank!"

Maggie jumped, startled, then sagged. She was always irritated when Reeve called her "Yank," but now she'd give anything to hear him say that word. "Will you take me to your brother?"

"Not on your life," Jamie answered immediately. "Right now my big brother is the last person on earth I want to see, with the possible exception of that heavy-handed no-gooder you were sharing a carriage with tonight. We ain't seen the last of him, I'll wager."

"It's 'haven't,'" Maggie pointed out primly, "not 'ain't.'"

Jamie looked annoyed. "You're his *boys'* nanny, miss, not mine, and I'll thank you to remember it."

Maggie could not afford to offend, not at this juncture, in any case. "I'm sorry," she said, and though she seldom resorted to artifice, she let tears pool along her eyelashes and bit her lower lip as she tucked her head.

Jamie clearly wasn't fooled, but he did come and sit down beside Maggie on the bed. She wasn't sure whether that was bad or good. "I'll see you get to Reeve, love—no worries. But I don't want you to tell him that you met up with me, understood? Reeve would be in grave danger if he found out about me now."

"But—"

The brogue was back, and a tiny muscle in Jamie's jawline leapt and then went still again. "I'll deal with Reeve in me own way and me own time, without you interferin', woman. If you do, never mind that me brother's bigger'n me, I'll paddle your sweet little rear end!"

Maggie swallowed. She believed him. "Well, let's go then," she said bravely, making to rise off the bed.

But Jamie caught her arm gently in his and tugged her back. "Not tonight," he said. "Your dapper gentleman friend 'as probably gathered 'imself an army and started lookin' up and down the street for us. I can 'andle 'im, and 'is driver, but I ain't up to a scrap with 'alf a dozen dockmen in the bargain."

The awful gravity of the situation began to dawn on Maggie. "You expect me to spend the night here, in this room, with—with you?"

Jamie was making a great production of pulling off his boots. If they were that tight, he ought to get new ones. "Aye, love, I do. Lay down."

Maggie tried to rise off the bed in a huff, only to be firmly pulled down again. "Of all the nerve—"

Jamie turned to her with laughter in his eyes. "Speakin' of nerve," he said, and Maggie thought it wasn't a good sign that he was still talking in a brogue, "you 'ave some yourself, love, leapin' out of a carriage that way, then flingin' yourself into the arms of a total stranger."

Maggie knew a hopeless situation when she saw one, and the truth was that she'd much rather take her chances with Jamie McKenna, in this seamy little room, than risk encountering Duncan outside. She squinted at the medallion that Jamie wore around his neck and saw that it was just like Reeve's.

"What is that?" she asked. Reeve had been secretive about the talisman; maybe Jamie wouldn't be.

"It's called a beggar's badge," Jamie answered, unbuttoning his shirt.

Maggie gulped and averted her eyes. "A b-beggar's badge? What on earth is that?"

Jamie's arms went up as he pulled the talisman off over his head. Unlike Reeve's, which hung on a chain of real gold, Jamie's was affixed to a string of leather. He handed it to Maggie in silence, apparently choosing to ignore her question.

She studied the writing on the coinlike piece carefully in the flickering lamplight. It said BLESSED IS HE WHO CONSIDERETH THE POOR. ST. PATRICK'S PARISH, DUBLIN.

"With that," Jamie said in a faraway voice totally devoid of the brogue, "a man could beg for his daily bread without being arrested."

"Beg?" Maggie couldn't imagine Reeve begging for anything, ever. "You were beggars?"

Jamie shook his head. "It didn't come to that. I was transported for pinching a gentleman's watch, and Reeve came out here as a cabin boy on a whaler."

"It's odd that you'd wear something like this," Maggie observed, frowning. "But I've never seen Reeve without his."

Jamie sighed. "He's a rich man now, Reeve is. I imagine the beggar's badge reminds him of leaner days and makes him thankful for all he's got. Now, lie down and get some sleep, Maggie-girl. I promise I won't lay a hand on you."

Maggie would never have believed that had it come from Reeve, but from Jamie it had a ring of truth. She wriggled over close to the wall and lay down with her shoes still on and her dress, torn and dirty now, twinkling in the lamplight. "Very well. I just hope you're a man of your word."

Jamie chuckled and stretched out on the bed beside Maggie with a sigh, leaving the lamp to burn.

A dreadful thought struck Maggie, and she bolted upright. "What were you transported for again?" she demanded.

"Picking a gentleman's pocket, love."

Maggie lay back down. "Oh. Did you pick a great many pockets, Jamie McKenna?"

He smiled and cupped his hands behind his head. "As many as I could get my fingers into, miss. But never you fear, I've reformed now. I've got sheep and a property of my own."

"Where?"

Jamie got up from the squeaky, lumpy bed to put out the lamp, and in the moments before he reached it, Maggie saw the long scars that crisscrossed his back. At some point Jamie McKenna had been savagely whipped. "You don't really think I'm going to tell you that, do you, and have you running to my brother with the news?"

Maggie sighed. "He loves you," she said into the darkness.

She felt Jamie's weight on the mattress beside her. "Aye," he said in a tone that indicated no emotion at all, and before Maggie could formulate another question, he was snoring.

Chapter 14 ❧

THERE WAS A SPLINTERY CRASH.

Maggie, sound asleep only a moment before, bolted upright on the bed she'd shared with Jamie McKenna. She felt him roll off the mattress, but it was the darkest hour of the night and she could see nothing save the outline of several hulking men filling the open doorway.

Too frightened to scream, Maggie simply tugged at her bodice to make sure it hadn't slipped while she was sleeping, and peered into the darkness.

Suddenly, she heard the sound of a match striking, and then the lamp Jamie had extinguished earlier was relit and she could see all too clearly.

Jamie was crouched on the floor beside the bed, a huge, savage-looking knife glinting in one hand. Duncan stood beside the lamp, and there were four enormous men with him, crowding the doorway, leering at Maggie and smiling toothless smiles.

"Take the girl outside," Duncan ordered.

Jamie rose slowly to his feet, the lethal knife still clutched in his right hand. "I wouldn't advise you to try it, mates," he said in a low voice that rumbled like lava forcing its way upward through solid rock.

One of Duncan's hooligans drew a gun from the inside pocket of his ragged coat and brandished it. "That blade ain't much use against one of these, now, is it?"

Maggie was inching toward the foot of the bed. She was ready to plead with Jamie. "Don't. They'll kill you!"

"Maggie!" Jamie warned, but she was out of his reach, awkwardly climbing over the brass bedstead to stand upright on the floor.

One of the thugs immediately grasped her already-bruised arm in a filthy hand, and she flinched. That tiny motion distracted Duncan from Jamie for the first time since the lantern had been lit.

"Take your hands off her," he said in a lethal tone, and the foul-smelling man let go of Maggie with a scowl. Duncan reached out and caught her around the waist with one arm, slamming her against his side.

"Leave this room with the woman, mate," Jamie warned Duncan in a calm voice, waggling the knife slightly, "and you'll go out wearin' this."

Maggie's heart stopped beating and then started again. "Duncan," she pleaded, knowing that Jamie meant what he said.

Duncan favored her with an icy smile that sent chills skittering up and down her back. "So at last you use my given name." He sighed. "Too late, alas—you've definitely fallen from grace."

In the next second Maggie was flung toward the door. She was still trying to recover her balance on the landing outside when she heard the hissing sound of a knife slicing through the air, followed by a sickening thud as it punctured flesh.

Duncan cried out, but then he staggered through the doorway and grasped Maggie by the hair with one hand. The knife was protruding from his left shoulder, his shirt was wet with blood, and Maggie felt bile rush into the back of her throat as her captor forced her down the outside stairway.

"What do we do about the sheepherder?" one of the scoundrels called after them.

In the first glimmer of dawn Maggie could see that Duncan was white with pain, but still he propelled her toward his carriage and thrust her inside. "Whatever you like," he groaned in response. "The bastard's all yours."

Maggie, flung onto the dirty floor of the rig, felt sick. Reeve had spent all those years looking for his brother, and now Jamie was about to die because of her. She screamed as Duncan lurched, half conscious, into the carriage and slammed the door. He backhanded her so hard that she tasted blood on her lip, and then moaned, swaying on the seat.

The carriage was rolling, and in the distance Maggie heard the sound of shattering glass. She prayed that Jamie had gotten away.

"Help me," Duncan mumbled, "please—"

Blood soaked the carriage seat, Duncan's clothes, and Maggie's as well. She groped her way onto the seat and saw that the knife had gone into his shoulder, almost to the hilt. She held down another surge of sickness and reached for the stained handle. Only then did she notice that she was clutching Jamie's medallion, still on its rawhide string, in her hand. Hastily, she dropped it into her bodice. "I'm not sure I'm s-strong enough," she managed to say.

Duncan's flesh had turned a pallid gray. "In the name of God, Maggie, try," he pleaded, and then he fell forward, kneeling on the carriage floor, his upper body sprawled across the opposite seat.

Trapped beneath him, Maggie had to squirm free. "We need a doctor!" she screamed out the window to the driver.

"No," Duncan rasped, "no doctors—oh, God, Margaret, *please help me—*"

As far as Maggie was concerned, this man was a murderer, among other things, but she could not ignore his pleas for help. Kneeling beside him, muttering a fervent and insensible prayer, she grasped the handle of Jamie's knife in both hands and pulled as hard as she could.

Duncan screamed as the dagger sawed its way back out of his shoulder, and then he slumped over, unconscious. It would have been the perfect time to escape, except that he'd fallen on Maggie, effectively pinning her to the floor between the carriage seats. Wriggle and fight though she did, she wasn't able to get out from under Duncan's weight, and she was freed only when the carriage came to a halt at the rear of the Kirk house, in the alleyway. The driver hauled Duncan out, supporting him by drawing one of his lifeless arms around his own shoulders.

Maggie's first instinct was to run, but she realized she couldn't do that as Bridget O'Malley, red hair flying free, came bounding down the path from the rear door of the house to help bring Duncan inside. Where could Maggie flee in a torn and rumpled dress splattered with blood? Besides, her things were still in her room. She might have left most of them behind, but she couldn't go without the little photograph of her parents; it was all she had left of them.

Bridget, wearing only a nightgown and wrapper, shot Maggie a killing look as she fell into step beside her and the carriage driver, who were supporting a moaning, delirious Duncan between them.

"What in the name of God happened?"

No one answered Bridget's question; instead, Maggie offered one of her own. "Where are the boys?" she demanded calmly. It would never do for them to see such a bloody spectacle as this, she thought grimly.

"Still sleeping," Bridget said tersely as they entered the kitchen. "Let's put him in my room," she told the driver.

201

Maggie bounded up the stairs while they were about the task of getting Duncan into bed. Moving more quickly than she ever had in her life, Maggie pulled the beggar's badge from its hiding place in her bodice and stripped off the once-beautiful dress that she'd worn to Government House. She poured water into a basin from the china pitcher on her dressing table. Frantically, she washed every trace of Duncan's blood from her body, and when that was done, she put on her own ugly gray woolen dress and snatched her reticule from the floor of the armoire. Into the valise went the medallion Jamie had worn.

The tentative rap at Maggie's bedroom door made her stiffen and bite her lower lip. If she didn't call out, perhaps whoever was there would go away.

Instead, the door squeaked open. Jeremy was standing there in his nightshirt, his green eyes wide. "I saw them bringing Papa in, miss," he said without preamble, "and you, with your dress all bloody—"

Maggie went to the child, put her hands on his shoulders. They quivered, warm and slight, beneath her palms. "There was an accident," she lied gently. The story she'd tell the police, of course, would be quite different.

Jeremy slipped out from under her hands and approached the discarded gown, still lying in a garish blue and crimson heap on the floor. "Did you get hurt in the accident too?"

Maggie sighed and sat down on the edge of her fancy bed, folding her hands in her lap in an effort to still their trembling, and Jeremy sat beside her. "No," she answered. "I wasn't hurt."

The moment the words were out of her mouth, Maggie was conscious of the bruises and scratches that covered her body, but of course she said nothing about those injuries. They were minor, and any mention of them would only confuse Jeremy.

The boy glanced at the reticule sitting on a table, its top open. "You're leaving?" he asked in a small voice.

Maggie was searching for a way to explain, when her bedroom door sprang open again, this time without a knock to forewarn her. Bridget was standing in the doorway, hugging herself, her wild auburn hair still tumbling loose around her waist. Her wrapper was bloody and her eyes were shooting fire. "Duncan is calling for you," she said to Maggie in tight, razor-sharp tones.

Maggie was about to say that she wouldn't go to Duncan no matter how loudly he called when she felt Jeremy's gaze and turned her head to search his face. If she refused to go to his father now, he would never understand.

With a sigh she stood up. "All right," she said, and she followed Bridget along the hallway and down the rear stairs into the kitchen. Bridget O'Malley's room was just beyond.

Duncan lay in the middle of a broad bed, his shoulder neatly bandaged, pillows propped behind his back. The blood had been washed away, probably by Bridget, and his hair had been combed. On the bedside stand was an open bottle of laudanum, which explained the glassy expression in Duncan's eyes and the idiotic smile on his lips.

"Leave us alone, Bridget," he said, and his words were only slightly slurred.

Bridget glared at Maggie for a moment, then stomped out of the room, slamming the door eloquently behind her. Duncan flinched slightly, and his grin broadened.

Now that Kirk appeared to be past the worst, Maggie hadn't a shred of sympathy for him. All her compassion was for Jamie, possibly lying dead on the floor of an ugly little room over a dockside saloon. The moment she left this house, she would go to the police and to Reeve, in that order. Stubbornly, she kept silent.

"My driver tells me that your friend got away," Duncan said. "Pity."

Maggie was so relieved, her knees wavered beneath her. She clasped the footrail of the bed to keep from sinking to the floor. "That is good news," she said coldly.

Duncan was still pale as death, and his chuckle sounded hoarse. "I wonder if it will be good news to Reeve—that you spent the night with a strange man."

The words struck Maggie with the impact of a blow, and she felt the color drain from her face. Within the space of an instant, however, she had drawn herself to her full height and jutted out her chin. "Reeve will understand, once I explain."

"So you're going to him?"

"I don't see any other option."

"There is a choice, Margaret. You can stay here and we can pretend that none of this ever happened."

Maggie's grip on the bed rail tightened until her hands ached. "That's madness," she breathed. "I won't spend another night under this roof."

"I think you will."

Maggie felt a quiver of fear in the pit of her stomach. "What are you trying to say?"

Duncan gave a dramatic sigh. "I would truly hate to have you arrested for stabbing me in the back, Maggie, but I'll do it if I have to."

"You know that's a lie!"

"Yes, I know it, and you know it. But my witnesses will testify as I instruct them. Prisons are unpleasant places, Maggie—especially for women. But they might put you in an asylum, of course, assuming that only an insane woman would have the strength, let alone the desire, to plunge a knife into the back of a man twice her size."

"I have a witness too," Maggie reminded him, but some instinct kept her from revealing Jamie's name. "You said yourself that he survived."

Duncan nodded, and his eyes burned into Maggie's face like green fire. "He did. But will you be able to find him? My guess is that your sheepherder is long gone by now."

Maggie thought of Jamie's determination to avoid Reeve and the promise he had extracted from her that she never mention his presence in Melbourne to his brother. Duncan was probably right, though she would have done almost anything rather than admit that. "I won't stay here," she said. "No matter what you threaten me with. I can tell Reeve all that's happened and he'll take my side."

"Are you so very sure of that?" Duncan asked, tiring now. He sagged back against his pillows and his eyes were hooded and strangely blank.

Maggie wasn't sure of anything except that she had to find Reeve and accept his proposal before he changed his mind. She would work on getting him to love her later. "I'm sure," she lied.

Duncan yawned. "Why act hastily, Maggie? I'm quite harmless in this condition, aren't I?"

That much was true. Maggie hesitated because she didn't want to leave the boys so suddenly, nor did she have any desire to go crawling to Reeve, entreating him to take her in. It would be better if she had time to wangle a second proposal. "I suppose you are, but—"

Just then Bridget rushed into the room, her face flushed, her gaze slicing Maggie to the bone before fixing itself on Duncan. "Reeve McKenna is here, Duncan," she said breathlessly, "and he's spitting nails. I tried to get him to leave, but—"

Duncan spread one hand in a generous motion and yawned. "By all means, send him in."

Bridget didn't need to go in search of Duncan's unexpected caller, for Reeve suddenly appeared in the doorway of the room. He glowered at Maggie and then at his wounded host. "I've got a message here that says you might be about to hurt the lady," he announced. His sea-green eyes took in Duncan's bandaged shoulder and went dark with an expression of puzzlement.

"Who would send such a message?" Duncan asked sleepily. "Obviously, the situation is quite the reverse."

Reeve took a folded paper from his pocket and tossed it onto the bed. The look he gave Maggie was not encouraging.

Laboriously, Duncan unfolded the message and frowned as he read it. "Hmmm. No signature." His green eyes moved to Maggie's face, filled with sleepy malice. "Must be from that sheepherder I found you in bed with," he said. And while Maggie flushed, he shook his head regretfully. "Nasty business, that."

Reeve's towering frame was rigid, and he didn't look at Maggie again. "What happened to you?" he asked in a tone totally void of compassion.

"Maggie stabbed me," Duncan said, smiling at her fondly.

Reeve glanced back at her over his shoulder. "She must have had reason," he said.

Maggie opened her mouth to protest her innocence where both the "sheepherder" and Duncan's stab wound were concerned, but Reeve interrupted before she could speak.

"Get your things," he ordered in a voice that brooked no argument. "You're leaving right now."

Maggie tossed Duncan a quietly triumphant look and left the room in a rush of gray wool. By the time she'd said tearful good-byes to both Jeremy and Tad and brought her reticule downstairs, Reeve was waiting.

His jawline tight, his eyes hard and oddly evasive of Maggie's face, he took her arm and ushered her outside, down the front walk, and into his own carriage.

"What's this about a sheepherder?" he demanded as the vehicle rolled away.

Maggie would have given anything to be able to tell Reeve about Jamie, but she couldn't: She'd given her word. Too, Jamie had implied that there might be tragic consequences if the secret was revealed. "He was just a nice man who tried to help me."

"Did you or did you not spend the night with him?"

Maggie was insulted. After all she'd been through, Reeve should have been offering her comfort and understanding. Instead, he was questioning her morals. "I did. I slept in the same bed with him, in fact," she answered coldly.

Reeve swore and Maggie saw his neck go red by stages. She realized that she couldn't afford to antagonize this man under present circumstances, and she relented.

"Reeve, there has never been any other man besides you," she said.

Reeve gave a long sigh. To Maggie's relief, he believed her. "Did you really stab Duncan?"

"No. The man I was with did that." Slowly, very carefully, Maggie explained how she and Jamie had met without mentioning his name or the beggar's badge he'd worn around his neck. She told Reeve everything else, however, and by the time the story was out, he wanted to go back to Duncan's house and tear his good arm out of its socket.

"We'll be married as soon as we get back to Sydney," he said when Maggie had talked him out of making the carriage turn around in the middle of the street.

Maggie felt hope leap in her tired heart. "Have you changed your mind, then, about—about loving me?" she dared to ask.

"No," Reeve said distractedly, clearly thinking of other things. "But that shouldn't matter—"

"It does matter!" Maggie spat out on the verge of tears. She drew herself into the corner of the carriage seat and huddled there, furious and weary and completely confused.

"Maggie." Reeve spoke her name gently and cupped one hand beneath her chin.

She promptly slapped it away. "Don't you touch me, Reeve McKenna."

Reeve sighed. "If you're not going to be my wife, Yank," he asked softly, "what are you going to do?"

"I certainly won't be your wife," Maggie huffed, "and I won't be your mistress either!"

"Then how will you justify living under my roof?" Reeve asked, smiling a little and arching one eyebrow. "You've got no place else to go, you know."

That was true enough. She probably wouldn't be able to get any sort of job, either, for Duncan would never sign her certificate now. Maggie gnawed at her lower lip for a few moments, and then inspiration struck. "I'll be Elisabeth's nanny!" she cried. "I'll get her to talk!"

"Elisabeth already has a nanny," Reeve pointed out reasonably, and though his lips were still, his eyes were laughing at Maggie. "But I guess you could have that part I offered you—Kate in *The Taming of the Shrew.*" He paused as Maggie's eyes lit up, then went on. "Of course, everyone will say that you're a kept woman."

Maggie was beyond caring what people said—for the moment at least. "Or you could give me back my papers," she suggested lamely. Actually, she wanted the part in the play and she wanted the shelter of Reeve's house as well, though it would have been scandalous, of course, to say so.

"Absolutely not," Reeve said with good-natured firmness. "I paid a lot of money for your freedom, Maggie, and I want something back on my investment."

Maggie's eyes widened. "Not—"

Reeve laughed. "Not that. If you come to my bed, it has to be because you want to be there. I wouldn't make love to you under any other circumstances, ever."

The stipulation didn't amount to much of a barrier between propriety and the passion Maggie felt for this man. She wanted him, even now, with her pride in tatters and her skin bruised and scratched from a tumble out of Duncan Kirk's carriage. But she could work through all that later; for now she was just glad to be safely away from that house and its half-mad owner.

Reeve and Maggie left for Sydney by train late that night. Reeve had engaged two separate sleeping rooms, and Maggie was grateful, though a part of her would have preferred to share one.

Alone in her tiny compartment, the windows covered for the night, Maggie took off her dress. Her arms were badly bruised where Duncan had grabbed them, and her knees and elbows were both scraped. The pain had not bothered her much before, but now that she had a chance to think about all she'd been through, she was very uncomfortable.

Maggie heard the compartment door close behind her before she realized that it had been opened, and whirled, wearing only her camisole and drawers, to face Reeve. He was looking at the bruises on her arms.

"I'll kill that bastard," he said under his breath.

Maggie relaxed a little, at least outwardly. Familiar emotions and needs and yearnings were churning within her. "You'd better go," she said, wishing that he wouldn't.

Reeve's eyes dropped to her knees, scabbed and sore beneath the ruffled bottoms of her drawers. "My God."

"Reeve, I'm all right," Maggie insisted softly.

"I'll get some disinfectant or something," he said, and then he left the compartment. Maggie could have latched the door, but for a reason she wouldn't have wanted to explain she failed to do so. She was sitting on her berth when Reeve came back carrying a brown medicine bottle and a clean white cloth.

209

"Take off your clothes," he said clinically. "I want to see how badly you were hurt."

Maggie's mind was screaming a warning, but her hands went to the laces of her camisole and untied them. Her brain might have wanted propriety, but her body yearned for comforting. She took off her drawers, once she'd tossed away her camisole, and lay down on the berth.

Reeve knelt beside her and, his brow creased with concern, dabbed at all her injuries with the cloth and the medicine. "My God," he breathed once as Maggie flinched at the sting, "you look like you've been dragged behind a runaway horse."

Maggie hadn't felt particularly sorry for herself before Reeve began fussing over her, but now her eyes filled with tears and every scrape seemed to be a gaping wound, every bruise a fracture.

"Roll over onto your stomach," Reeve said, not appearing to notice her tears or her bare breasts reaching toward him so openly and so eagerly.

Obediently, Maggie rolled over, expecting more gentle attention. Instead, she got a smacking swat on her naked bottom and a jovial, "No damage here!"

She turned over again, more vulnerable than she'd ever been. "Stay with me," she whispered.

Reeve shook his head and got to his feet. "Not tonight, Yank—you've been through enough as it is. Time you got some rest." With that he opened Maggie's reticule and pulled out the first nightgown he found. "Here," he said, tossing it, as something made of metal clattered to the floor. "Put this on."

Maggie sat frozen on the berth, clutching the nightgown in front of her and watching helplessly as Reeve stooped to pick up what had fallen to the floor: a beggar's badge identical to his own.

The expression on his face was horrible when he

looked up from the medallion lying, still splattered with Duncan's blood, in his palm. His aquamarine eyes scored Maggie, and a white line of fury edged his jaw.

"Jamie," he breathed. "Your sheepherder—was he Jamie?"

Maggie shifted so that she was kneeling on the narrow berth, her nightgown still in her hands. Her heart was hammering against her rib cage and her breath burned its way in and out of her lungs. Slowly, she nodded her head.

"And you weren't going to tell me?" The low words were not spoken so much as flung at Maggie, like a hissing snake.

Maggie felt tears of frustration bloom in her eyes. Her scrapes and scratches were forgotten. "He made me promise—"

Suddenly, Reeve strode toward Maggie and grasped her chin hard in his hand. "He did what?"

A tear streaked down Maggie's cheek. "He made me promise that I wouldn't tell you that I'd seen him."

Reeve held up the bloody beggar's badge. "Did he give you this, Maggie? Or did you take it off his body after Kirk was through with him?"

He saw her as an accomplice to Duncan, and that wounded Maggie more deeply than anything he could have said or done. "You don't understand," she whispered, trying to shake free of Reeve's grasp on her chin and failing miserably. "Jamie isn't dead—that blood is Duncan's, not his—"

There was a flicker of relief in the aquamarine eyes, but no compassion and no forgiveness. "You would have gone to your grave without telling me that you'd seen my brother," he marveled, "when you knew how hard and how long I've looked for him!"

Maggie had no defense. What could she say beyond telling Reeve that Jamie had made her promise to keep their encounter a secret? "H-he said you would be in d-danger if you knew—"

Reeve set Maggie free with a force that terrified her. Then, after giving her one scalding look of utter contempt, he left the compartment, the door crashing shut behind him.

Chapter 15 🌿

Maggie had half expected to be left to her own devices at Sydney Station, so cold had Reeve's manner been since his accidental discovery of Jamie's medallion the night before in that tiny train compartment. Instead, she was shuffled into a carriage and whisked off to his town house overlooking Rushcutter's Bay.

In the entryway of that grand house, Reeve spoke to Maggie for the very first time since he'd stormed out of her compartment. "The housekeeper will see that you're properly settled," he said, his eyes avoiding hers, his voice tense. "Report to the Victoria Theatre tomorrow morning and Philip Briggs will tell you what to do."

Maggie sucked in her breath. "I—I have to work with Philip? But I thought you'd given him the sack—"

Now the aquamarine gaze was fixed on Maggie, seeming to pin her to the elegantly papered wall. "Hired him back," was the succinct answer. "As for working with Briggs: beggars, as they say, cannot be choosers, Miss Chamberlin."

It hurt terribly to be spoken to in such a way, as intimate as Maggie had been with Reeve. But she had pride, if nothing else, and she returned his glare with one of her own. "Very well, Mr. McKenna," she said icily, turning to start up the broad stairway, her pitiful reticule in hand.

Reeve stopped her by grasping her elbow. She flinched, the skin was so tender there, and he loosened his hold slightly, though he did not release her. "The servants' quarters are reached by the rear stairway," he said.

The servants' quarters. Maggie felt as though she'd been slapped, and the high color of humiliation throbbed in her cheeks. Things certainly had a way of turning about, she thought to herself. Not more than forty-eight hours before, Reeve had asked her to be mistress of this house. Now she was being relegated to the servants' quarters, doubtlessly a cramped, unventilated place on the uppermost floor. "Of course," she replied airily, determined not to cry. There would be plenty of time for that later.

She made to move past Reeve, but he was still holding on to her arm. "I know you must have had finer accommodations at Duncan's," he told her in an angry whisper.

Inside, Maggie was seething, though she kept her outward appearance cool. "What are you implying?" she asked loftily.

"I'm implying nothing," Reeve replied, thrusting her elbow free of his hand in one savage motion. "I'll be at sea for a while," he said. "If you need anything, ask Philip."

Unconsciously, Maggie was rubbing her sore elbow. She was very near tears, though she prayed she could hold them off just long enough to get out of this man's sight. "I shall," she promised with a lift of her chin.

This time Reeve let her pass. She got as far as the kitchen before she cried.

* * *

Maggie's room in the attic was hot and small, with ceilings that followed the slant of the roof. There was one tiny window, which overlooked the rear garden, but it was sealed shut.

The floor was bare, splintery wood, and there was no armoire here—only a series of pegs hanging on the back of the door. Maggie hadn't the spirit to unpack her reticule, instead, she collapsed on the narrow cot tucked under the harsh line of the roof and buried her face in the coverless pillow.

Past weeping now—she had never been able to sustain a crying jag for more than a few tumultuous minutes—Maggie simply lay still, wishing that she'd never left England for this godforsaken place where beautiful birds had no song to sing and lush flowers no fragrance. She had been lost in her singular misery for some minutes when she heard the door of the garret open with a squeak.

Maggie stiffened, afraid to look. But the hope was there in her heart, the hope that Reeve had relented and decided to forgive her. It was dashed when she felt a tiny hand come to rest on her back.

Slowly, Maggie rolled over. Elisabeth was standing beside the cot, her lovely little face full of concern. Her dark hair glistened in the dusty attic light, and her blue-green eyes were wide.

Smiling despite everything that had happened to her in the past few days, Maggie took the child's hand. "Hello, Elisabeth," she said.

Elisabeth smiled and nodded. Though she seemed shy as a doe, she made no effort to pull free of Maggie's hand.

"I was hoping that you and I could talk together," Maggie ventured. Her throat felt raw, her eyes puffy and swollen.

The little girl shook her head.

"You do know how to talk, though, don't you, Elisabeth? You're just pretending that you can't."

With no sign of rancor Elisabeth drew her hand

from Maggie's and retreated a step. She looked as
though she might actually speak, and Maggie was
waiting, holding her breath, when a gray-haired
woman in a navy-blue bombazine dress suddenly
filled the open doorway.

"There you are, you little scamp!" the woman cried
good-naturedly, and the moment was spoiled.
Elisabeth gave Maggie a long, searching look and then
turned to face her nanny.

The governess smiled at Maggie. "Hello, there,
miss," she said in an accent that might have been
American or Canadian. "I'm Miss Cora Fielding.
Who are you?"

Maggie rose to her feet, smoothing her skirts, very
conscious of her mussed-up hair. "Maggie
Chamberlin," she said. "Pleased to meet you."

"Merciful heavens," Cora breathed, putting one
hand to her sizable breast. "We hail from the same
part of the world, you and I."

Maggie nodded, just as pleased as Cora to find
someone from home.

Cora was flushed, and her bright blue eyes shone
with delight. "I was born and raised in Chicago,
myself. What about you?"

"I've lived all over," Maggie said, a little self-
conscious about her early life. "My family traveled
with a—with a circus."

At this Elisabeth's eyes widened. Maggie knew that
it was all the child could do to keep from asking about
the animals, the performers, the big tents. She saw the
little girl bite down on her lower lip.

"A circus!" Cora crowed, giving Elisabeth a gentle
nudge. "Did you hear that, Miss McKenna?"

Elisabeth turned and scampered out, and Cora, of
course, was obliged to follow. She did linger in the
doorway for moment, though, her fleshy hand gripping the knob, her expression sad.

"Poor little mite," she observed distractedly.

216

"What do you suppose could have happened to her that she'd freeze up her tongue like that?"

Maggie didn't have an answer, of course, but it seemed that none was expected of her anyway. She opened her reticule and began unpacking, and Cora closed the door softly and went after her charge.

It took very little time to hang up her spare dress and tuck her nightgowns into the trunk at the foot of her cot—Maggie had brought along none of the things Mr. Kirk had bought for her, of course—so when the task was done, she got out her much-read copy of *The Taming of the Shrew* and quietly let herself out of the stifling attic. Three steps led down to the rooms where the servants stayed, and then there was another stairway, long and steep, that brought her to the kitchen.

The room was empty, and Maggie was hungry. After a quick look around she helped herself to a biscuit and jam and slipped out the rear door into the garden. Arranging her skirts carefully around her, she sat on the ground beneath an acacia tree in full leaf and opened the book to read.

She studied the dialogue carefully, even though she knew the entire play almost by heart, and then nodded off into a fitful sleep. She hadn't rested well the night before, of course, or the night before that, and she was exhausted.

A tickling sensation along Maggie's cheekbone awakened her. She focused on the frame of a man, crouching in front of her in the grass, and again knew the hope that Reeve had forgiven her.

It was a fleeting fancy, for the man who had tickled her with a blade of grass was much smaller than Reeve, and of fair coloring. Maggie came wide-awake with a wrench. "Philip!"

Her erstwhile suitor smiled at her. "Hello, Magpie," he said softly.

Flushed, Maggie fussed a moment with her skirts

217

and her tumbledown hair. "What are you doing here?" she asked.

Philip chuckled at her uneasiness, as if to reassure her. "We're going to be working together. Given that, I decided that it would be a good idea to make amends for what I did. Or didn't do."

Maggie composed herself while she watched Philip consider the question, and when it appeared he'd decided, she said, "I'm glad we didn't marry, Philip. We both would have been unhappy."

Philip nodded, and the expression in his amber eyes was gentle. "You're in love with Reeve McKenna, unless I miss my guess. But things aren't going too well, are they, Mag-pie?"

Dropping her eyes and biting down on her lower lip, Maggie shook her head. "Not well at all," she confirmed in a whisper.

Philip curved an index finger under her chin and lifted it. "I'd box his ears for you if I dared," he said. "Since I don't, I'll set myself to making things as easy for you in the production as I can."

The play was the one thing Maggie had left of this debacle that had overtaken her almost the minute she'd stepped off the ship from England, and she brightened at the thought of it. Perhaps if she threw herself into the role of Kate, if she allowed it to consume her, she would forget Reeve McKenna. Why, by the time he came back from his sea voyage, she might have progressed to disdaining him. She might even be the toast of Sydney, with men twice as handsome and twice as rich seeking her hand.

She sagged. It didn't really matter how handsome or well-to-do those other men might be: None of them would be Reeve. "When will we start work, Philip?" she asked, her voice small and uncertain.

"Tomorrow," Philip answered, rising from his crouching position to his full height. "I'll send a carriage 'round for you at half past nine, so be ready."

"I will," Maggie promised, entangling her feet in

her skirts and nearly falling when she tried to stand. If Philip hadn't been quick to catch her arm, she would have tumbled into the grass.

Surprisingly, Philip bent his head to give Maggie a soft, tentative kiss. "Be very careful, little one," he warned. "There are sharks in the waters you're sailing, and they have big teeth."

With that cryptic remark Philip turned and walked away, taking the stone walkway that led around the side of the house. Maggie closed her book and sighed. She hated it when people made ambiguous statements like that and then just walked away.

She started back toward the house, only to have the idea of visiting Tansy dawn upon her. Tucking her book into the pocket of her dress, Maggie decided to try to find her friend. She would telephone Lady Cosgrove for the address.

In the kitchen she found Cora sitting with a cup of tea, her shoes off, her face pallid.

Pleased to see her new friend, Maggie smiled. "Hello, Cora."

Cora gave a cordial nod and smiled wearily. "I may be too old to look after a four-year-old," she confided out of the blue. "Maybe I should have stayed in Chicago."

Still set on finding and using a telephone, Maggie was somewhat inattentive. "Have you been in Australia long?"

"Only a few months," Cora replied, taking a delicate sip of her tea. Her expression was serious again. "Meant to marry Henry Carver, a missionary. But he passed on, poor dear, while I was still at sea."

Maggie's mind had stopped its wandering. "Oh, Cora, that's terrible—I'm so sorry. Do you ever think of going back?"

"Hardly anything but that," Cora confided. "If I can keep this job for six more months or so, I'll have my passage saved."

Maggie remembered a time when Reeve had offered

Cora's position to her and deduced that the governess couldn't have been in residence long. "Are you making any progress with Elisabeth?"

Cora shook her head. "No, but then, I've been in this household for only a fortnight. She's a strange child, Elisabeth. She's intelligent—I suspect she can read, at least a few words. When I brought out my alphabet cards, with an apple for A and such, she looked at me as though I were a fool. But she mouthed the letters, even if she wouldn't say them aloud."

"She must have suffered some kind of trauma, though I can't imagine what it would have been," Maggie said thoughtfully.

"It certainly wouldn't have anything to do with Mr. McKenna," Cora replied. "The man's the soul of kindness with that child."

Maggie felt cold and lonely all of a sudden, and she wrapped her arms around herself and answered, "There was a woman here—Loretta Craig was her name—and it occurs to me that she might have upset Elisabeth somehow."

"Miss Craig," Cora reflected. "I've heard the maids talk about her. Maybe they know something that would help me reach Elisabeth."

The distant jangling of a telephone reminded Maggie that she'd planned to contact Lady Cosgrove and ask for Tansy's address. After excusing herself politely, she hurried off to follow the sound.

The chase led to an enormous room boasting a billiard table, a cluttered desk, hundreds of books, several settees, and a number of leather chairs. She stopped cold in the doorway as Reeve snatched the receiver from its hook and growled, "Yes!"

Maggie watched as his brawny back went rigid. "I want no excuses, Wilkins," he said after a few more moments had passed. "If you have to turn every pub in Melbourne on end, you do it. I want my brother found."

The man on the other end of the wire was talking so

loudly that Maggie could hear him, though she couldn't make out the words. Reeve grew more and more annoyed as he listened, then boomed, "Damn it all to hell, I don't care what it costs! And I expect to find a report waiting when I come back!"

The receiver crashed into its hook beside the telephone and Maggie turned to flee, only to be stopped by a clipped, "Not another step, Yank."

She was frozen by the glacial words, but she didn't have to speak. She lifted her chin and remained stubbornly silent.

Reeve had to come around and face her, and he did, his eyes snapping, his hands on his hips. "Did you want something? A different room, perhaps?"

Maggie raised her chin another notch. "My room is fine," she said. Reeve McKenna would roast in hell before he got a word of complaint out of her. "I merely wanted to use the telephone."

Reeve gestured toward the apparatus with a sweeping move of his arm. "Help yourself, Miss Chamberlin. Never let it be said that I am an unreasonable master."

"You are not my master," Maggie pointed out in a chill fury as she rounded Reeve and swept into the huge, masculine room, passing the billiard table to stand facing the telephone. She had never used one before, and she felt stupid and awkward for hesitating now. She whirled, her hands on her hips, and started because Reeve had been right on her heels. He was standing so close, in fact, that she could see the tiny specks of silver in his aquamarine eyes. "I'm an actress, not a servant, and I'll thank you to remember it."

"I own you," Reeve immediately retorted, "lock, stock, and barrel, you saucy little wench, and I could just as well make you a scullery maid or a mistress, if that's what I wanted to do!"

There was a limit to what one person could endure, Maggie reflected to herself, deliberately keeping her face impassive as she drew back her foot and planted it firmly in the middle of Reeve McKenna's shin.

A stunned expression crossed his face and then, an instant later, he howled with pain and reached for the injured portion of his anatomy.

Maggie turned and walked imperiously over to the telephone, taking up the receiver and putting it to her ear. After that she had no idea what to do.

Reeve reached past her shoulder to turn a little handle affixed to the side of the hulking machine, which in turn was attached to the wall.

"Central!" said a nasal voice over the wire, and Maggie jumped, her eyes rounding.

Reeve, standing entirely too close, smiled down at her in a way that could be described only as impudent. Clearly, he intended to eavesdrop on the conversation, should Maggie manage to have one.

"Central," repeated the disembodied voice, sounding impatient now.

"I would like to speak with Lady Cosgrove, at the Girls' Friendly Society, please."

Reeve arched an eyebrow at this, and the set of his mouth had softened slightly, Maggie noticed. A series of clicks and whirrings met her ear as the call was put through.

Lady Cosgrove came on the line only after Maggie had spoken to her assistant first, and she was chagrined at interrupting an apparently busy day. She stated her name and was about to ask after Tansy when Lady Cosgrove suddenly cut her off with, "Oh, yes—Margaret Chamberlin. Mr. Kirk has sent word that you abandoned his household—at a very inconvenient juncture—to become an actress."

The chill in the woman's voice was withering. Maggie was very careful not to meet Reeve's eyes. She tried to explain. "Lady Cosgrove, there were extenuating circumstances," she began, only to hear a loud crash at the other end of the line.

It was too much. Maggie hung up the receiver and turned away, chin high, meaning to escape. She had to succeed as an actress now, for there was no hope of ever earning a certificate.

"Maggie?" Reeve's voice stopped her, unexpectedly gentle. "What is it?"

Maggie looked back at him, her eyes brimming, and said, "You'll be pleased to learn that I have just been shunned by the one woman who could have given me another means of earning my living."

Reeve was standing directly in front of her now, and he inclined his head to one side. "You don't want to be an actress?" he asked, and he sounded genuinely concerned.

Maggie wanted only to be Reeve's wife, at that moment at least, but of course she couldn't say that outright. She dashed at the embarrassing tears with the back of one hand and said plaintively, "I was only trying to find my friend Tansy."

"The one you were with in Parramatta?" Reeve asked, and now his hands were resting on her shoulders. Maggie was beginning to hope that he'd forgiven her after all.

She nodded and sniffled once, quite inelegantly.

"That's easy, Maggie. She works for my friend Adam Beckwith. I can drop you off there on my way to the wharf."

Maggie remembered that Reeve was going to sea, and a new fear overtook her. "Will your journey be a long one—or—or dangerous?"

Reeve smiled, and his hands rested on the sides of her face. One thumb smoothed her tremulous lower lip and Maggie felt a shiver go through her. "Whalers are not crafts built for sight-seeing," he said quietly. "I'll be gone a week or two, I suppose."

"Reeve—" Maggie paused, swallowed. "I'm sorry that I couldn't tell you about Jamie—"

He tipped his head to kiss her lips, sending another

spasm of desire flowing through her body, in the wake of the first. "You did what you had to do, love," he said. "I know that now."

"Then you're not angry with me anymore?"

Reeve's wonderful eyes were fixed on the ceiling as though he were pondering the question. But there was a twitch of amusement at one corner of his mouth. "I didn't say that, Yank. After all, you just kicked me soundly in the shin."

He drew Maggie close and held her, his strong hands splayed on her back. Maggie's breasts were touching his chest, and even that much contact made her nipples harden beneath her clothes. "Aren't you going to say that you're sorry for kicking me too?" he prompted.

Biting back a grin, Maggie shook her head from side to side. "You deserved it. After all, you've given me a room the size of a mousehole."

"I think there might have been some mistake," Reeve said, pretending to be very serious. "Would you mind showing me this room?"

Maggie's senses were leaping and her face felt hot. She had a good idea of what would happen if she led Reeve to that attic room, but she couldn't find it within herself to refuse him. She loved him too much and needed him too badly. Still, she hesitated. "I'm not sure."

He laid an index finger to the tip of her nose, and though that wasn't an intimate contact, it stirred responses in other parts of Maggie's body that longed to be touched in just that way. "I'm going to sea, Maggie," he said hoarsely. "I want to make sure that all these little domestic matters are settled before I go."

Maggie began to think that she might have misinterpreted Reeve's insistence on seeing her room. She led the way through the house to the kitchen and up the first set of stairs but faltered at the foot of the three steps leading to her room. "Where are all the servants? I haven't seen anyone except for Cora since I arrived."

Reeve gave Maggie's bottom a surreptitious pinch. "This is their day off," he said.

Maggie's cheeks were flaming. "I'm not going into that room, Reeve McKenna, unless you promise me something on your honor!"

He reached out boldly to caress her breast. "What?"

"You have to swear that you'll marry me the minute you get back to Sydney," Maggie blurted out, and she was afraid to breathe while she waited for his answer.

"Done," he said, just when he had stretched her patience to the breaking point.

Maggie pulled him into the little room and closed the door, and Reeve looked around with a mock frown on his face. Even while he was doing this, he was unbuttoning the bodice of Maggie's dress.

"This will never do," he said as he lowered her camisole, baring her breasts. "No air, no light—"

Maggie drew in a sharp breath as he suddenly bent his head and took greedy suckle at her right breast. Her fingers knotted in his hair. "The—door, Reeve—" she managed to choke out. "Someone might—come in—"

Easily, he maneuvered her so that her back was to the door. While he teased and tasted her puckered nipple, he slowly lifted her skirts. She felt the ties of her drawers give way and then he was pulling them down, kneeling before her.

"Hold your skirts, Maggie," he ordered gruffly, and she did, bunching the stiff gray fabric in her fists. Her drawers were around her ankles now, like filmy hobbles, and Reeve made no effort to free her. All his attention was focused on baring the hidden rosebud he sought.

Maggie felt his breath on that nubbin of flesh and whimpered. The position of vulnerability was delicious, as was the suspense with which he teased her, giving her an occasional flick of his tongue but otherwise withholding the attention she longed for.

"Ooooo," she gasped, lifting her skirts higher and trying to step out of her drawers.

Reeve took one of her ankles into his hand and lifted it free, setting her foot down a good distance from its counterpart. Then, with his fingers, he fondled and caressed Maggie until she was moaning senselessly.

"You'll move your things to my room, Maggie," he said gruffly, between brief, fiery tastings of her sweetness.

"Ummm," Maggie pleaded, and then she gave a little cry as Reeve took her full into his mouth and began drawing at her.

She flung her head back and forth against the door, and her hair, always ready to tumble down, flew about her shoulders in cascades. Still, Reeve feasted.

"Oh, please, oh, please—" Maggie begged, all but blinded by the force of her need.

He drew on her in a long, excruciatingly pleasant motion of his lips, again and again, saying gentle and wicked things between samplings. By that time Maggie was feverish; she forgot about holding her skirt and plunged her hands into Reeve's hair, desperate to end the teasing.

With an arrogant masculine chuckle, Reeve set about driving Maggie to the very edge of madness. There was a blinding burst of passion, an explosion that hurled her toward the sky, and she descended slowly, quivering.

Reeve rose to his feet and Maggie's skirts fell back into place, though her breasts were still bare and proud. She was almost disappointed when he reached out and closed her hand over her bodice so that she was covered, but a second later he was lifting her off her feet, carrying her out of that dismal little room, and down the stairs to his spacious one.

Early the next morning Maggie awakened to find herself alone, and she knew before she read his note that Reeve had gone to sea. She was sad and frightened, but then she remembered his promise that they would be married as soon as he returned.

Humming, Maggie dressed hastily. Later that day the housekeeper moved her things from the attic room to Reeve's.

Chapter 16 🍂

THE MOMENT MAGGIE ARRIVED AT THE VICTORIA THEA-
tre and walked in through the stage door, she was set
upon by two costume women, clucking and sputtering
over her gray woolen dress. "Not fit for a cleanin'
rag," said one.

"It will never, never do," added the other.

Maggie flushed with embarrassment and then felt
true relief when she saw Philip walking toward her, an
angelic smile lighting his face.

"Good morning, Maggie," he said, taking both her
hands in his and giving them a reassuring squeeze.
His amber eyes took in the pair of fluttering seamstresses with an expression of amusement. "Time for
a fitting, is it?"

"Time and past, Mr. Briggs!" complained the
smaller of the two women, giving Maggie's dress a
truly rueful look. "My goodness, but that's ugly!"

Maggie thrust back her shoulders and lifted her
chin. Before she could say anything that she might
have come to regret, Philip took her arm and hurried
her away, placating the seamstresses by calling back
over one shoulder, "Mr. McKenna has left orders for

Miss Chamberlin to be provided with an entire wardrobe. You might want to consider suitable colors and fabrics."

Giving Philip a sidelong look, Maggie stopped in her tracks. "An entire wardrobe?" she whispered, awed.

Philip gave her a gentle pull to get her moving again, and soon they were entering a small office backstage, near the dressing rooms. "That surprises you?" he asked politely, closing the door behind them. "You're his mistress, aren't you?"

Maggie went a dull red. She supposed she was Reeve's mistress, but it was role she didn't like playing. "We're to be married as soon as Reeve gets back to Sydney," she said. "He promised."

Philip was behind his desk, fussing with a stack of papers and politely averting his eyes from Maggie's obvious discomfort. "Well, well," he said without a shred of conviction in his voice.

"You don't believe me?" Maggie challenged.

At last Philip met her gaze directly. "I think it's unlikely that Mr. McKenna would permit any woman he took as his wife to pursue a career," he said.

Maggie felt as though she'd just been punctured by a pin; all the spirit went out of her, like the air from a balloon. "Oh," she said.

Philip's look was a kindly one. "Maggie—"

"It's all right," she said too hastily, spreading her hands. "A-am I to have a dressing room?"

"Only the best," Philip replied with an exuberant smile. Obviously, he was relieved that the subject of Maggie's relationship with his employer had been dropped. "Come along—I'll show you."

The dressing room was spacious indeed, with gaspowered lights surrounding an enormous mirror and a bathroom of its own. There was space for an enormous collection of costumes and even a chaise longue, upholstered in dark blue velvet, for resting between rehearsals and performances.

Maggie was impressed, but she was also unnerved. This dressing room, she was certain, had belonged to Loretta Craig. Out with the old mistress, in with the new.

"I'll give you a few minutes alone, then send in the costume people. Would you like some tea or something, Maggie?"

Philip was being so kind; Maggie had almost forgotten that it was his fault that she was in Australia in the first place. If not for him, she'd probably still be working in London. She shook her head. "Nothing, thank you."

The moment the door had closed behind Philip, Maggie dashed into the bathroom and threw up.

Nerves, she thought to herself as she rinsed her mouth and splashed water over her face. Just nerves. Nothing to be alarmed about.

The seamstresses, who turned out to be sisters from northern England, kept her busy the rest of the morning. They measured and draped and pinned until Maggie thought she'd faint if she weren't allowed to sit down.

An unexpected visitor served to revive her. "Maggie!" Loretta Craig sang as though they were the oldest and best of friends as she swept into the dressing room without bothering to knock. She was a vision in emerald-green velvet trimmed in black braid, carrying a matching parasol and wearing an elegant little hat with a green feather affixed. "How nice to see you again!"

The sisters from the north of England fled, leaving a trail of measuring tapes and pincushions behind them.

Maggie drew a deep breath, preparing herself for what would undoubtedly be a difficult interview. "Hello, Miss Craig," she said, stepping regally down from the stool on which she'd been standing. Keeping her dignity was no easy matter, since she was wearing only her camisole and drawers and petticoat.

Loretta sat down on the foot of the velvet-covered chaise with a pretty little sigh and began tugging off her dyed-kid gloves.

Maggie could bear it no longer. "What are you doing here?" she asked forthrightly.

Loretta smiled a charming smile. Maggie might even have gone so far as to describe it as dazzling. "Why, I've come to help you with your lines and such, child. Being by far the more experienced actress—"

"I don't need any help with my lines," Maggie interrupted firmly. "I can practically recite the entire play."

Loretta arched one raven-black eyebrow. She really was beautiful, Maggie thought to herself, and far more sophisticated than a nineteen-year-old raised in a traveling circus could ever hope to be.

Apparently, Loretta had already spotted Maggie's weakness. "You are very young for the part of Kate, I must say. I could see you as Bianca, but—"

There was a rap at the door, and Maggie snatched up her discarded woolen dress and dodged behind a changing screen, pulling the garment hastily over her head.

"Hello, Loretta," Maggie heard Philip say. "To what do we owe this—pleasure?"

From the rustle of velvet Maggie discerned that Loretta had stood up. As she buttoned the front of her dress, she heard the older woman say wearily, "I had planned to offer the benefit of my training and experience. Apparently, Miss Chamberlin feels no need for the guidance of someone wiser."

"And older," Philip added wickedly.

Maggie peeped around the edge of the changing screen just in time to see Loretta level a killing look at Philip and then walk, with imperial grace, out of the dressing room.

"Do you think this is going to happen often?" Maggie asked, coming out from behind the screen.

Philip chuckled. "I doubt it—Loretta has a role of her own, at another theater."

Maggie felt like throwing up again. "One that belongs to Mr. McKenna?"

"Actually," Philip began somewhat reluctantly, "title to the other theaters has been transferred to Loretta. It was a parting gift, of sorts."

Maggie wondered sadly what Reeve's "parting gift" would be to her once he grew tired of their romance. She brought herself up short, however—Reeve had asked her to marry him. She was not going to be his mistress, but his wife. "I see," she said.

Rehearsals began shortly thereafter, and Maggie found that while Philip Briggs was gentle at all other times, he was a hard taskmaster when it came to the blocking of scenes and the delivery of lines.

The actor playing the role of Petruchio was an Englishman named Samuel Fairmont, and Maggie found a friend and mentor in him. Tall and blond and very handsome, Samuel was the perfect hero.

When the work had ended for the day, he walked Maggie to her dressing room door. "You really are very good," he said gently.

Maggie was exhausted and quite discouraged. All this time she'd prided herself on knowing the play so well, but Philip had railed at her from the beginning —everything she'd done had been wrong. "Thank you," she said in a dispirited voice.

"May I buy you supper?" Samuel asked, lingering at Maggie's elbow.

At first she was inclined to refuse. But then some inner spark of rebellion struck itself against the possibility that Reeve might indeed be planning to keep her as he had kept Loretta, and Maggie's pride ignited. Besides, her doubts about the sincerity of Reeve's marriage proposal aside, a simple supper with a new friend seemed innocent enough, and it sounded like fun. "I'd like that," she said.

"Excellent." Samuel smiled. "I'll wait for you at the stage door."

Maggie ducked inside her dressing room and made quick work of straightening her hair. There was nothing to be done with her dress, really, but she gave the stiff skirts a rueful shake and went out.

Samuel was prosperous for an actor; he took Maggie to one of the nicer hotel dining rooms and ordered roast duck for them both, along with wine.

"You will make a marvelous Kate," Samuel said, lifting his glass to Maggie in a graceful toast. "You have the spirit, the fire—"

"I think Philip sees me as Bianca," Maggie confided wearily. "That was the role he originally intended me to play, you know."

Samuel smiled, looking dapper in his rust-colored waistcoat. The soft gas lighting flickered in his wheat-blond hair. "What changed his mind?"

Maggie couldn't bring herself to tell Samuel the whole truth, of course. What would he think of her if he knew that she was Reeve McKenna's woman, playing the part only because the owner of the theater had chosen to favor her with the role? "I don't know," she lied. And then, to change the subject and because she was honestly curious, Maggie asked, "How did you come to be in Australia, Mr. Fairmont?"

"Please," he reprimanded her gently, "my name is Samuel. And I'm in Australia because I wanted an adventure. After I've earned my passage I'm going on to America. Always wanted to see the place."

For a moment Maggie felt a terrible, keening homesickness. She put it down immediately, for it was silly to be lonely for a place where one had no family and no friends. "That will be exciting," she said.

"Do you ever miss your own country?" Samuel asked softly, holding a glass of shimmering purple wine in his hand.

Maggie nodded, lowering her eyes. "Yes—but I

233

have no one there anymore." Briefly, she explained her unorthodox childhood and the loss of her parents later on.

Samuel sighed. "It's a lonely world we live in, Maggie, a lonely world indeed."

Maggie felt uncomfortable and concentrated on eating what remained of her dinner. Samuel was right, in a way; there were so many people in the world, but few of them touched one another's lives in any lasting way. "Yes," she said.

Before the conversation could go on, Philip appeared beside the table, looking frustrated and annoyed. "What the devil do you think you're doing?" he demanded of Maggie in an agitated whisper, sparing narry a look or a word for Samuel.

Maggie felt too tired and too subdued to be angry at Philip's intrusion, as she would have been at any other time. "I'm having dinner," she said, stating the obvious.

Samuel had risen to his feet; he was quite tall and muscular and the look he'd turned on Philip was not a friendly one. "I trust that you have some reason for imposing so flagrantly," he said.

Philip was trying to be brave, though it was clear that Samuel's superior size intimidated him. He glared down at Maggie and said through his teeth, "We are leaving, Miss Chamberlin. This very moment!"

Maggie flung down her napkin. "I beg your pardon!" she hissed, conscious that people were turning to stare. This kind of attention she could do without.

Philip studiously ignored Samuel, who looked as though he'd like to strangle him. His face was red, and his amber eyes were fairly crackling with vexation. "You have caused enough gossip for one night, Maggie," he said evenly. "Don't make it worse by creating a scene."

Maggie sighed. She had no idea what Philip was talking about, but suddenly her appetite was gone and

234

she felt extraordinarily tired. "If you'll excuse me, Samuel," she said, rising from her chair.

Samuel rose, too, making no protest, though his gaze swung toward Philip again, dangerous as a lance. "We'll discuss this, Briggs," he warned.

Philip nodded dolefully. "So, unfortunately, will the whole city of Sydney," he said as Maggie placed her hand on his arm. "Good night, Mr. Fairmont."

Samuel made a disdainful sound and sat down to finish his roast duck and his wine.

Outside in the street Philip fairly dragged Maggie toward a waiting carriage. "Do you want to find yourself scrubbing floors or wiping a lot of snotty noses in some nursery?" he demanded without preamble.

Maggie stood stubbornly still on the wooden sidewalk, furious. "Exactly what are you saying?" she cried.

"I'm talking, you little idiot, about your reputation. And about your—your status with Reeve McKenna. If he comes back and hears that you've been seen in public in the company of another man, he'll be livid!"

Maggie's mouth dropped open. "That's what this is about?"

Philip gestured for the carriage driver to stay in the box, and opened the door for Maggie himself. "Yes," he answered on a sigh.

Maggie refused to be stuffed into the carriage and dispensed with quite so easily. "Of all the unmitigated gall—Samuel is my friend!"

"Samuel is a womanizer," Philip argued flatly. "He will take advantage of you and of your position in Reeve McKenna's household if he can."

"You're a fine one to be pointing a finger, Philip Briggs. If you hadn't taken advantage of me, I wouldn't even be here!"

With surprising strength Philip took Maggie by the waist and forcibly lifted her into the carriage. "No," he said through the window, "you would probably be

235

dying of consumption in some back-alley room in the West End. Go home, Maggie, and don't make the same mistake again—I'm warning you. Mr. McKenna will not tolerate philandering."

"Philandering?!" Maggie cried, outraged, but the carriage was moving by then and there was no way to carry on the argument, save shrieking insults after Philip like a fishwife.

The great house near the bay was lonely that night, with Reeve gone away, and Maggie could not bear the prospect of traipsing off to his room to sleep in his bed like a good little mistress. She would go there only to fetch the things the maid had carried in that morning.

There was a tiny package, gaily wrapped in silver paper and tied with a red bow, resting in the middle of the neatly made bed. Maggie was sure it hadn't been there before, and she approached it warily.

The name on the tag was her own. Her fingers trembling, she opened the package and found a little black velvet box inside. She held her breath as she lifted the tiny lid, gasped when she saw the gleaming diamond shimmering and twinkling in the dim light.

"It came while you was out, miss," a female voice said, and Maggie whirled to see a maid standing in the doorway of what was probably the bathroom, a stack of neatly folded white towels in her arms. "I'm sure the master had it sent."

Maggie sank down on the side of the bed, her knees too weak to support her. "Did he—Mr. McKenna— ever give Miss Craig such a ring?"

The maid's short black curls bobbed as she shook her head. "No, mum. But then, he never meant to marry her, like he does you."

Suddenly, all Maggie's confusion fell away. She felt like whirling around the room and singing, but, of course, she didn't. She took the magnificent ring from its bed of black velvet and slipped it onto her finger. "Wait until Tansy sees!" she whispered, forgetting that she wasn't alone.

"Tansy, miss?" the maid asked, a lilt in her voice. "Do you mean Tansy Quinn?"

Maggie nodded. "She's a very good friend of mine."

The young girl's face was suddenly wreathed with smiles. "Ain't that somethin'! She's coming by this very evenin', mum, to play whist with the rest of us."

Maggie beamed, admiring the flash of her engagement ring. "Could I play too?"

The towels went tumbling gracelessly to the floor, and Maggie realized that the maid was staring at her in shock. "Play, mum? Play cards in the servants' quarters? The master would have a thing or two to say about that, once he found out!"

"He won't say anything at all," Maggie answered blithely, helping to pick up the towels and even to refold them. "I want to see Tansy and, anyway, I like a good hand of cards now and again."

"Yes, miss, but—"

Maggie assumed a fierce look. "What is your name?" she demanded.

"Caroline, miss. It's Caroline. You won't be getting me into dutch, now, will you, for droppin' the towels like I did?"

Maggie couldn't sustain her glowering expression. She laughed, full of joy because Reeve really meant to marry her and because she was going to see Tansy again. "Of course I won't, silly," she said. "But I'd better be invited to that card game!"

Caroline paled and backed out of the room, the towels clutched to her flat little bosom. "Yes, mum, whatever you say," she prattled, and the moment she was through the doorway, Maggie saw her burst into a breakneck run.

Later that night, the long, austere room shared by all the maids employed in that house was abuzz. Everyone fell silent the moment Maggie walked in.

It was Tansy who recovered first. Bounding off one of the cots, where she'd sat cross-legged, she hurled

237

herself at Maggie and cried, "Ain't it good to see you, though! And you almost the mistress of this grand 'ouse!"

Maggie laughed and hugged her friend. "I've missed you," she said, blinking away the mist that had gathered in her eyes.

Tansy returned the hug and then whirled to face half a dozen wide-eyed maids. "I told you, didn't I?" she reprimanded them good-naturedly, spreading her hands wide of her body. "She's a regular sort, our Maggie! We've nothin' to fear from 'er."

The other girls, Caroline among them, did not look convinced. "She's the master's lady," one of them, a very plain girl with acne-scarred skin, dared to say.

"I ain't so sure she's a lady," someone else put in, and there was a twitter of giggles.

Tansy, as insulted as if the remark had been directed at her, bristled at Maggie's side. "Is that 'ow it is, then? You're too good, the lot of you, to play a 'armless game of cards with me friend?"

Another girl came forward, shyly, with a faltering smile on her lips. "My name's Shirley," she said, offering a friendly hand to Maggie as her eyes took in the tired gray dress. "Ain't he goin' to fix you up properlike, like he did Miss Loretta?"

There was a communal groan at the mention of Loretta, and then Caroline piped up. "You all know he's gotten Miss Maggie a ring—I told you at supper!"

Tansy's eyes were wide as she turned to face Maggie. "A ring, is it? Let me see!"

Maggie showed the magnificent ring not only to Tansy, but to all the others as well. There were *ooos* and *ahhhs* aplenty, and then Tansy said, "Well? Is me friend to join in the game or not? If she ain't, we'll just go off, 'er and me, to see what we might see!"

"She can play," sighed the girl with the poor complexion, and soon Maggie was a part of a rousing game of whist, having more fun than she'd had in weeks.

When it grew late, the games ended, and Maggie walked Tansy as far as the rear garden, where her new beau, Jack Fly, was supposed to be waiting to see her home.

"Coo," Tansy breathed, admiring the ring one last time in the light of the broad February moon. "Ain't this goin' to curl Lady Cosgrove's 'air. She'll 'ave to accept you as an equal!"

Maggie doubted that Lady Cosgrove would ever accept her, married to Reeve McKenna or not. She'd gone beyond the pale as far as that good woman was concerned.

"About time, it is!" complained a male voice from behind a row of bushes. "I've got 'orses to groom tonight, you know!"

Tansy smiled. "Come out, Jack, and meet me friend, the future Mrs. McKenna."

The bushes rustled and then Jack appeared. He was a brawny young man, good-looking in a rough sort of way, and he rubbed one hand down his pants leg, offered it to Maggie, and then withdrew it again before she could reach out.

Tansy laughed at Jack's nervousness and linked her arm through his. "I'm gettin' married too, Maggie. Durin' the jubilee in June."

Jack shivered. "It's cold in June," he complained.

"At 'ome," Tansy sniffed, lifting her nose, "ladies gets married in June. Don't they, Maggie?"

Maggie nodded. It was clear that Tansy was in love, and Maggie couldn't have been happier. She hugged Tansy again and they said their farewells and Maggie scampered off to the room on the second floor.

She undressed quickly, yawning as she put on her ragged old nightgown, then went into the bathroom. There, she cleaned her teeth and washed her face and marveled at the size of the bathtub. The thing was big enough for half a dozen people.

That night Maggie tossed and turned, uncomfortable in the massive bed, missing Reeve. In the morning she left for the theater, where another round of rehearsals would be held.

Mercifully, the sister seamstresses had made her a new dress, a lovely cambric creation with sprigs of English holly embroidered on its full skirts, and Maggie was spared wearing her trusty gray woolen.

She worked hard all that morning, and Philip didn't holler at her so much as he had the day before, though he did reduce the young woman playing Bianca to tears on several different occasions. Samuel looked as though he wanted to punch Philip Briggs in the nose, but he kept his composure on that score and poured all his passion into the part of Kate's determined suitor.

At midday, when the cast was set free to have their noon meal, Maggie couldn't resist showing Philip her engagement ring. Now let him imply that Reeve had no intention of marrying her!

Philip sighed. "Lovely. But things like that aren't hard for a man to come by, Maggie—not if he's got the kind of money Reeve McKenna has."

Thwarted again, Maggie stomped off to her dressing room and slammed the door shut. Her lunch was brought to her, but she ignored it, feeling slightly sick to her stomach.

The afternoon was as difficult as the morning had been, but Maggie survived it somehow. When the workday was over, she got into the waiting carriage without speaking to either Samuel or Philip, and went home.

That night there was no card game in the servants' quarters to distract her. But there was another package on the bed.

Seeing no reason to stand on ceremony, Maggie ripped the large box open and found a beautiful blue velvet cloak inside, trimmed in some luscious white fur. She draped the garment over her shoulders and whirled round and round in delight.

Her delight soon faded when a sudden rush of

nausea flowed into her throat. Maggie dropped the cloak on the floor and dashed into the bathroom, arriving just in time.

When the spate of sickness was over and she'd rinsed out her mouth, Maggie went despondently back into the bedroom and sat down in an enormous leather chair facing the bed. For the first time, she allowed herself to count days, and the tally was an alarming one. She should have been bleeding a week before.

Trembling, Maggie undressed and crawled once again into that big, lonely bed, turning down the lamp before snuggling underneath the lightweight comforter and silken sheet. In the moonlight flowing in through the windows she could see her engagement ring flashing, and she comforted herself with the promise Reeve had made. If she was going to have his child, she was also going to have his name.

The following day was much like the two that had preceded it. Maggie worked hard, she was sick once, and there was another present waiting on the bed when she got home. This one was a tiny silver music box, and there was a note tucked beneath its lid.

Maggie opened the note. "Maggie," Reeve had written in his forceful hand, "I've arranged for something to be delivered every day until we can be together again. Though I'm writing this ahead of time, I know I'll be missing you by the time you read it. If you see Jamie again, don't let him leave. Sincerely, Reeve."

Maggie would have felt better if the note had been signed with love, but she was willing to wait for that. With a sigh she wound the music box and let its tinkling notes carry her far away, to a place where she and Reeve could be together always.

Chapter 17 🌱

THEY'D BEEN AT SEA THREE DAYS WHEN THE GREAT, rolling hulk of a whale was sighted off the starboard bow. A spray of water shot twenty feet into the air, glistening in the midday sunshine, and Reeve stood stock-still on the deck of the *Elisabeth Lee,* his hands gripping the railing.

Behind him, the crew raced to reset the sails, to lower the dinghies into the water, and to load the harpoons. Reeve felt sick, looking at that majestic creature as it plunged far beneath the surface and then rocketed skyward, as if to issue a challenge.

"Comin', Cap'n?" a crewman asked, swinging a leg over the side of the small ship. He held his harpoon in one hand as he made his way down the rope ladder dangling above the sea.

Reeve followed the man down into the dinghy and took hold of the oars. The tiny boat moved swiftly toward the mammoth creature frolicking in the sun-spattered water, two other small craft bobbing in its wake.

Again the whale sounded, and there were moments

of unearthly silence before the enormous beast broke the water in a burst of power that set the boats rocking violently from side to side. With a shout the man who had spoken to Reeve earlier on deck lunged to his feet and fired the harpoon. It punctured the sleek water-filmed flesh of the whale, and there was a cry of anguish that Reeve felt in the very core of his soul.

The water turned red with blood, and it took all Reeve's determination not to bend over the side of the dinghy and heave. Two more harpoons found their marks, and the magnificent animal rolled onto its side, one great eye covered by a crimson sheen.

"Oh, God," Reeve muttered. "God."

"Haul her in, mates!" shouted the man who had fired the first harpoon. "Ain't she a marvel, though?"

Reeve had never liked whaling, not since his first experience with it at fourteen. Now he was finding it intolerable.

His hands shook as he climbed the ladder to board the *Elisabeth Lee* again, and he had barely swung himself over the rail when he heard the screams and the horrible churning of the water. He whirled.

"Sharks!" screamed one of the men still below. The water bubbled like hell's caldron, and the dinghies were flung this way and that. Most of Reeve's crewmen made it up the ladder; the rest—a dozen or so—were hurled into the water.

What followed was the stuff of which nightmares are woven. Men on deck fired rifles at the frenzied sharks, while the predators tore at the carcass of the whale and at the crewmen who had been thrown into the sea. Reeve watched in horrified helplessness as a young man was dragged beneath the surface. Moments later bright red bubbles boiled up.

"Jesus," sobbed one of the men standing beside Reeve on the deck, and his words were more prayer than blasphemy. "Holy Jesus, help 'em."

The fury of the sharks drew other sharks, and the

frenzy went on and on. Reeve stood frozen at the rail, unable to look away.

When the horror had finally ended, there was little left of a whale longer than the *Elisabeth Lee* and nothing left of the men who had died in that roiling mess of blood and gore.

"Come away, Cap'n." The first mate spoke quietly, his hand resting on Reeve's arm. "Cap'n?"

Reeve shuddered. No matter how much he longed to, he couldn't step away from the rail or the memory of what he'd seen. In twenty years of whaling he'd watched more than one man die, that was true, but he'd never witnessed anything remotely like what had happened that day.

The first mate tugged at his arm. "Cap'n, we're settin' sail for Sydney—is that all right?"

Reeve managed a brisk nod, but that was all. His muscles were still as taut as though they'd been cast of iron, and there was a queer buzzing sound in his head. Underlying this were the shrieks of men dying a nightmare death.

It took several men to pry Reeve's hands loose from the railing. They led him, like a child, to his quarters below deck.

"We'll put in at Auckland," he heard the first mate say to the other men. "We're closer there than Sydney. The cap'n needs a doctor."

"It be 'is mind that's needin' treatment, mate, and there ain't no doctors for that," responded someone else.

Reeve wanted to lift his hand, to tell them that he was all right, that he didn't need a doctor, but he found that he could neither speak nor move. He was trapped inside himself.

"We're going to Auckland," the first mate insisted, and though Reeve could see Jacob's face looming over him, he couldn't respond in any way. Even the flicker of an eyelash was beyond him.

"I've seen this before," put in a swabby standing at the foot of Reeve's berth. "Some never get over it."

The sailor's words echoed through Reeve's mind; the thought of staying this way for the rest of his life filled him with desperate fear. *Maggie,* he cried, from the depths of his soul. *Maggie.*

The days passed quickly for Maggie, she was working so hard on the play, but the nights were long and filled with doubts and fear. She was sure that she was pregnant now, and once she was in bed, she was tormented by wild imaginings. Almost invariably, when she did manage to sleep, she dreamed that she was playing the role of Kate, her stomach burgeoning out in front of her, while the audience booed and hissed and threw vegetables.

When a week had gone by, Maggie began to look for Reeve, but he didn't arrive, though more presents and more notes did. The gifts were always frivolous and expensive, and the notes always mentioned Jamie.

Ten full days had slipped by when Philip let himself into Maggie's dressing room late one afternoon without bothering to knock. He was holding a piece of yellow paper tightly in one hand and the expression on his face was ghastly.

Maggie had been using her free moments to try on the new dresses the seamstresses had been making for her, now that most of her costumes were done. At the sight of Philip, reflected in the glass of her mirror, she whirled and demanded, "What is it?"

"The *Elisabeth Lee* ran into some trouble, Maggie. Part of the crew was killed."

Maggie felt the blood drain from her face and the strength flow from her legs. She sat down heavily on the bench in front of her mirror. "Reeve?" she asked in a whisper.

Philip shrugged miserably and held out the piece of paper. Maggie snatched it from him and read the telegraph message thereupon. CALAMITY THREE DAYS OUT. TWELVE MEN DEAD, REST SAFE IN AUCKLAND. JACOB HUGHES, FIRST MATE, THE ELISABETH LEE.

Staring into space, her throat thick, Maggie managed to ask, "Who gave you this?"

"It was sent to Mr. McKenna's offices, Maggie. A clerk brought it over."

The telegram was crumpled in Maggie's hands; carefully, she smoothed it out on her knee. "You think Reeve is dead, don't you?" she accused Philip in wooden tones.

Philip sighed and came to stand close by, his hand resting gently on Maggie's shoulder. "Jacob Hughes is the first mate, not the captain. If Reeve were alive, he'd have sent the wire himself, wouldn't he?"

Maggie wanted to attack Philip like an animal, kicking, biting, scratching. How dare he suggest that Reeve was dead! She sat perfectly still instead, drawing in one deep and shaky breath after another. "I'm going to Auckland."

Philip sat down on the end of the chaise longue and then reached out to catch one of Maggie's hands in his own. "You can't, Maggie, and you know it. You've got the play to think about, and besides, what good could you do in Auckland? The *Elisabeth Lee* will sail back to Sydney as soon as she's manned and fitted for the voyage; it's her home port."

"To hell with the damned play!" Maggie cried out, plunging to her feet and pacing the dressing room, tears welling in her eyes. "To hell with everything and everybody except Reeve McKenna!"

Philip gave another sigh, this one ragged and long. "Maggie, I know how you feel, but you've got to stay here. You've got to wait for news!"

"I can't bear to wait!"

"You'll have to," Philip said firmly, rising to take her quaking shoulders into his hands in an attempt to steady her. "Maggie," he began again, his voice reasonable and quiet, "suppose you did set sail for New

Zealand this very day. Do you know what would probably happen?"

Maggie was trembling. She shook her head.

"Your ship and the *Elisabeth Lee* would pass each other. You'd be no closer to learning the truth than you are right now."

Maggie lowered her head with a despondent sob, and Philip drew her close, wrapping his arms around her. "My poor Maggie," he whispered hoarsely. "What have I done to you?"

Her face buried in Philip's shoulder, Maggie wailed. "There's a child—oh, Philip, I think there's a child—"

Philip's embrace tightened. "My God," he breathed.

Maggie had already come to regret blurting out such a confession, and she thrust herself away from Philip and sniffled, trying to recover her composure. The first thing she had to do was go directly to Reeve's offices and find out if anything else was known about the disaster at sea. "I'm leaving now," she said, her chin high.

Philip caught her arm in his hand. "Let me go with you, Maggie," he pleaded softly.

Maggie shook her head, pulled free of his grasp, and crossed the dressing room to open the door. Philip's next words stopped her where she was, her hand grasping the knob.

"If you are expecting McKenna's child, Maggie, I'll marry you. I owe you that much."

Maggie could not bear the thought of marrying anyone but Reeve, but she understood that Philip was being more than kind, he was being noble. She turned to look back at him with puffy, red-rimmed eyes. "Thank you," she said, and then she left the room.

Tansy was standing beside Maggie's bed, bathing her head with a cool, damp cloth. "There now," she said sadly, "that's it. You're comin' 'round at last."

247

Maggie had a headache, and she felt sick to her stomach. "Reeve—"

"I know," Tansy said gently. "I know."

Maggie struggled to sit up, and the room spun around her, making her sink back onto the pillows and gasp for breath. "He's not dead, Tansy," she insisted. "If Reeve were dead, I'd know it."

"There now, we'll just have to wait and see, won't we?" Tansy was fussing with the covers, and Maggie slapped her hands away, trying to get out of bed.

"I've got to speak to the people at Reeve's business—"

Firmly, Tansy shoved her friend back into bed and put the covers in place. "No, Maggie. You tried that once and, to 'ear your Philip Briggs tell it, you got no farther than the sidewalk before you collapsed in a heap. There's a love, now just rest."

Maggie groaned. "I can't rest!"

"Do you want to lose that baby as well as the man you love?" Tansy demanded, drawing up a chair and plunking herself down in it. "You will if you keep this up."

Maggie's eyes had gone wide. "How—"

"I knew by the look o' ye. It ain't like I 'aven't seen this before now. What'll you do, Maggie, if Mr. McKenna is dead?"

The memory of Philip's second marriage proposal flashed in Maggie's mind, but she put it aside immediately. Neither she nor Philip would be happy in such a situation, much as she'd once dreamed of being his wife and bearing his children. "I don't know," she said.

"I shouldn't 'ave asked," Tansy said, looking angry with herself. "Lord knows, this ain't the time for it. Rest, Maggie, and don't give the man nor the babe narry another thought. Tansy Quinn will take care of everything."

Maggie settled back against her pillows and sighed. She could think of nothing but Reeve McKenna and his child, and she doubted that anyone other than God could set things right.

Jamie sat beside Reeve's bed, his battered sheepman's hat dangling from his fingers. It had been more than twenty years since he'd had a close, clear look at his older brother, and to find him like this was almost unbearable. Reeve had always been so strong, so certain of where he was going and what he wanted.

"His soul done froze up inside him," Cutter O'Riley observed from just inside the door of the room in Jamie's house. "Never seen anything like it in all my days."

Jamie kept his eyes on Reeve's immobile face, thinking of all the effort he'd gone to to evade the detectives. The reasons for avoiding his brother hardly seemed important now. He was glad that Peony kept her ear to the ground, knew what was going on in the seafaring world. He might not have learned of Reeve's tragedy if it hadn't been for her.

Convinced that his brother should be looked after by someone of his own flesh and blood, Jamie had gone directly to the newly docked *Elisabeth Lee* and claimed Reeve, then brought him home.

"Damn you," he breathed, addressing his brother, "don't you die now. Don't you give up and die. You've got Maggie to live for—"

"He can't hear you," Cutter complained, weary of standing around in the house when there was so much work to be done. "And who, pray tell, is Maggie?"

Despite the heartache he felt over Reeve, Jamie permitted himself a small smile. "She's the hell-kitten my brother loves," he said. "Lucky for him, she loves him back."

"Peony ain't gonna like it one little bit if she hears you talkin' so fond about some other woman, Jamie-boy."

"Peony and I have an understanding," Jamie replied, tossing his hat aside to lean closer to his brother. Had he seen a flicker of movement there by Reeve's lower lip?

"I'll wager that understandin' don't include your spendin' a night with a woman what loves your brother," Cutter said.

"Get out of here," Jamie replied.

When Cutter was gone, he reached out to turn up the bedside lamp. Light spilled over Reeve's face, and this time Jamie was sure of what he'd seen before; Reeve's eyes, closed by the doctor like a dead man's, were open.

Jamie's own eyes had misted over, but he managed a lopsided grin. "So you found me. You never give up, do you, brother?"

Reeve's face might have been carved of granite, it was so still, but Jamie could feel his brother's struggle in his own spirit.

"I know what you want, mate," Jamie said, his voice hoarse. "I'll take you back home as soon as you can travel."

"When'll that be?" demanded a man from the doorway.

Jamie looked back over his shoulder to see Jacob Hughes, Reeve's first mate, standing where Cutter had been minutes before.

"We gotta get back to Sydney, mate. The men got families there, wonderin' and waitin', and there's some that have to be told bad news."

Jamie sighed. "Sail whenever you're ready; I'll see that my brother gets back when he's well enough for the trip." An image of saucy gray eyes and tangled hair the color of moonlight rose in his mind. "He's got a woman. I want you to tell her that Reeve's alive."

"I'll see that it gets done, Mr. McKenna," Hughes answered, and then he was gone.

Jamie swung his gaze back to Reeve's face, still as impassive as a stone statue. "At least Maggie won't be worrying that you're dead," he said.

Reeve closed his eyes and Jamie bent closer, squinting. Sure as hell, there were tears glistening along Reeve's coal-black lashes.

"So Reeve managed to survive, did he?" Loretta smiled broadly at the crewman dispatched by the first mate of the *Elisabeth Lee.* "Why, that's just wonderful news!" She turned briefly to the man behind her, who was dressed for an evening at the theater. "Isn't it, Duncan?"

Duncan's green eyes were thoughtful. "Yes," he replied, "wonderful news."

The man who had carried the message nodded his head nervously and turned to leave. He ran down the walk to the street and disappeared into the night.

Duncan's shoulder was still stiff from that unfortunate incident in Melbourne, and he rubbed it distractedly with his hand. "There is never going to be a better opportunity," he said in that odd, faraway voice that had become his usual way of speaking.

Loretta was annoyed. "Really, Duncan, your obsession with that little twit is really quite tiresome. She loves Reeve, and she'll never want you, not after what happened in Melbourne."

Duncan smiled absently, looking through Loretta to something else, something that was out of her sight and her reach. "She must be devastated, believing that Reeve is dead. And vulnerable."

Loretta snapped open her fan and fluttered it angrily back and forth in front of her face. She looked her best, and here was Duncan, not even noticing. All he could talk about was Maggie. "I think," she ventured to say, "it might be better if we don't go to the theater tonight, Duncan. I can assure you that Maggie makes a very naive Kate."

That stupid grin was still on Duncan's face. "If you don't want to see the play, Loretta, that's fine with me. Personally, I wouldn't miss it for all the tea in China."

Loretta stomped one delicately slippered foot. "I don't like being made a fool of, Duncan. Just what, exactly, are you planning to do?"

Duncan gave an odd, slanting shrug and winced at the pain in his sore shoulder. "Offer my sincerest sympathies, of course."

Loretta rolled her eyes. She had half a mind to stay home that evening, but there was always the possibility that dear little Maggie would botch her opening performance completely, and Loretta didn't want to take a chance on missing that. She reached for the bell cord and pulled for a carriage to be brought around. "Don't make any foolish mistakes, Duncan," she warned acidly. "Maggie may think Reeve is dead, but we know better. And his revenge is something you'd rather not experience, believe me."

Duncan opened the front door of Loretta's town house and gestured grandly, with his good arm, for her to precede him.

Maggie's own pallid face stared back at her from the lighted mirror. The makeup she'd applied for tonight's performance gave her a garish look, and her stomach was gyrating crazily. "I can't do this," she said softly.

Behind her, Philip Briggs laid his hands on her shoulders. Her costume, a lovely thing of plush gray velvet, left them bare. "What do we say in the theater, Maggie?" he prompted as though she were a slow child and not a woman who'd been widowed before she'd even had a chance to be a wife.

Maggie sighed. "The show must go on," she recited forlornly.

"Exactly. This is your chance, Maggie, to make a real place for yourself in the world. Don't ruin it."

She bit her lower lip. What Philip said was true; with Reeve gone, her only chance to offer her baby a good life was to make a success of her acting career. If this play went well, she would be on her way.

Philip bent his head and planted an innocuous kiss on the curve where Maggie's neck and shoulder met. "You'll be the toast of Sydney, darling," he said.

Maggie slipped away from him to fuss with her elaborately coiffed hair and examine her makeup. "Yes," she repeated obediently, woodenly, "the toast of Sydney."

Maggie's performance was brilliant. Duncan clapped enthusiastically when she took her bows, as did the rest of the audience—except for Loretta. She sat, stiff with disdain, in the seat next to his, her elegantly gloved hands lying still in her lap.

"I'm going backstage," Duncan announced when the lights came up. "Are you coming with me?"

Loretta's program was now crumpled in one hand. She gave Duncan a sharp look and shook her head, and he left her there to make his way through the crowds, climbing the steps at the side of the stage. Moments later he was standing in the wings, his feet riveted to the floor by the sight of Maggie Chamberlin. God, what a fool he'd been to let her get away.

He smiled and straightened his tie. He would not make the same mistake twice. "Maggie?" he called, pressing his way through the throng of admirers to stand at her side.

Maggie looked up at him blankly, her gray eyes full of misery. Duncan realized that she was totally indifferent to him and was stung; her outrage would have been better than this empty stare. Far better.

"Maggie," he said hoarsely, taking one of her hands to lift it for a kiss. By that time Duncan was hoping that Maggie's memory of him had indeed faded away. It would be wonderful to have a second chance to win her affections.

But he saw the fury spark in her stormy eyes as she recalled her experiences in Melbourne. She wrenched her hand free and spat, "Let me go, you bastard!"

Duncan was momentarily taken aback. He'd known that Maggie had spirit, of course; she'd defied him too many times for him to believe otherwise. But he had never dreamed that she hated him this much. "If you'll just give me an opportunity, Maggie, I'll make up for everything. I promise you I will."

Just then the actor who had played Petruchio appeared, still wearing his cape and dashing feathered hat. Possessively, he took Maggie's arm, and Duncan didn't like the way she leaned against the man.

"Miss Chamberlin is really not up to dealing with her admirers tonight," the actor said coolly.

Duncan seethed, though he kept his gentleman's smile firmly in place. "Are you ill, Maggie?" he asked indulgently.

Her gaze was as cold as the blade of a sword. "A few more moments of your presence, Mr. Kirk, and I will surely vomit."

A slap across the face would not have outraged Duncan more. Color surged up from under his elegant collar and flowed hot along his jawline. Still, he bowed politely before turning to walk away.

If Maggie wanted a battle, she would have one. And she would lose.

Duncan smiled to himself as he left the theater by a side door and leaned against a brick wall, striking a match and lighting a cheroot. Queensland, he thought as he drew deeply of the smoke. Queensland was just the place for the taming of a certain very fetching little shrew.

Of course, it would take days, maybe even weeks to make the necessary arrangements. Duncan threw down his cheroot and ground it out with his heel. There was no point in wasting time.

Maggie lived for just two things during those first difficult days following her acceptance of Reeve's death: the child growing within her and the surcease

254

of pain that was achieved each night when she walked onstage. The newspapers were calling her portrayal of Kate a triumph, but she only sighed when she read the articles.

One of the English sisters was letting out Maggie's costumes, and she turned obediently in the direction indicated by the woman's tug at her gown. There were flowers on the table in front of her dressing room mirror, beautiful hothouse orchids, fragrant and white as snow.

Maggie turned up her nose. If Duncan Kirk thought that a few fancy blossoms were going to change her mind, he could just think again. Wistfully, she looked down at the diamond ring she hadn't had the heart to take off, and sighed. Soon enough, she supposed, she'd be asked to leave Reeve's house, and she might need to pawn the ring at some point. She wouldn't be able to play the role of Kate once she was noticeably pregnant, of course, and then how would she earn her living?

Maggie pushed the question aside. She would think about that later.

Philip burst through the door at exactly the moment she'd made that decision, his face alight with excitement. "Maggie, would you believe it? You've been invited on a tour!"

She drew in a breath, let it out again. "A tour?" she echoed blankly.

"Of the United States, Maggie!" Philip blurted out. "If you want to go home, this is your chance!"

For the first time in days Maggie was jarred out of her walking stupor. She stared at Philip, her eyes wide. "You mean my passage would be paid and everything?"

Philip nodded eagerly. "And I'll go with you, as your manager and"—he glanced at the wardrobe woman, who was listening shamelessly—"your husband."

255

Maggie paid no attention to Philip's constant hints that they should be married, and she brushed this one aside as well. Would America really be home? She had no friends there, and no family.

On the other hand, she would not be a foreigner in the United States as she was in Australia. She sighed. "When do we leave?"

Chapter 18 ❧

LORETTA DIDN'T KNOW WHETHER TO BE ELATED OR ENVI-
ous. Maggie Chamberlin, invited to tour America!
Why, it was preposterous. The chit had no theatrical
experience to speak of, and very little talent.

Thoughtfully, Loretta folded her newspaper and
laid it aside. On the other hand, the fact that Reeve
was alive couldn't be kept from the girl forever; one
day soon, he would return to Sydney and take up
where he'd left off. And then there was the matter of
Duncan's growing preoccupation with the little bitch.
Loretta was concerned about that; Duncan was just as
rich and almost as powerful as Reeve, and if she
couldn't have Reeve back, she most certainly wanted
Duncan.

She sat back in her chair as a maid came into the
dining room of her small town house to clear away the
breakfast dishes, and a smile curved her lips. Under
the circumstances, Maggie's tour of America might be
the most fortuitous thing that could have happened.

Just then Duncan came into the room wearing the
trousers and elegant dress shirt he'd worn the night

before to the theater. There was no sign of his coat. "Good morning, Loretta," he said with a dismal sigh.

He had been considerably more pleasant in bed, Loretta thought peevishly, but she smiled. "Good morning, darling."

Duncan gave her a quizzical, wary look. Though they had been friends for years, they apparently hadn't reached the stage where Loretta could address him with an endearment. "Let me see the newspaper," he said as the maid set a plate of sausage, eggs, and scones before him.

Loretta knew there was no way she could keep news of Maggie's invitation to America a secret from him; she could only hope that he wouldn't be prompted to do anything rash. With a small sigh she handed him the *Sydney Times*.

Duncan opened the newspaper to the section where theater news was printed, and Loretta braced herself. She watched in helpless pique as the color drained from his face and his jawline tightened. He swore and flung the periodical back over one shoulder, and Loretta flinched.

"Blast it to bloody hell!" he growled.

Loretta sighed. "Now, Duncan—"

"That little imbecile!" Duncan yelled, rising from his chair so quickly that it toppled over backward and nearly struck the maid, who was still trying to gather up the newspaper he'd tossed moments before. "I have half a mind to go down to that theater and drag her out by the hair!"

Loretta called upon all her years of training and experience to summon up one sweet smile. "Duncan, do calm down. Maggie will have to finish the run of her play before she leaves, and that will take weeks."

Red from his collar to his hairline, his wonderful emerald eyes flashing, Duncan righted his chair with narry a glance for the shivering maid and sat down in it heavily. "She's just foolhardy enough to take the next ship, Loretta, and you know it!"

"Would that be so awful?" Loretta asked in a small, tremulous voice. "After all, Duncan, you have me."

Duncan gave her an exasperated look and began eating, glowering into space as he chewed. Loretta knew he was plotting, and that worried her.

"Duncan," she said softly. "Marry me."

He stopped chewing, and his fork was poised in midair as he stared at Loretta in amazement. "Marry you? Damn it, Loretta, if I've told you once, I've told you a hundred times—I mean to marry Maggie!"

Enough was definitely enough. Loretta surged to her feet, hot color pulsing in her face, her dark eyes venomous. "It isn't Maggie you've been bedding these past few weeks, is it?"

Duncan hurled his napkin into his plate and stood up. "More's the pity," he retorted, and then he turned and stormed out of the dining room.

Loretta squeezed her eyes shut tight when she heard the front door of the town house slam.

Maggie wasn't exactly looking forward to traveling to America; it was more a case of being resigned to her fate. Philip and Samuel would both be going along, though, and that meant that she would at least have friends. Standing in the center of Reeve's bedroom, she laid both her hands on her stomach. The baby would be her family.

She was just getting dressed for another long day of rehearsals when the door squeaked open and Elisabeth crept in. The child was more subdued than ever now that Reeve was gone, and Maggie felt a pang at the thought of leaving her.

Her enormous aquamarine eyes round and sad, she approached Maggie and held up a shiny red apple and one of Cora's alphabet cards. "Apple," she said clearly.

Maggie sat down on the edge of the bed, agape. Tears sprang into her eyes and she held out her arms. "Elisabeth," she said as the child scrambled into her lap and huddled against her in silent despondency. "Oh, Elisabeth."

Elisabeth began to cry. "Papa," she sobbed. "Papa, Papa!"

Maggie embraced the child. "I know," she said. "I miss him too."

Elisabeth tilted back her head and reached up with one tiny finger to touch a teardrop on Maggie's cheek. She didn't speak again, but her expression said volumes. Somehow she'd sensed that Maggie was planning to leave Australia forever, and she was asking her not to go.

"I don't belong here, in this house," Maggie said sadly, praying that the child would understand somehow. "I've got to go."

Elisabeth clutched at the front of Maggie's dress, letting the apple and the corresponding alphabet card fall to the floor. Her small face was contorted with grief and fear. "Mama!" she whispered.

Maggie hugged Elisabeth close again, her chin resting on top of the little girl's dark head. "Oh, Elisabeth, I wish I were your mama. I truly do. Then we could be together always."

Elisabeth was still sobbing and Maggie rocked her in her arms, softly singing a lullaby that she'd learned from her own mother long ago. When the child had fallen silent again, she laid her gently on the bed and covered her with a satin comforter. Elisabeth slipped her thumb into her mouth and fell into a sound, exhausted sleep.

"Poor little darling," Cora said from the doorway. "I don't think she's been sleeping well lately."

Maggie bent to kiss the small forehead and dashed away her tears with the back of one hand. "It's going to be dreadful to leave her," she confided.

"I know," Cora replied quietly. "There's a man here to see you, Miss Margaret, from Mr. McKenna's offices."

Maggie steeled herself for some gruesome accounting of Reeve's death and walked bravely out of the bedroom and down the front stairway. The clerk was standing just inside the parlor.

"If this is about Mr. McKenna's death," she said abruptly, "please be very brief." Maggie raised her chin. "I must get to the theater."

The young man was gazing at her in amazement. "Mr. McKenna's—*death?*" he said, marveling.

Maggie felt an odd, wiggling sensation deep inside her, as though her frozen spirit might be thawing. She dreaded the pain that would result. "Yes," she answered stiffly. "Surely you know that he was killed at sea."

"Miss Chamberlin," the visitor breathed, aghast, "Mr. McKenna is very much alive. He's being brought home from New Zealand within the week!"

The entryway swayed and undulated around Maggie, and wild hope leapt within her. "Alive?" she choked. "Reeve is alive? Why didn't someone—"

The clerk took Maggie's arm and supported her until he'd led her to a sofa in the nearby parlor and helped her to sit down. "Dear God in heaven, madam —don't tell me that this household has believed Mr. McKenna dead these past few days!"

Maggie nodded, her throat too thick with tangled emotions for her to speak.

The bearer of glad tidings offered his hand in an agitated and very belated introduction. "Simon Coates, at your service, madam. Good heavens, I cannot understand how such an error could have been made."

Maggie's spirit was rejoicing wildly, though outwardly she was quite calm. After some struggle with her constricted vocal cords, she managed to say, "You said that Mr. McKenna is being brought from New Zealand. Was he injured?"

Sadly, Mr. Coates shook his head. "He wasn't

injured, miss. But apparently the sight of his crewmen dying in such a horrible way did something to his mind. My reports say that Mr. McKenna doesn't speak, and he's confined to an invalid's chair."

Maggie stood up slowly, her heart pounding. If she'd thought it would get her to his side faster, she would have swum out to meet his ship. "When will Mr. McKenna be arriving?" she asked.

"Probably on Friday, though ships' schedules are sometimes quite difficult to predict—"

Friday. Maggie's life would begin again on Friday. "I must tell Elisabeth," she muttered, starting to leave the parlor without so much as a fare-thee-well for Mr. Coates.

He stopped her with an anxious, "Miss Chamberlin, there are some matters that need immediate attention, and since Mr. McKenna is unavailable—"

Maggie turned slowly to face her caller. "I don't see how I can be of help, Mr. Coates."

For the first time, Maggie noticed that the man was carrying a case of some sort. "There are papers that need signing, Miss Chamberlin, and Mr. McKenna did leave word that in case of extreme emergency, your signature was to be accepted in place of his own."

Maggie's mouth dropped open. Few men allowed their wives any say at all in their business affairs, and yet Reeve had trusted his fiancée with the sweeping power of his own name. Staggered, Maggie reached out for the newel post on the banister and held on until her knees felt steady again.

"V-very well," she said shakily, "take the papers into the study, please, and I'll look at them in a moment. Before I do anything else, I have to tell a little girl some very good news."

Simon Coates smiled and nodded his head, and Maggie went carefully up the stairs to the room where

Elisabeth slept so fitfully, her thumb still in her mouth.

Gently, Maggie pulled the little thumb free and whispered, "Elisabeth?"

Dark, thick lashes fluttered open. "Mama," Elisabeth said firmly.

Maggie gathered the child close, her eyes brimming with tears again. But this time they were tears of joy. "Elisabeth, your papa isn't dead at all—it was a mistake. He's coming home to us this very Friday!"

Elisabeth gave a gleeful shout and hurled her arms around Maggie's neck. "Papa!" She laughed.

Drawn by the uproar, Cora dashed into the room, wringing her hands. "What on earth—"

"Reeve is alive!" Maggie cried, spinning around once, clutching Elisabeth, for the sheer, miraculous rapture of it. "He's alive and he's coming home!"

"Oh, miss," Cora breathed, her plump cheeks flushed, "that's wonderful."

Maggie gave Elisabeth another hug and then set her on her feet. "I've got papers to sign," she said brightly. "Cora, will you do me an enormous favor and call Philip Briggs for me? Tell him, please, that I won't be going to America after all, and I won't be coming in for rehearsals today. He'll argue with you about the rehearsals; just tell him that I know my lines well enough and I'll be there in plenty of time for the performance."

Cora nodded and she and Elisabeth left the room hand in hand. Maggie took a moment to say a prayer of thanks, then went to stand in front of the mirror over Reeve's bureau.

Pale and peaked only minutes before, she was now glowing with happiness. There was the matter of Reeve's illness, but that would heal in time; plenty of love and care would hurry the process.

After a short interval had passed, Maggie felt composed and businesslike. She went downstairs to the study to meet with Mr. Coates. Cora was just turning away from the telephone, and she was flushed again, though this time with annoyance.

"He says you'd better be in that theater within the next twenty minutes," she confided tightly in passing, Elisabeth trotting along at her heels. "If you're not, he's going to come here and fetch you himself."

"If Philip tries anything like that," Maggie answered blithely, "it will cost him a layer of skin and at least one eye." She swept past the frazzled nanny to the desk, where Mr. Coates waited politely.

Maggie took Reeve's chair. "Now, then," she said. "I'll have a look at those papers."

To Mr. Coates's suppressed annoyance, Maggie insisted upon reading every word of every document before signing, and what she didn't understand, she asked to have explained.

Philip arrived, unannounced, just as Mr. Coates was leaving.

"What the devil do you mean by holding up the entire cast this way?!" he shouted.

Maggie smiled warmly. "Yes, Philip, it is good news that Reeve is alive after all. Thank you for saying so."

Philip had the good grace to look chagrined. "Of course it's wonderful news, Maggie. I'm very happy for you. But—"

"But nothing. I'm not going to rehearse today, and if you press me, I won't perform either."

Philip's amber eyes narrowed. "Maggie Chamberlin—"

"Soon to be McKenna."

"You'd like to think so," Philip challenged her as he sank into the chair Reeve's secretary had just vacated.

Maggie took a moment to admire her ring. "It seems that Reeve left word at his offices that my signature was to be as good as his when it came to matters of business."

Philip's mouth dropped open. He had never believed that Reeve really intended to marry Maggie, but now he was forced to face the truth. "That means that the man has virtually handed over everything he owns!"

"He trusts me," Maggie said, glorying in the words. "He must think that I have a very practical nature."

Philip made a rude snorting sound. "More likely, he's so besotted that he doesn't know what he's doing. And you haven't got a 'practical nature,' Maggie—if you had, you wouldn't be throwing away a chance to set America on its ear!"

Maggie smiled, perched now on the edge of Reeve's desk, her arms folded. "I'm sure there are lots of other actresses who would like to go," she said cheerfully. "Loretta Craig, for instance."

"The people involved want you, Maggie. If you don't go, neither do Samuel and I."

Maggie felt just the slightest guilt. "I'm pregnant, Philip," she reminded him quietly. "Just how much are they going to want me when I have a stomach out to here?"

"You could have taken a short sabbatical and then left the child with a nanny somewhere and—"

"Leave my baby with a stranger?" Maggie was stiff with outrage. "You can't be serious, Philip—I never intended to do that for a moment!"

Philip was now leaning forward in his chair, his head in his hands, his fingers entangled in his hair as though he might be planning to tear it out. He was making an odd groaning sound that made Maggie stoop to look into his face, concerned.

"Philip?"

"Why me?!" he wailed. *"Why?"*

Maggie patted the top of his head compassionately and swept out.

The rest of the week crept by. By day Maggie helped Cora in her work with Elisabeth, coaxing the child to add more and more words to her still-limited vocabulary. At night she threw herself into her performance

265

in the play, and every evening at curtain time there were more flowers and more offers to travel to other parts of the world as an actress.

Maggie was pleased by this acclaim, of course, though she had no intention of leaving Australia. Though success was what she'd dreamed about all her life, Reeve was more important now.

On Friday afternoon, having missed another rehearsal, Maggie was pacing the sidewalk when the carriage drove up. To her surprise, Jamie got out first.

He patted her cheek and then muttered, "Oh, hell," and kissed her forehead.

Maggie was craning her neck, trying to see inside the carriage. Jamie took her shoulders in his hands and made her look at him.

"Maggie, Reeve isn't himself. You're going to have to be very, very patient."

By then the waiting had become unbearable. Maggie shrugged free of Jamie and hurried to the door of the coach, which stood open. One seat had been removed, and Reeve was there, sitting rigidly upright in an invalid's chair. There wasn't a flicker of recognition in his face, and Maggie felt her heart sink.

She would have climbed into the carriage, but Jamie and the driver shuffled her aside to lift Reeve's chair out. He didn't react to the jostling motion at all, he just stared vacantly into space.

"Reeve?" Maggie whispered.

There was no response at all, not even a look or a twitch of a muscle. Reeve looked like one of the wax figures Maggie had once seen in a London museum.

Jamie gave her a gentle look and then he wheeled Reeve toward the house. On Maggie's instructions he and the driver took him upstairs to his room.

"Leave us alone, please," Maggie requested hoarsely, and both men obediently went out.

"Reeve."

He was staring not at Maggie, but through her, as though she were invisible. Her heart twisted painfully, and she stepped up to him and took his hand gently into her own, laying it to her stomach.

"There's a child growing inside me, Reeve," she said. "Your child."

She saw a muscle beneath his ear move almost imperceptibly, and once again joy swelled within her. She bent to kiss Reeve's forehead. "I love you," she said. "I love you now and I'll love you always."

One tear pooled in Reeve's eye and slipped down his granite cheek. Maggie then knew for certain that he was going to get well.

It was her farewell performance, and by the time it was over, the audience was on its feet, shouting and clapping. With the others, Maggie took her bows.

In the wings, Samuel lifted her off her feet and planted a smacking kiss on her cheek. "You were sensational!" he said.

Maggie laughed with happiness. She was going to miss Samuel very much; he'd been a true friend, helping her with her performances and never making the kinds of demands that other men might have. "So were you," she answered somewhat breathlessly once her feet were back on the floor again. People were pressing all around, but she lingered, looking up into Samuel's face. "You're not angry with me? About— about the tour, I mean?"

Samuel smiled and took her upper arms into his hands. "How could I be angry with you when your eyes shine like that? Your tragic little face was breaking my heart."

Maggie reached up to touch his smooth-shaven cheek. "Be happy always, Samuel," she said softly, and then she turned to leave.

Her carriage was waiting in the alleyway behind the theater, but so, alas, was Duncan Kirk. He was leaning against the brick wall of the building, smoking a cheroot, and when he saw Maggie, he tossed it to the ground.

He looked so tormented that Maggie couldn't find it in her heart to be angry with him. She settled her shawl around her shoulders and said, "Hello, Duncan."

Duncan's throat worked for a moment, and his lips moved, but no sound came out.

Maggie, feeling generous, smiled and started past him. She wanted to get into that carriage and go home to Reeve, and the sooner the better.

But Duncan stopped her with a rasped, "Maggie, don't go."

She paused, then turned to face him. In the light of the moon he looked haggard and upset. "I must," she said gently. "Reeve is waiting."

"Damn Reeve!" Duncan exploded suddenly. "The man is a cripple! What can he give you?"

Behind her Maggie heard the carriage door squeak open, and the sound made her braver. "He can give me love, Duncan," she answered.

Duncan's face went gray. "No," he breathed. "You and I were meant to be together—you've got to believe me."

Maggie only shook her head.

Duncan started toward her then, blindly, furiously, and Maggie was afraid. Suddenly, she found herself looking at the broad expanse of Jamie McKenna's back as he made a barrier between Duncan and herself.

"Is there a problem, mate?" he asked cordially.

"You again!" Duncan spat.

The powerful shoulders moved in a shrug. "I'm likely to turn up in the damnedest places. How's your shoulder, then?"

Duncan cursed and spun on one heel to stride back into the theater, and Jamie turned to look down into Maggie's face with a reprimand in his azure eyes. "Can't you go anywhere without getting into trouble?" he demanded.

Maggie lifted her chin and was about to come back

with a snappy retort when she realized that Jamie was teasing. She gave a nervous giggle and let her forehead rest against his strong shoulder for a moment. "So far, I haven't managed that," she said.

Jamie chuckled and helped her into the carriage, then climbed in after her. He gave the wall behind him a firm rap with his knuckles, and the vehicle was in motion.

"I have something of yours," Maggie said, opening her handbag and rummaging through it. A moment later she held out the beggar's badge, still suspended from its rawhide string but washed clean of Duncan Kirk's blood.

Jamie took the medallion and slipped it on over his head, touching it fondly before dropping it inside his rough-spun shirt. "Thanks, Maggie. I didn't feel right without it."

"How is Reeve?"

Jamie shrugged, though there was a shadow of misery in his eyes. "Just the same. You'll have to be more careful once I leave, snippet, because my brother is in no shape to be pulling you out of fixes."

Maggie leaned forward. "Once you leave? Jamie, you're not going, are you?"

Jamie gazed out at the lights of Sydney for a few moments before answering. His voice was hoarse. "I have to, Maggie-girl. I have a property of my own—I told you that."

"In New Zealand," Maggie confirmed despondently.

Jamie nodded.

A despairing sort of curiosity overtook Maggie. "Why have you been hiding from Reeve all these years when you must have known how badly he wanted to find you?"

Jamie sighed. "You're not going to leave me alone until I answer, I suppose?"

"That's right," Maggie replied.

Unexpectedly, Jamie unbuttoned the cuff of his

right shirt-sleeve and began rolling it up. Even in the dim light from the streetlamps, Maggie could see the jagged scar that covered his forearm.

Maggie gasped, touching the mark with tentative fingers. "What happened?"

"Reeve."

Maggie's heart stopped beating and then started again. "Are you saying that your own brother did that to you?"

Jamie nodded, rolling the sleeve back down, buttoning the cuff in a methodical way that made Maggie want to scream with impatience. Finally, his answer came. "He had his reasons, love. And he didn't know that the man who jumped him in a back street in Brisbane was me. He was only defending himself, and he did a right proper job of it."

"Why would you attack Reeve, of all people?"

"Didn't know it was him at the time. I meant to rob him, Maggie. I wasn't the same man I am today."

Maggie reached across the carriage seat to take one of Jamie's hands in her own. "Reeve probably doesn't even remember the incident, Jamie—and even if he did, I know he would forgive you."

"You may think that, but I'm not so sure," Jamie answered distractedly. "Reeve can be a hard man, Maggie. And I'd rather have him looking for me than hating me for what I used to be."

Maggie lowered her eyes. "Jamie, he's been searching for you for twenty years. He almost didn't forgive me when he found out I'd seen you and told him nothing about it."

"Like I said, Reeve can be hard." There was a finality in his tone, a stubbornness as ungiving as Reeve's.

"He loves you!"

"And I'd like to keep it that way."

Maggie sighed. "Jamie," she began again reasonably. "He's been with you in New Zealand. He'll know where to find you."

"He'll never remember," Jamie said, and Maggie had a terrible feeling that he was right.

"You told me that Reeve's life would be in danger if I told him I'd seen you," she accused him, thinking of all she'd gone through in an effort to keep that secret.

"I lied," Jamie answered flatly.

Chapter 19 ❧

THE BED WHERE REEVE LAY WAS AWASH IN MOONLIGHT.
Maggie planned to sleep upstairs, in the attic room
she'd originally been given, but she needed to touch
Reeve, to assure herself that he was indeed back, safe,
if not sound.

She sat down on the edge of the bed, wondering
whether he was asleep or awake, and tentatively
touched his forehead. She saw his eyes open, and she
smiled. "Hello, Reeve," she said softly.

Maggie thought she saw his lips move, and she was
quick to light the lamp on the bedside table. He
looked exhausted, but stronger, too, and he was
definitely trying to say something.

His struggle tore at Maggie's heart. She touched his
lips with her fingers and whispered, "It's all right,
darling. You're home now, and you're safe."

The word was torn from him in a breathless rasp.
"Yank," he said.

Maggie's tears threatened to overflow, but she bat-
tled them staunchly. Reeve's doctor, who'd visited
just before she left for the theater that evening, had
said that there must be no emotional displays in the

patient's presence. She drew a very deep breath and said brightly, "We'll be leaving for Queensland in a week's time. Your doctor tells me that the sunshine and the sea are just what you need now."

The change in his face, so long awaited, was terrible to see. Reeve paled, and there was a wild expression in his eyes. Maggie wondered what she'd said wrong, and then realized that the incident that had done injury to Reeve's mind had happened at sea. She could have bitten off her tongue. "I'll go now," she said, standing up, "and let you rest."

His left hand made an almost imperceptible movement, then groped for her, catching hold of her skirts. "Stay," Reeve struggled to say.

Maggie couldn't leave him, not now. She began removing her clothes and his eyes watched her hungrily as she shed each garment and laid it neatly over the back of a chair. Though she knew that Reeve couldn't make love to her, there was something intimate and sensual in undressing before him that way, in the light.

She was naked when she turned out the lamp, rounded the bed, and crawled in beside him, cuddling close and running one hand idly up and down his broad chest. He made a low, throaty sound of pure pleasure, and as Maggie's fingers moved over his abdomen, she felt him responding to her touch.

On impulse, she took him full into her hand and caressed him, heard the rumbling groan come from the depths of him to echo in the dark room. Giving Reeve pleasure became, at that moment, the whole reason for Maggie's existence. She slipped beneath the covers to give him an impish nip with her teeth, and she felt a shiver run the length of his body.

"I—need you—" he said, and the words were like a gruff sob.

Maggie continued to pleasure him, accelerating her efforts as she felt his rigid muscles begin to lose their stonelike quality and come alive again. When she knew he was ready, she moved to sit astraddle of Reeve, slowly taking him inside her.

"Yank," he pleaded.

Maggie had sheathed him in velvet, and every motion of her hips was exquisite delight for her. "I—love you—" she gasped, lifting his hands to her bare breasts and holding them there, letting him feel the nipples harden against his palms.

Reeve groaned and she sensed his struggle to move beneath her. "Relax," Maggie whispered, rising and falling upon him gently, glorying in the way he filled her. "Let me do it all."

Slowly, sweetly, she carried Reeve closer and closer to the sky, still holding his hands to her breasts, her head flung back as she climbed toward her own pinnacle. Just as her body buckled in fierce response to his, she felt Reeve shudder powerfully and then spill his own passion within her.

She sank to his chest, gasping for breath, and buried her face in the warmth of his neck. His hands went tentatively to Maggie's back, made their way slowly from the curve of her waist to the round plumpness of her bottom.

Maggie slept that way, linked to Reeve, and awakened in the morning to find that he'd hardened within her. Startled, she sat up, and the motion caused her such pleasure that she moaned and rolled her head back.

She heard Reeve chuckle, felt his hands cup her breasts, this time without help. And coupled with the sweet sensations he was arousing in her body was the joyful knowledge that Reeve was truly getting well.

Staring down at him, Maggie saw an impish light in his eyes and a grin on his mouth. Her breasts blossomed against his palms, growing heavy, and, with him still inside her, she bent forward. His hand slid aside and Maggie felt his mouth close over her nipple, taking slow, hungry suckle.

She made a whimpering sound as he swelled to even

greater magnificence inside her, and instinct caused
her to rotate her hips. Reeve's groan vibrated through
her breast as he continued to draw at it.

"Oh," Maggie whined as the sweet pressure built
within her. "Reeve, Reeve—"

He grazed her nipple gently with his teeth and gave
a hoarse cry as she began to move her hips faster and
faster. She would have withdrawn her breast so that
she could sit up, but Reeve would not allow that.
Stubbornly, he held her with his mouth even as he
drove her mad with his heat and his length.

Release was upon her in a moment of fiery fever
that left her shuddering. She sagged against Reeve as
he continued to suck her, his powerful body quivering
ferociously as he, too, was satisfied.

When she had the strength to rise, Maggie levered
herself upward with her hands. Reeve's fingers immediately found her breasts, kneading the soft, warm
flesh there, plucking at the pebble-hard peaks.

"Oh, no, you don't!" she scolded good-naturedly,
removing herself from Reeve and from the bed before
he could have her again.

That mischievous light was shining in his eyes, and
Maggie blushed from her toes to her hairline as she
felt his gaze sweep over her, telling her without words
that he knew he could have her at any time and under
virtually any circumstances.

"You think you're so smart," Maggie threw out just
as if he'd teased her aloud. "Well, we'll see how you
react to a thorough bath, Mr. Reeve McKenna."

He grinned, and Maggie stomped into the bathroom and ran water for a bath of her own. When she'd
finished, she put on a long wrapper of soft rose-
colored flannel and brushed her hair. Then, with a
joyful sort of spite, she filled a basin with warm water
and carried it, with a sponge and soap, to the bedside
table.

Reeve watched her impassively as she tossed back
the comforter and sheet to reveal his nakedness.

"Can't have the doctor knowing what you've been up to," Maggie said cheerfully as she soaped the sponge.

He grinned, and the sight filled Maggie with happiness, even though she was still pretending to be outraged. Deliberately, she began washing his abdomen and inner thighs, and, to her delighted amusement, his manhood swelled to a splendid length, wanting a bath of its own.

Maggie bathed every part of Reeve, except for his back, before deigning to wash the straining evidence of his passion. That she did at her exquisite leisure, delighting in the way Reeve's eyes rolled closed as he gave himself up to the sweet agony she was causing him.

She was quite unprepared for the strength in his arms when he suddenly caught her around the waist and propelled her toward him. She landed with her knees pressing into his pillow, one on either side of his head, and shivered when she realized what vengeance he was going to take. Maggie felt her wrapper being nuzzled aside and grasped the headboard of the bed in both hands to anchor herself.

"Reeve," she pleaded, "don't—"

The first glancing touch of his tongue silenced her. She tried to shift away, but his hands slid beneath her wrapper to close over her bare hips and hold her fast in the position he wanted.

Maggie knew that Reeve wasn't going to release her. Her breath came in quick gasps as he began his gentle reprisal.

Maggie was dressed, with her hair up in a coronet at the back of her head, when the doctor arrived. There was nothing she could do about the high color in her cheeks or the sweet humming sensation in the very core of her that made her words come out with a squeaky breathlessness.

Dr. Claridge, an elderly man with a balding pate

and dancing blue eyes, examined Reeve and said, smiling at Maggie, "Remarkable. What on earth did you do?"

Maggie went red as brick, and Reeve chuckled.

"Love will work miracles," said Dr. Claridge politely. "I've always said so."

Maggie made a dash for the door and fled down the rear stairs, her skirts clasped in her hands. There was a strange woman sitting at the kitchen table with Cora, sipping tea.

Feeling like a bounding schoolgirl, Maggie came to an abrupt halt, staring at the woman and feeling an uneasy premonition. The visitor's hair was dark, like Loretta's, and her eyes were a crystalline blue. Though she wore a very sedate dress, there was no hiding the shapely lines of her body.

"Maggie, this is Miss Eleanor Kilgore. She's going to be taking care of Mr. McKenna until he's up and around again."

Maggie nodded politely. Though it was completely frivolous, she felt an urge to drag Miss Kilgore to her feet and shuffle her out the back door. "I had meant to look after Mr. McKenna myself," she said.

Eleanor smiled, revealing tiny, perfect white teeth. "Caring for an invalid is quite exhausting, miss. Not to mention that it requires a rather strong stomach. Have you ever emptied a bedpan?"

Maggie had just been challenged, though only she and Eleanor seemed to know it. "I—I could," Maggie said uncertainly.

"But you haven't," Eleanor replied, her tone placid. "I imagine the servants have been taking care of that."

Maggie was very conscious of her tenuous position in Reeve's household. If she'd been his wife, she could have ordered Miss Kilgore out; as his fiancée—a slow blush crept up her face—and his mistress, she had no such right. "I'm taking Mr. McKenna to Queensland in just a few days. I'm sure you wouldn't want to travel so far, when the assignment will surely be a short one."

Eleanor was unmoved. "Dr. Claridge tells me that the recovery could take some considerable time, if it happens at all. Besides, I rather like the idea of living in a sunny, tropical setting. I'm told Mr. McKenna's estate borders the ocean."

That was more than Maggie had been told; she knew nothing at all about Reeve's Queensland property, except that he raised sugar cane there. She bit her lower lip and then walked purposefully over to the stove to get the kettle. She brewed a cup of tea before forcing herself to join Cora and the nurse at the table.

"Mr. McKenna seems to be recovering nicely," she said belatedly and in somewhat defensive tones.

"Physical responses," drawled Eleanor complacently, "can be misleading."

Maggie felt as though she'd been slapped, and her cheeks burned. "Dr. Claridge was quite pleased, actually," she said when she'd taken a moment to compose herself.

Before Eleanor could answer, Cora betrayed Maggie by rising to her feet and announcing cheerfully, "Well, I'd better look into packing Miss Elisabeth's things if we're making a journey."

Maggie tossed her a pleading look, which Cora missed completely, and then stared down into her teacup when she and Reeve's nurse were alone.

"I saw one of your performances in *The Taming of the Shrew,*" Eleanor said when the interval of silence grew awkward. "You were really very good."

"Thank you," Maggie responded woodenly.

"I can't help wondering why you would create such a stir and then turn your back on the theater entirely, Miss Chamberlin. According to the newspapers, you had quite a future in front of you—and in your native America too."

The answers that came to Maggie's mind all sounded childish and petulant. For the first time since

Reeve's return, she began to doubt her place in his affections. In retrospect, she realized that all the romantic gifts he'd sent had one thing in common: a note mentioning Jamie. He might only have given her the power to sign his name because he'd no reason to think she'd ever be called upon to use it and, as for the lovemaking, well, Reeve was a virile man, even in his illness. He might have responded to any other woman in just that way—Eleanor Kilgore, for instance.

Shaken, Maggie stood and carried her teacup to the sink. Eleanor was still waiting for a reply to her remark about Maggie's career in the theater.

Maggie held out her left hand, the magnificent ring shimmering on her finger. Even that didn't give her any peace; Philip had said that gems were easy for a rich man to acquire, and he was right. Nonetheless, as Eleanor inspected the ring, Maggie said, "I'm going to marry Mr. McKenna. So, of course, I'll have no time for the theater and certainly no inclination to travel all the way to America."

The light in Eleanor's stunning blue eyes was smug; there was no other word for it. "Mr. McKenna, according to the doctor, is a long way from being well enough to undertake the—er—rigors of marriage, Miss Chamberlin."

That's what you think, Maggie wanted to say, remembering the events of the morning, but of course she couldn't mention that. It was simply too personal. "Have you ever met Reeve before?" Maggie asked, following a hunch.

Eleanor sighed. "No. But of course I've seen him—he's well-known in Sydney, after all. He's a magnificent man."

"Yes," Maggie replied. "If you'll excuse me, I have things to do." She had nothing to do, if the truth were known, now that she'd given up her role as Kate, but she would have died before admitting that to Miss Eleanor Kilgore.

Eleanor smiled and rose from her chair. "I wonder

if you could spare the time from your busy schedule—I do hate to impose—to show me the way to Reeve—er—Mr. McKenna's room?"

Seething, Maggie nonetheless smiled her most fetching smile. "Of course," she said, and she gritted her teeth as she led Reeve's nurse up the stairs and along the second floor hallway. Why couldn't Dr. Claridge have engaged someone different, someone matronly and plain, she wondered as she indicated the door of Reeve's bedroom.

Eleanor knocked and then went in, at a summons from the doctor, and Maggie was left standing in the hall, wondering what to do.

She finally made her way down to the study, where the walls were lined with books. She chose a volume of fairy tales and went in search of Elisabeth, only to learn from a maid that Cora had put off packing the little girl's clothes to take her to the park instead.

At a loss, Maggie returned the book to the proper shelf in the study and then went outside. She longed to visit Tansy and pour out all her doubts and fears to her friend, but of course she couldn't. Tansy was working, and her duties would not be fulfilled until nightfall.

Jamie had apparently left for New Zealand already, and Maggie missed him. She would have been able to confide in Reeve's brother, and she craved his reassurance.

Opening the gate, Maggie set out in the direction of the corner where the streetcar stopped. She had money in the pocket of her skirt; maybe this was a good day to shop or visit the menagerie.

She rode into downtown Sydney in something of a stupor. Was it possible that Reeve had made all those promises and given her all those presents just because he thought she knew something about Jamie? Had he changed his attitude so abruptly, after his first furious reaction on learning that she'd encountered his brother in Melbourne, only because he hoped to persuade her to confide some secret concerning Jamie that he thought she was hiding?

Maggie sighed as she followed one street sign and then another, finally finding the trolleycar connection that would carry her to the menagerie. The glint of her diamond ring blurred as she looked down at it.

"Maggie!" hailed a man's voice as she stepped down from the car a short distance from the menagerie. "Is that you?"

Maggie looked around and saw Samuel Fairmont striding toward her, his face wreathed with smiles. She managed a faltering smile of her own, very glad to see her friend. "I came to see the animals," she said witlessly.

The expression in Samuel's eyes revealed that he'd guessed that she was upset, though his dazzling smile remained in place. "So did I. A happy coincidence—we'll see them together."

Maggie burst into unceremonious tears. She'd held them in check for so long that now they flowed uncontrollably. Samuel frowned, took her arm, and escorted her swiftly to a secluded bench, providing her with a fresh white handkerchief.

"What is it, little one?" he asked ever so gently. And that very tenderness made Maggie wail with grief and confusion.

Haltingly, she told Samuel her deepest secrets: how she was carrying Reeve's baby, how she wondered if he'd only pretended to want her because he thought she knew more about his missing brother than she was admitting, how threatened she was by Eleanor Kilgore, the nurse Dr. Claridge had engaged.

Samuel listened compassionately until the whole story had been told, and then he held Maggie close in an effort to comfort her. "Poor child—what a life you've had. Perhaps you should come to America with us after all."

Maggie shook her head, sniffling, and drew back from Samuel's comforting arms in an effort to compose herself. "I couldn't go, Samuel—I think I knew all along that I couldn't leave Elisabeth, let alone Reeve. Besides, such a journey would be too much to ask of a little baby."

Samuel used his thumbs to dry Maggie's face. "I have no idea who Elisabeth is, and Reeve clearly doesn't deserve you. As for the baby—Maggie, infants have been making crossings like that for centuries. They're really remarkably resilient, you know."

"Elisabeth is Reeve's niece—oh, it's all too complicated! Samuel, I just can't go—it would break my heart."

"It seems to me that your heart is already broken." Samuel sighed, but then he stood up and offered his hand. "Come. Let's have a happy afternoon, shall we? We'll see all of the animals and then we'll have a nice supper somewhere and I won't say another word about America or the theater."

Maggie smiled, knowing that her eyes were red-rimmed and puffy, that her face was mottled. "You really are so kind. I'll miss you terribly when you go away."

Samuel executed a sweeping, Petruchio-style bow. "We shall not speak of partings and other sadnesses, m'lady. This is a day for making merry."

Laughing, Maggie slipped her arm through Samuel's and allowed him to escort her inside the menagerie. She had a wonderful afternoon, seeing zebras and elephants, monkeys and wombats, koala bears and kangaroos.

Remembering Mathilda, the kangaroo she had petted at Parramatta that recent day that seemed so far in the past, Maggie felt her spirits sag just a little. Things had not been quite so complicated then.

Samuel was quick to try to cheer her. "Did you know that the Aborigines have a legend about the 'roos, and how they came to be?"

Maggie shook her head, at once touched at Samuel's unflagging concern and intrigued by the prospect

282

of a story. He led her back to the same bench and they sat down again, Samuel's hand holding Maggie's own.

"It seems there was a terrible windstorm," he said, in his storyteller's voice. "Strange animals were blown through the sky, and their hind legs grew longer and longer, they were trying so hard to reach the ground.

"It was a dreadful storm, tearing grass and bushes from the ground and even uprooting trees. The Aborigines hid in the rocks, watching in horror, as you can imagine."

Maggie smiled and nodded, and Samuel went on. "As it happened, to the utter amazement of the onlookers, one of these odd animals became caught in the branches of a tree that was still clinging to the earth, and it was hurled to the ground. The creature looked all around, and then went hopping away."

Maggie laughed and clapped her hands. "Samuel, that was marvelous."

"Of course it was," he said with gentle humor. "Now, let's go and have something to eat. As it happens, I am quite ravenous."

Samuel's prosperity extended to having a carriage at his disposal, and he ushered Maggie to it and seated her inside. They drove to a restaurant in a hotel overlooking Rushcutter's Bay, and Maggie quite forgot her troubles as she laughed at Samuel's stories and consumed an enormous supper of roast beef, potatoes, and corn.

At the end of the meal Samuel invited Maggie to attend a performance of the play and see how her understudy was carrying on, but she shook her head. It was time to go back to Reeve's house and face things as they were.

Samuel got out of the carriage and escorted her to her door, planting a gentlemanly kiss on her forehead.

"Thank you, Samuel," she said softly. "You made an impossible day better."

He smiled. "I'm off to convince yet another Kate

that the moon is not the sun," he said, and then he strode back down the walk to his carriage.

Maggie let herself in and made her way slowly up the stairs, braced for another encounter with Eleanor. She didn't see her, however, and by the time she reached Reeve's door, she was brave enough to go in.

Eleanor was standing at the window, one side of the draperies still caught back in her hand, and Reeve was staring stonily at the ceiling. It was as though he'd made no progress at all.

Angered, Maggie went to his bedside and touched his hand. Reeve drew it away, and Maggie's eyes lifted to Eleanor's face.

"I was just telling Mr. McKenna that you'd arrived home in a gentleman's carriage," she said brightly, letting the drapery fall back into place.

Maggie could well imagine how the caring Miss Kilgore had phrased that bit of information. "Please go," she said steadily, and, to her surprise, Eleanor shrugged and left the room, closing the door quietly behind her.

Maggie smoothed dark locks back from Reeve's forehead and then kissed his stubborn, ungiving mouth. "You can't imagine how pleased I am that you're jealous," she teased.

His whole body trembled with the effort to speak. "I'm not—jealous!" he insisted.

Maggie smiled. "You are too. You're wondering who I was with and what I was doing. I went to the menagerie, if you must know, and there I encountered my friend, Mr. Samuel Fairmont, who is an actor."

Reeve was scowling, and his blue-green eyes snapped.

"He's quite handsome," Maggie went breezily on, "and very attentive. He bought me supper and listened to my tale of woe."

Reeve made a disgusted sound and tried to push Maggie off the bed, but she settled herself firmly and kept right on talking.

"My heart's broken, you know. I'm in love with this wonderful man—he's the father of my unborn child, incidentally—but I have a terrible suspicion that he's only using me because he thinks I know a great deal about his missing brother."

Reeve didn't react, but he was listening with his whole being.

"Oh, yes!" Maggie cried tragically, as if he'd said he didn't believe her. "It's quite true. But the truth is, I don't know anything about his brother. All I know is that I love this man who's sired my baby, but he freely admits that he doesn't love me."

Slowly, Reeve's hand rose to her face, and she thought she saw the hint of a smile on his mouth.

Maggie got up and walked to the door, summarily turning the key. Then, as the room filled with the first shadows of early evening, she began removing her clothes.

"I don't think much of Miss Kilgore's therapy," she teased as she tossed her dress aside and then slipped out of her petticoat. "It's not nearly so effective as mine."

She took a long time unbuttoning her camisole, and then went to sit on the bed, in only her drawers. Cradling Reeve's head in her arms, she lifted it to her bare breast, and he took the offered nipple hungrily into his mouth.

Chapter 20 🌿

THE NIGHTMARE REPLAYED ITSELF BEFORE REEVE'S MIND'S eye, day and night. He saw the water, seeming to boil with blood, and he heard the screams of his crewmen. The unforgettable stench of carnage filled his nostrils, and he could not turn away from the ship's rail. Not, that is, unless the Yank was loving him. She provided his only respite from the gruesome scene that plagued both his mind and his spirit.

He couldn't remember her name. She was lying beside him in the bed; he knew that. If he could just call out to her, she would drive the haunting spectacle from his mind for at least a few minutes.

"Loretta," Reeve rasped after a few minutes of desperate mental groping.

The light was turned up and the dreamscape became less intense, less brutal. He felt her hands on his bare shoulders, warm and reassuring.

"I'm Maggie," she said.

Reeve could see her clearly then. Her silvery-blond hair was tangled and soft, and her gray eyes were filled with a teasing sort of reprimand.

"Maggie," he repeated, puzzled.

286

She laughed softly and kissed his chin. "That's better," she said, twisting so that she sat with one soft hip against his side, looking down at him. Her hand stroked the hair back from his forehead. "We're off to Queensland tomorrow."

Reeve willed her to keep talking, about anything and everything. She had a way of absorbing his every thought and emotion.

She reached for a book on the bedside table and leafed through the pages, knowing somehow that the sound of her voice and the sight of her face were all that kept the horrors of the night at bay.

"The Lord is my shepherd," she read, "I shall not want.

"He maketh me to lie down in green pastures: he leadeth me beside the still waters.

"He restoreth my soul: he leadeth me in the paths of righteousness for his name's sake.

"Yea, though I walk through the valley of the shadow of death, I will fear no evil: for thou art with me; thy rod and thy staff they comfort me.

"Thou preparest a table before me in the presence of mine enemies; thou anointest my head with oil; my cup runneth over.

"Surely goodness and mercy shall follow me all the days of my life: and I will dwell in the house of the Lord for ever."

The familiar words rolled over Reeve's troubled spirit like a balm. He reached for Maggie's hand and held it tightly, and she understood. She began to read the same passage over again, and Reeve dared to close his eyes. For the first time he was not met with the grisly sight of sharks tearing at the carcass of a whale and at living men; instead, he saw green pastures, dotted with sheep.

And he slept a deep and healing sleep.

At Maggie's insistence the trip to Brisbane was made by train and not by sea. As a consequence, it took much longer, and everyone was exhausted on arrival.

Arrangements had been made for the party to spend one night at a local hotel and then journey on, the following day, to Reeve's property. From what Maggie had been able to discern by talking to Simon Coates, the plantation was a good ten miles due north of Brisbane. Reeve had recovered to the extent that he needed only a cane instead of the invalid's chair, but he still spoke rarely, and when he did, it was in monosyllables. Maggie suspected that he was just being cussed.

The hotel, as fate would have it, looked out over a crystal-blue sea, and after searching the entire upper floor of the building, Maggie finally found Reeve standing on the porch, gazing out at the rolling, white-capped waves.

"This is an incredible place," she said, drawing in the scent of burned sugar that filled the air. In a nearby gum tree, parrots alighted, like robins might in America or England, their plumage colorful and their songs raucous.

Reeve made a sound that indicated nothing more than that he'd heard her and kept his gaze fixed on the horizon.

Just then Cora came out of the hotel with Elisabeth, and the little girl hurled herself at Reeve, wrapping her arms around his legs and looking up at him adoringly. "Apple!" she crowed, demonstrating her progress. "Shoe button, potato, kangaroo!"

Reeve smiled wanly and ruffled her hair, and Cora removed the child and started down the steps. "We're going looking for seashells, Elisabeth and I," she announced.

"Seashells!" yelled Elisabeth.

Maggie laughed and linked her arm through Reeve's. "You're not fooling me, you know," she said quietly. "You could talk much more than you do if only you wanted to. I would think Elisabeth's efforts would shame you into trying harder."

He touched her nose. "Shoe button," he said, obediently, his eyes dancing. "Potato, kangaroo."

"That isn't funny," Maggie huffed, though secretly she thought it was.

"Marry me, Maggie," Reeve jarred her by saying. "Now, tonight."

Hope swelled within Maggie, but before she could reply, Eleanor appeared at the base of the steps. She'd been out walking along the beach, and her beautiful dark hair was windblown. Ignoring Maggie completely, she smiled at Reeve, smoothed her hair back from her cheek with one hand, and said, "I think you're overextending yourself, Mr. McKenna. Perhaps you'd best go to bed."

Reeve's attention, Maggie was relieved to see, was all for her. "That's a fine idea," he agreed, touching the tip of her nose. "But first I want to talk to a preacher."

Two splotches of color appeared on Eleanor's flawless cheeks. The look she gave Maggie would have scorched the hide of an elephant. "To confess your sins?" she drawled before she snatched up her skirts in her hands and stomped up the steps.

Maggie smiled warmly. "We'd be delighted to have you for a witness, Miss Kilgore," she said.

Eleanor marched inside the hotel, her chin high, her skirts rustling.

"I'm warning you," Maggie said, standing very close to Reeve. "The first thing I'm going to do as your wife is give that woman the sack."

Reeve laughed. "Jealous?"

"Never!" lied Maggie. But her good spirits were plummeting. Yet she was troubled by the fact that Reeve had still not said he loved her. She sat down on the swinging bench the hotel had provided for its guests' comfort and sighed.

Reeve immediately sat beside her. "What is it, Yank?"

Maggie whispered, "Do you love me?"

He picked up her hand, his thumb toying with the magnificent diamond on her finger. "I gave you this, didn't I?"

"You've probably given a lot of women a lot of baubles, Reeve."

"Never an engagement ring." He sighed.

Maggie repeated her question doggedly. "Do you love me?"

"I'm not sure I know what that means, Maggie, but insofar as I understand the word, yes."

Maggie closed her eyes. It certainly hadn't been a flowery declaration, but considering that she loved Reeve desperately and that she was carrying his child, she was relieved. Still, there were other hurdles. "About Jamie. Reeve, do you remember being with Jamie? Coming home with him on the ship after your—your experience?"

Reeve was staring at her as though she'd grown an extra nose. "What?"

"It was Jamie who brought you home. He looked after you before that too—until you were well enough to travel."

All the color that remained in Reeve's taut face drained away. "My God," he breathed. "I was with Jamie?" He grasped Maggie's elbow hard. "Why don't I remember?"

Maggie could only shake her head.

"There's a lot you can tell me, isn't there?" The words were sharp with suspicion and mistrust.

The wedding, a shining prospect only moments before, suddenly seemed impossible. "Reeve—"

He was propelling her inside the hotel, his cane stumping on the floor as they walked. Since the dining room was still empty, he chose that spot for his inquisition. Flinging Maggie down in a chair, Reeve leaned against the table and ordered, "Tell me everything!"

"He lives somewhere in New Zealand, Reeve—probably near Auckland. That's all I know, I swear it!"

Reeve's hand caught under Maggie's chin. "It had better be," he said through clenched teeth.

Maggie slapped his hand away, her eyes stinging with tears. "Damn you, Reeve," she spat out, leaping to her feet, the table between them for a barrier. "You have been using me all along!"

His face changed; Maggie saw him weaken. "No," he protested. "That isn't true."

"It is!" Maggie cried, wiping away her tears with the heels of her hands. A moment later she wrenched the ring from her finger, hurled it at Reeve, and fled the hotel.

She didn't stop running until she'd reached the beach, where she slumped to her knees in the pure white sand and covered her face with both hands. Her grief and her fury were noisy, and Maggie made no attempt to control them.

"I knew it would come to this," observed a voice behind her.

And Maggie whirled at the familiarity of the tones and cadence of that voice. "Duncan!" she gasped, scrambling up from her knees.

He was dressed for Queensland, in a pristine white suit with an elegant string tie. He came toward her and, with a handkerchief as pale as his suit, dried her face as though she were a lost and errant child. "Come back to us, Maggie," he said softly. "I swear there'll be no more episodes like the one in Melbourne."

Maggie shook her head, amazed that she'd been tempted, for just a moment, to go with Duncan. "I couldn't. I love Reeve."

Duncan's face tightened almost imperceptibly. His eyes slipped over the bodice of Maggie's simple cotton dress to her thickening waistline. "Good God, you're pregnant, aren't you?" he asked in a stunned whisper.

Maggie dropped her eyes. "Yes."

There was a dreadful silence, during which she could feel Duncan's fury, but when he spoke, his voice was even. Composed. "All the more reason for you to come with me, Maggie, right now."

Maggie looked at Duncan in wonder. "How can you suggest that when you know—"

"I know that McKenna will tire of you just as he tired of Loretta. What will you do then, Maggie? Raise your child alone, on the generous stipend Reeve always provides for his former mistresses?"

Maggie swallowed. "I won't accept anything from him!"

"That would be foolish indeed. Unless, of course, you'd already made other arrangements for your own support and the child's."

"Your tenacity never ceases to astound me, Kirk," Reeve said.

Neither Maggie nor Duncan had heard him approaching, and both were stricken to silence.

"Go back to the hotel," Reeve said to Maggie, though his gaze was fixed on Duncan Kirk. "The preacher will be arriving at any minute."

Maggie stayed where she was. "There won't be any need for a preacher, Reeve."

Duncan had recovered his aplomb by then; he was smiling at Reeve. "I should think you'd want the services of a priest, being who you are. But that kind of marriage wouldn't be quite so easy to annul, would it?"

Reeve's hand tightened on the handle of his cane, and for one awful moment Maggie thought he was going to club Duncan over the head with it. For her part, she was reasoning out what it might mean for a Catholic to be married by a preacher instead of a priest. In the eyes of the church the ceremony would not be valid.

Maggie looked covetously at the cane. Oh, to grab it and twist it around its owner's neck!

"I'll be damned, Kirk," Reeve breathed, "if I'll explain to you!"

"You can explain to me, then!" Maggie cried, planting herself directly in front of Reeve.

"Go back to the hotel and wait for the preacher, darling," he said with an acid smile.

Where once Maggie had gloried in the idea of marriage to this man, now she felt trapped. She had no real choice but to do as he said; leaving with Duncan was unthinkable, and she'd missed her chance to go on tour as an actress. She lifted her skirts and stomped back toward the hotel, and Reeve followed, though at a much slower pace.

Inside her room, which adjoined Reeve's, Maggie quickly locked the door to the hall and the one that linked her quarters to his. Then, steaming, she opened her trunk and riffled through it, passing up all her pretty new things for the tattered nightgown she'd brought from England. Quickly, she stripped off her clothes and put it on.

The key in the door between Maggie's room and Reeve's toppled to the floor with a warning clink, and then he was standing there in the opening, brandishing a key of his own.

His wonderful blue-green eyes narrowed at the sight of the nightgown she wore. "What the hell—"

"Bed is all you want me for, isn't it?" Maggie snapped, taking down her hair and brushing it. "I thought I'd dress appropriately!"

"I prefer you naked, but if you insist on being married in your nightgown, I guess that's your business. Explaining the wedding pictures to our children will be something of a problem, but I'm sure you'll come up with a story or two."

Maggie had reached the limit of her endurance. She hurled her hairbrush at Reeve and it went wide of him, crashing against the woodwork that framed the door. "I despise you," she said.

"I've asked for a priest," he answered, unmoved.

"Good! He can perform your last rites!"

Reeve laughed. "Oh, Yank, you are full of fire. I'm looking forward to the warmth in my bed."

Maggie picked up the pitcher from her bureau top and hurled it with a mighty effort. Unfortunately, she missed again, and the crockery shattered on the floor at Reeve's feet.

"You must have been smashing as the shrew," Reeve said, leaning one shoulder against the door-jamb. "I suppose the part came quite naturally to you."

Maggie reached for the basin and held it high above her head, ready to throw. "Get out!" she screamed.

Grinning, Reeve scuffled through the shards of glass on the floor, his cane making that familiar thump-thump sound. With one hand he pulled the basin from Maggie's grasp and purposefully dropped it. "I can afford a few bits of crockery, love," he said, catching his hand under her chin and lifting her face for his kiss. "And," he added when he'd stolen Maggie's breath from her lungs and set her heart to hammering, "I can tame you."

"You'll spend the rest of your life trying!" Maggie sputtered.

"Open your nightgown, Maggie. I want you."

Maggie trembled, so great was the need to do as he said, even though it would mean utter defeat for her pride. "No."

Reeve let the cane clatter to the floor, and his fingers were remarkably deft as he unfastened the tiny buttons. Maggie's camisole was underneath, and he chuckled at this flimsy barrier.

Maggie drew in her breath and closed her eyes, the

battle lost before it had even begun. She felt the camisole being lowered, and then the touch of Reeve's tongue on the peak of her breast. He sucked freely for a while, and then, as easily as he had before his illness, he lifted Maggie up into his arms and carried her to the bed.

She landed hard on the mattress, knocking the wind from her. It was several moments before she managed to say, "You charlatan! You didn't need that cane at all—"

Reeve grinned, kneeling beside her on the edge of the bed and rolling her nightgown up until nothing of her was left to his imagination. "I think it makes me look distinguished," he said, caressing her.

Maggie was writhing now, helpless with passion. "And it—occurs to me—that you're speaking—very easily—for a man—who was silent for so—long."

Reeve chuckled. "You've caught me out, Yank," he answered smoothly. "I've been practicing."

"Oh!" Maggie gasped, and from that moment on, she was the one who could not speak coherently.

Father Shaunassey wore a priest's cassock and a crucifix; otherwise, Maggie would have asked to see his credentials. As it was, she simply stood beside Reeve in the hotel dining room, her face still flushed from the prenuptial episode upstairs, while the holy words were recited.

Cora served as a witness, Eleanor as a grudging wedding guest, and Elisabeth as a delighted one.

The priest pronounced Maggie and Reeve to be man and wife, and Reeve availed himself of the groom's prerogative: a kiss.

Lips still moist from that, Maggie shook her dazed head in an effort to clear it and marched over to Eleanor.

"We won't be requiring your services after today," she said bluntly. "Your passage home to Sydney will be paid and, of course, you'll be given any wages due you."

"But I've another month!" Eleanor sputtered.

Maggie smiled broadly. "Then you shall have leisure time. How wonderful for you!"

Eleanor turned in a sweep of skirts and outrage and left the room, nearly colliding with Duncan in the doorway.

"My heartiest congratulations," he said, kissing Maggie on the cheek before she could fully take in the fact that he'd had the gall to show up.

"I knew you'd be happy for us," Reeve said dryly, standing behind Maggie and slipping his arms around her waist. She felt his hard length and sighed, resigned to the wonders of the night to come.

"You'll be traveling to the property tomorrow, I presume?" Duncan asked.

Reeve's breath was warm on the nape of Maggie's neck. It set her tingling. "Maybe," he answered gruffly.

Even though Duncan's face was gray with suppressed rage, he smiled. "You'll want to look out for the bushrangers, of course. Lots of lonely stretches along that road."

Maggie gulped. "Bushrangers?" she echoed.

"At home we call them outlaws," Duncan was helpful enough to point out. His eyes, fiery in his pale face, slipped to Reeve. "I hope you're strong enough to protect your womenfolk, McKenna."

"I expect I'll manage."

Duncan shrugged, though the expression on his face was anything but nonchalant. "I have quite a company of men with me. If you'd like, we can escort you as far as your place."

"Thanks," Reeve answered tightly, "but no thanks."

Duncan turned and walked away and Maggie remembered the maps the Kirk boys had drawn when she was still their governess. The place they'd marked as being their father's land couldn't be far from Reeve's.

"He lives near you?" Maggie asked, inexplicably frightened.

"On the plantation next to mine," Reeve replied. And then, as unconcerned as a child, he began cutting the small cake provided by the hotel's kitchen staff.

He gave a piece to Maggie and then to Elisabeth, setting his own aside. Though it couldn't have been later than four o'clock in the afternoon, he gave an exaggerated yawn.

Maggie turned bright pink. "Don't you dare suggest it!" she warned him.

Reeve touched an index finger to her upper lip, coming away with a speck of icing, which he touched to his tongue. The subtle sensuality of the motion made Maggie lower her eyes, suddenly as shy as if she'd never been touched by this man. To her utter mortification, she yawned.

Reeve laughed and kissed her on the forehead, then turned and lifted Elisabeth up into his arms. She pointed to Maggie and chirped triumphantly, "My mama!"

Forgetting her serious doubts about Reeve's love in particular and their marriage in general, she kissed the little girl soundly on the cheek. Maggie knew she would always cherish that moment.

After making slow, sweet love, Reeve and Maggie lay still on their marriage bed, their bodies damp with exertion. Reeve's hand caressed Maggie's slightly rounded abdomen.

"When will this child of mine be born, Yank?" he asked quietly.

Maggie was full of happiness and faith in the future. "November."

"Summer." Reeve seemed to dream the word rather than say it.

Maggie smiled. "I can't get used to November being summer. Australia is such a strange place."

"Aye," Reeve agreed. Then the dreamy expression left his face and he frowned. "Maggie—"

Maggie braced herself for more questions about Jamie.

"I think you should let Eleanor stay on awhile. Half the time there aren't any servants at the property—"

"Eleanor?" Maggie interrupted pointedly. "Just when did 'Miss Kilgore' become Eleanor?"

Reeve chuckled. "The first time she bathed me," he teased.

Maggie stiffened. "I'd rather slave from dawn till dusk than have that woman under my roof for another day!" she spouted.

Reeve traced the pouting lines of her lower lip with a fingertip. "And I'd rather you carried our child to full term, Yank, instead of working yourself into an early birth."

"Eleanor would never condescend to be a servant," Maggie bristled. "She's a nurse."

"All the same, I'm going to ask her."

Maggie could imagine her own humiliation if that should happen. "Reeve, you can't. I gave her the sack, showed her the road—"

"All right. We'll see if we can't find someone in Brisbane."

"Thank you." Maggie sighed.

"Of course, I'll have to go and take care of the matter tonight, since the coach leaves first thing tomorrow morning."

Maggie didn't want to give up her groom even for a few hours, but she found the prospect far more palatable than that of having Eleanor Kilgore traipsing along with them when they left. She made a face.

Reeve chuckled. "Naturally, I'll make sure you've been thoroughly loved before I go." He bent to give the peak of Maggie's right breast a gentle lashing with his tongue, and she groaned. His hand strayed downward to caress her most vulnerable part. "How shall I love you, Maggie?"

Trembling, her hands entwined at the nape of his neck, Maggie told him. Soon Reeve was inside her, entering with one smooth, powerful thrust, and they were moving together in the first throes of rapture.

Maggie's hands moved from Reeve's neck to the broad, muscular expanse of his back, her nails digging into his flesh as her passion grew to intolerable levels. "Oh—Reeve—please," she begged. "Please!"

He withdrew until he was barely inside her, silently taunting her for long moments. Then, in a long stroke, he moved inside her again.

Maggie grasped at his buttocks, frantic, but he pulled back once more, lingering there, at the very brink of leaving her. "Why?" she whispered wildly. "W-why are you d-doing this?"

He favored her with a long, sweet stroke of friction. "It's all—part of your taming—little shrew."

Maggie's head was thrust back, her eyes closed. She felt the roughness of Reeve's chest chafing her sensitive nipples as he sheathed and unsheathed himself in her aching warmth. She raised her fingers to touch his flat male breasts and began caressing them, and the teasing stopped.

With a rumbling groan Reeve slid his hands under her bottom and lifted so that he could possess her fully. Again and again he plunged inside her, and Maggie made a whimpering sound in her throat as each stroke set another, hotter blaze inside her.

Finally, she erupted with a lusty gasp, flinging her hips up to meet his as her back arched. A cascade of sensation pounded within her, and then Reeve cried out as he, too, reached the limits of his self-control. Shuddering, he sank to Maggie's soft and pliant body.

She wound a finger in the hair at the nape of his neck. "Who's taming whom?" she teased.

Reeve made a growling sound and slipped downward to kneel between Maggie's legs. Grasping her by the ankles, he forced her to bend her knees, then kissed the tender flesh on the inside of one thigh. "We'll see," he said.

"I'd like to withdraw my challenge," Maggie struggled to say.

"Too late," Reeve replied, and he didn't sound at all regretful.

Chapter 21

THE OVERLAND COACH WAS DRAWN BY A TEAM OF EIGHT bay horses. Maggie watched, holding Elisabeth's hand, as trunks and valises were loaded atop the vehicle and strapped into place. Eleanor was in evidence, but there was no sign of the woman Reeve had promised to hire as housekeeper.

When he would have handed Maggie inside the coach, she hung back until Cora and Eleanor had both been seated. Reeve lifted Elisabeth through the open door, and then turned to his bride, a somewhat sheepish look on his face.

Maggie glared at him.

"She said she doesn't mind being the housekeeper," he whispered, irritated. "Great scot, Maggie—it's only for a month!"

"You promised!"

"I had no chance to find anyone else, now, did I?"

Maggie folded her arms stubbornly. "I'm your wife. I'll look after your house!"

"You're my wife, all right. And you'll get your backside into that coach before I blister it, with all Brisbane looking on!"

She got into the coach, disdaining her husband's offer of help, and met Eleanor's gaze evenly. Eleanor smiled and inclined her head—Tansy would have called her expression "cheeky"—and if Cora and Elisabeth hadn't been present, Maggie would have reached out and slapped the woman right across the face.

Reeve, no more a fool than Maggie, rode up top with the driver.

The weather, so mild the day before, was rapidly turning nasty. An eerie wind howled in the trees and great gray clouds fretted and rumbled in the sky. Remembering her first experience with an Australian rainstorm during the camp meeting at Parramatta, Maggie felt warm color rise in her cheeks.

After a time her throat began to feel a bit raw and her head ached, but she would have died before complaining.

The coach hadn't traveled far when the angry clouds burst and a driving torrent began, striking the ground so hard that it sounded as if a great fire were burning all around them. A cool mist filled the coach.

"I hope we don't get bogged down in the mud," fretted Cora, fiddling with her gloves and then straightening her hat. She glanced down at Elisabeth, who had fallen asleep in her lap, her head resting against Cora's sizable bosom. "We'd be sitting ducks if any bushrangers happened along."

Eleanor smiled indulgently. "The driver carries a rifle," she said.

"Piffle," said Cora. "What good would that be against a dozen or more men?"

"I'm sure we're quite safe," Maggie put in.

Of course, it was exactly then that the coach lurched violently to one side and, with a sickening sliding motion, settled into a deep rut. Even Eleanor blushed at the words the driver bellowed at his team, trying to spur them onward.

The coach didn't move, except to settle deeper into the mud.

Men in broad-brimmed hats and long canvas raincoats appeared on every side then, mounted on horseback and carrying guns. Maggie held out her arms to a confused, just-awakened Elisabeth, and the child scrambled from Cora's lap to hers.

Cora's chin was quivering, though she was obviously trying to maintain a brave front for Elisabeth's sake. "Bushrangers," she whispered.

"Nonsense," said Eleanor with a cool smile. "It's only Mr. Kirk and his party, stopping to offer assistance."

Maggie wondered how Eleanor had come to know Duncan so well that she could pick him out of a dozen men in raingear in the middle of a rousing storm. Given the animosity between Duncan and Reeve, she'd almost rather the horsemen had been bushrangers.

The door of the coach opened and Reeve was there. Maggie was very glad to see him, in spite of the fact that he'd brought Eleanor Kilgore along as housekeeper after she had expressly asked him not to. He was wearing a canvas raincoat, Maggie was relieved to note, though his hat was sodden and dripping.

"There's an inn just up the road!" he shouted over the thunderous rain. "Duncan's men will take you there on horseback, and we'll catch up once we've got the coach out of the mud!"

Maggie's mouth dropped open. He meant to send the women into the bush with strange men, in this weather? "I'll stay here, thank you very much!" she shouted back. "And so will Elisabeth!"

Reeve answered with a scowl and reached for the child, who went to him before Maggie had a chance to restrain her. "I'll deal with you later, Mrs. McKenna, when I don't 'ave water runnin' down me back!"

So the brogue was back, was it? Not quite daring to

challenge Reeve when he was annoyed enough to slip back into the Irish, Maggie allowed herself to be lifted out of the coach and hauled onto the heaving, rain-slickened back of a horse. She felt the rider's canvas coat open to enfold her and ducked her head as close to the man's chest as she could, the rain having lashed the very breath from her lungs.

She could feel Duncan's heart beating against her cheek. Because he was warm and relatively dry, Maggie wrapped both arms around him and held on as the horse began picking its way through the deep mud.

It seemed a hundred miles to the inn, but finally they arrived. Maggie was set on her feet, and she dashed toward the shelter of the roof overhanging the porch, close behind Elisabeth, who had been carried by another rider. Eleanor and Cora followed.

Pausing in the doorway, Maggie looked at Duncan, sending a grudging thank-you with her eyes. He grinned and touched the battered-down brim of his hat, and then turned and rode away, his men following.

The innkeeper's wife was bustling about, building up the fire and shouting to her husband to brew fresh tea. Cora, wet to the skin herself, was kneeling on the hearth, hastily peeling away Elisabeth's drenched clothes and wrapping her in a blanket brought by a little girl wearing a mobcap and an apron.

Maggie wasn't about to undress in the middle of a public tavern, but Cora and Eleanor showed no such qualms. Soon they were shivering before the fire, stripped to their underthings and wrapped in blankets, just like Elisabeth. They were sipping tea while Maggie huddled close to the fire, hugging herself, her skirts dripping water on the polished wooden floor.

"Not that I care," Eleanor said in an tone that carried to Maggie's ears alone, "but if you don't get out of those clothes, you'll die of pneumonia."

Maggie was damned if she'd die of pneumonia or

anything else and leave Eleanor a clear path to Reeve's affections. She snatched up a blanket of her own and stormed over to the innkeeper's wife, who directed her into the kitchen. It was too busy a place for Maggie's liking, so she found a pantry and slipped inside to take off her clothes and wrap herself in the blanket. Soon, standing as far as she could from Eleanor without leaving the warmth of the fire, she was sipping tea with the others.

"Mrs. McKenna is expecting a child," Eleanor told the mistress of the small inn forthrightly. "Is there a place where she could lie down?"

"I don't want to lie down," Maggie protested, but the fact of the matter was that she felt a bit dizzy, on top of having a sore throat and a pounding headache. A sneeze loud enough to shake the rafters escaped her.

"There, you see," clucked Eleanor, grasping Maggie officiously by the arm. "She's already falling ill."

"Two and six for the room," said the innkeeper's wife, leading the way upstairs to a little chamber under the slant of the roof. Maggie was dragged along after her by Eleanor, who was stronger than she might have suspected.

The narrow bed looked warm and inviting, though the room was musty and the rain hammered furiously at the roof. Maggie shed her blanket and her damp camisole and drawers once she and Eleanor were alone in the room, and crawled under the covers.

The walls seemed to undulate, and Maggie closed her eyes. Within moments she'd lapsed into a queer state halfway between waking and sleeping, and she began to feel too warm. Every time she tossed back the covers, however, strong, deft hands replaced them again.

By nightfall, Maggie was burning with fever.

Reeve had found few things impossible in the course of his life, but prying that coach from the mud was that and more. Finally, an early darkness set in, and there was nothing to do but unhitch the exhausted team and ride on to the inn. He arrived with the angry driver, Duncan, and all his men hours after the women had been brought in.

Cora, Eleanor, and Elisabeth were all sitting at one of the inn's trestle tables. Elisabeth was looking through a picture book, while Cora and Eleanor played cards.

"Where's Maggie?" Reeve demanded instantly.

Eleanor stood up gracefully and swept through the crowd of sodden men to stand facing Reeve. "She's resting. You must get out of those clothes, Mr. McKenna. After all, you're not well."

Maggie, resting? Stubborn, energetic Maggie? Reeve thrust away Eleanor's hands when she would have taken off his rain slicker. "Where?"

Eleanor sighed. "Upstairs. First room on the right."

Reeve took the stairs two at a time, driven by some instinct that warned of trouble. He found her lying, half covered, in a cot pushed against the sloping roof.

Slipping out of his canvas coat, Reeve covered her and then stepped back, not wanting to drench her in rainwater. He flung his squishy hat aside and dried his hair with a towel he found in the cupboard beneath the washstand.

"Maggie?"

She opened her wondrous gray eyes and looked at him in an unseeing way that chilled Reeve as his wet clothes hadn't. "Saints in heaven," he muttered, touching her forehead with one hand.

Her flesh was hot beneath his fingers.

Whirling, Reeve raced out of the room and back down the stairs. "Eleanor," he ordered, "go upstairs and see to my wife. She's running a high fever." He turned to Duncan, who, like himself, was still dripping wet. "Kirk, is there a doctor around here?"

Duncan shrugged, but his face was drawn, and at that moment Reeve knew he cared about Maggie in his misguided and volatile way. "I don't spend any more time around here than you do, McKenna."

"That missionary fellow over on Squatter's Ridge," said the innkeeper's rotund wife, "he's a doctor, ain't he, Angelina?"

A young girl in a servant's cap nodded her head. "Yes, mum."

Before Reeve could react, Duncan rounded on his men and ordered, "Bring him here."

Two of them donned their canvas coats and wet hats without complaint, and went out.

Reeve went back upstairs to Maggie, stripping to his trousers and then pulling up a chair to sit beside her bed. He knew that Duncan was behind him, but he said nothing.

"She's so like my wife," Duncan observed.

That made Reeve look back over his shoulder at the man who had once, a long time ago, been his friend. "So that's why you're so obsessed with her," he said hoarsely. "She reminds you of Elena."

Duncan stiffened at the sound of the name Reeve knew was almost holy to him. "She was carrying your child too—just like Maggie is. It's an odd sort of justice, isn't it, McKenna?"

They had been over this ground a thousand times before. Reeve closed his eyes and sighed. "I never touched Elena," he said patiently, bracing himself for the reply he knew would come.

"She told me herself that the baby was yours. She said you were taking her to America—"

"Duncan, for God's sake, listen to me. I don't know why Elena lied to you, but there was nothing between us. Ever."

"She chased after you! Do you know how humiliating that was?"

Reeve touched Maggie's face again, and alarm made his voice gruff. Elena Kirk had indeed pursued him, but he'd never been in the habit of bedding other men's wives, and he'd rebuffed her as gently as possible. "She wanted to go home, Duncan. Back to England. Not America. England. It affected her mind."

"Now you're saying that Elena was mad?" Duncan rasped in a furious whisper.

"Not mad. Lonely."

"She had our sons and she had me!"

"She may have had the boys," Reeve agreed without taking his eyes from Maggie's fevered face, "but she never had you. You were too busy mining opals— too busy cavorting with your various mistresses. Little wonder Elena took to making up stories about lovers of her own."

"Dear God, I wish I could believe that she'd never given herself to you."

Reeve stood up and turned slowly to face Duncan. "What possible reason could I have for lying about it? After all you've done to me to avenge your imagined wrongs, I'd take pleasure in being able to tell you that your wife preferred me."

Duncan looked taken aback, and when Eleanor entered the room an instant after Reeve had spoken, he strode out without another word.

Eleanor was carrying a bowl of water and a cloth. Without speaking at all she took the chair Reeve had left vacant by the bed and began bathing Maggie's forehead. He wondered why his wife disliked the woman so, when she was obviously a competent and caring nurse.

"Could she lose the baby?" Reeve dared to ask.

Eleanor dipped the cloth in the basin and wrung it out, then laid it to Maggie's face again. "More to the point, Mr. McKenna," she remarked without looking up, "she could die."

That, the unthinkable, had not occurred to Reeve. His knees suddenly weak, he scanned the room for another chair and, failing to find one, knelt beside the bed. "No," he whispered, remembering another cot, in another room and another country, where another woman had died of a fever, long ago.

"We'll do our best to prevent that, of course," Eleanor said airily. "The blunt truth is that the doctor won't be able to do anything for Mrs. McKenna that I can't. She'll reach a crisis and then she'll either live or die."

Some of the mysteries of Maggie's antipathy toward this woman were solved. "How the devil can you speak of life and death that way, as if this were a choice between two kinds of tea cakes?" he demanded in a raw whisper.

Eleanor's slim shoulders moved in a shrug; she went right on trying to cool Maggie's fevered flesh. "One learns to be philosophical in my vocation, Mr. McKenna."

"Damn it, I don't want you to be philosophical—I want you to fight for her!"

She lifted dark blue eyes to his face, and he saw a weariness of soul in their depths. "You really do love Maggie, then?" she asked softly.

"Yes," Reeve answered, really sure of the fact for the first time.

Eleanor stood up, offering him the basin and the cloth. "Reeve, I think it might be best if you do this," she said, her eyes lowered now, her face virtually without color.

Reeve took the basin and sat down, gently applying the cloth to Maggie's forehead.

He knew that Eleanor had opened the door, though he didn't turn and look.

"I would advise you to keep very close watch on your Maggie," Eleanor said in parting. "You have enemies, Mr. McKenna, and some of them are people you seem to trust."

The door closed with a quiet click, and Reeve, pondering her words, went on tending his wife until Cora arrived, some minutes later, with fresh water.

He wondered who it was that Eleanor had referred

to before; Duncan was the obvious choice, but, of course, Reeve wasn't foolish enough to trust him. He'd let Kirk bring Maggie from the coach to the inn, but there'd been no real choice, and Duncan wouldn't have been foolish enough to try anything with the lady's husband so close by.

He glanced at Cora. She was harmless; just an aging spinster far from home and trying to make an honest living. Besides the retinue of servants staffing his various houses, that left only Eleanor herself. Had she, in some perverse way, been warning him that she was not what she seemed to be?

He sighed and stood up.

"No change, now, is there," Cora said regretfully, sitting down to take Reeve's place for a while. "You go and get yourself something to eat, Mr. McKenna. Stand by the fire for a bit. You'll be no good to Mrs. McKenna if you lapse into sickness yourself."

Reluctantly, Reeve left the room and went downstairs, where he forced himself to eat a bowl of stew and a biscuit. The warmth of the fire did feel good against his chilled flesh.

Duncan left a hand of cards to join him at the trestle table. "How's Maggie?"

"No better," Reeve responded woodenly, without looking at the man. An uneasy truce existed between them, but both knew that they would never again be friends. "And no worse."

"I regret what I said about Maggie's illness being a sort of justice. It isn't and I'm sorry."

Reeve glanced up from his stew, still deep in thought. "You do care about her in your way, don't you?"

Duncan nodded. "I'd have married her, but she wouldn't have me."

"After what happened in your carriage in Melbourne that night, Duncan, you shouldn't be surprised."

Duncan was holding an enamel mug of coffee between his hands. He lifted it to his mouth and took a steadying draught before answering. "I'm sure you'd agree that passion can do very strange things to a man."

"What would you have done—if my brother hadn't interfered?"

Duncan set the mug down with a thump. "That sheepherder was your brother?"

Reeve nodded. "I asked you a question."

His face twisted with a memory of pain suffered, Duncan unconsciously rubbed the place in his shoulder where he'd been stabbed. "The truth is, I intended to raise welts on her bare backside. I hadn't thought much beyond that, frankly."

"Maggie thought you meant to rape her."

Duncan sighed. "Maybe it did appear that way from her viewpoint. She made me so crazy—"

"That," Reeve said, "I can understand. But if you ever force yourself on her, Duncan, I'll kill you."

Duncan indulged in a speculative, thoughtful silence for a few moments, then asked, "Suppose I can woo her? Suppose she gives herself to me, Reeve?"

"Then I wouldn't want her," Reeve replied, and with that he shoved his half-finished stew away and went back upstairs.

It was the middle of the night when the missionary doctor arrived. He was surprisingly young, with an earnest face and a small, agile build. Briskly, he examined Maggie and then tucked the covers in around her again.

"Pneumonia?" Reeve hardly dared to ask.

The doctor shook his head. "No, mate. Just exhaustion, I'd say, and a very bad cold. Has she been under a great deal of strain or tension in recent days?"

Reeve considered all that Maggie had been through and nodded.

"There you have it, then. Your wife needs a good

long rest and lots of sunshine." The physician made a wry face at the intruding clamor of the rain on the roof. "That is, if the sun ever chooses to come out again."

Reeve was weak with relief. He paid the doctor a generous fee and, when he was gone, stripped off the clothes he'd put on earlier and crawled into bed beside Maggie. The space was scant, considering the width of that cot and his own size, but Reeve didn't care. Though she was hot as a cheap pistol, he held her close and fell asleep.

The next day the sun was out with a vengeance, drying up the muddy lakes that filled the roads and turning the mud to cracked dirt. Maggie was awake, though not nearly well enough to travel.

She made a face at the bowl of broth Reeve held out to her. "Tastes like dishwater," she said.

Reeve chuckled, too glad of her recovery to be annoyed at her sullen mood. "The doctor said you need to eat. Are you going to take this yourself, Yank, or do I have to pour it down your throat?"

Maggie took the bowl with a wrenching motion that slopped some of the broth over onto her bedclothes. "When I married one of the richest men in Australia," she said testily, "I expected better things to eat than a chicken's bathwater."

Reeve grinned. "Did you, now? Pity. It's a steady diet of bathwater from here on out, though we'll try to vary the meat. Sometimes we'll dip a kangaroo into the pot, now and then a wombat."

Maggie was trying to frown, but she didn't succeed. A sheepish grin curved her mouth. "Have I been too impossible?"

"Much. I've never believed in beating women," Reeve joked, "but I may take it up."

"Lay a hand on me, Reeve McKenna," Maggie retorted cockily, "and I'll skin you with a paring knife."

He laughed. "It's good to have you back, Yank," he said hoarsely.

She looked toward the window, which was aglare with the light of the fierce Queensland sun. "Have the others gone?"

"Eleanor went on with Duncan to get the house ready. Cora is still here, looking after Elisabeth."

Maggie sighed, and the sound was forlorn. She clearly wasn't used to staying in bed while life went on without her. "I never get sick, you know," she said. "Even on the ship out from England I was up and around every day, while most of the others lolled in their berths."

"Lazy no-gooders," Reeve commiserated, hiding a grin. "I suppose if they weren't in bed, they were hanging over the rail."

Maggie nodded quite soberly. "It was disgusting," she said.

Reeve couldn't help laughing. "You're an arrogant chit, do you know that?"

She lifted her stubborn little Yankee chin, and at that moment Reeve had no doubt what he felt for this woman: It was love, pure and simple and dizzying in its scope. "I was merely recounting circumstances as they happened," she said.

Reeve restrained his mirth. "Of course," he said primly. "If we ever take a sea voyage, Mrs. McKenna, I'm sure you'll acquit yourself in a heroic manner."

Maggie's silvery eyes widened. "You'd do that?" she whispered. "Take a sea voyage after what happened to you?"

She clearly didn't intend to have any more of the broth, and Reeve took it away, lest she spill it. "I won't go after a whale again," he said seriously. "They're magnificent creatures, Maggie, too special to be made into lamp oil and corset stays."

Her small hand crept out to cover his. "It was the whaling that made you rich, wasn't it?"

Reeve nodded. "Aye, but its time is past. From now on I'll be a gentleman farmer and invest my money in sheep or something."

Instantly, Maggie lowered her eyes, and Reeve knew she was thinking of Jamie.

"So he has sheep, does he?" he asked hoarsely.

She looked at him with an expression of dread. "A great many, I suspect," she said.

Given Maggie's recent illness, Reeve found it easy to keep his voice calm and gentle. "You know something more about Jamie, don't you, Maggie? Something you're afraid to tell me?"

She swallowed, her eyes averted now. "It's not me I'm afraid for, Reeve. It's Jamie. He's sure that if you know, you'll never forgive him, and he'd rather you didn't find him at all than to have you hate him—"

Reeve held up his hands in a bid for silence. "It's all right, Maggie. I won't ask you anymore. When you're ready to tell me, you can."

"I promised I wouldn't," she said sadly.

"Then I'll have to accept that for the time being," Reeve replied. "But I'm warning you, Yank: I won't always be this charitable."

A small smile quirked one corner of her mouth. "I know," she answered. "Come here and kiss me, please."

Reeve shook his head. "And catch your cold? Never!"

"If you don't kiss me right now, I'll be forced to do something truly decadent and even bawdy," Maggie announced firmly.

Reeve cocked an eyebrow. "Such as?"

She tossed aside the covers with a gesture of daring, only to find that she was wearing a nightgown. "How did I get into this?" she asked. "I was naked—"

Reeve laughed and pulled the bedclothes back into place. "Eleanor put it on you when you fell sick. Decent sort, Eleanor."

Maggie crossed her eyes.

Chapter 22 ❧

REEVE'S HOUSE, BUILT OF WHITE STONE, LAY AT THE END
of a red dirt road lined on either side with banana
trees. Beyond the structure were acres and acres of
sugar cane, standing as tall as corn. Riding beside
Reeve, in the box of a wagon borrowed from the
innkeeper, Maggie drew in her breath at the sight of it.
"You run a place like this with no servants?"

Reeve grinned at her and, with a swift motion of his
hands, brought the reins down on the backs of the
two-horse team, urging them to go faster. "No house
servants to speak of. Field workers are another matter."

"Aborigines?"

Reeve nodded, then frowned slightly. "They're a
migratory people, though. When the spirit moves
them, they just put down their tools and leave."

In the distance Maggie caught the shimmer of
sunshine on blue-green water. She remembered that
the ocean was near, and looked forward to walking on
sandy beaches and searching for shells. "Does this
place have a name?" she asked, spotting Elisabeth and

Cora up ahead, waving from the porch of the house. Smiling, she waved back.

"Aye," Reeve said quietly. "It's called Seven Sisters, because of a story the Aborigines tell. A legend from the Dreamtime."

"The Dreamtime?"

"That's what the Aborigines call the period before recorded history."

"Tell me about the legend," Maggie pleaded, for she loved such stories. Samuel's tale about the kangaroos, told to her that day at the menagerie, had delighted her.

They were nearing the house, and Reeve's expression was suddenly sober. Maggie followed his gaze and saw Duncan Kirk standing on the porch with Eleanor. "Another time," her husband told her. He brought the wagon to a stop in front and leapt agilely from the box to walk around and lift Maggie down.

Perhaps because he had a bent for the traditional—or maybe because he wanted to remind the lookers-on, most notably Duncan, that Maggie was his wife—Reeve suddenly swept her up into his arms and carried her up the porch steps, Elisabeth scrambling happily at his heels. He paused at the door to give Maggie a quick kiss, and then he carried her over the threshold.

"Welcome home, Mrs. McKenna," he said gruffly.

Happy tears filled Maggie's eyes, for there had been so many times when she'd thought this occasion would never come. Her hand lingered on the nape of Reeve's neck even after he'd set her carefully on her feet. "There were moments," she confessed, "when I thought that if anybody carried anybody over a threshold, it would be me toting you."

Reeve laughed and gave her a surreptitious swat on the bottom, and then Maggie took her first look around her. The house was spacious and rustic, lacking the marbled elegance of the place in Sydney, and Maggie loved it on sight. There was an enormous fieldstone fireplace, and from the dining room she could see the ocean. The kitchen was in a building separate from the main house, reached by a footpath. There were, of course, no gaslights and certainly no indoor plumbing fixtures.

Seven Sisters was an outpost of sorts, but that didn't dull its appeal to its new mistress. Maggie had a real home for the first time in her life, and that made her throat tighten with emotion.

In the master bedroom upstairs she knelt on a window seat, looking out over the sugar cane and the sparkling sea. She felt Reeve's hands on her shoulders and his breath on the nape of her neck as he bent to kiss that sensitive place.

Sighing with contentment, Maggie lifted her hands to cover Reeve's. "I feel as though all my life has been a road, leading here, to Seven Sisters," she said softly.

"I feel the same way," Reeve reflected, nibbling gently at the side of her neck. "But just since I carried you over the threshold, Mrs. McKenna."

Maggie turned, looking up into Reeve's face with tear-bright eyes. "I want our child to be born right here, in this room."

"Aye." Reeve chuckled, lifting her chin for his kiss. "And is there a better place to conceive a dozen more?"

The kiss sent a shiver of desire through Maggie, and she mentally counted the hours until the night. Reeve's hands cupped her bottom, pressing her close to him and, after circling her tingling lips once with the tip of his tongue, Reeve added in a throaty whisper, "I'll make you very glad you married me, Yank."

Maggie slipped her arms around his neck. "I'm already glad of that," she replied softly. And then she arched an eyebrow thoughtfully. "In many ways, tonight will be our wedding night."

Reeve was about to kiss Maggie again when someone cleared her throat. Startled, Mr. and Mrs. McKenna remembered that they were not alone and turned to see a flushed Eleanor standing in the doorway.

"There's a meal ready," she said with unparalleled timidity, "if you'd care to join us."

Maggie was hungry, though she would have preferred to be alone with Reeve for the rest of the day, and she took her bewildered husband's hand and led him toward the door.

The meal consisted of roasted poultry of some sort, as well as potatoes and peas, and scones served with jam and fresh cream. Maggie was forced to compliment Eleanor on her cooking. She couldn't help noticing that both Duncan and Reeve were quick to agree.

Once they'd eaten, Reeve and Duncan left the dining room, by some tacit agreement, to have a private discussion. Cora announced that Miss Elisabeth needed a nap, as did her nanny, and hauled her protesting charge upstairs. That left Maggie with Eleanor, and, in an effort to be gracious, she helped clear the table.

For all that, the moment was awkward.

"You really shouldn't be doing this," Eleanor said remotely as she scraped plates and stacked them. "You're the mistress of the house, after all, and you haven't been well."

Maggie felt an unexpected sympathy for the woman, and, holding a bowl of leftover potatoes in one hand and the platter the scones had been on in the other, she asked, "Eleanor, why do you want to be here so badly that you'd reduce yourself to a servant's status?"

Eleanor met Maggie's gaze for the first time since the meal had ended, and there were tears sparkling in her eyes. Maggie, who would never have been able to imagine this formidable woman crying, was taken aback. "Sometimes," she said, "we have to settle for what we can get, Mrs. McKenna." Eleanor's look sharpened. "And when you're big with child and not quite so receptive to your husband's attentions, I expect to get plenty."

Maggie was so stunned that her fingers went slack and the potato bowl dropped to the hardwood floor with a clatter. "You want to be Reeve's mistress?" she marveled.

Eleanor smiled and wiped away her tears. "Wives wear out rather rapidly in the bush," she observed coolly. "I suspect the day will come when you're glad to have your husband in my bed instead of yours."

Dazed by the woman's gall, Maggie bent and picked up the bowl she'd dropped, setting it on the table with a thump. "Your confidence in your charms is quite amazing, Miss Kilgore," she replied. "But even if Reeve should ever feel the need to take a mistress— and I assure you, I'll do whatever I have to to prevent that—you'll be far away from Seven Sisters. In fact, you may be leaving today."

Eleanor's smile was firmly in place, and the brightness in her eyes now was spawned by determination, not tears. "Do you imagine for one moment, Mrs. McKenna, that your doting husband will send me away and allow you to endanger his child by scrubbing floors and cooking meals? If you do, you underestimate his devotion."

"Once I tell him what you're planning—"

Eleanor interrupted with a dismissive laugh. "Even if you do, and he goes into a towering rage and shows me the door—which is unlikely since there are few white women who would be willing to live so far out in the bush—I'll have only to apply to Mr. Kirk for a position in his house. He'll hire me, rest assured, and that may prove even more convenient for Mr. McKenna, since Mr. Kirk's residence is less than a mile's walk from this one. He'd be able to visit his mistress without flaunting her in his wife's face."

Maggie knew that Eleanor's threats carried weight; for the very reasons she'd stated, it was most unlikely that Reeve would send her away. She'd only have to lie if he were to confront her about her intentions, and Maggie, being the younger of the two women, would seem the jealous and unsophisticated bride. Reeve would believe that her pregnancy was causing her to imagine things.

"You won't have him," Maggie vowed proudly, color throbbing in her cheeks, and then she turned and left the dining room.

Reeve and Duncan were just coming out of the small study, and Maggie could see no indication of what they'd discussed in either of their faces. She was too upset to look beyond their expressions.

"I'm going for a walk," she announced somewhat petulantly, folding her arms.

Duncan offered his hand to Reeve and, after a moment's hesitation, Reeve took it. At any other time Maggie would have been curious about what they were agreeing to between themselves. She turned and set out for the back of the house.

Reeve caught up to her as she was starting through the cane field, moving steadily toward the sea, which called to her with a low, soothing voice.

"There are snakes out here," he commented, falling into step beside her.

The cane rustled and raised a sugary smell as Maggie marched onward. "And I was wondering what to give Eleanor for Christmas," she muttered sarcastically.

Reeve grasped Maggie's arm at the elbow and stopped her progress, spinning her around so that she came bumping up against his chest. He laughed and entangled his fingers in her falling-down hair. "What is it that's got you in such a fuss, Maggie?" he demanded with a grin.

Maggie considered telling him, but she could guess what would happen if she did. Reeve would either think that she was exaggerating or he would send Eleanor on her way—to Duncan's nearby house. "Are there really snakes here?" she asked, hedging.

Reeve nodded, and, except for his eyes, which were still dancing, his expression was serious. "Don't be wandering off on your own again, Maggie. It isn't safe."

Unable to bear a reprimand then, Maggie bit her lower lip and fought back tears. "Sometimes I don't think there's anyplace in the world that's safe," she said sadly.

Reeve touched her nose and his voice was gentle and hoarse with concern. "Yank, what is it? What's troubling you?"

Maggie brightened because she had to; she meant to fight for this man she loved with every resource that she possessed. She smiled and twisted her hips mischievously against Reeve's, then went bounding through the towering sugar cane at a dead run, her laughter ringing out like music behind her.

"Come back here!" Reeve yelled furiously. "I wasn't kidding about those snakes!"

Maggie ran until she reached the edge of the cane field; there, she stopped, breathless. The sea was spread out before her in all its splendor, lapping, crystal-blue, at the white sands. "Thunderation," she whispered, stricken by the beauty of the place.

Then, hearing Reeve storming through the cane behind her, Maggie skidded down the short hillside to the beach and turned to watch her husband's descent, her hands on her hips, her face shining with mischief. At that magical moment it was as though there were no Eleanors in the world, and no Lorettas; Maggie had found her safe place.

"I ought to turn you across my knee!" Reeve raged, his nose an inch from Maggie's.

"But you won't," she chimed, her hands caught together behind her back, "because I'm pregnant."

"You're right," Reeve confessed, looking both exasperated and disappointed. He ran one hand through his dark hair and muttered a curse word, and Maggie laughed, taking his muscular arms in her hands.

"This is paradise!" she crowed, catching Reeve's hand in hers and dragging him toward what appeared to be a cove, sheltered by rocks and towering trees, just down the beach.

Grudgingly, he smiled at her. "Maggie," he said, stopping her and turning her in his arms so that she was looking up at him. "I love you."

Maggie's throat swelled with emotion and she swallowed. "Really, Reeve? Do you really love me?"

He nodded, his hands strong on her shoulders. She took one of them and placed it flush with her stomach.

"When I'm big and very fat, will you still want me?" she asked timidly.

"More than ever," he answered, and then he was ushering her down the beach, through a gap in the rocks and into the cove Maggie had suspected was there. It was the Garden of Eden, shut off from the rest of the world; exotic flowers of the richest purples and crimsons nodded from the bushes on the hillside behind it, and parrots of every color squawked in the trees.

Maggie plopped down in the snow-white sand and began unlacing her shoes. "Oh, Reeve," she breathed, awed, "it's so beautiful here."

He dropped to his haunches beside her and, with slow, sensuous motions of his hands, removed both her shoes, then rolled down her stockings and tossed them away.

Maggie's heart was hammering and her breath had already quickened to a gasp; all her instincts bid her to lie back in the warm sand and let Reeve love her.

She resisted those instincts because she wanted this time to last.

Bolting to her feet, Maggie lifted her skirts and went splashing into the water up to her knees. Reeve hung back, his face suddenly taut with unpleasant memories, and some of Maggie's joy faded away. She made her way slowly back toward him.

"You have shadows in your eyes," she said softly, placing one hand on each side of his face.

He dragged her to him and held her close for a moment, his grip fierce, but after a few seconds he relaxed. His hands went to her hair, and he plucked away the last remaining pins, watching as her pale hair tumbled down around her shoulders and breasts in shining waves. "You can drive the shadows away, Maggie," he said, his voice low and husky. "You and only you."

She began unbuttoning his shirt, and when she'd opened it to his muscle-ridged stomach, Maggie laid her hands to Reeve's flesh, caressing him. He groaned as she toyed with his taut nipples.

"Oh, God, Maggie," he rasped, "I need you."

Maggie stepped closer, touching one button of flesh with the tip of her tongue and taking delight as Reeve shuddered with pleasure. She grew bolder then, kissing her way across his chest to the other nipple and tasting that as well. Beneath her hand, the muscles of his stomach tensed to a hardness as dense as granite. When she took hold of his belt buckle, he gently displaced her hand and opened it for her.

They drifted downward until they were kneeling in the sand, and Maggie reached inside Reeve's trousers to catch him gently in her hand. He moaned and thrust back his head as she freed his straining magnificence to the air and the darting touch of her tongue.

"Maggie," he grated. "Oh, Maggie—"

For long, sweet minutes Maggie McKenna pleasured her husband, and during that time he unfastened the buttons at the back of her cotton dress and slipped it from her shoulders. When Reeve could bear not another moment of the dizzying torment to which she subjected him, he raised her head with his hands and kissed her. She shivered as his tongue searched the warm moistness of her mouth and his hands smoothed the dress downward to her waist. Having anticipated just such a moment since morning, Maggie had worn no camisole.

He cupped the warm fullness of her breasts in his hands, chafing the nipples with his thumbs.

Maggie had no memory of being lowered to the sand, but she felt its gritty heat against her bare back, and the sun became a dazzling illumination framing Reeve's head. She made a throaty whimpering sound as he eased her dress down over her hips and thighs and then tossed it away. Upon discovering that she was wearing no drawers, he drew in his breath and then chortled raggedly. "You little vixen—you knew this was going to happen."

"Ummm," Maggie crooned, closing her eyes as the warmth of the sun and of Reeve's love washed over her in delicious waves. His hands stroked her thighs in whisper-soft touches and then, with a groan, he bent his head to her breast, circling the pulsing nipple with his tongue.

Maggie's entire body hummed with the sensations he was stirring inside her, and she clasped both hands behind Reeve's head to hold him close while he sucked. In the trees the parrots screeched and the waves washed in and out on the shore, setting a primal rhythm for Maggie and Reeve to follow.

Finally, with a lusty motion of his body, Reeve rolled onto his back, holding Maggie above him, and he caught her untended breast in his mouth, nibbling at its peak with his lips. Still, driven by some instinct older than the sand beneath them, she pulled free of Reeve's mouth and mounted him. Driven to a delirium of need himself, he lunged inside her in one powerful, heated stroke.

Though Maggie wanted to race toward the dizzying finish that she knew would come, Reeve controlled not only his own desperation, but hers too. Grasping her hips in inescapable hands, he set her pace to match his slow, lingering thrusts.

Maggie was trembling as each stroke of his manhood tantalized her at excruciating leisure but refused to gratify. "Oh, Reeve—I beg of you—I need you so much—"

Still, he moved at the same even tempo, granting her no quarter. He knew, as Maggie did, that the final moments of their loving would be all the more gratifying for the long delay.

Maggie grew fevered as she was trained to the exact motions that Reeve wanted of her. Her nails delved into the hard flesh of his shoulders as he moved beneath her, driving her inexorably toward sweet madness. As the passion became too piercing and too intense to be borne, she began to toss her head back and forth wildly, and Reeve's hands tightened on her hips as she tried to accelerate the pace and wrest his control from him.

Finally, Maggie's whole being convulsed as her body buckled in one spasm of elation after another. On and on the glorious tumult went, until Maggie sagged, exhausted, to Reeve's chest.

He was approaching his own pinnacle, and, in a frantic shift of his body, he set her beneath him and lunged into her depths. Reeve's torment ended with a great shuddering in his body and a rush of senseless pleas from his mouth, and then he fell to lie, gasping for breath, beside Maggie in the sand.

She let her hand rest on his quivering, granitelike belly, and her head found its way unerringly to his shoulder.

Perhaps because her emotions were so raw, and so

close to the surface, Maggie remembered that Eleanor planned to take this from her and she began to cry. Several moments had passed before Reeve felt her tears against the flesh of his shoulder and raised himself to look down into her face.

"Tell me," he commanded, his voice ragged.

"I never want to lose you," Maggie wept, shaking her head against the sand. "Never. Oh, Reeve—I love you so much!"

Tenderly, Reeve brushed tangled strands of golden hair back from her face. "And I love you," he said, his breath warm where it touched her lips. "Maggie, don't cry."

She trembled. "You'll never take a mistress?" she whispered, and if she was begging, she didn't care. She touched the charm dangling from his strong neck with the tip of her finger. "Promise me, Reeve, that you'll never betray me."

He kissed her lingeringly, and then said, "I believe I've already made that promise, Yank. Before a priest, if I remember correctly."

Tears were slipping through the sand that coated Maggie's face with a fine layer of grit. "S-someone told me that you'd t-take a mistress when I get f-fat and—"

"Whoever told you that is wrong, Maggie."

She sniffed. "I couldn't bear it, Reeve, if I had to share you. I kn-know some women can look the other way when their husbands stray, but I c-couldn't."

He kissed her eyelids and one of his legs lay sprawled across both of hers. "Maggie, do you think I'd ask total fidelity of you if I couldn't give it in return?"

"Lots of husbands do exactly that," Maggie mourned.

"Well, I'm not lots of husbands. I'm *your* husband. And I'm not such a randy bastard that I can't restrain myself when there's a need for it."

Feeling better, Maggie began to laugh. "You've never restrained yourself with me," she accused him.

He raised himself from the sand, pulling Maggie with him, and led her to the shore. They knelt, facing each other, in the shallows, and Maggie let her head fall back as Reeve bathed her in the tepid water, washing away the sand and the residue of their loving, washing away Maggie's doubts and fears.

An hour later they were dressed again and walking back toward the house through the rustling cane, hand in hand. Maggie could not have been happier, and she was humming when she entered the kitchen to see how dinner was progressing.

Eleanor was racing back and forth between stove and worktable, her hair clinging damply to her cheeks and her neck. Sensing Maggie's presence, she stopped, holding a kitchen towel in one hand, and took in her rumpled dress and unlaced shoes with a glower of understanding. "Can I help you with anything?" she demanded shortly.

Maggie smiled. "Only the cooking and cleaning," she said, and then she turned and walked on toward the main house.

The next morning Reeve left the house at dawn to supervise the work in the cane fields, and Maggie began to learn the realities of living on a sugar plantation. She had her breakfast and wrote a long letter to Tansy, and then there was nothing left to do. Elisabeth was busy going over her numbers with Cora, and Eleanor was hardly Maggie's idea of congenial company.

Maggie decided that a walk was in order and, since snakes were to be avoided, she chose the long driveway for her stroll. If she reached the main road and still felt restless, she would go on.

The banana trees rustled companionably on either side of her, their fruit covered with canvas bags to protect it from the birds. As quiet as Seven Sisters

327

was, Maggie could have spent all her life there without complaint; the peace of the place was healing some mysterious wound of the spirit that she'd never known she'd suffered.

The distant rattle of carriage wheels on the hard dirt of the road made Maggie stop and listen, hoping for a visitor. But the sound faded away and she went on walking.

She was startled when she looked up and saw a black woman coming toward her, carrying a battered valise and trailing two little girls behind her. Maggie could hardly contain her relief when she recognized Kala, the housekeeper from Parramatta. The children, Goodness and Mercy, she remembered with a grin.

"Kala!" she cried, about to throw her arms around the woman.

Some kindly reserve in Kala's dark, dark eyes stopped her.

"We walked all this way, missus!" crowed either Goodness or Mercy; Maggie had no way of knowing which was which.

"All the way from Parramatta?" Maggie was boggled at the enormity of such an undertaking.

Both little girls nodded, but it was Kala who spoke. It was the first time Maggie had heard her utter a word. "We hear of wedding, we come."

Maggie was touched. She was also looking forward to seeing the expression on Eleanor's face when she encountered Kala. "You must be very hungry and very tired," she said to the three travelers. "Come, and I'll see that you get something to eat."

"Lemonade?" asked one of Kala's young companions with a hopeful expression on her face.

Kala made an angry shushing sound and swatted at the child, who dodged her easily. "Pardon, please, missus," she said.

When Maggie entered the kitchen building with Kala and the children behind her, Eleanor stopped her frantic cooking and smoothed her lank hair back from her face with both hands. "Well," she muttered, clearly reading the situation for what it was. She took off her apron and marched out of the kitchen without a word. When Maggie checked her room, an hour later, Eleanor's things were gone.

Chapter 23 🌿

ELEANOR'S PRIDE WOULD NOT PERMIT HER TO WALK around to the rear of Duncan's house as a prospective servant might do. She set her bags down on the porch and, after smoothing her hair and her skirts, she rapped at the front door.

Her knock was answered by a sullen-looking boy with bright red hair and eyes of the same intriguing emerald green as Duncan's. "What?" he snapped.

Eleanor sighed. "I would like to see Mr. Kirk, please."

"He's in Mr. McKenna's field," the boy said, "helping out with the work. Can you cook?"

About to turn away in discouragement, Eleanor was caught off guard by the lad's question. She just stared at him.

"Can you cook?" the urchin repeated, this time indulgently. Eleanor enjoyed a brief fantasy, during which she boxed the little bleeder's ears.

"Yes, I can cook," she said coldly. "But since you haven't the authority to hire me—"

"I've got that all right," the boy insisted, swelling his little chest. "Papa said you might come here once you'd learned how hopeless it is, what you're up against—"

Eleanor arched one dark eyebrow and bent to look directly into the lad's freckled face. "What," she asked, "am I 'up against'?"

"You want Mr. McKenna for your own, I think. Just like Papa wanted Maggie. He's learned that there's no separating those two—best you learn the same, mum."

"You are an impudent little scrap, do you know that?" Eleanor jutted out her chin. She was not used to being insulted.

"Yes, mum. My name is Tad and I'm the eldest son, so someday I'll own most of Papa's property. Won't you come in now and make us some lunch?"

Eleanor pushed a strand of damp hair back from her forehead and bent to grasp the handles of her suitcases. "You'll inherit, all right," she replied under her breath, "if some deranged cook doesn't poison you in the meantime."

"Beg pardon?" Tad asked sunnily, looking back at Eleanor over one thin shoulder.

Eleanor smiled a winsome smile and ignored the question. "Show me the way to the cookhouse, lad, and I'll see that there's a fine meal awaiting your father at midday. I'd like you to go and tell him so, in fact. That way, he won't be eating at the McKennas' when he needn't."

Tad grinned. "First let me show you to your room, miss. You look some the worse for the walk, if you don't mind my saying so."

"Would it matter if I minded?"

The obnoxious grin widened. "No, mum."

Tad Kirk was a challenge, but Eleanor had dealt with far worse in her lifetime. "At least we understand each other, don't we, Master Kirk? That's more than a lot of people can say."

In a hurry to begin cooking, and thus impress Duncan with her skill and assure herself of a place a stone's throw from Seven Sisters, Eleanor set her suitcases down in the room Tad indicated without even looking around.

Duncan arrived at noon, covered in a mingling of soot and sweat. As he washed up at a bench in the corner of the kitchen, Eleanor was, for the first time, aware of him as a man rather than a means to an end. He was a well-built specimen, she reflected, watching the play of muscles in his back as he splashed water over himself and then shrugged back into his filthy shirt.

He grinned at her from beneath a thatch of soot-blackened hair as he sat down at the trestle table to eat the stew and biscuits she'd prepared for him. "So, you've made the same discovery as I, Miss Kilgore," he observed not unkindly. "Do sit down and have a bite of lunch—I can't abide people pacing while I'm trying to eat."

Eleanor sat, but she hadn't the appetite for stew and biscuits or anything else. "What discovery is that, Mr. Kirk?" she responded.

Duncan was chewing. When he'd finished, he replied, "You want Reeve and you'll probably never have him. I, on the other hand, wanted Maggie—but fair as she is, she's not worth my life, so I've had to give up the idea."

"I have an advantage over you, Mr. Kirk," Eleanor said frankly. "When Mrs. McKenna grows fat with his child, and not so eager for her husband's loving attentions—"

Duncan arched one skeptical and quite dirty eyebrow, interrupting without apparent chagrin. "The advantage," he pointed out flatly, "is Maggie's, I'm afraid. I can't imagine her turning that man away for any reason—she adores him—but even if she were to do that because of a difficult pregnancy, at any rate, Reeve would even be more indulgent, not less so.

"You waste your valuable time seeking McKenna's

bed, Miss Kilgore. Especially when you would be so welcome in mine."

Color surged up over Eleanor's bosom and into her face. If the truth be known, she didn't find the prospect at all untoward. "Rumor is," she said primly nonetheless, "that you've taken Miss Loretta Craig for a mistress."

Duncan laughed. "Alas, that *affaire de coeur* is over. Loretta's sold everything she has to organize her own theater troupe—I confess to contributing a few hundred pounds to the cause. She is sailing off to America, there to become a sensation." He spread his marginally clean hands. "For all I know, she's gone by now."

Eleanor folded her arms. "Why have you stayed on here, all this while, if you've given up on having Maggie for yourself?"

"Good Lord," Duncan breathed, "am I really so transparent as that?"

Eleanor only nodded.

Duncan sighed philosophically. "One always hopes, I guess. One always hopes. Some terrible accident could befall McKenna and leave his lovely wife widowed. Besides, I really rather enjoy working the land—it's a welcome change from the stiff-collar doings in Sydney and Melbourne."

"Perhaps," Eleanor agreed, hiding a smile. "But I think there's more—you want to be nearby so you can get reports from your spy. Tell me, Mr. Kirk, is Cora your mother, or your maiden aunt?"

Duncan's mouth fell open.

"You didn't think anyone knew, did you?" Eleanor asked, her tone sweet as marzipan. "It's really not such a staggering deduction—after all, Cora is an American and so are you. And, of course, I've seen the two of you meeting—as if by accident—on a number of occasions."

Duncan gave a long sigh and pushed away his bowl.

He scowled at Eleanor. "Cora is my aunt," he admitted grudgingly. "She came to Australia, at my request, to look after my sons. By the time she'd arrived, I was in love with Maggie and I asked her to seek a position in Reeve's house—so I'd always know that she was safe."

"We're birds of a feather, you and I."

"I don't think so, Miss Kilgore. Whatever I've done, it's been because I care for Maggie. You, on the other hand, would as soon see her drowned in the ocean as tip your hat to her."

Eleanor sighed prettily. "Are you implying that I would murder?"

Without warning of any sort, Duncan grasped Eleanor by the bodice of her dress and, using both hands, he hauled her across the table. Her feet dangled off the floor and she could feel his breath in her face as he warned, "Do anything to hurt Maggie—anything, Miss Kilgore—and you'll find me a relentless and formidable enemy."

Besides fear, Eleanor felt a certain excitement. She nodded and Duncan let her slide the length of him, until her feet touched the floor again. Her heart was beating too fast and she couldn't seem to catch her breath.

"There is only one way to keep you out of mischief, miss," Duncan informed her in a hoarse undertone as his lips drew ever closer to hers. "And that's to keep you so busy that you'll have no time left for scheming. I'll want a bath when I get back from the fields, and I'll want you."

Sweet shivers went through Eleanor as she lowered her eyes and permitted herself a half smile. "Your bed and your bath will be as you wish, Mr. Kirk," she said softly.

Duncan caught his hand under her chin and wrenched it upward. She saw emerald fires burning in his eyes. "Who are you?" he demanded. "You know my secret; I want to know yours."

Eleanor had not craved any one man as much as this—not even Reeve McKenna—since Jamie. Duncan's hand strayed inside the bodice of her dress and cupped her breast and she closed her eyes, half sick with the wanting. "The child—Elisabeth. Sh-she's mine—mine and Jamie's."

Duncan's fingers tightened and then went slack. "My God—you're Jamie McKenna's wife?"

"I was only his woman," Eleanor confessed, and she was surprised that so much of the pain lingered even after more than four years. Desperately, she covered Duncan's hand with her own, at her silent urging, and he began to caress her again.

Mercy burst into the cookhouse, where Maggie was peeling carrots. "He's back, missus. Mr. 'Kenna's back!"

Hastily, Maggie threw down both carrot and paring knife. She hurried through the doorway opposite the one where Mercy had entered and waited outside until Reeve and the other men were seated at the long trestle table and Kala was serving them their midday meal.

Then, after smoothing her tumbledown hair and drawing a deep breath, Maggie entered the cookhouse, smiling. The men sitting on either side of Reeve made room for her, and she sat down at his right.

"You're filthy," she remarked.

Reeve chuckled and looked her over. "You've worked up a bit of a sweat yourself. I didn't know that was possible with embroidery."

Maggie bit her lower lip and dropped her eyes. Her conscience smarted, but she couldn't quite bring herself to confess that she hadn't worked a stitch the whole of the morning. "Could I go back to the fields with you, just to see what it's like?"

"No," Reeve answered in a bland tone as he ate. "And mind you don't go wandering through the cane to the sea either. There'll be snakes aplenty, trying to escape the flames."

Maggie had sweet memories of the white beach beyond those fields, and she felt color rise in her cheeks. She glanced at the black men sitting all around, some dressed in loincloths, and said, "I'd like to send for my friend, Tansy Quinn, if that would be all right."

Reeve gave her a distracted look; it was obvious that he was thinking of other things. "Good idea. Someone for you to talk to."

"We'd have to pay her wages—employ her as a servant—"

"Aye. I can manage that, I think. Send for the girl, Maggie, and give a man some peace."

Maggie was stung. Tears welled in her eyes—she'd become overly sensitive in recent days—and she bounded to her feet. "I'll give you all the peace you want, Reeve McKenna!" she hissed.

The Aboriginal men sitting around the table dipped their heads, studiously ignoring the drama going on under their very noses. Reeve got up with a long-suffering sigh, caught Maggie by the arm, and propelled her outside into the glaring sunshine.

"In the name of God, Yank, what is it that you want from me?" he asked patiently.

Maggie jutted out her chin. "A little of your attention, Mr. McKenna," she whispered fiercely. "Every time I say anything to you, it's 'give a man some peace, Maggie'! At night, instead of loving me, you just turn over and snore!"

Reeve grinned, his teeth startlingly white against his smoke-blackened face. "So that's it. Maggie, I'm working long hours—when I get to bed, I want to sleep."

"That's obvious," Maggie complained, folding her arms. "Don't you love me anymore?"

"You know I do, Yank."

Maggie looked in all directions before whispering,

"Eleanor's been gone to Duncan's for a week. You haven't touched me since the day she left!"

Reeve's grin was gone. A glower formed in his features as dark and dangerous as the clouds before a Queensland storm. Taking an ominous step toward Maggie, making no effort whatsoever to keep the matter private, he roared, "By God, Yank, if you're implyin' that I've been flingin' up that woman's skirts—"

Maggie was hastening backward and trying at the same time to smile. She hadn't meant to go so far as to invoke the brogue. "Reeve, keep your voice down, please."

"I won't keep me voice down, woman!" he bellowed, still advancing. "And I sure as 'ell won't 'ave me morals questioned every time I'm too tired to make love to you!"

Maggie turned a rich crimson color, embarrassed beyond all bearing. "Reeve, please, you're shouting—"

He glared at her and, at last, lowered his voice. "I'll spend tonight at the inn," he said in a hiss, "so don't be thinkin' that I'm with me nurse! On the other hand, Yank, think whatever ye damned well please!"

"Reeve!"

He was turning, striding away. Maggie waited in the house, forlorn, until all the men, Reeve included, had gone back to the fields. Then she returned to the kitchen to help clear the tables.

Kala slapped her hands away. "Sit down, missus. My girls can do this."

Goodness and Mercy took over the work and Maggie slumped into a chair. It was too near the cookstove, but she was too upset to care. She began to sob. "My husband hates me!" she wailed.

Kala chuckled. "No, missus."

"Yes, he does!" Maggie wept noisily. "He's going to sleep at the inn tonight!"

"No, missus," Kala said again. She heaped copper

kettles in a pile on a table beside Maggie's chair and then handed her mistress a cloth and a tin of dark powder. "Make shine," she added.

Sniffling, Maggie began to polish the copper, rubbing the powder against the metal until each pot glistened. The work helped to distract her from her troubles, as did the soft songs Kala and the girls sang as they went about their own labors.

Goodness and Mercy had gone off somewhere, and Kala was out dumping the dishwater, when Maggie finished her polishing. She felt much better, and she was smiling as she threw several blackened polishing cloths into the cookstove.

The stove lids jumped as a series of startling explosions went off. Kala immediately ran inside the cookhouse, caught Maggie by the hand, and dragged her out. The men, Reeve included, were running from the fields.

"What happened?" Reeve demanded just as the loud popping finally stopped. There was no visible damage to the cookhouse.

"I was only polishing the copper," Maggie said huffily, folding her arms and looking away from Reeve. "I threw the rags in the stove when I was done, and then all hell broke loose."

Kala started to laugh. She laughed so hard that she sank to her knees in the tall green grass, clutching her stomach and rocking back and forth. It was perfectly obvious that she wasn't going to be any help to anybody.

Maggie stomped back into the kitchen building and grabbed up the tin of polishing salts she'd used, holding it out for Reeve's inspection.

He shook his head. "Can you read, Yank?"

Maggie bridled. "You know very well that I can!"

"Then perhaps you wouldn't mind reading this," he said, tapping the front of the colorfully painted tin with a forefinger.

Maggie's eyes widened as she read the single, ornately written word: *Gunpowder.*

"Oh," she said lamely.

Reeve grinned and ruffled her hair with one dirty hand, and it began to fall in lush curls of silvery-gold all around her shoulders. For a moment there was a familiar heat in his eyes, but it faded away with his grin. "Try to stay out of trouble, woman. Just for a few hours."

Maggie was insulted and hurt. "I'll make things easier for you, Reeve. You have our bed, and I'll sleep at the inn!"

"Set a foot off this property," Reeve warned in response, "and I'll forget me convictions and take a switch to you! And you needn't think, love, that I'm joking, because I'm not!"

Maggie had no doubt that he wasn't, and she sighed. Having nothing more to say, she turned and walked into the main house.

It wasn't the prospect of a bed that took Reeve McKenna to the inn that night, but the need for a few drinks and a barkeep to listen to his woes. "I married a Yank, you know," he told the innkeeper.

The man nodded sympathetically. "Aye, mate, I know you did. You'll be wanting a room tonight?"

Reeve shook his head and lifted his second mug of ale to his lips. He was just about to take a sip when Eleanor appeared at his side. She was standing right there at the bar, bold as brass.

"Hello, Mr. McKenna," she said.

Reeve could only gape.

"I suppose your next question, should you manage to utter one, will be 'What the devil are you doing here?'"

"Aye," Reeve managed to say, "that would be the question."

She lifted her chin and Reeve thought to himself

that if it hadn't been for Maggie, he might have wanted this woman very badly. As it was, he felt only numbness toward her. "I'm here with Mr. Kirk," Eleanor explained. "We came to fetch the post—one does look forward to getting letters, doesn't one—and poor Duncan fell quite sick."

"Sick? Where is he?" Reeve still didn't like or trust Duncan Kirk, but if the man had fallen ill, he couldn't just turn his back on him. Kirk was his neighbor, if not his friend.

A flicker of triumph showed in Eleanor's dark blue eyes, and Reeve wondered at it. "Upstairs," she said. "We've put him to bed—he's out of his head with fever, you know."

Reeve glanced at the barkeeper, who was studiously polishing a glass and would not meet his gaze.

Eleanor led the way up the stairs, with Reeve following. She opened a door at the end of the hallway with a brass key and went in. The moment Reeve was inside, too, she closed the door again and leaned back against it.

He was looking at the bed. Fatigue and two stout ales notwithstanding, he knew an empty mattress when he saw one. Reeve turned to look at Eleanor, more in puzzlement than anger.

She spread her hands. "Duncan's not really sick, Reeve," she confessed in a very small voice. "He's downstairs somewhere, playing cards."

"Then why the hell—?"

Eleanor took the mug from Reeve's hand and splayed her fingers over the front of his sooty, sweat-dampened shirt. "I want to be your mistress, not his."

Reeve felt pity, though he tried to hide it. "Step away from the door, woman. I've got serious drinking to do."

"I could make you forget Maggie."

"Nobody," Reeve replied soberly, "could do that. And for all that I'd like to wring the Yank's stubborn little neck a lot of the time, I love her."

For Reeve that closed the subject, but Eleanor's midnight-blue eyes pleaded with him. "Don't go, please," she whispered.

Reeve removed her hands from his chest and set her gently aside. As he opened the door, she said, "I know your brother."

He turned, disbelieving and a little angry now. "What?"

Eleanor lifted her chin. "That's all I'm going to tell you, Reeve McKenna. If you want to know more, you'll have to come to me on your knees."

"Don't balance a stick on your nose while you wait," Reeve replied, though he wanted to grab the woman and shake some word of Jamie out of her. He closed the door, hurried down the stairs, and rode home. The fresh air cleared his mind.

Whether or not Eleanor really knew anything about Jamie's whereabouts was a question he would consider later. For now he just wanted to be near Maggie.

She flung a basin at him when he opened the bedroom door, and it shattered against the woodwork.

Reeve chuckled, using the door as a shield of sorts. "Still angry, love?" he called sweetly. "Or are you hinting that you'd like to relive our wedding night?"

Something hard struck the door, and Reeve flinched.

"Now, there's no sense in being difficult, Yank. I've come to tell you that I'm sorry."

Silence. Was the little scoundrel appeased, or just preparing another volley?

"Maggie?"

Nothing.

"The moment I got to the inn," Reeve went on, grinning, "Eleanor Kilgore tried to get me into bed."

There were footsteps and then the door opened. Maggie was standing there, glaring up at him, her bare feet surrounded by shards from the broken basin. "Did she really?"

Reeve nodded somberly and lifted Maggie into his arms. "You'll cut your feet," he scolded, laying her gently on the bed and then turning away to pick up the pieces of broken crockery littering the floor. "We're going to have to do something about your temper, Yank. It's more than a hardworking man should have to bear up under."

He could feel her curiosity, her impatience, and her fury. Since Maggie couldn't see his face, he grinned. "Never mind my temper. What did that trollop say to you?"

Reeve went right on picking up glass. "Spirited me off to a room, she did, saying that Duncan was sick and all. When we got there, no Duncan. She threw herself at me."

Maggie made a growling sound. "I'll strip off a layer of her skin, that vixen!"

Reeve set the pieces of crockery carefully on the bureau top and started toward the door. "I'm going downstairs for a broom. Stay in that bed, Maggie, unless you plan to put some shoes on. There might still be glass on the floor."

Maggie was kneeling in the middle of the bed, looking winsome and flushed in her pink cotton nightgown. "I want you to take me to the inn so that I can tear that woman's hair out. Right this minute!"

Reeve shook his head and laughed, and when he came back, minutes later, with the broom, Maggie was lying placidly in bed, staring up at the ceiling. "You made that whole story up, Reeve McKenna, just to get me jealous."

Reeve shrugged. Maybe it was better for her to believe that. He didn't want Maggie getting into a rough-and-tumble with Eleanor and hurting herself. "Whatever you say," he answered.

"I suppose you're too tired to make love to me," Maggie ventured as Reeve swept up the tiny bits of glass. He carried them to the hearth in the corner of the room and disposed of them in a dustbin.

"Tonight, Yank, I'd sooner turn you across my knee than make love to you."

Her lip jutted out. "Then tell me the legend of the Seven Sisters. You promised to the day we came here, but you never did."

"I need a bath, Maggie. And Kala's prepared one for me out in the kitchen."

She was stubbornly silent.

Reeve sat down on the edge of the bed in his filthy clothes, and sighed. "Once there were seven emu sisters—"

"Emu?"

"Those big birds," Reeve reminded Maggie patiently. "You probably saw them at the menagerie."

"Oh," nodded Maggie, waiting.

"Anyway," Reeve went dutifully on, "the Dingomen wanted them for wives. The sisters hid under the outcropping of a giant pile of boulders, but their suitors were clever and they built a fire, planning to drive the sisters out into the open. The emus grew long legs so that they could run very fast, but they couldn't escape the Dingo-men, who pursued them. Finally, they rose into the sky and made themselves into a constellation of stars still called by the name of Seven Sisters."

Maggie yawned. "What about the Dingo-men? Did they give up?"

Reeve smiled and kissed her forehead. "And shame their gender? Of course not. They took to the sky, too, and became Orion."

"My goodness," said Maggie, closing her eyes.

"I love you," Reeve told her, his own eyes strangely misted over, his throat thick. There were times when his feelings for this troublesome woman-child nearly overwhelmed him.

"Ummm," Maggie replied, snuggling down into her feather pillow.

Reeve kissed her cheek and went quietly downstairs and across the yard to the kitchen, where his bath was waiting. He chased Goodness and Mercy away, then stripped off his clothes and climbed into the tub. As he washed, he considered the events of the day and wondered if Eleanor Kilgore had been telling the truth when she'd claimed to know Jamie.

There would be time to find that out later; Reeve wasn't as obsessed with locating his brother now that his life was so full. He remembered the basin shattering against the bedroom door and grinned. Aye, his life was full.

Chapter 24 ❧

THE SCENT OF SUGAR SMOKE FILLED MAGGIE'S NOSTRILS from morning till night during the days and weeks to come, as the cane fields were systematically burned off in preparation for harvest. The soil in Queensland was so fertile that two crops could be brought in if the rainfall had been adequate and the Aboriginals were moved to work. That year luck was on the planters' side.

While Reeve would have preferred his wife to sit back and embroider as she awaited the birth of their child, Maggie worked long hours in the kitchen every day, helping Kala prepare food for the workers. Goodness and Mercy labored alongside the women, getting in the way more than anything, but Maggie tolerated them easily. Eleanor Kilgore was another matter.

She arrived early one morning when the cane was still being burned off, with Duncan and the workers he'd been able to garner. Marching into the kitchen just as if she belonged there, Eleanor took up an apron and tied it around her slender waist.

Maggie, who was peeling potatoes and already suffering from the heat, though it was only half past five, stopped her work to ask pointedly, "What are you doing here?"

Eleanor—true to her word, she had become Duncan's housekeeper immediately after leaving Seven Sisters—smiled and replied, "I'm part of the agreement between Mr. Kirk and Mr. McKenna. They're sharing their workers until both their crops have been harvested, and I'm a worker."

"We don't need you," Maggie said in somewhat haughty tones. She was already growing thick around the middle, and Reeve usually collapsed into bed at night, too exhausted to make love to her. Constant exposure to Eleanor, who was, of course, still as shapely as ever, was the last thing she wanted for him.

"Maybe you don't," Eleanor replied blithely, and then she began scraping carrots and there was nothing Maggie could do short of throwing the woman out bodily.

Maggie turned back to the mountain of potatoes before her, seething. She'd known that Reeve and Duncan had made some sort of gentleman's agreement, but she'd never dreamed that it included Eleanor.

At noon Reeve appeared unexpectedly in the sweltering kitchen, something he had never done in all the time Maggie had been at Seven Sisters, and he was furious to find his wife there. Blackened from head to toe by the sugary-scented soot of burning cane, he caught Maggie by the elbow and dragged her out into the dooryard. Eleanor's indulgent little smile added to her umbrage.

"Let me go!" she hissed, wrenching free of Reeve's grasp. Somewhere nearby Goodness and Mercy giggled.

"Do I have to send you back to Sydney?" Reeve demanded in a rasp caused by the constant inhalation of smoke. "Is that what I have to do, woman, to keep you out of trouble?"

"I'm not in trouble!" Maggie cried. If Reeve sent

her away, or even confined her to the house, she was going to die of boredom and frustration. "I'm only helping with the work!"

"Damn it, you're carrying my child and I won't have you lose it because of your stupid Yankee pride!"

"Reeve—"

"If I catch you out here again, Maggie, I'll take you to Sydney myself, I swear it."

Maggie's eyes filled with tears. Surmounting this man's towering will would be an impossible task, but she had to try. "Reeve, I feel just fine, I really do—"

Ominously silent, he raised one smoke-blackened arm and pointed toward the house just as he might have had he been dealing with Elisabeth. Maggie was furious.

Rooted to the spot, she crossed her arms over her chest and jutted out her chin. "I'm tired of being ordered around, Reeve McKenna. I'm a grown woman and if I want to peel potatoes, *I'll peel potatoes!*"

He took a step toward her, glowering, and Maggie's courage flagged slightly. She retreated a step, but insisted, "I won't go in there and sit bandying a needle about while everyone else is doing real work!"

In one lightning-swift movement Reeve swept her up into his arms, then began striding toward the house. "Thank your lucky stars you're pregnant, Yank," he raged under his breath, "because if you weren't, I'd paddle you within an inch of your life!"

Reaching the parlor at the front of the house, he set a kicking and wriggling Maggie in a chair and held her there, one hand on her shoulder. Her good dress was stained with soot from his trousers and shirt.

"Brute!" she spat out, helpless against his strength and his formidable resolve.

"Defy me again and you'll find out the extent of it!" he retorted, glaring down at her.

"I'll defy you, all right!" Maggie hissed. "The moment you're out of sight I'll do what I want to do!"

Reeve gave a long, ragged sigh. "There's only one way to manage you, isn't there, Yank?" he reflected with a shake of his sooty head, and then he pulled her out of the chair and once again hoisted her into his arms.

"What are you doing?" Maggie demanded. This time she didn't struggle; she knew it was a waste of energy.

"Guess," Reeve replied, and he carried her, bold as brass, up the front stairway and into their bedroom. There, he tossed her onto the bed and began unbuttoning his shirt.

Maggie was wide-eyed with an untenable combination of fury, surprise, and plain, ordinary desire. "Don't you dare try to make love to me," she ordered without real conviction.

Reeve's flesh, she soon saw, was as sweaty and dirty as his shirt. Apparently unconcerned with such things as personal cleanliness, he unbuckled his belt and opened his trousers.

Sitting up now, Maggie squeezed her eyes shut. "Leave this room right now, Reeve," she said magnanimously, "and I won't take you to account for this."

Reeve chuckled. "That, Yank, is a profound relief." She heard the belt buckle jingle and then the clunk of boots being kicked aside. "However, I think I'll risk your terrible revenge. Just this once."

Maggie opened her eyes and swallowed at the sight of him. He was magnificent, and even her anger at being put in her place in this age-old way wasn't enough to nullify her wanting of him. "D-do you honestly think, for one minute, that this is g-going to make me pay any m-mind at all to your arbitrary—rules?"

Kneeling on the bed beside her, Reeve tossed up Maggie's skirts with an arrogance that would have made her scratch his eyes out if she hadn't needed him so badly. It had, after all, been more than a week since he'd touched her, except to kiss her good night. "Yes," he answered flatly.

Maggie batted her skirts away from her face, sputtering, as he deftly undid the ties of her drawers. "I'm warning you, Mr. McKenna—"

The drawers slid down and Maggie shivered involuntarily as she felt Reeve's hands on her bare thighs.

"Open your dress, Maggie," he said, beginning to caress her in the most intimate way possible. "I want to see your breasts."

Maggie swallowed a moan as her hips began to writhe in response to his touch, and her hands went obediently to the buttons of her dress, even though she willed them not to. She bared herself, except for her thin camisole, and clutched at the bedclothes with frantic hands as Reeve laid his tongue to the shadow of one nipple, then gently scraped it with his teeth. The fabric of her camisole clung moistly to the tender peak as it hardened and strained toward Reeve's mouth.

And still he fondled her.

Completely lost, Maggie whimpered his name and arched her back so that he had ready access to her muslin-covered breasts. He undid the tiny ribbon ties and she sighed as the camisole was thrust aside by the swell of her bosom.

Greedily, Reeve took one pulsing peak into the warm moistness of his mouth to cosset it there, and with a cry Maggie flung her arms up over her head and grasped at the headboard of the bed in order to anchor herself. When she would have lowered them again to tangle her fingers in Reeve's hair, he held them in place, her wrists imprisoned in one of his hands.

He spoke against her nipple, his every breath making it tighten into a keener sensitivity. "I'll leave you too exhausted to rebel again, little Yank," he promised in a husky whisper.

Maggie clung to the last shreds of her pride, even as

her body leapt to obey his every command. "You'll exhaust—yourself—as well—" she gasped.

Reeve laughed. "Not so," he replied, and then he sucked at Maggie's breast until she was half wild with the need of him. Then, and only then, he moved to kneel on the floor and shifted Maggie's hips so that they were resting on the very edge of the bed. She was totally vulnerable to him.

"Your first lesson in being an obedient wife," he grated out, and then he nuzzled through her softness to catch her in his mouth.

An electrical jolt went through Maggie as he nibbled at her, and her back arched as if in spasm. Groaning, she grabbed at the bedding with her fingers, sure that she would float away if she didn't hold on. "Oh, Reeve," she choked, "my—God—Reeve—"

He enjoyed her at his leisure until she reached a slow, scalding release, and then he pleasured her again, with the same infinite patience. She was still quivering from that, and praying that he would take her now, when he shifted positions so that she was kneeling over him, and he partook of her yet again. In his own time, and his own way, he drove her over the edge of madness for the third time.

Maggie began to plead softly for quarter, but Reeve granted none. Her body was his playground, and he had no qualms about taking what he wanted. And what he wanted, it soon became evident, was to love Maggie until she was totally beyond rebellion. He made her reach climax after climax, until she had lost count, until she couldn't think or do anything but respond to him, and then, at last, he took her.

Like the lappings of his tongue, the strokes of his manhood were slow, leisurely ones. The pinnacle Maggie reached that time, as Reeve stiffened upon her and groaned at his own gentle pleasure, was the most violent of them all.

He slipped from her with seemingly renewed vigor, climbing back into his filthy clothes and humming an impudent little tune as he put on his boots. Maggie lay still on the bed, too sated and too spent to move, let alone speak.

Just before he left the room, Reeve gave Maggie's perspiring bottom a little pat and kissed her forehead. "I hope you'll stage another rebellion soon, Yank. I do enjoy taming my own personal shrew."

If she'd had the strength, Maggie would have hurled something against the door. As it was, she could only lie there, trying to regain her breath and plotting revenge. She fell asleep in the middle of that, and when she awakened, it was dark outside and she could hear the strange chanting songs of the Aboriginal workers floating on the warm night wind.

She sat up, yawning, and her eyes widened. Reeve was sitting in a tin washtub at the foot of the bed, happily washing away the day's soot and grime.

Kneeling on the mattress, Maggie wrestled her way out of her tangled dress. Her drawers and camisole had disappeared entirely. With a flouncing motion she got off the bed and wrenched on a white eyelet wrapper. It was scant covering, but it took the arrogant glint from Reeve's eyes.

"Pity," he said, soaping a sponge and proceeding to scrub his underarms. "You've smudged that lovely thing with soot."

Maggie looked at herself in the mirror and was appalled to see that much of the blacking had rubbed off Reeve's body and onto hers while he was making love to her that morning. The pristine white wrapper was now splotched with black, especially in the areas of her breasts and thighs. Embarrassed, she plunked down on the bed and glowered.

"I hate you."

"Alas," Reeve sighed philosophically, "you lie with your lips, but your body tells the truth."

Maggie turned crimson. "You had no right!"

"I had every right, love; I'm your husband. And don't play the wronged maiden; you weren't carrying on the way you were because you didn't like what I was doing."

Caught with no way to deny that she'd responded to Reeve's loving with her entire body and soul, Maggie lowered her eyes. "I wasn't carrying on," she protested weakly.

"You were howling like a dingo," was the blithe response, and then Reeve was rising out of the water with an inordinate amount of splashing. Maggie watched warily, seething, as he dried his superbly muscled body and began to dress in clothes too elegant for a quiet evening at home.

"Where are you going?" Maggie asked suspiciously.

There was a most inopportune tap at the door, and Reeve only grinned at his wife before opening it. Goodness and Mercy came in, giggling, and carried out the bathtub full of sooty water.

"You need bath too, missus," Mercy said. "We bring back new water."

Maggie longed for a bath, but she wasn't about to take one in front of Reeve McKenna. Not after the sweet, endless ordeal he'd put her through that morning. "Thank you," she said briskly, and the little girls went out, lugging the tub between them and slopping half the water on the floor.

Reeve, heedless of the small lake on the costly Persian rug, was standing in front of a mirror, frowning as he grappled with his fashionable string tie. "You ought to wear the pink silk, my love," he said offhandedly.

The pink silk was the best gown Maggie owned. Trimmed at the hem and bodice with tiny diamond-like beads, it was very formal. "To dinner?" she asked, examining her fingernails idly. "It's hardly the thing. Cambric is more suited."

"Not to a party at Duncan's house, it's not," Reeve replied, and his marvelous aquamarine eyes were sparkling as Maggie leapt off the bed, unable to hide her excitement.

"A party?" She beamed.

Reeve laughed. "A party," he confirmed. "We're celebrating the harvest."

Maggie was pacing the floor. "Where are those girls with my bathwater?" she fretted.

Reeve stopped her, taking her shoulders gently into his hands, and kissed her. "I love you," he said.

Maggie stiffened, remembering how he'd taken over her soul so easily, shamed by her own surrender. "Because I'm such an obedient little wife?" she drawled, glaring up at him.

"Because you're such a hellcat," he replied, his eyes laughing at her. Then he shrugged. "Of course, if you don't want to dance with me tonight, I'm sure Eleanor will be more than happy to—"

"Don't you dare dance with that woman!" Maggie interrupted, stomping one foot.

Reeve laughed, laying a hand to his heart as if to still its thudding beat. "Tell me that you love me, Maggie McKenna, and I promise I won't."

Unable to sustain her snit any longer, Maggie chuckled and shook her head. "You know I do, you waster," she answered. "Why else would I endure your overbearing and officious manner?"

Reeve was just about to kiss Maggie when Goodness and Mercy arrived with a tubful of fresh water. Maggie winced as she watched them slip and slide over the wet floor, and was much relieved when they set their burden down without incident.

"We bring mop?" Goodness asked.

"You bring mop," Maggie confirmed with a sigh.

"Later," added Reeve with a warning waggle of his index finger.

Goodness and Mercy fled in a gale of giggles.

"I have no idea what they see in you," Maggie observed.

Reeve took a step toward her, grinning devilishly, one eyebrow arched. "Don't you?" he challenged.

Maggie flushed. "Get out of here," she snapped.

353

To her surprise and relief, Reeve did leave the room. Maggie promptly locked the door behind him, then slipped out of her wrapper and stepped into the bathwater. It was tepid, but given the sweltering heat of an Australian summer, that was fine with Maggie.

As she bathed, Maggie thought of the last party she'd attended, at Government House, in Melbourne, and smiled at how much things had changed since then. She hoped that Duncan's sons, Jeremy and Tad, would be at the party; it would be wonderful to see them again.

There was another knock at the door just as Maggie was drying herself. "Who is it?" she asked suspiciously.

"Kala, missus, come to help with your dress."

For Kala, who could be silent for days on end, that was a virtual diatribe. Wrapping the towel around herself, Maggie went to the door, turned the key, and admitted the housekeeper.

Kala's coffee-colored eyes took in the mussed bed. "You sick, missus?" she asked.

Embarrassed, Maggie shook her head. "I was just— just tired," she answered.

Kala went to the giant armoire, one side of which was filled with Maggie's clothes. "Baby inside make tired," she said, looking back over one shoulder. Just the flicker of a smile moved on her lips. "Baby outside make even more tired."

Maggie laughed and nodded, and she was, at that moment, completely happy. She loved her husband, he loved her, she was carrying his child within her, and tonight she would go to a party in a pretty silken dress. After all the years she'd spent alone, living from hand to mouth and wearing whatever she could afford to buy from the secondhand carts on the streets of London, she felt inestimably wealthy.

"The pink silk," she said when Kala's eyes questioned her.

The lovely gown rustled as Kala took it carefully

from the armoire and laid it on the bed. Its pretty crystal beads glimmered in the dim light of the lamps Reeve had lit before Maggie awakened from her stuporous sleep.

Behind a lovely changing screen of polished acacia wood, Maggie replaced her towel with taffeta drawers, a camisole, and petticoats. She would have worn a corset, too, but Reeve forbade that, considering them silly at best and harmful at worst.

"Are you coming to the party, Kala?" she asked as the servant came around the screen and held out the magical pink dress. Maggie stepped into it.

"No, missus," Kala said in a tone that was almost indulgent. "No dark peoples at white party."

Maggie felt sad. After all, Kala had worked as hard as anyone. She deserved to dance and wear pretty things too. "Oh," she said.

Kala chuckled as she did up the tiny crystal buttons at the back of Maggie's dress. "We have party of our own, missus," she said by way of reassuring her mistress.

Maggie was heartened as she sat down at the dressing table to do her hair, which had been flowing free ever since Reeve had taken it upon himself to "tame" her. Before she could lay a hand on the brush, however, her husband came through the open door.

"Thank you, Kala," he said, and though the words were said kindly, they were a dismissal nonetheless.

Kala went out on soundless feet and Maggie sat at the dressing table, stricken to stillness by the impact of this man's presence. Not since the first day she'd seen him, aboard the *Victoria* at Brisbane, had that impact lessened. Each time she encountered Reeve McKenna, it was as though she were meeting him for the first time.

"Do you know," he began in a smoky whisper, closing the door, "how incredibly beautiful you are?"

Maggie recovered herself and made a face. "You needn't think that compliments will make me show you mercy, Mr. McKenna. I intend to have my revenge."

Reeve laughed and, when she reached for her hairbrush, he was there to take it from her. He began brushing her hair as he had done that morning in his wagon, during the camp meeting at Parramatta, and Maggie closed her eyes for a moment, remembering.

"What sort of revenge will this be?" Reeve asked softly, a hint of laughter causing a corner of his mouth to twitch slightly.

"The unexpected kind," Maggie answered, watching his reflection in the mirror and wondering how she could possibly have lived nineteen years without this man to love her, to enrage her, to pamper her.

Reeve chuckled. "That sounds ominous," he said.

Maggie was as aroused by Reeve's brushing her hair as she would have been by his hand caressing her breast or his lips nibbling at her earlobe. She took the brush from him and made short work of braiding her hair into a single shining plait and then winding it into a coronet. "I mean to catch you unawares," she answered belatedly.

Reeve drew her to her feet and gave her a lingering kiss that stole her breath away. "How about now?"

Maggie pushed herself away from him by pressing her palms to his chest. "That would be much too convenient for you," she answered airily, and then she swept to the door and out into the hallway, and Reeve had no choice but to follow her.

Duncan's house might have been merely a mile away if one was on foot, but by carriage the trip involved a much longer distance. Maggie sat primly in the seat beside Reeve, smiling at his obvious agitation. It was clear that Mr. McKenna didn't like the idea of being taken unawares.

The Kirk house, a rustic structure much like Reeve's place, was alight at every window when they arrived. There were a lot of buggies and wagons in the dooryard, but no other carriages.

Reeve was scowling as he helped Maggie down and tucked her arm through his, and she laughed. "Are you very worried, Mr. McKenna? How lovely, if you are!"

"You little—" Before Reeve could finish whatever it was he had been planning to say, two boys came running down the walk, fairly hurling themselves at Maggie and shouting for joy.

Smiling, Maggie kissed Jeremy's forehead, and then Tad's. "I was hoping to see you here tonight," she said, resisting an urge to ruffle their carefully combed red hair.

"Maybe you can teach us, instead of Miss Kilgore," Jeremy suggested.

"I hate her," Tad put in.

"You once said that you hated me," Maggie reminded him wryly. "Have I changed so much?"

"Not that I can tell," Reeve added, sounding sour.

Maggie elbowed her husband subtly and smiled at the boys. "You both look so very handsome that I probably won't be able to resist teaching you. Since I'm not allowed to help with the harvest in any way" —she paused, looking up at Reeve for an angry moment—"why don't you ask your father to bring you to our house in the morning? We'll have our lessons just as we used to in Melbourne."

Jeremy and Tad were so delighted by this prospect that they ran off immediately in search of their father.

Reeve gave Maggie a look and escorted her up the porch steps. "Teaching is work," he pointed out.

"You'll have to settle for it," Maggie replied. "You can't spend every morning of your life loving me senseless just to keep me from helping out in the kitchen."

"Pity," Reeve agreed pensively.

Duncan met them at the door, looking handsome in his white suit, and immediately claimed a dance with Maggie. Arching an eyebrow at Reeve, who was still irritable, he said, "It's my prerogative as host."

Reeve subsided and somewhere in the crowd of laughing, chattering people, fiddles began to play. "So it's come to this, has it," Duncan teased as he and Maggie began to turn in a slow waltz through a parlor that appeared to run the length of the house. "We're only friends and neighbors, allowed to dance once or twice a year." He sighed pragmatically.

Maggie laughed. "There was a time, Mr. Kirk, when I thought we could never be friends."

"You're right," Duncan conceded, frowning. "What's the matter with Reeve anyway? He looks as though he could bite a railroad tie in half."

Maggie pretended she hadn't heard the question, and when that dance ended, she was immediately pulled into her husband's arms for the next.

"Jealous, darling?" she teased.

"Don't push your luck," Reeve replied.

Throughout the evening he stayed close to Maggie, claiming her every dance and ignoring wistful glances from Eleanor, who had obviously had plans of her own for the night. Maggie gave the woman a winning smile every chance she got, and when the hour was late and the McKennas were back in their darkened carriage beginning the drive home, she took the promised revenge. It was to be hoped that the driver couldn't hear Reeve's moans of helpless pleasure.

Chapter 25 🌿

THE WHITE-CAPPED WATER WAS A JADE-GREEN COLOR under a sky of the fiercest blue. Jamie McKenna stood at the railing of the small, fleet steamer, scanning the horizon for any sign of land.

"Suppose he isn't there, Jamie?" Peony asked, moving to stand beside him. The wind blew her golden hair back from her face. "Suppose he's in Sydney?"

Jamie didn't feel like talking; he merely shook his head, expecting Peony to understand because she was the oldest and dearest friend he had. Instinct had prompted him to look for Reeve in Brisbane instead of Sydney.

Peony, a beautiful woman of forty, stared wistfully out to sea. Jamie saw her give an involuntary little shudder and then hug herself.

"Cold?" he asked, ready to take off his suit jacket, a garment he despised, and lay it over her shoulders.

Peony shook her head, but she lifted her lacy shawl into place. "I was just—remembering."

Jamie had his own memories of Queensland, and all of them were painful. He smiled and slipped a reassuring arm around her. "We agreed there'd be no looking back, didn't we?"

Her expression was pensive as she gazed upon some horrific sight that Jamie couldn't see. "Increase is still alive," she reflected, in a near whisper, "and if he gets wind that you're in Australia, he'll have you killed."

"Not before he'd had a good bit of vengeance, I suspect," Jamie answered. He wasn't afraid of Increase Pipher or of any other man—except possibly Reeve.

Peony shivered and squeezed her eyes shut in response to whatever pictures were looming in her fertile mind, then turned, placing one hand on Jamie's back. Though the scars from Increase's whip were hidden beneath his coat and shirt, Peony had never forgotten them. "Nothing and no one is worth the chance you're taking, Jamie McKenna," she whispered, and her bright green eyes brimmed with tears.

The brogue began to creep back into Jamie's voice, as it often did when he was irritated or upset. "I'll not 'ave the blighter dictatin' where I can go and where I can't, then!" he flared.

Peony subsided and turned her face resolutely toward the sea. The rocky shores of Queensland were now visible in the distance.

Once the sugar cane had been harvested from both Seven Sisters and Duncan's neighboring plantation, Reeve began to brood. Often, Maggie found him standing at a dark window, in the middle of the night, gazing toward the sea. She knew he was thinking of Jamie, and she worried. It was only a matter of time, Maggie was certain, until he would decide to go to New Zealand in search of his brother. Because of her pregnancy, he would surely leave her behind.

On one such night, awakening to see Reeve standing at the bedroom windows, she got up, sliding her arms around his middle and letting her forehead rest against his back. He stiffened in her embrace, and Maggie wondered briefly if he'd started visiting Eleanor.

Her eyes filled with tears, but she forced them back. She was smiling cheerfully when Reeve turned to face her. "Thinking of faraway places?" she asked softly.

"And faraway people," Reeve confirmed. His arms encircled Maggie, but he was not really with her. His mind and spirit were in New Zealand, with Jamie.

"When are you going?" Maggie hadn't planned to ask the question; it had simply popped out.

Reeve tensed again, but this time his hands rose gently to the sides of Maggie's upturned face, caressing her. He hesitated, then answered with a sigh of resignation, "Soon."

"I want to go along," Maggie said stoutly.

Reeve shook his head. "That's out of the question, Yank," he told her in a gentle voice. "And furthermore, you know it is."

Maggie lowered her eyes, lest he see the tears that had gathered there again. She didn't trust herself to speak.

Her husband held her, one hand stroking her back, moving the silken fabric rhythmically along her skin. "I won't be away long, love, I promise. And you can pass the time in Sydney, shopping and the like. Wouldn't you enjoy that?"

Maggie was full of despair, despair she felt honor bound to hide. "No, I wouldn't," she answered stiffly. "But I do have business in Brisbane."

Reeve arched one dark eyebrow. "What kind of business?" he asked, his tone rife with suspicion. Maggie couldn't think why he never trusted her not to get into mischief the moment he turned his back.

She lifted her chin. "I'm going to speak to the people at the orphanage where Elisabeth was found. I want to know why she's silent so much of the time."

Reeve let out a sigh. "Good luck, Yank. The best

detectives in the country weren't able to find that out. Leave it alone, Maggie—she was probably upset because her mother abandoned her."

Maggie had to admit that his theory was entirely possible. After all, being left was a small child's greatest fear. "What do you suppose she was like?" she mused in a faraway voice. "Elisabeth's mother, I mean."

His wide shoulders lifted in a shrug. "When and if I find Jamie, maybe I'll ask him. We'll set out for Brisbane in a couple of days, Maggie, and you and Cora and Elisabeth can travel on to Sydney from there."

Maggie stomped one foot. "No! Reeve McKenna, I'm your wife and I have every right—"

He laid one finger over her lips, silencing her, and shook his head.

In a sudden fury of indignation, Maggie knotted her hands into fists and batted impotently at Reeve's chest. A sob escaped her, ragged and hoarse, and he lifted her into his arms. Sinking onto the side of the bed, Reeve held Maggie in his lap like a shattered child.

She wept in earnest.

To Maggie's huge annoyance, Reeve chuckled, and his hand entangled itself in her hair as he held her against his chest in an effort to comfort her. "There now, Yank, it's all about that baby growing inside you, isn't it? Makes you pettish."

"The baby's got nothing to do with it, you lout!" Maggie wailed. She sniffled noisily. "It's your leaving, though I can't th-think why I'm not overjoyed to be r-rid of you!"

Reeve laughed and kissed her forehead. "Maybe you will be once I'm gone and you have the run of every shop in Sydney Town. You can see that friend of yours too—what's her name again?"

"Tansy," Maggie answered grudgingly. She'd

wanted her friend to come and live at Seven Sisters, but Tansy had refused because it would have meant leaving her intended. Acting on a mischievous hunch, she added, "I think I'd rather stay right here at home."

Reeve went rigid so suddenly that Maggie was nearly flung off his lap. "With Duncan Kirk living a stone's throw away? Not on your life, Yank."

Maggie batted her eyelashes. "I thought Duncan was your friend," she said innocently. "Don't you trust him?"

"I'd sooner leave you in the care of a band of drunken pirates," Reeve replied. "You're going to Sydney Town, and that's the end of it."

Though Maggie argued and even resorted to tears on at least one more occasion, Reeve's decision stood. After three days of hectic preparation, they set out for Brisbane by way of the coach, Cora and Elisabeth accompanying them.

The journey was uneventful, if exhausting, and Maggie was in a sullen mood as she got ready for bed at the hotel. The room she and Reeve shared had been theirs once before, on their wedding night.

Maggie tried to turn away from Reeve when he touched her, so great was her anger and her fear, but his caresses, as always, set her afire. After a fevered blaze of loving, she lay still in his arms, wondering at the power he wielded over her. It seemed there was no way to defy him and thus retain some pitiful semblance of self-respect.

Reeve's ship was to sail early, and he was up and dressed when Maggie awakened. She sat up in bed, yawning.

"How long will you be away?" she asked casually, averting her eyes so that Reeve wouldn't see the plot of rebellion brewing there.

"Long enough to find Jamie and work out why he's stayed away these twenty years," Reeve replied, his voice quiet. Firm. His aquamarine eyes transmitted a warning when Maggie finally dared to look into them. "Don't even think of trying to stow away on board that ship," he told her.

Maggie's last splendid hope was dashed, and her disappointment must have shown in her face because Reeve chuckled and shook his head.

Maggie hurled back the covers and scrambled awkwardly out of bed. Although the baby would not be born for months, she was already losing the agility that came with being slender. "I can tell you why Jamie didn't want to face you," she volunteered desperately, "and then there'll be no need to go!"

Reeve looked at her with something disturbingly like contempt. "Only now, when it serves your purpose?"

Maggie wanted to weep at his coldness and the distance she saw in his eyes. She thought she knew then how Loretta had felt when she'd been sent packing, and she wondered if the time was coming when Reeve would send her away too. She drew herself up. "Very well, then, I won't tell you."

She started to turn away, but Reeve grasped her by the arm and wrenched her around to face him. "I told you that the day would come when I'd ask what you know about my brother, Maggie. That time is here."

Maggie bit her lower lip. Reeve was like a stranger; she couldn't believe he was the same man who had loved her, who had tended her when she was sick. Tears burned in her eyes and Reeve's hands closed over her shoulders and then fell away.

"Tell me," he rasped.

Maggie's knees felt weak; she went to the bed and sat down. "You've found Jamie again without even knowing it," she said, dashing away her tears with the back of one hand. "He was the man who tried to rob you, right here in Brisbane a few years ago, and he has a nasty scar to show for it."

Reeve's muttered exclamation seemed to fill the

364

room. A moment later, without a good-bye, much less an apology for his high-handed behavior, he was gone.

Maggie was crushed. She'd wallowed in abject misery for several minutes when there was a tap on the door and Cora came in at a dispirited invitation.

"Good heavens," the older woman gasped, peering into Maggie's pallid face. "What's happened?"

Reeve has stopped loving me, Maggie wanted to answer, though of course she couldn't bring herself to say the awful, poisonous words aloud. "Nothing," she lied. "Nothing at all." She paused, drawing a deep breath. "Has Elisabeth had her breakfast? I've an errand to attend to, and I'd like her to go with me."

Cora's concern still showed in her face. "She's downstairs, Mrs. McKenna, with Eleanor."

Maggie stiffened as a distinct feeling of danger rippled through her. "Eleanor is here? In Brisbane?"

"Yes," Cora answered, looking surprised at Maggie's reaction. "She's on her way to Auckland this very morning. Says she has business there, with Mr. Jamie McKenna, mind you, though I can't think what it could be—"

Maggie's alarm deepened. Though she couldn't have given a specific reason, her trepidation went far beyond the fact that she didn't want Eleanor traveling in Reeve's company. She began wrenching on her clothes while Cora watched in amazement.

"Don't just stand there!" Maggie cried as she struggled with her shoes. They were never easy to put on, with all their buttons, but now that her ankles were swollen, they were impossible. "Go downstairs and make sure that Elisabeth is all right!"

But Maggie couldn't wait for Cora to follow her orders. Hair flying free, shoes still unfastened, she dashed down the stairs ahead of the governess, through a lobby full of stunned wayfarers, and into the public dining room.

Elisabeth and Eleanor were nowhere in sight.

Maggie whirled, full of fury and fear, and collided

365

hard with Duncan. Laughing a little, he steadied her by taking her shoulders into his strong hands.

"So it's true," he muttered. "There is a beautiful harridan scurrying about this hotel with her hair falling around her waist and her shoes untied."

"She's taken Elisabeth!" Maggie cried. "She's—"

Duncan's face was instantly sober. "Who, Maggie? Who's taken Elisabeth?"

"Eleanor!" Maggie managed to cry. "She told Cora she had some business with Jamie McKenna—"

Duncan remained thoughtful, and he spoke very slowly. "That means she's boarding the same ship as Reeve," he reasoned. "Elisabeth is safe."

Maggie tried to go around Duncan in pursuit of the child she loved as her own, but he stopped her, holding her fast by the shoulders. "I'll take you to the wharf," he said. "I have a carriage right outside."

"No," Cora whispered, but nobody paid any attention. Maggie ran to the carriage and climbed inside without help. "Please," she implored Duncan, who followed and settled himself comfortably in the seat across from hers, "tell the driver to hurry!"

"No need for that," he said, brushing off the sleeves of his impeccably clean white coat. "The ship has already sailed. Look at the horizon and you'll see."

Maggie fairly dived for the window. There was a vessel on the horizon, as well as several at anchor in the harbor. The carriage, meanwhile, was moving away from the sea instead of toward it.

She drew a deep breath and let it out slowly. She'd let her guard down and this was what had come of it. After her first ride in a carriage with Duncan, Maggie reasoned to herself, she should have learned.

"Where are you taking me?" she asked coolly.

Duncan smiled at the demand, examining his fingernails. "Home," he said.

Panic gnawed at Maggie's insides, but she forced herself to remain calm. "My home is with Reeve," she pointed out. "Now, stop this nonsense, please, and drive me to the harbor."

Without looking at Maggie, Duncan shook his head. "The trouble with you and me, my love, is that we've never had a chance to get to know each other. That's why Eleanor and I worked this plan out."

Maggie's eyes rounded. "You knew Eleanor was going to kidnap Elisabeth?" she asked in utter shock.

Duncan bristled and, at last, met Maggie's gaze. "Elisabeth is her daughter—it's hardly kidnapping."

Maggie's shock was consummate. Her mouth dropped open and she forcibly closed it again.

Duncan laughed and the sound was low and harsh, frightening Maggie.

"Elisabeth never let on," she muttered.

"That's because she doesn't remember."

Maggie locked her hands together in her lap and moved forward a little on the seat. "What happened, Duncan? Why is it so rare and difficult for Elisabeth to speak?"

He hesitated, then evidently decided that there was no reason to keep the secret anymore. After all, he had Maggie and Eleanor had Elisabeth. "Eleanor had left the child before." He sighed. "Often for weeks. That time Elisabeth must have guessed that her mother was never coming back."

Maggie thought back over all the days Eleanor had spent in Reeve's household, both in Sydney and at Seven Sisters, and she was awed at the woman's capacity to ignore her own child. Never once had Eleanor shown the slightest curiosity about Elisabeth, or affection for her. "Whatever could Jamie have seen in her?" she mused.

Duncan only glared at her. He didn't like being reminded of the man who'd plunged a knife into his shoulder.

Outside the carriage, open spaces stretched in every direction. In the far distance two kangaroos hopped across the ground at amazing speed. "Take me back, Duncan," Maggie said at length, in an attempt at reason. "Reeve will be furious if you don't."

"Reeve is on his way to Auckland," Duncan answered smoothly, and that seemed to settle that.

"Reeve!"

Some note or nuance of that voice was vaguely familiar. Reeve paused on the ship's ramp and turned to assess the crowd gathered on shore.

A tall man with fair hair and azure eyes stepped forward, one suntanned arm lifted in tentative greeting. A slender blond woman stood on tiptoe to kiss the stranger's cheek, then walked away toward the ticket office.

Reeve froze where he was, other passengers boarding the ship surging around him. "Jamie?" He muttered the name softly.

As the man who might be his brother drew nearer, Reeve broke the strange paralysis that had held him and started down the ramp. His throat felt thick and his stomach jittery.

Finally, the two men stood facing each other on the wharf. The stranger looked uncomfortable in his suit and fancy hat.

"Hello, Reeve," he said quietly.

It was a moment before Reeve could speak. All the waiting and searching and hoping were behind him now; saints in heaven, this was Jamie standing before him.

Jamie's eyes misted over, though he was grinning in that cocky way that Reeve remembered so well. "I didn't expect you to come to meet me," he observed.

Reeve's anger was sudden and fathomless. "Damned if I did that," he hissed, lapsing into the brogue. "I was off to New Zealand to find you and break your—"

Jamie flung back his head and shouted with laughter. Reeve was overwhelmed by a raging joy that blurred his vision and made his eyes sting. He stood stiffly in his brother's embrace for a moment before returning it.

Eleanor watched the reunion, tightly clasping Elisabeth's hand.

Reeve and Jamie were face to face, two towering men with broad shoulders and an aura of power about them. It was that faculty, mainly, that had attracted Eleanor to each man in his turn. Her heart climbed into her throat as she waited for Jamie to turn and see her standing there, with his daughter. Her daughter.

"So it was you that tried to rob me in that Brisbane alley, was it?" Reeve accused him, but his hands were gripping Jamie's shoulders. The talisman he wore around his neck, a twin to Jamie's, glistened in the bright Queensland sunshine.

Eleanor felt an ache in one corner of her heart as she watched Jamie smile. "Aye, mate—that was me." In a wink he was out of his jacket and rolling up one sleeve to show off the scar Eleanor remembered so well. "Made a job of it, didn't you, now?"

Reeve swore as he assessed the injury he'd done his brother.

Elisabeth began to fret at her mother's side, and Eleanor knew it was time to step forward. She assembled a sweet expression and started toward Jamie, only to have the little girl at her side pull free and dash toward Reeve, shouting, "Papa! Papa!"

Reeve's face was a study in surprise as he lifted the delighted child into his arms. Frowning, he scanned the people milling along the wharf and on shore. "What are you doing here, shoebutton?"

While Elisabeth was prattling out her answer, Jamie's robin's-egg-blue eyes at last found Eleanor. Instead of the welcome she had hoped to see there, though, she discovered a glacial hardness. *This is our child,* she wanted to scream out, but she didn't dare. It was clear that Jamie still hated her, would always hate her.

She turned from the scene on the wharf to flee, looking back only once. Reeve and Jamie were striding along a good distance behind her, engaged in an earnest conversation, Elisabeth riding happily on Reeve's shoulders.

On the path leading to the hotel Eleanor encountered Cora, who was blubbering and wringing her hands.

"First you take off with little Elisabeth, and now Duncan's gone and kidnapped Mrs. McKenna—where is that child, Eleanor Kilgore? What have you done with her?"

Eleanor wiped the tears from her cheeks with the back of one hand. "Elisabeth is with Reeve," she said quietly. She didn't ask where Duncan might have gone with Maggie, because she knew; she'd guessed his plan, seen it written in his eyes the moment he'd learned that Maggie was to be separated from Reeve for a period of time. Together, they'd plotted the rest.

It wasn't far, the little hideaway Duncan had taken for the occasion of winning the fair Maggie. Eleanor decided to go there and have vengeance on all the men who had scorned her: Duncan, Reeve, and Jamie.

It would be so easy.

"I shouldn't have done this, Maggie, and I'm sorry." Duncan was so contrite that his captive was hard put to be furious with him, though she knew she should have been. Her main concern was Elisabeth; she prayed that the child was safe.

The small farmhouse Duncan had brought her to stood in the middle of a field of towering and neglected sugar cane, and Maggie settled herself at the kitchen table. There was just one room; from where she sat she could see both the bed and the cookstove. "You're very fortunate that Reeve is on his way to Auckland, Duncan Kirk, because he'd have your hide for this."

Duncan sighed and shook his head. "I seem to

suffer from a certain madness where you're concerned."

Maggie was annoyed and she longed for a good stout cup of tea. "Don't be melodramatic," she said, getting up from her chair to riffle through the various tins stored on the shelves beside the stove until she found one that contained orange pekoe. "We'll never get all the way back to Brisbane before dark, and that means we'll have to spend the night. It's a fearsome bother, Duncan—Elisabeth's at sea, Cora will be worried sick and, of course, I've missed my ship to Sydney—"

Duncan sank forlornly into a chair. "The driver's taken the carriage back to Brisbane for the night anyway." He sighed. "I'll sleep in the barn, of course."

"Of course," Maggie agreed primly. With that, determined to make the best of a difficult situation, she took the teapot from the back of the stove and set out to find the pump. The kettle would require a good rinsing, having sat unused for a time. She found the wellhouse and was pumping cold water into the pot when she saw a horse and buggy careen through the whispering cane and stop in the dooryard.

Eleanor was standing in front of the seat brandishing a small handgun that glistened blue-black in the fading sunlight. "Duncan!" she screamed.

Maggie's heart began to pound. She dropped the teakettle, ready to run, just as Duncan came out of the cabin, his thumbs tucked into his vest pockets, his attitude plainly condescending. "Now, Eleanor, don't make a fool of yourself—"

A shot whined in the otherwise still air, and Maggie cried out in utter shock as Duncan folded to the ground and Eleanor turned toward her, holding the pistol in both hands. Maggie plunged into the cane, running as fast as she could.

To her horror, she heard Eleanor in wild pursuit; the overgrown sugar cane rustled and snapped as it fell beneath the horses' hooves and the floor of the buggy. Maggie's heart burned in her throat as she zigzagged this way and that, trying to stay out of her pursuer's path. Please, God, she prayed as she stumbled on, don't let me die. Don't let my baby die.

Just as Maggie burst into a clearing, where a small gully had been worn away in the ground by the driving Queensland rains, she heard a shout in the distance. Reeve. The voice was Reeve's.

She screamed his name as Eleanor's horse and buggy crashed through the sugar cane into the clearing. The tired, frightened animal went wild with panic as it stumbled into the gully, landed on its side, and struggled to rise to its feet. The buggy held it down.

Eleanor, meanwhile, was flung free, and she scrambled to stand, her skirts and face covered with dirt, the gun still in her hand. "You," she said, glaring at Maggie with all the hatred of hell in her face. "I'll kill you for what you've done to me!"

Maggie was in the open; if she ran for cover, Eleanor would surely shoot her before she could escape. She gasped for breath and willed her heart to slow to a reasonable meter. Before she could ask what it was that she'd done to Eleanor, she heard Reeve's voice again, heard the cane shifting as he ran through it.

"Maggie, where are you?"

"Stay away!" she called back, both relieved and terrified to know that she hadn't imagined his presence. "Eleanor has a gun—she'll kill you—"

Reeve didn't listen, and everything happened, it seemed to Maggie, in a split second. He entered the clearing on her right, about twenty feet from where she stood, and Eleanor spun and fired at him wildly. Maggie screamed as he fell and lunged toward him, forgetting her own safety.

"Reeve!" she gasped when she reached the place where her husband lay, a crimson stain pooling around his right shoulder in the dirt. Maggie hurled herself on him in a desperate attempt to shield him.

Eleanor laughed like a madwoman; Maggie heard her approaching and knew that she was going to die. She looked up and saw such rancor in the woman's once-beautiful face that she had to look away. It was then that she spotted the snake, dark and sleek, slithering over the ground toward Eleanor.

"Look out," she choked, clinging to the unconscious Reeve, determined to absorb any bullet that was fired at him. "There's a snake—"

Eleanor only laughed again. The sound was wicked and cold. "I was almost a McKenna once, did you know that?" she asked. "Did you know that Elisabeth is my little girl?"

Maggie could not look away from the snake. "In the name of God, Eleanor, behind you—"

"You don't think I'm going to fall for that old trick, do you? If so, you're sadly lacking in that ingenuity Americans are so famous for."

There was a hiss and the snake struck, not from a coil like a rattler, but in one flying black line of vicious fury. Eleanor shrieked in pain and shots peppered the ground around Maggie and Reeve as her hand convulsed on the trigger of the pistol.

Maggie awaited pain and death and felt nothing. She watched as Eleanor sagged to the ground and lay staring up at the sky, her eyes widened and blank.

Maggie had no time for Eleanor or the snake; she was examining Reeve. She found that he was breathing, to her great relief; he'd been shot through the shoulder and the bleeding was already slowed to a trickle.

Hearing a whistling *thunk* of a sound, Maggie looked up to see Jamie pulling his knife from the ground, where it had severed the snake's head from its body. "Is my brother alive?" he asked.

"He is—no thanks to you," Maggie responded,

pulling up her skirts to tear off strips of her petticoat for binding Reeve's wound. "Where the devil have you been, Jamie McKenna?"

Jamie took his time answering. He went and freed the poor struggling horse from beneath the over-turned buggy. "I was lookin' after me mate, Mr. Kirk. He's going to get well, by and by. Bullet barely touched him."

Out of the corner of her eye Maggie saw that Jamie was kneeling beside Eleanor now; she didn't want to look too closely, sensing that the moment was a private one, but she did see her brother-in-law gently close the woman's eyes and smooth her tangled hair back from her forehead. "I'm sorry things weren't different for us," he said to the dead woman, his voice detached and hollow with some secret pain.

Reeve was just coming around. "What the hell—" he muttered.

Maggie smiled with relief and with love. "My hero," she said, bending to kiss his furrowed fore-head. She paused and drew a deep breath, then rushed on. "I want you to promise me that you won't hurt Duncan for abducting me. He was carried away by passion, that's all, and he's quite sorry."

Reeve sat up, wincing a little at the pain in his shoulder, and his aquamarine eyes took in Maggie's thickening waistline, her tumbledown hair, her dirt-smudged face. "Passion, is it?" he reflected, and then he chuckled hoarsely and shook his head. Maggie would have boxed his ears if he hadn't already been injured.

Jamie was utterly silent. He lifted Eleanor gently into his arms and started back toward the cabin. Maggie watched him go with a feeling of sadness as she helped Reeve to his feet.

"How did you know where to look for us?" she asked.

"Cora told me that Duncan had tricked you into getting into his carriage and she guessed that he was headed here because she'd heard him making arrangements to buy the place."

Maggie looked at the carcass of the snake and winced. "I hope there aren't any more of those around," she said.

Reeve leaned on her slightly, his flesh pale as death from the pain as they made their way out of the cane field in the direction Jamie had taken. He said nothing.

"Eleanor was Elisabeth's mother," Maggie said, because she needed to make conversation.

Reeve nodded. "Jamie never knew there was a child until today, when I told him."

"Why do you suppose a woman would abandon her own daughter that way, and let everyone believe that she was dead?"

"I don't suppose we'll ever know exactly," Reeve answered quietly. "She obviously wasn't the motherly sort. Maybe that's all there was to it."

"Jamie sent her away, didn't he? Eleanor, I mean?"

Reeve nodded. "Found her in a compromising situation, you might say."

A horrible thought struck Maggie. Now that Jamie knew Elisabeth was his daughter, maybe he would want to take her back to New Zealand to live. Maggie would be devastated if he did that, for she'd come to cherish that child with her whole heart. "Is he going to—will he want to—"

Reeve looked down at Maggie and smiled despite the set of his jaw that plainly said he was in severe pain. "Elisabeth stays with us," he assured her. "At least until she's old enough to decide for herself. After all, I'm the only father she's ever known, and she's taken to calling you Mama, hasn't she?"

Maggie nodded, her eyes brimming with tears of weariness and relief and a thousand other emotions. She remembered Reeve's coldness that morning in the hotel room, and her feeling that he didn't love her anymore. "Are you going to dismiss me from your

375

life, Reeve McKenna," she dared to ask, "the way you did Loretta?"

Reeve stopped there in the cane that rose all around them and turned to face Maggie. "I married you, Yank. For me, that means a lifetime of loving you. I'll never send you away, and I'll never leave you."

Maggie stood on tiptoe to kiss her husband. "Promise?" she asked in a whisper.

Reeve kissed her passionately. "I promise," he answered, and Maggie knew he meant it.

Seven Sisters—*November 1887*

"HE'S FUNNY-LOOKING," SAID ELISABETH MCKENNA, peering into the face of the new baby Reeve held so carefully in his strong arms. "What's his name?"

Maggie watched fondly as Reeve looked down at the tiny, wrinkled infant, his handsome face alight with joy and pride. "His name is James," he said. "James Chamberlin McKenna."

"Can I take him outside and show him my new pony?"

Maggie, still confined to her bed even though she felt strong and healthy, smiled and patted the comforter. Elisabeth came and sat beside her, gazing up into Maggie's face with an expectant expression.

"James will have to be just a bit older before he can properly appreciate anything so wonderful as your pony," Maggie confided.

"Oh," replied Elisabeth with an air of importance. Satisfied, she scrambled down from the bed and dashed out of the room, bored with babies.

Reeve put his newborn son carefully into the cradle and then stretched out on the bed beside Maggie. Sighing with contentment and smiling up at the ceiling, he said, "I wish I could make love to you, Yank. Then everything would be perfect."

Maggie laughed and bent to circle his lips with her

tongue. "Perhaps you can't make love to me," she whispered, "but I can make love to you."

Reeve looked at her in shock. "Good God, woman, what are you saying? You just had a baby—"

Maggie was kissing his jawline. "I know," she answered in a throaty voice. "It's an experience that's almost impossible to overlook."

Reeve chuckled. "That it is. Stop that!"

Maggie continued to kiss him, unbuttoning his shirt, trailing the path of her fingers with her lips. She delighted in the shivering groan he gave. "I think you'd better lock the door," she said.

"I think you're right," Reeve replied, moaning as Maggie's tongue traced the circumference of his nipple. He got up, locked the door, and came back to the bed, where his wife immediately began loving him again. "Woman," he implored hoarsely as she tugged his shirt free of his trousers, "will you have mercy on me?"

"No," Maggie answered. And she was true to her word.

Author's Note

In both *MOONFIRE* and the upcoming *ANGEL-FIRE,* I have tampered with history by extending the transportation of criminals from the British Isles to Australia by some twenty years, this being necessary to the stories.

Reeve, Maggie, Jamie and I all beg your kind indulgence.

Linda Lael Miller
P.O. Box 2166
Bremerton, WA 98310